Eve Hogan
Author of *Intellectual Foreplay*

"If you know anyone who is recovering from an addiction, an illness, a relationship issue, being laid off, if you have an anniversary, holiday or gift occasion, if you simply wish to deliver a dozen perfect 'roses for the soul', then the florist is *Diamond Heart!*"

Vincent Gerard Molina
Author of *Communicating with a Former Spouse*

"The most important ship you will ever sail upon in your life is your RELATION SHIP. If you are seeking more complete, loving, supportive RELATION SHIPS in your life, then you will find calm seas and a safe harbor with *Diamond Heart*."

Rand Brenner
Vice President of Licensing, Saban Entertainment

"I have invested a lifetime with such projects as *Batman* with Warner Brothers and *Power Rangers* with Saban Entertainment, entertaining millions of children worldwide. Alan Dohrmann's **lessons** for the child in all of us, do more than entertain...for they train us...to seek and find the miracle that is locked within the human soul. Unlock your miracle!"

Jim Britt
Author of *The Master's Key;* Fortune Trainer, Featured
with *Denis Waitley*

"Having taught the MASTER KEY program to
global audiences for years, I find Alan Dohrmann's
lessons help every adult and child to place the MAGIC
KEY into the MASTER LOCK of human potential, and
to throw the doorway of opportunity open WIDE once
again....."

Barry Spilchuk
Author of *Cup of Soup For the Soul*

"*Cup of Soup* readers MUST read this book! The
healing work of the stories in the *Chicken Soup for the
Soul* books, in my opinion, is further expanded with the
stories in *Diamond Heart!* The **lost** lessons from the man
who coached Walt Disney and Napoleon Hill are now
available to the public. The word WOW comes to mind
with every story!"

Mitchell Santell
Host of *Do The Dream, National Radio Program*

" '*Do the dream*' is one of Walt Disney's famous
sayings. I was present when Academy Award winning
photographer Bill Bacon presented Bernhard Dohrmann
with rare photographs of Walt Disney taken when his
father Alan Dohrmann was on location with 'Uncle Walt'.
Diamond Heart speaks one message to everyone...THE
DREAM **IS** ALIVE!"

Diamond Heart

MY FATHER'S STORIES

...AN ADULT FAIRY TALE...

Bernhard Dohrmann
ST Productions • Alabama

© 1997 Pending, Bernhard Dohrmann
ISBN 1-890465-40-2
Library of Congress # Pending.

Diamond Heart is a work of fiction; no reference to any third-party place or thing is presented other than to entertain the reader of an adult fairy tale.

This book is dedicated to Lynn Dohrmann, whom if my father could have known her, would have completed his belief in life ... *that perfection CAN be HAD.....*

Acknowledgments

I wish to thank the LORD GOD for tickling my aging memory so many times, that the detail for each story came alive again. I pray special grace resides within these pages.

As 100% of my proceeds for each DIAMOND HEART book sale, is donated to the International Learning Trust, I wanted to thank the ILT for planning to install Super Teaching Systems into classrooms for school children all over the world.

I wanted to thank every Income Builder Super Teaching Instructor for their tireless coaching all the way through the final draft. IBI proved once again Teamwork does Make the Dream Work!

I would like to thank Jack Canfield, author of *Chicken Soup for the Soul,* as he reaches ten million readers, for being the key inspiration to FINISH it.

As with any project there are many people that make the magic of the completed work. Cloudsifter Flood, the most amazing editor, brought her native American heritage into the message. Thanks to my wife, Lynn, and our children (especially Ryan and Justin), for hearing my fathers stories time and time again - just to make sure they were correct in each and every telling. Barry Spilchuk, author of *Cup of Soup For the*

Soul, and Eve Hogan, author of *Intellectual Fore-play,* for coaching throughout the process.

I want to thank all the runners in my life, too many to name, who contributed to the magic of *Diamond Heart*. To Debbie Hudson for putting the book into final form. To Geof, Mark, Carl, Susan, Sally, Mellissa, Terry and Pam for being my family.

To Phylis Dohrmann for loving my Dad with her whole heart, her whole mind and her soul until the day he "graduated".

And finally, to my father, Alan G. Dohrmann for teaching the world that the 21st Century is not a place for adults to work at making a better future, but rather a place for children to play at creating a happier playground.

Foreword

I can still remember what I felt like the first time I saw a bookstore with *Chicken Soup for the Soul*, with my name on the cover, in large   display racks outside not one, but almost every major bookstore in the world. I can remember what the feelings were like when USA TODAY and my hometown paper both reported how many weeks *A 3rd Serving of Chicken Soup* had remained on the NEW YORK TIMES Best-Seller List, and how fast it had risen to number one.

It felt GOOD! Very, VERY GOOD!

As a bestselling author, I receive many requests for endorsements and I have taken great care in choosing which books I will endorse, especially in the rare moments when I "step inside" a new book and write a forward. This care is part of the "quality control" I wish to make to my many millions of *Chicken Soup* readers.

I want my readers to know that one reason I chose to write a forward for DIAMOND HEART is that I see the book as more "healing soup" for millions of readers. *Diamond Heart*, like *Chicken Soup for the Soul*, features many stories, each appealing to different emotions and each teaching different and valuable life lessons.

Another reason I encourage you to read DIAMOND HEART is part of my own individual story. For many years I have had the privilege to "learn" powerful lessons taught as *My Father's Stories* by Bernhard Dohrmann. These stores have touched my life. I have also watched these stories touch the lives of many thousands of others over the years. As a result, I feel the healing power contained in these messages deserves a wide readership.

The reader should know that I never met Alan Dohrmann when he was alive, although I often feel that in some magical manner he has adopted me and mentored me for a long while. I have known or know of many of the people who were Alan Dohrmann's students - the late Val Van de Wall, Tom Wilhite, William Penn Patrick, Alexander Everett, Earl Nightingale, Dr. Edward Deming, John Hanley and Walt Disney to name only a few. I have also had the honor to know Jane Wilhite with whom Alan Dohrmann worked for so many years, and through her eyes have gained a bit more insight into this special teacher.

I have primarily been able to know Alan Dohrmann and his work through the eyes of his oldest son, Bernhard Dohrmann, with whom I have taught many powerful personal development seminars. Over the past five years I have tasted the words of Alan Dohrmann as if he were still teaching them himself. If ever you have an opportunity to hear the spoken stories, do not hesitate to make a date with destiny! If Bernhard Dohrmann is teaching live, cancel other plans and make it a point to attend the lecture. You'll find it one of the most unique experiences of your life.

I never knew the author, Brother Al Dela Rosa, the Benedictine Monk who brings each story to life once again, although I know his godson, Tony Dohrmann, Bernhard's oldest son. In knowing various members of the Dohrmann family, including the late Alan Dohrmann's wife, Phylis, I have a closer context for the stories you are about to enjoy. I know enough of the history, to know that even though *Diamond Heart* is labeled a work of fiction, much of the "story" is based on the real life experiences of the Dohrmann family.

Perhaps the cornerstone reason I want you to read *Diamond Heart* is simply to invite you to return to the lost innocence of your own childhood. My partner, Mark Victor Hansen, and I believe in our "diamond" hearts that the world needs a new *Alice in Wonderland* adventure, to take us all collectively and each individually into the twenty-first century.

In the end, it might be only through the eyes of the magical child that hides just beneath the surface in all of us that we once again rebirth our own connection to the miracles taking place all around us. *Diamond Heart* is above all, an adventure - a magical safari into the inner reaches of the heart, that compels the reader to return to what is most heroic within us - the child who is always the hero.

As you hear the words, see the colors, feel the heart throb, and embrace the magic one more time, the natural child in your own "diamond heart" is likely to be re-awakened. For some it may only be for a moment in time, but like any fairy tale, a precious memory that lasts for an entire lifetime.

For others, *Diamond Heart* may become a fork in your life's journey. It is for you, that I write this forward.

My hope is to leave a simple fingerprint upon your soul. My request is that you embrace *Diamond Heart.*

Own each story through the "inner" eye of your childhood imagination. Allow each miracle, each message to reside at the deepest level of your own pure heart, to become one of the many Diamonds, forever held in your eternal divinity - your Diamond Heart.

As I close, my wish is that *My Father's Stories, an Adult Fairy Tale* be told and retold by the adult readers to the children of the world for generations to come. If this special dream for the *Diamond Heart* stories becomes reality for the children of the world, then, like the loaves shared by a simple carpenter's son two thousand years ago, it will feed the entire world with abundance and love.

Your work is to serve the loaves!

Jack Canfield
Author, *Chicken Soup for the Soul*
Santa Barbara, California

Table of Contents

INTRODUCTION

"Tonight, children, we will hear the story of Brother Al Dela Rosa." Bernhard Dohrmann sat in the overstuffed easy chair, the same chair his own father had used when he was the storyteller. Berny's wife, Lynn, was perched on the arm of the chair, her tiny frame and uptilted eyes riveted toward her husband. The semicircle of children before them in the large living room was silent in anticipation.

"Brother Dela Rosa was a Benedictine monk in the Catholic church for virtually all of his adult life, and our family was blessed to have him spend time with us over many years. Children, do you know what it is like to live the life of a Benedictine monk? Does anyone have any ideas?" (Heads shook from side to side ... no, they did not know.....)

Flashing an impish grin at his audience, Bernhard opened an old and faded family photo album. The album crackled as the plastic covers marked age with sound. The pages however, were timeless, as they showed the children's late grandfather, Bernhard's father, Alan Gerrard Dohrmann, sporting a wide brimmed hat and smoking a pipe.

Their famous grandfather was standing beside a strange little man wearing the traditional robes of the Benedictine order. As pages were turned, they saw the long flowing robes, the large hood hanging down his back, his simple sash and rosary beads, all seemed incongruous somehow with a man so very short in stature.

Each page held the shining round face marked with a huge smile, introducing Brother Dela Rosa in 1950's repose to the curious children peering at an old photo album they had never seen before. Bernhard continued to gently flip the pages of his family album, as he shared even more views of a forgotten period. The children saw many moments of laughter, family, and friends, including all their uncles and aunts, memories undiscovered 'til now, and carrying with them that intriguing scent of past secrets and unknown events.

As children do, the young ones pointed to their own father, sitting in Brother Dela Rosa's lap, gazing up as if listening to a story too sacred to turn away from in order to please a photographer.

Mr. Dohrmann continued as he closed the old photo album with a reflective thump.

"It was Brother Al Dela Rosa who became the godfather to my oldest son, Tony......" He shook his head as if remembering something ... and then decided to go on past the thought.

By flipping the pages of the photo album, Bernhard had been able to show the children a family gathering of another time; a time when magic people in the children's lives were still very much alive. The children's grandmother appeared, and their late grandfather appeared again and again, like some elf from another world. Brother

Al appeared, and once he was holding a tiny baby at a Christening font as the baptismal waters were being poured upon Tony's baby head. (The captions explained it all to the attentive children for the very first time).

"Brother Al lived most of his life, children, never speaking a word," (Bernhard next showed them the stone walls of the peaceful Montclair Abbey at San Moritz) "living most of his life under a sacred vow of silence. Brother Al lived all of his time, inside a cloistered monastery high on an ancient mountain, never receiving visitors. Never having contact with the outside world. Never speaking a word, except in prayer or chant."

"However, there was a time, children, when Brother Al was asked by his reverend abbot to receive a 'special instruction'.... from a great mentor for the church, which would take him away from Montclair Abbey, as he would travel halfway around the world...special instruction to be provided by none other than your grandfather." (Bernhard tapped the picture of his father) "...Alan Gerrard Dohrmann."

"That was how it began. As Brother Al was granted permission to leave Montclair Abbey...and a magical relationship was formed between the monk and your grandfather... and, of course, with each of us who were honored to know that gentle, scholarly, funny, wise old man."

Now Bernhard reached behind his chair and pulled out an old faded parchment, a soiled scroll that looked like "real" Egyptian parchment. The children heard the slight, raspy noise as he laboriously unrolled the delicate scroll. He was quickly on his hands and knees beside them, huffing dra matically and making the children laugh as the scroll was laid flat. Next, he placed one heavy golden chess piece, from his father's chess set, onto each of the four corners of the scroll, which was finally revealed; an artistically embellished masterpiece. The children pored over it eagerly, soaking up the detail. The sight was amazing: hand-scribed letters much like an ancient bible, illustrations of great detail appearing here and there like inspirations.

They quickly became disappointed, however, for the entire scroll was written in the ancient and beautiful script of scholars. A special twinkle entered into Bernhard Dohrmann's eye as he said,

"Children, ALLOW me to translate......"

PREFACE

(From the scroll of Brother Al Dela Rosa):

I am now in my last years, the final twilight of a contemplative lifetime. At the age of eighty-seven, my own story is almost complete, as are these many scrolls. My goal in these final years has been to draw events from a memory that no longer works as I wish to command it. My gnarled fingers try to record something important, little Heart Diamonds which I believe represent tiny treasures for the world. A kind of adult fairy tale, the like of which has not been told.

I see this work as a gift to the children, and to every child inside the adult, that child who lies hiding under the older, more cynical surface, waiting to respond to childhood magic once again. For this reason, I have chosen to create these scrolls, in an attempt to convey some of the feeling of enchantment that those days possessed.

Not covered in my true-life adventure are details about the actual history of the family which precedes my own experience with the Dohrmanns. I have added only glimpses of a summary nature. It is my hope this addition to my more important effort produces some further color for the more ambitious "stories" that follow.

My hand hurts now when I write, and I am no longer sure of many specifics. My failing faculties permit me to write for only a short time each day.

My spare walls, home these many years, are constructions of stone and time. As my gaze wonders around an all too familiar chamber without the distractions of the world outside, I have only a small writing table, a sparse wood night stand and a familiar old bed comfort to these ancient bones these many years. Even so, I am angered as my memory fades; I fear a detail may be left out, or an important truth may now be forgotten. Such ramblings are the thoughts of a silly old man. For now regardless of how incomplete..... I must release the work for others to ponder. This will be my very last scroll.

For this reason, I saved until last the beginning work you read now, to assure that the manuscript contains the truth of it all. I complete these last words knowing that your adventure is about to begin....... as did my own a long, long time ago.

My gift of these writings....these adventures...so they may help you, guide you, inspire you...remains a gift to "the nine" (Terry, Pam, Bernhard, Mark, Geof, Melissa, Carl, Susan and Sally) the Dohrmann children....and then to the rest of the world.

I speak ever to the raw potential of your inner child. May you discover your own DIAMOND HEART as "your" journey begins...

Chapter 1

The Rose Garden

THE FIRST DAY

He was a peculiar child, in the very best sense of the word. Everyone who knew him at age four and a half thought of him as precocious. He asked adult questions. He would carry on adult conversations. At one point, in 1952, his mother, fearing that he might be departing from reality into a world of illusion, engaged a special child psychologist to provide direction. Dr. Eldeson would ultimately ask that the little boy cease his visits, stating:

"... because, Mrs. Dohrmann, I am starting to join Bernhard in conversations with his imaginary playmates....and I really think he is right as rain. Encourage his imagination and you will have so many new worlds to explore yourself...I do think YOU should keep seeing me however, for a few more weeks, to adjust to the mission of raising your special family....." (and she did).

I think it was around this time in 1952 that my part in this family's history began. I am trying to write the record down before my memory for dates is gone completely.

I write each day in this tiny room by sun and candlelight across huge spans of time. The stories are not all in sequence, I know, but rather in the chronology of the heart. With each scroll I find I leave these stone walls and travel to what it once was, a long, long time ago.....

I came into the tale when I was a much younger man focusing on my vocation at secluded Montclair Abbey, my cloistered home for many years. My abbot had referred me, without discussion or much explanation, to Alan Gerrard Dohrmann. It was related to me in a short meeting, called in Montclair Priory, that Mr. Dohrmann was a dear friend of the Church, and a special mentor to my abbot himself. I was selected by some process never revealed to me, for "special" training.

I can remember how it was in those days as if I were still living them.....

Although many traveled the Golden Gate Bridge route to Marin County from San Francisco, upon arrival in the city I had elected to take the old fashioned method of the ferry on my first visit. I longed for the view from the water as we passed by the red-orange shadows of the monumental steel span, called by someone, "One of the few human constructions ever to improve upon nature."

I enjoyed the coffee that was served by uniformed stewards in that more gracious time, as I sat within the salon of the Tiburon Ferry and looked forward to the conversations a ferry trip would deliver. For the time I would be out in the world, Father Abbot had released me from my vow of silence. A monk in robes always attracts fellow Catholics, and often those of other faiths, to lively discussions. Indeed, conversations of substance with relative strangers often glittered like polished diamonds in the sun in those days when conversation was still looked upon as an art form in some circles. One was never alone as a member of the Church wearing the robes of office, and talking was a luxury in which I was happy to engage.

A number of my fellow travelers were regular commuters on the ferry, and were familiar with the sight of Mr. Dohrmann and his guests going back and forth. One gentleman noted that Napoleon Hill had traveled just the week before to visit with him. Another mentioned having met Walt Disney and Mr. Dohrmann on a ferry ride several months before.

As the day warmed, we passengers went out on the foredeck to watch the choppy currents in the bay, and to feel the sun against our faces. The Golden Gate Bridge loomed to our left. About halfway through our journey, between our ferry and that loveliness arching overhead, passed the squat desolation of Alcatraz. As we slipped by, I said a prayer for all the souls within, who lived lives in superficial ways similar to my own ... regimented hours within stone walls. I reflected on how my life gave me peace and joy, while theirs were filled with anguish ... a matter of the soul's perspective and reaction to circumstance.

It was an uncharacteristically balmy day, although about three quarters of the way across the fog sent a finger to tease us with a chill, a sliver of white to remind us that this was still San Francisco. Sea gulls followed the ferry, hoping for a reckless moment of food-flinging from the tourists.

I became convinced before we landed at the charming Tiburon Ferry Terminal, that my stay at the Dohrmann home was going to be even more of an adventure than I had imagined. I invested a little more time in the quaint shops that lined the waterfront while waiting for the electric train to arrive. Back then, it all was "unspoiled." The emerald hillsides of Marin County were speckled with villages reminiscent of Europe, in timeless repose above the water. Unspoiled in a time of resounding innocence. It was all delightful.

The ceremony of boarding and departing in the old electric cars was a feast for an untraveled Benedictine living in a cloistered abbey. The conductors searched for even one stray passenger, and then the loud call of "ALL ABOARD!" marked the exit through the green chessboard land of Marin County, California. My compartment was empty, which allowed me to bask uninterrupted in the endless variety of nature along the way. It was as if I had moved from Montclair Abbey into the Looking Glass world within which Alice herself had journeyed. There was virtually no noise in those electric vehicles. The transition from lurching cars and metallic clanking to the flowing movement of our train at full power was marked by the smooth rythmn of wheels on rails. Marin County's extraordinary beauty unfolded around each curve, and the scents of redwoods, eucalyptus, and woodland herbs tweaked my nose through the opened windows of the compartment. I closed my eyes to the sights from time to time in order to fully enjoy the smells...both were intoxicating to one accustomed to the cloistered life...a fully-sanctioned intoxication, moreover, since it came direct from the hand of God.

Mount Tamalpais dominated the entire ride. First fully present in the twist into the hills of Mill Valley, and then playing hide and seek along the way through valleys on tributaries of the electric train tracks. Early Native Americans described it as a sleeping maiden who resides in perfect repose, silhouetted against the sky. I could see the contours of her face, her lips, the sweep of her body down to the little "foothills" ... a perfect word in this case, as they formed the small feet of the figure. So lovely and lifelike was she that I almost expected her to stand and greet us each time I spied the mountain from another viewpoint.

Clickity-clack, the train coasted between the summer home communities for San Francisco's emerging elite, past the old-money mansions in Ross, through the village of San Anselmo and onward to Mr. Dohrmann's outpost village, Fairfax. The final point in the line, at the Fairfax Bay station I was deposited in a roundhouse turnabout, next to an old creek bed. Nearby stood gigantic oak and bay trees. I was glad for the shade that day when I stepped off the train, as the summer heat was a constant reminder of the weight of a monk's robes, almost equal to the weight of our vows. Off to the side I noted a new "Woody" station wagon with windows down, which appeared to be waiting for me. As I waited for my luggage to be taken off the baggage car, I noted that I was the only passenger who had exited at the Bay Street Terminus station.

As the Woody wagon doors opened, a small boy, not put off by my strange habitual robes, ran the short distance to the train platform. I can recall the sunbeams bouncing off his perfectly blonde hair, and even from a distance the glimmer from his flickering blue eyes was engaging.

Stretching an arm out for a handshake, the young scamp said, as if years beyond four in age, "You must be Brother Dela Rosa....my name is Bernhard Dohrmann".

Then an unusual thing happened (remember, this was 1952) which may have been my first lesson from the Dohrmanns. The lad reached up to embrace me and said, to a complete stranger, "I'm a hugger, Brother Dela Rosa."

I found I was on bent knee almost before thinking, complying with the request for a hug, and feeling the strong little arms squeezing my neck, hearing the whisper in my ear, "You're going to love The Apartments, Brother Dela Rosa. Forest has your rooms all prepared ... we've all been waiting all day for you to come and play with us....."

I folded young Bernhard's hand in mine with a broad smile and said, "I've been hearing stories about you, Bernhard, and I can already divine that some of them must be true".

Smiling back and reaching to carry a suitcase bigger than he, as if we had done this routine a thousand times, he proclaimed, "Is this your bag, Brother Dela Rosa?" dragging it along the planks of the plat-

form in the dry Marin heat, never waiting to confirm
whether it was my bag, or not.....

I took the bag from him, not without a brief
struggle. I allowed him to carry a small "reading" suitcase, and pride was restored. We sauntered like old
friends to the waiting Woody station wagon. As the
driver door opened, a man stepped out wearing a broad-
brimmed hat, dressed in khaki shorts as if ready for
an African safari, with one hand holding a smoldering
red pipe and the other extended in my direction. Thus
began my very first dialogue with Alan Gerrard Dohrmann.

I was immediately put at ease by the strength
and light that flowed from the man. I felt warmed by
his sweeping smile which seemed to have no borders.
The way the light danced in his eyes, told me from
where the boy had received his magic. Both emanated
a strength of spirit that struck a chord in my heart.

After the shortest of pleasantries and a brief
pack-up of the Woody wagon we were off, and my life
with the extraordinary Dohrmann family began with
a carload of children and the scent of pipe tobacco.

I wasn't prepared for the shortness of the ride
from the train platform to the Dohrmann estate. The
little conversations about my trip evaporated as we
drove up the old buggy road to the converted stable
(now a garage) at the foot of the grounds. The car drove
up from Old Olema Road onto a steep circular driveway, past the old stables, and then down on the far side
back to the intersection of Bay and Olema. Old barn
lumber had been used to create the enormous garages.
Each of the two garages were cut into the side of the
hill, and looked like military bunkers with their vast
cross-beamed wooden doors. The huge redwood cross
bars suggested that when the doors were sealed, it
might be for eternity.

I noted two porters who stood on either side of
the gated stairway that led up to the home rising from
the surrounding gardens. Each was eager to take my

belongings up the many levels of stairs. As I followed in this procession, I noted how the many individual stairs and landings led up to the higher redwoods, which shrouded the Dohrmann estate. It was then that I first saw the main house that stood towering three stories over the cliff.

Walking into the compound on that first day felt as though I had stepped into a movie, which I perhaps, would rather have paid to observe, than to appear in. I can't remember anything that held the same feeling for me as the quiet procession into the Dohrmann estate that perfect summer afternoon. The feeling came not from the wealth which had created the buildings, but rather from the impression of peace within natural surroundings which pervaded all the area. Redwoods have a humbling effect upon even the most ambitious constructions of man.

I was escorted to The Apartments, about which I had heard from Father Abbot prior to my arrival. He had cautioned me not to be impressed by, nor to become accustomed to, the luxuries that would be mine to command during my stay. Mr. Dohrmann and the children passed by the turn I made to The Apartments; they mounted a different outside stairway to the main house. I was as yet too unfamiliar with my new environment to know that they were in all likelihood on their way to the play yards and the outside lath house, which served as a focal point for the entire Dohrmann family. I was presently occupied in being made comfortable with my own new surroundings.

The servants explained that Mr. Dohrmann had requested I rest until the dinner hour that first evening. Dinner would be served in the main house precisely at six. I felt a military precision in the way the message of "precisely" was imparted.

During the explanation of the amenities and workings of my new temporary home, my bags had been unpacked for me. My garments hung neatly or were placed into dresser drawers, fresh hand towels laid out for my immediate use. A huge bowl of fresh fruit was set with a welcoming card from Mrs. Dohrmann on the circular table in the kitchen, and another in the bedroom. There was fresh chocolate to tempt me.

As the servants departed, I considered a shower and a short nap. One could not help but explore, and I noted that all rooms included fifteen-foot double windows, opened and screened, with majestic views across the Marin County valleys. As I looked through a number of them I noted one could see from the main room all the way to San Francisco Bay. Five of these enormous windows had built-in window seats with colorful cushions that invited one to snuggle down into the perfected charm of it all.

It was more than a contrast to my routine lodgings of stone and wood in the Montclair Abbey, whose severe simplicity was calculated to constantly remind us of our vow of poverty. My one small cot and writing table held all the wealth of my personal estate back home. As I started for the shower, I recalled it was a long walk down an often very cold hallway to arrive at the amenities in the Abbey. Father Abbot's words of warning came back to me in force. It was not many minutes before I was refreshed, fully asleep and dreaming of the events to come.

I remember counting my blessings ... like sheep.

THE DINNER

Having showered before my nap, I was so completely refreshed that it was as if my long journey had never taken place. I remember that I fell to reading my assigned passages from the Bible on that first late afternoon in the Dohrmann Apartments. Father Abbot would have approved that my monastic routine was unmoved by time, location or circumstance.

The sounds of that first day remain with me more clearly than almost any memory: The background of the whispering redwoods, swaying and groaning with soft summer songs. The bees kept humming into my meditations, music of the Lord, accompanied by the soft rustle of leaves and occasional twitterings from birds that flitted in the branches. Occasionally there came from above childish giggling and shrieks of laughter, additional notes that cascaded down to my sitting room; wonderful sounds for a cloistered monk who heard children so rarely. There was a sound of expansion and contraction that was deep and sober, the resonance of an ancient redwood home. Each tone in this music of family life would come, after time, to be a treasured possession of my life.

I remember looking around the structure often as I read. A guest in The Apartments was always conscious of those who had preceded them. Works from famous men and women furnished the libraries in every room. Each hand-signed memento held its special note to Mr. Dohrmann. Presidents, kings and corporate notables adorned a dresser, a bathroom wall, or lined a hallway. From words of John Muir to Harry Oppenheimer of South Africa, the eye could catch something new at almost every corner of The Apartments.

You had a feeling of sitting in the rocking chair that had only recently cradled Walt Disney or William Penn Patrick. You had a respectful awareness that you slept and showered where days before Napoleon Hill had contemplated the same views. These thoughts would wander in and out as I tried to fix attention to my reading of Scripture. I pulled my reading glasses off and reflected on the "feeling of the place." I believe I could have challenged the Cheshire cat in a smile competition.

Eventually a light, correct knock came upon the door; I noted the time was 5:50. Forest, one of the gentlemen who had escorted me earlier, and head of Mr. Dohrmann's staff, requested my presence for dinner in the main house. I indicated that I was ready, and was promptly escorted up several exterior flights of stairs with wide, wood-paneled landings. We ended our climb upon the large porch area at the rear doorway to the main family living space. From this large porch with its lazy hanging sofa, amidst so many flower stands and urns, one could turn and literally see forever. The vista was breathtaking. I found myself guided by a touch from Forest, as I must have lingered a bit too long. Time had disappeared for me, but this was to be only the beginning.....

Walking in through an equally gigantic sun room, past two large ballroom-size living rooms, and into a large, formal dinner room, I was shown to my position in the center of the formally set dining table. As with all rooms of the Dohrmann house, the wall facing the dining room table opened to ceiling-high windows that faced a forest of tall trees and a vista embracing the lovely scenery beyond. The children (all nine of them) were already positioned, with two of the "babies" residing in hand-carved and painted antique high chairs. I was pleasantly impressed to note that Mrs. Dohrmann was a hands-on helpmate with her servants as she worked beside them in the preparation and presentation of the meal ... all the while taking time to welcome me and introduce me to each child.

I was moved that the children had "dressed" for dinner. Although I believed it was for my honor (a bit of pride which would have to be atoned for in my next confession), I would come to discover that this convention was family ritual for those meals in which Mr. Dohrmann was at home, presiding as head of family.

After being introduced and seated, I was left by myself to become acquainted with each child's personality. Terry was curious about my life in the monastery. Bernhard wanted to know why I didn't wear my hood raised. Pam wanted to know what we ate at the Abby. The helpers were constantly watching the "babies" with a napkin at the ready.

Geof wanted to play with my rosary beads. Mark was interested in my crucifix, asking "Had it been blessed by the Pope?" Susan and Sally sought to know who made my clothes, while Carl said I "looked funny". Baby Melissa banged her spoon into her plastic dish again and again.

At the exact moment specified for the dinner hour, Mr. Dohrmann arrived. He was dressed even more formally than I had anticipated, with a unique Sulka silk gray-on-black smoking coat. As he entered the room, the children became immediately silent (or what the family described as Nature Tone F). It was much like a Geary Street stagehouse play, all coming into the dining room and waiting until the main actor came onstage. I learned that such appearances were part of the theater of sharing time with this family and its legendary teacher.

Taking his place as if in a timeless routine, Mr. Dohrmann tapped his water glass and bowed his head. Folding his hands, he offered a blessing...

"Bless us, oh Lord, for these Thy gifts, as we appreciate the bounty You have placed before us. We thank You for our nourishment and our opportunities. We thank You for the health in our family and that all our members are strong and well. We thank You for bringing Brother Dela Rosa into our family and for permitting us the privilege of adopting him as one of us on this night. We ask that You provide special blessings to Brother Dela Rosa each day of his journey throughout life. We also pray that from his time with us here in our home...our prayers beseech You, Father, to guide Brother Dela Rosa so that he be blessed to discover his most perfect possible future through Your grace. We also pray, Lord, that Brother Dela Rosa attract the most perfect possible companions, partners and friendships with whom to share this most perfect future... Amen."

Then, with his beaming grin, while passing a bowl of mashed potatoes to me, he said simply, "Let's begin, shall we?" I would learn that when Mr. Dohrmann was not "away", dinner was always a formal affair, except once each week the family would have a "picnic" dinner in the outdoor lath house he had constructed for such occasions.

At all meals, dining was a time for family gathering, conversation, and tradition. I can think of no meal routine that was other than as I just described. The children were always dressed, the ladies in pretty dresses and the gentlemen in short pants with neat white shirts and suspenders. Mr. Dohrmann always came in last. Immediate quiet was expected as he opened each meal with his blessings.

It was from the first a routine with which I felt a comfortable familiarity. Even now I simply do not have the words to convey how it FELT to receive that first blessing on that evening of my first meal with the family. In an age gone mad with television and the destruction of imagination, the impact of old rituals of conversation and fraternity has been lost to so many of us. The memory of that time when they still prevailed is precious.

At some point during that first meal I recall the discussion between Mr. and Mrs. Dohrmann turning to the trouble that young Bernhard had gotten into the preceding afternoon. After hearing the description of the events in summary form from Mrs. Dohrmann, I sensed the serious penetrating stare that Mr. Dohrmann bent upon his oldest son. Mr. Dohrmann said words I would come to hear him recite often in the visits to follow: "Nature tone F, children, nature tone F." I would later learn from the immediate silence that Mr. Dohrmann had instructed the children to know that there was an absence of NATURE TONE F in the Universe and a call for it meant abrupt silence from the entire household, servants included.

Still holding his gaze on the young boy, Mr. Dohrmann said to the four-year-old ("Almost five," he would quickly correct if called upon) to recount the tale in his own words. The rest of the meal consumed most of an hour, during which time the boy failed to eat or, it seemed, to take in air, as the words flowed from him like a water fall.

I was delighted as the story unraveled, by the manner in which young Bernhard would bob his head up and down, fling his arms about for emphasis, and take us all in as his gaze shifted along the length of the table, as if the story were being told privately just for the one who held his eyes for the instant. I noted most of the children and even his mother, leaning "into" the story halfway through, and only Mr. Dohrmann continued to eat and ultimately relax back into his chair in an uninvolved, observational repose.

The candles were not really needed when we began to dine at 6:00, but as the story neared its conclusion I noticed their flickering back and forth over the childish faces, made the words even more magical than they otherwise might have been. Still, perhaps the magic was always there, and I just became more aware of it as the tale progressed.

THE GINGERBREAD HOUSE

The way it was told that night, it was really Ricky Brown's fault. The Dohrmanns lived at 555 Olema Drive. Ricky Brown lived down Bothine Drive and right at the end of Old Bay Road. The front driveway of the Dohrmann estate was a long and winding one that ended almost directly across from the Tobin estate. Hal Tobin was a promising young lawyer with two children, Robin and Doug.

Doug, although two years older than Master Dohrmann, was Bernhard's very best friend. Ricky was the local team leader, two years older than Doug. In the world of a four-year-old, the difference between ages six and eight are light years spanned only with unbridled imagination.

It seems that yesterday afternoon, Ricky Brown had wandered up to the Dohrmann estate, opened the large iron gates, and ventured down the terraced walkways to the play area. It was his custom to arrive unannounced and to take over directing affairs for the children, to the accompaniment of disapproving frowns from ever-watchful household staff.

The staging area for the beginning of our story was located out and above the Dohrmann main kitchens. This colorful area was a magnet for all the neighborhood children. Delightfully appointed and surrounded by beds full of flowers, this circle held the family swing sets, sandboxes and play areas. There were games, toys and play sets which were, of course, wildly attractive to the neighborhood children, so the place served more like a community park than a private family play area. Each of the swing sets, merry-go-rounds, and spring-rider horses was freshly painted and meticulously maintained, so that the children always had the feeling of playing with new toys.

Doug Tobin had already arrived and was playing with a group of older neighborhood boys, led by Larry Piambo. The Piambo family owned a huge estate adjacent to the Dohrmann home, and would on occasion entertain 500 Shriners in their outdoor picnic area, complete with permanent picnic tables. The children would frequently act as "Indian scouts" during these large Piambo events ... making raids on the chicken and dessert opportunities.

The action of young Bernhard's story was soon to move from the play yard to the forest area, but as I was about to learn, to get to the forest area, you had to walk across the Dohrmann grounds, through the double-lined walkways of flowers, past the vegetable garden, in between the lath house and the compost pile, and out the back way, through the barbed-wire fence to the trail. Once you got to the trail, you would climb one of the three giant stones called The Boulders, that sat like border guards to the long, sloping field beyond.

It wasn't really the open meadow that drew your eye, however. It was the adjacent Piambo mansion that sat off to the right of the trail. The Piambo home rose like a lighthouse from the dense Redwood Forest to suggest an old world tower which would block your path to the trail that lay in front. Bernhard explained that you wanted to see if old man Piambo was out working in his vegetable garden, or his flowers, or his glassed-in greenhouse, or anywhere else in sight.

Old man Piambo had built the mansion with funds from the large, well-known California construc-

tion company that bore his name. Although his sons ran
Piambo Construction in those days, the "old man" held
his hand on everything, and was treated with old style
Italian respect; a "Don of Dons" in his empire. In broken English, this imposing old man could spark any
trespassing child into flight with a single word from another country ... one that required no translation. Old
man Piambo loved his grandchildren (Larry being the
youngest), but believed strongly that the grace of young
children was that they should be SEEN, but never
HEARD.

The Piambo Estate sat like a gate on the freedom trail that led into the forests beyond. If the children could see the trail was "clear", they would run in
single file, like an army platoon, to the large chain-link
gate at the bottom of the long, sloping field.

Ricky had the lookouts holding the barbed wire,
as the "youngers," including Master Dohrmann, scampered through to the trail. The olders were already
upon the tallest of The Boulders, taking stock of the
Old Man Piambo situation this warm, late Wednesday
afternoon in the summer of nineteen hundred and fifty-
two.

The "safe" signal blew through the summer
wheat in the field. The safe sound was made by taking
a clean, young blade of summer wheat grass into
overlocking thumbs and blowing the "call." The
youngers knew this sound and were ready to RUN!

The trail invited the scouting party to venture
quickly and quietly past the long, wire fence of the
Piambo vegetable garden on the right, past the orchard
further down the trail, and finally out of the double
gates (young boys could squeeze through, the binding
chain was just long enough) and out across the old
Manor Road

Once on the other side of the old country road,
and past the stand of redwoods on the rising knoll, the
scouting party ventured up the steeper trail that led

into the real forests, the elders in the lead. The youngest in the Ricky Brown scouting party was six, save for
four-year-old Master Dohrmann. Crouched in a circle,
the elders paused to sniff out the way into the forbid-
den forest.

Even in the blistering heat of the late summer
afternoon, the sun seem to wink out in the shadow of
the towering redwoods. The coolness leached out into
the heat of the dusty trail. After only a few seconds of
deliberation, the party was sucked into the primordial
eternity of the original forest in Marin County. And still
the trail rose, higher and higher, turn after turn, until
the sound of the scouting party was lost to civilization
altogether.

A breeze like midnight rippled through the
shadows of the forest. Tiny monsters spread themselves from the upper boughs and teased the trail dust
with images from another time. The insects were a
hazard of the trail, giving occasional bites, but most
often simply an annoyance. Still, the relief from the
heat was welcome to the boys as they toiled on their
upward climb.

The shade was almost total as they turned the
bend, and the sun was captured completely in a shroud
of redwoods. The darkness was not foreboding at first,
because the end point still leaked light upon the entrance to the forest. However, it was only a few bends
before the focus of attention was the large ferns that
lined the way. Each footfall made a separate sound,
softened and muffled by the dust and fallen needles beneath. The trunks lined the passageway in Gothic
splendor, cathedral images almost inescapable as the
light filtered down in intermittent shafts. Each boy was
conscious of the stories that they'd heard, that these
trees had been present during all the wars of all time,
back before the time that Jesus Christ was alive in the
world, all the way up to the last war their fathers
fought in.

Ricky suggested each boy pick up a "magic stick" and strike the trees as they went. This act, he suggested, would protect the scouting party from the known dangers from wood witches and the evil spells they might cast on young boys. Most of the party complied immediately, carefully selecting sticks to match their own height. Each was tested on a tall tree trunk for sound quality. The weaker sticks were discarded in favor of stronger ones with greater "power." These boys were veterans of the ancient forest ... at least in theory.

And so the party wound their way ever higher, through the delicate ferns and redwood giants, tapping the trees for luck and protection as they explored their way. No one in the group had asked for or given an explanation of why they were taking this excursion or where the expedition might end. On only a few occasions, earlier journeys testing the way into these forests had been tried, but each had terminated far short of the point where sight of the entrance to the forest was lost.

After more than an hour of walking, the boys paused on a large stone outcropping to use their belt canteens in the spring-fed stream that peeked out from the cool, mossy stones, disappearing from time to time as it ran underground. Acquired from an army surplus store, the heavy metal containers were filled with water collected along the way, and this was a perfect spot. Looking back down their trail, they felt that a long journey into primitive times had already been accomplished. Going forward seemed more compelling when balanced against the prospect of returning downward along the now foreboding shadow line.

As it does in Marin, the sun abruptly changed its angle of attack around three o'clock. The sun dipped just beyond the high mountain line and a new shade descended upon the land. The new shadows cast themselves instantly like a battalion of demons, spreading into pockets of sunshine and devouring them. Each tree

became accentuated as if painted with new pitch, stain-
ing the leaves of life with tar. The renewed coolness
gave only a momentary warning before the hue altered
to dim the horizon with less optimism for small boys
in their scouting work. A pause with tangible vibration marked this moment for the boys. A hand went up.
A whispered command. Some small talk about, "What
was that?" and "Did you feel anything?" and "Let's keep
moving....."

"It's the witching hour," said Ricky, in a raspy
whisper on the far side of the bend. "This is the time
they are free to come out....."

"Yeah, and every tree must be tapped twice now
if we are ever going to get out of here," said the usually fearless Doug Tobin.

"My magic is stronger than any old witches,"
chanted young Dohrmann, who strolled with leadership authority to the front, tapping trees on both right
and left to reassert his claim as he went past.

"If a four-year-old can take it ... so can I," said
leader Brown, but copying each tree struck by young
Dohrmann as he followed, no longer in the lead.

In fact, the younger Dohrmann had wound away
ahead, and was now over a rise in the trail and out of
sight. The others ran to catch up, and as they came to
the top of the knoll and peered beyond, they noted that
the trail sloped downward on the other side for the first
time. Some twenty yards or so ahead was young
Dohrmann, with hands woven into great four-inch
squares of wire fence. The scouting party had found
something. Ricky was certain it was the purpose of the
entire mission.

Bernhard turned with his finger on his lips, and
the shhh-shing noise made sense to each of the young
scouts. They bent to scurry forward, knees low to the
ground and lower still, as they approached to the right
and left for their own fence positions.

The wire squares were eternal in appearance, like some painting, some giant mural that stretched along the horizon. Held in position every ten feet by giant green fence posts, each wire block of fence spread itself like a separate canvas. The fence wove its way on uneven terrain, as far as the eye could see, enclosing an area of many, many acres. The entire forest here was framed away, contained within the borders of this new perimeter. The barrier went on at odd angles, following contours far down in the valley, and way above on the high knolls beyond the view of what the boys, in their crouching position, could follow.

"What is it?" said young Dohrmann with some need for confirmation.

Still holding his hands through two square frames of the wire fence, Ricky said, "You're seeing what I am; you can see what it is as plain as I can."

"Yeah," said Doug Tobin with a long drawn-out whisper. "It's all true. Every word of it. It's the gingerbread house they took Hansel and Gretel to for sure," and his eyes went wide with wonder. For there it was, nestled in a grassy meadow, waiting all this time for discovery!

Ricky turned his eyes to follow the trail under the fence. His gaze continued in true scout fashion, down the fern paths and on to where the rock walls began. There seemed to be miles of trails inside the bastion of green fence posts. Each new trail was framed with rock terraces. Rock walls festooned with clumps of roses lined every inch of every trail, as if a bridal procession were soon to pass through each. Pools of green lawn would interrupt the pattern at random positions, as would clumps of redwoods, each with hammocks creaking back and forth in the gentle breezes.

"I could smell them before we got here," said Ricky as if his personal authority had somehow been restored with that observation.

"Me too," said Doug Tobin, to cement the good will of the leader even further.

"I could feel them," said young Dohrmann, and each looked at him as if he were perverted and then turned back to the awesome vista.

ROSES

Over two thousand rose bushes, but the scouting party was too stunned to count even ten. Roses! Showers of color filled every tier of every layer, along every trail within the fence. Some of the roses were far off, at the same level as the boys, at what seemed to the eye to be half a mile in the distance. A few of these pools of color framed orchards of apples and peaches in deep late-summer leaf. Additional rose beds framed the soft green lawns, as lower and lower the circles of stone-walled trails spiraled like a protective cocoon around the brown and green "gingerbread" home that sat dead square in the center of the garden.

Ripples of color and a thousand scents filled the air. Virtually one of every species of rose alive in the world was represented in this magical place, but the scouting party was far from possessing this arcane knowledge. Bright reds and pinks from Ecuador, striped roses from London, blue roses from India, yellows and whites from South Africa, green roses and the rare coral and chartreuse from around the world ... purple and orange ... black and burgundy and all the hues of any rainbow ever dreamed were captured in petals within the stunned vision of the young boys. Smells and sights too strong for young explorers to ignore.

It seemed even more magical that every red-wood-chip trail on every descending tier of the symmetrical garden was drifted with fallen rose petals, summoning young feet to run the gauntlet.

It might have ended there. The scouting party could have turned and taken their secret back home with them, precisely at that moment. Would have in fact. Almost, in truth, did.

But they paused to look and whisper about the..........Roses

Like the world has never seen.

So many.

So perfect.

In gardens nothing this side of Europe had ever imagined.

But it was not only the roses that swept them up. If it had been the roses and nothing more, the boys almost certainly would have dashed back over the crest of the trail behind them. Boys in quick flight, running full tilt to take the unearthed secrets of their scouting party to higher authorities.

These thoughts were flickering through each young mind when almost simultaneously they spied the TREE FORT!

THE TREE FORT

It looked terribly old. Made from barn wood, holding in its mossed boards the romance of a prairie cabin, it called to the boys in a way the garden never could.

The trail's end lay immediately in front of the boys. It insinuated itself under the wire fence, and downward into the forks of many trails that branched this way and that among the roses. In tier after tier after tier of stone embankments, lined by roses and fern trees, one fork led off to the left.

It was this fork which, when followed, led to the wider trail, the open trail that led among the high ferns to the SENTINELS. Three giant redwood spires of wisdom beyond time ... you could feel it. Redwoods so ancient they had stood the test of storm and time and fire to rise over two hundred feet in height above the cliffs and hills. These three, only these, were knitted together by man-made rooms.

The detail of the structure was inspiring to the young souls. Man-made rooms with quaint pitched roofs, and rope-held stairways, the most mystical tree house any scouting party of boys had ever laid eyes on. Little latches held shutters up above each of six windows in the magical tree home. Every detail was created with the tinkering of a child in mind.

"Get down!" Ricky exclaimed in his Full Command voice. "We have got to see if anyone is IN there. If no one is around we have to go and explore that tree house before we come home. If no one is around we can CLAIM it as our FORT of ROSES. It will belong to us!"

There was more than a little debate about whether it was "proper" to go and explore someone else's tree house. Some of the debate centered on the notion that a fence that was either very high or very long, to say nothing of being both, must be in place to keep people out as well as to keep people in.

The olders reasoned the fence might be only to keep the deer from eating the roses. It seemed a bit extravagant to the leaders that such a huge effort would have been made ONLY for the purpose of keeping trespassers out.

"It's magic, pure and simple," Doug Tobin concluded. "This fence was put here by magic." He looked so certain as he turned on his tummy to face the others.

"No one is going to argue with you, Dougie," said Ricky Brown. "That's why we have our magic sticks, just for this kind of thing." He tapped his stick against the green fence post near him, and a loud dull thud echoed into the forest. In the gingerbread house a dog barked twice, and then silence returned.

When Ricky looked back, young Dohrmann was on his back and already half-wiggled under the wire fence, struggling to stay centered in the trail that went beyond.

"What do you think you're doing?" the Brown boy hissed roughly, now standing and poking the younger child with his magic stick.

"STOP THAT!" Dohrmann was in no mood for debate. He had already pushed his own magic stick beyond the threshold, both for convenience and as a prudent measure against malign influences which might need strong opposition.

"I know what I'm doing," he huffed as his legs came free on the other side, and he stood with his own magic stick extended. "If you're smart, you'll follow me," but Dohrmann made no move away from the scouting party, rather huddling closer to the fence line.

"The fence is not here to keep people out," he said stoutly. "The fence is here to keep children IN," as he pointed far down to the gingerbread house.

"We found the secret way out. If we use our magic sticks we can always find our way back here, and the opening will appear if we tap it." The smile on the four-year-old was so compelling that it warmed the others. Everyone knew truth when they heard it spoken.

Doug Tobin was the next to worm his way under the small place where the wire bent back in. If you wiggled right on your back, you made it up and under and into the garden, which is exactly what Doug Tobin did.

Slowly all six of the party managed to squirm and wriggle their way past the fence line, and each stood in silence waiting for the last to "cross over."

Once fully inside the world of the roses, it was Ricky who assumed the leadership role, riled to be "one-upped" by a four-year-old. Crouching in Indian style, trained by Hopalong Cassidy and Roy Rogers, the party moved toward the big fork that led down to the tree house ... way down, past the fern line. They went as far as the point where the roses started. They turned however, off to the wide trail on the left ... the high trail ... the trail farthest from the Hansel and Gretel house below.

Circling far above the splashes of circular green lawns, and the framing rose rock walls that bordered them, they finally stood at the foot of the old wooden stairs. The stairs hung down to the forest-needle floor of the grotto by huge ropes that must have been made by pirates. The craftsmanship of the entire structure was totally satisfying, both outside and inside...the model of every boy's dream....

Rope-work banisters lowered or raised the wooden gangplank of a stairway. The rope rails made it appear easy to race up or down in haste to the pitched double doorway that led inside. Windows with flung-open, lattice-worked shutters rimmed the tree house. Little latches held the large double doors open against the wind ... inviting the boys to rush up and inside.

Ricky again took up the creaking lead, as he plunged ahead into the shadows of the open doors, and disappeared entirely inside the tree house.

"Hey, guys," he said to the timid at the foot of the gangway, still whispering as if his life depended on decibels. "You've got to see this. Hurry UP!" There was a compelling urgency in the tone that only young children fully understand. Compliance was immediate as they raced up the roped stairway, one and all, until all had disappeared into the dark coolness within.

INSIDE THE TREE HOUSE

It took a few moments to shake the energy that seemed to crackle in the air. Inside the tree house was EVERYTHING young boys would ever hope for. Without words, but with just eye contact, they each had agreed that if their lives were to end this instant, everything was now PERFECT. They were complete with this discovery. Their young lives had meaning now. They were, for the moment, filled with the overwhelming emotion of BEING CONTENT.

Their young eyes were soaking in details like a submarine periscope. There was a miniature sink with miniature handles featuring running water inside the tree house. There stood a table to snack or color upon. As if by the casting of a childhood spell, someone's four-color game board was carefully carved into the surface of this special table. Large flaps could be folded up and fixed into place to enlarge its surface. Every part was a fantasy for all those under ten. Large, wooden, hand-carved checker pieces, each heavier than any boy had ever seen before, were laid out as if for them alone. Little drapes of cloth skirted the open windows and fluttered in the breeze. The high pitched roof gave a church-like, mystical feeling to being "inside."

A fresh vase of roses, recently cut, sat in the center of the table and filled the tree fort with fragrance.

Little buckets of fruit sat off in the corners, as if waiting to be tasted.

Little towels were hung on little racks.

A small treasure chest of games that spilled over onto the floor stood over against the far wall.

Drawings of board games appeared in the floor as if burned by a witch's fire.

The guarding SENTINELS shot creaks and groans with each fresh breeze into the open windows and along the floorboards. This constant "shaping noise" provided a musical quality to the background, like an old ship's planks straining against the sea. As all this was soaking in, it took a while for the boys to speak.

MAGIC TREES

"We're going to come back here over and over. You know that, don't you?" blurted Dohrmann, in an almost machine-gun like exclamation.

"Yeah, we know, we know," Ricky exclaimed, resting his chin on his arm at the window sill, as he looked down upon HIS recently discovered rose garden. He was like a ship's captain long at sea, who had just heard the cry of, "Land ho!"

"We can bring stuff from home and make this place totally ours," Doug Tobin chimed in. He was gasping for breath as he spoke.

"Wait, you guys ... this tree house must have been built for other children. We are all going to get in trouble for just being here," said Jeffrey Roberts from New Marin Drive.

"Nah," Ricky waved his arms with authority. "LOOK at this place. It's old. Really old. And look," his index finger picked up some dust upon the game table as he held the soiled digit high in the air. "Any children who came to this place must be all grown up by now," which seemed to settle everything for Ricky. He scrunched back down to look out at the slopes of the rose garden, and far past the orchards to the valleys beyond.

Dohrmann almost sighed, with his head propped up, looking around the tree house as he pointed and said, "What about the fresh roses, Ricky? What about that fruit? Who put THOSE in here if this is so OLD?"

Lying flat on the floor to peer out through a knot hole to the lower part of the garden, Doug Tobin, the lawyer's son, hissed, "If that IS the Gingerbread House, we won't have much time to get away if the witch comes out."

Ricky moved to the window for a better view of the house and poked his head out, stating with inner certainty, "Well, if it IS the Gingerbread House, and if we hear even one sound, I want the entire scouting party out of here like Flash Gordon, everyone understand?" He looked around until everyone had their heads nodding, before a leader's satisfaction allowed him to turn back and look down into the garden one more time.

... *And then it happened.....*

The deep howling voice could scarcely be described, even in young Bernhard's words, as the "Dog From Hell" started barking. The barking never stopped, becoming more frantic once it started. The boys could see the enormous black and white head as it lunged to break through the windows of the Gingerbread House, obviously with perfect "knowing" of who the boys were and where they now huddled. It was odd for the boys, because it was not a bark like any they had known before. It was like a demon dog accusing the scouting party of some impossible violation. At some level each boy, now shaking with fear, knew that a wrong had been committed. A violation had been effected. Retribution was the only atonement possible. The deep baying was eager and knowing and urgent in the definition of its inner need. Each boy held a sense the dog was huge and powerful and cunning. It was the Hell Hound ... on the path to exact amends.

Frozen as the frantic wails continued to rise and rise, the boys felt the tree fort walls closing in upon them. What was once a cozy, welcoming space seemed now to be shrinking, compressing time and space in additional punishment to the assault on their ears and nerves coming from the Hound.

To compound the change in circumstances that had befallen the scouting party, the large green door on Gingerbread House slammed open so hard its window panes vibrated with a wicked clatter. A black and white, oversized, overfed spaniel from the nether regions roared out onto the lower lawn, showing fangs fully bared, vigilant in the protection of its Gingerbread domain. The spaniel lurched and lurched, threatening the tree house with ravenous eagerness, glaring hauntingly at the boys.

This was all bad enough; the impact of the next event was far beyond the ability of the scouting party to absorb.

For next, the witch came out! ... her voice already rising directly to the magical tree house as if nothing in the universe was hidden from her.

In a flash of recognition the scouting party identified the witch: plump with short, cropped, gray hair, that in its odd way of coming to points here and there, seemed to have been coifed by a butcher, or possibly a gardener with dull hedge clippers. A very broad hat with a point on top was snatched from its hanging position on a peg in the outside wall and placed upon the aging head.

The grapefruit face squinted and strained to see the upward distance to the tree house. For the first time, the boys noticed the red brick master walkway that tied all the Rose Garden trails together, the master walkway that led directly from Gingerbread House to the wide trail from their no-longer-secret position.

The boys, as if on a single command, had fallen flat to the floor when the thundering opening of the door to Gingerbread House had rumbled across the clearing. Each member of the scouting party now peered through a crack or knot hole, and more than two were visibly shivering. They were thinking,

"*So is THIS it?*"

"So it all ends here ... just like Hansel ... just like Gretel."

Each knew the witch in the core level of their being. There was no possibility for error.

"So this is iT!" Dohrmann gasped out ... to no one listening. Too much hell-hound barking. All attention on the witch ... no one was hearing any more.....

The dog never stopped, but also never strayed from her master's side. The boys concluded the giant dog was held in check by an invisible leash.

Grabbing an upside-down broomstick that was held by pegs similar to the ones that had held her pointed witch's hat in place, her voice cracked with age and yet powerful enough to halt the wind, cried out:

"Boys ... boys ... I can SEE you in there. I know you're up there. You can't fool me!" and then she pointed her broom handle directly at the tree fort in a threatening motion. (Ricky would later declare he was certain that spells were leaping off the rounded end directly into the wind).....

Still waving her broom stick wildly in the air and flinging her arms all about for emphasis, the witch cried, "Boys, you'll hurt yourselves. You're too little and that's too high for you to play unsupervised. Now you come down here this minute or I'll have to come up there and get you out!"

At this point, according to Mr. Dohrmann's young son, she grasped the broomstick, and was all set to jump up and fly directly around the tree house. However, as the report was delivered to me by only one, and that the youngest of all the participants, there may be room for doubt. I believe it was Ricky who finally broke the hypnotic moment with his declaration.....

"She's not going to lock me in that old iron cage and eat me ... I'm telling you, she's NOT going to eat

ME....." At which point Ricky flew down the trap door stairs, and blistered the ferns in his exit through the point of entrance to the Rose Garden. Young Dohrmann said...the speed of his exit seemed swift enough to set the redwood chips ablaze.

No one is quite sure what the other members of the scouting party said, but it was noted that each said something. There were words floating in the air, no one quite remembers who said what or when ... but it went something like:

"I told you not to come into this place,"

and,

"I'm not sticking no bone out through a cage for the rest of MY life,"

and,

"You better come on, Bernhard,"

and,

"Ricky ain't seen a day when he can outrun me when I'm really, really scared,"

and,

"Bernhard, ain't ya comin'?"

and,

"Do you think that demon dog can fly?"

and,

"Forget the dog, do you think SHE'LL fly after us all the way down?"

and,

"Don't forget your magic stick or we're doomed!"

and,

"Bernhard, ya better come now ... you're the last one....."

Each cry followed by footfalls like hooves at full gallop, as the little legs and shoes swallowed up the distance from the bottom of the rope-held stairs to the exit from the Rose Garden at the end of the far, Wide Path.

Now, at this point everyone had a different memory of what had taken place. It seems pretty clear that it was almost at the bottom of the trail, near the first stand of Redwood trees that the scouting party caught up to one another. Near old Manor Road and the safety of the chain link double gate to The Boulders at the top of the way to the Dohrmann estate.

Even so, it was some moments catching their breath before Ricky began heaving for air between coughs with, "I wasn't really scared, you know," and others with their predictable "Me neither's", and with small talk for some minutes before Doug Tobin chimed in with, "HEY ... where's BERNHARD?"

Doug remembers that Ricky's face turned a bit ashen as his gaze went back into the shadows of the deep forest. Some say Ricky even started back up the trail a bit, but others say he never did. Finally, everyone agrees, Ricky was slapping his hands at his sides, washing away the dust which floated around his hands. Shaking his head no, no, and even OH NO, he circled the group, secure and safe in the lower Redwood stand opposite old Mr. Piambo's yard ... looking upward ... upward to the trail that led into the darkest forest anyone had ever known.

"You can't know if he is even still up there," he turned and pointed at the forbidding trail, drenched in shadows. "We don't know which WAY he might have run. Bernhard didn't stay THERE, you all know that! You all KNOW that, right?" There was unanimous nodding. They all KNEW.

Sounding a little more confident, Ricky continued with, "He could have run AHEAD of us, you know! He could even be home right now while we stopped to wait for each other. He's the one that's going to get in trouble."

Doug Tobin added, looking really depressed and sounding worse, "No one is going to believe us, you know. No one. We can't say we found a magic garden and a witch and the REAL Hansel and Gretel house.

We'd be grounded for weeks. Especially if she has already eaten Bernhard."

A younger member of the original scouting party added woefully, *"I'm pretty sure that if grown-ups went up there, the Rose Garden would be invisible to them. Like in Flash Gordon. It would drop out of time and vanish from their being able to see it. I think kids are the only ones who can see the garden or get in ... or out."*

"Yeah," exclaimed Doug Tobin in a best-friend kind of voice. "But what about Bernhard? WHAT!? He could be trapped up there with that old witch in that magic garden in and out of time place. Where is that going to leave all of US?"

"I'll tell you where that is going to leave all of US," said Ricky Brown, certainty returning to his voice. "We're going to all face the music together. Each one of us is going to tell anyone, if they ask, and ONLY if they ask, the same story, and here is the story:

1. The olders went on a scouting party like we always do.

2. Bernhard was told he couldn't come, so he took a nap. We left Bernhard with instructions to wait as lookout at The Boulders 'til we got back, like he always DOES.

3. We got back to The Boulders and he was gone and we didn't know where he had gone off to. We called around but he was gone. We figured he went back inside to sleep.

4. We just played in the children's yard until it was time to go home.

5. We don't KNOW what happened to Bernhard, and that's the TRUTH. We don't KNOW ... so let's get on with it!

"That's it ... everybody got it?" Ricky was glaring, on tiptoes, with his tallness towering over everyone in the scouting party for effect. His hand was raised waiting for agreement.

The others just looked at the ground and agreed with the body language of sad eyes and sunken, nodding heads. No one said a word. Ricky was already walking toward the big, double chain-linked gate. The others were being led up the trail to The Boulders and past to the Dohrmann home. They followed slowly, as if by looking back and lingering they would see young Master Dohrmann rush from the wooded trail and leap out of an ancient forest that just may have swallowed the four-year-old forever.

ALICE MAHONEY

As soon as the last boy had vanished beyond the line of green fence posts, the eyes of the witch returned to the tree house. The great demon dog had become even more agitated, as if stung by hornets. The invisible leash upon which the black and white spaniel strained continued to hold, but it appeared to the mind of young Master Dohrmann to have greatly weakened. The Giant Animal was precluded from rushing head on, up to the tree fort and forthwith devouring the young boy only by invisible threads of the witch's binding spell, that was now becoming dangerously stretched and frayed with each new burst from the animal.

After what seemed an eternity to the one frozen in fear inside, the witch placed the broom against the side of Gingerbread House, as if she sensed the spectacle she was making of herself. A great tension seemed to go out of the moment with this friendly gesture. At this point of it, young Bernhard was so wild-eyed it seemed his heart had ceased to beat. Certainly his last breath had been drawn at least ten minutes before.

The witch's skirt whirled as she spun with impossible agility and disappeared inside the darkness of the house. The dog continued to lurch at unnatural angles of attack and with each lunge increase the fury of its protest. The invisible leash continued to hold.

Sometimes the dog would seem to lurch off its front feet and leap with only its back feet in place as if to demonstrate the impossible strain upon the witch's magic tether. The barking was never-ending, with each deep-throated howl a protest from another dimension.

Lying crouched on the floor of the tree house beneath the games table, young Dohrmann held his head in both little hands, as if the rehearsed protections against a nuclear blast that his older siblings had told him about would somehow serve him well in this equally catastrophic situation. Shaking in a fetal ball, he would from time to time revisit the knot hole to see how long it would take for her to place him into the iron cage. He was uncertain whether she would use magic, or come up in physical form and simply carry his limp body to its final place of torment.

While the witch was gone there was a snatch of time to assess the situation. Looking backwards over his shoulder, he concluded that all of the scouting party, his "friends" had long since vacated this terrible spot. Not even one companion was left for comfort. In fact, thinking about it at the dining room table, great emphasis was placed on noting that NO ONE in the scouting party had seemed to care or notice that they had left him, alone, the youngest ... left behind to die. Or perhaps worse than die!

Next, during those fragile seconds, Bernhard searched the pathways for routes of immediate escape. There were many teasers. All paths had a particular property he had not noticed earlier. Each path led to a central wide red brick path, the MASTER PATH, which led in only one direction. Down, ever downward, directly to Gingerbread House.

"All roads lead to Rome," he thought ... not really knowing what it meant but recalling it having some reference to what he was seeing.

and,

"Go directly to jail, stick a bone out, not your finger, before you die, do not collect two hundred dollars, never buy Board Walk....."

and,

"Ring around the Rosies, pocket full of Posies, ashes ashes, we all fall down ... *dead*" (he had added for emphasis).

For some reason he did not feel SAFE trying to run for escape as the others had done. He longed to make the run to the fence line and back to his old world but he could not uncurl from his balled position. Leaving the safety from under the table seemed an impossible feat at the moment. His limbs would refuse to obey if ordered to do so. He KNEW that at a heart level of intelligence.

There seemed to be a sense of destiny, of being frozen in place with a standoff that had to shift in order to start TIME again. Bernhard was convinced that the witch had stopped time.

He was no longer certain how long it took to resolve the contest of will. The result could still be that he would be home in time for dinner ... or the result might be he would lose his eternal soul to the witch. He gulped, hoping he was not to become soul food for the howling demon dog. He was, as he said afterward, a "tiny bit" nervous, holding his fingers just so far apart to let us all know exactly how much a "tiny bit" actually was.

Bernhard's attention was abruptly called back to the porch when the witch suddenly, as magically as she had departed, returned to the scene. She was holding something in her hands. In fact, she held the "something" up towards the tree house and when she did, a miracle seemed to happen. The Demon Dog STOPPED barking and stared at what she held in her uplifted hands.

"Boy!" the witch cried in a loud voice. "BOY? I have something here for you. I am holding a plate full of warm cookies. They just came from my oven. I won't hurt you. My dog, Flower, won't hurt you." (Bernhard remembered the impact of learning a demon dog's name was FLOWER).

"I promise, Boy, I will not hurt you in any way," (shaking her cookie plate slightly, as if to waft its fragrance towards him). "If you come down right now, I'll give you all the cookies you can eat. I promise on my word of honor, Boy, I'll show you a short cut how to get home. In fact I'll walk you all the way back to your house so you won't be afraid if it gets dark. My name is Alice Mahoney and I WON'T HURT YOU! I swear it ... in fact, I will only protect you if you will just come down ... I give you my word! I'm so afraid that you will fall and hurt yourself, so please come down from our tree house!"

Bernhard could plainly see the cookies. The effect on young Dohrmann was nothing like the one they were having on the dog Flower. Flower's entire body was shaking as if some kind of convulsion had come upon her. She was rolling over on the lawn, doing her "good girl" tricks on the grass like the best dog ever. Her tail was wagging back and forth so hard, that the entire back end of the giant spaniel was awash in leaves and dirt as she "spilled over" into the trail by the side of the lawns.

Bernhard shifted his gaze back to the witch, as if something in his memory made him think that any witch with a name like ALICE might turn out to be a good witch. There were, as he knew, good witches, like Glinda in *The Wizard of Oz*. As a matter of fact, young Dohrmann recalled from some fairy tale or other, that if a witch gave you her name, the person who received this secret name held immediate power over the witch. He was sure only good witches ever gave you their name. He spent some time explaining his rationale to all of us at the dinner table, as if it were more significant than other parts of his story. We all nodded as if we were quick to grasp the concept.

He also remembered that witches who swore and gave you their word of honor, became BOUND by the Law of the Universe. Such witches could lose their power if untrue to their own word. This more than any other memory caused young Dohrmann to uncurl from his ball under the tree house table and begin to descend. He wanted us to understand his choice had been made after considerable reflection on the foregoing wisdoms.

It was as he was taking his last look at the Tree House domain, that he remembered his magic stick.

In fact, all the magic sticks from the scouting party were in the tree fort. Everyone in the scouting party had scampered away without their protection. Young Dohrmann was fearful none of them had made it back home alive.

He reached back into the tree house and scooped up his personal magic stick, as if his own life depended upon it. He was certain, in fact, that this act would later be the saving of this day.

"I'm taking insurance," he said to himself as he descended, holding on to the rope banister, aware of the redwoods' haunting groan as each breeze taunted the silence. Alice sat on a step by the gingerbread house with her overgrown dress spilling over her like a circus big top.

Even though "Bee" (as the family called him) wasn't sure what "insurance" really meant, he tapped the ground and all three redwood trees carefully before he began to take the wide trail down toward Gingerbread House. He never took his eyes off Alice Mahoney, although his senses were bombarded by the smells of two thousand living roses and a plateful of chocolate chip cookies. Seeing her head bob under the enormous straw hat, Bernhard thought for a moment, if only a moment, that Alice Mahoney might be a circus clown rather than a witch. Then he remembered his father's stern condemnation, in several pointed remarks, of those who judge others only on external appearance. He decided to give the witch a chance to show her goodness. We who were listening to the tale were given to understand that this decision had NOTHING to do with the chocolate chip cookies.

"No, no! You awful dog. You're going to frighten the boy!" Alice cried out with a another bob of her head and a wave of her hand. Her pointed hat and long rumpled sleeves made her a character from Lewis Carroll.

"Now stop it this minute. STOP IT or no cookies for you!" Alice's pitch was so stern that young Dohrmann paused in his winding way downward to the rising aroma of fresh cookies. Upon Alice's multiple commands or by some secret spell (Bernhard wasn't quite certain which) the dog fell to the grass and ceased its commotion, keeping a watchful eye on the boy first, and then, and more importantly, the cookie plate. Flower's eyes had turned woefully pathetic, removing almost all of the red demon fire that had been so evident from the tree house.

Standing erect, which was not "tall" (Alice Mahoney was a small, old witch) and motioning with her hands to the boy she said softly, "Come around THIS way, young man ... come THIS WAY." She gestured towards the pathway that led between isles of roses, to the wide sloping brick path, surrounded by rose gardens on either side, all the way down to the house.

The setting of Gingerbread House was like a Greek theater in which all the seats were overbooked by roses. Row after row of sold-out theater tickets had been taken up by virtually one of every breed of rose bush in the world. They all seemed content to sit and watch the play house that Alice had built in the very center. Their applause was the fragrant breeze and their standing ovation petals as bright as any sunshine. It was as if a photographer's pose had trapped Gingerbread House in a bathtub of flowers and the home itself drained all that beauty to Alice Mahoney.

Bernhard's timid steps set a peculiar flow of thoughts into motion in his four-year-old mind. He found himself wondering what it would be like (he later explained to us) to wake up in Gingerbread House. He found himself comparing his own room in the Dohrmann home, to the fabulous small viewing window in Alice Mahoney's cottage. He felt, in this real-life Wonderland garden, as if a magic rabbit had led him here. With each step he took, Bernhard was becoming less and less afraid.

(I noticed Mr. Dohrmann was becoming very attentive to the story as his young prodigy displayed the courage to face his fears in an unknown fairyland of roses.)

"Sit, boy. Sit!" commanded Alice, like a grandmother speaking The Law to a grandson. "I know you're scared, so here, you eat these cookies." She held one out directly to young Dohrmann's mouth, conveniently open with astonishment.

"As many as you want. Eat! I'll get some milk," she said pleasantly, "and mind the dog doesn't get ANY while I'm gone!"

Turning to Flower, she scolded, "You've been a bad, bad dog and you're not getting cookies now as a reward for being a rascal!" With a long huff like the wind near Half Dome, she rose on her short, stubby legs and propelled her frame into Gingerbread House. The floor boards creaked within.

Returning instantly, she snatched one of the cookies from the plate she had left on the steps just below Bernhard's feet, and bit a corner and smiled and winked as she ate, saying "They're not poison, you know." She turned and the brown shingled cottage, with its green shutters and bright green door swallowed her up. The sounds of a refrigerator being opened and milk bottles clinking and glasses tinkling came out the door, as Bernhard sat under the ever-watchful eye of Flower. Flower had become the saddest of all dogs watching the cookie plate and its shrinking supplies.

The boy, teased by the smell of fresh cookies, tasted one, and then another. By the time Alice returned with the much-desired milk, the boy had eaten several. Looking up with a belated smile on a face showing more chocolate than skin, Bernhard said, as if he had been familiar all his life with the garden of roses, "Can I give Flower a cookie?"

"Well, I don't know," replied Alice, fixing the dog sternly with her magic stare. "Flower, you know better than to be such a bad, BAD dog?" Alice seemed to carry on rather long conversations with Flower on such subjects as being BAD, being VERY BAD and being in a condition known as AWFUL.

"You have been a very naughty dog! What do YOU think you deserve for being so very naughty? So you think you deserve even ONE cookie for being so awful today?" She paused, waiting for her answer.

Flower, meanwhile, was stirring up a cloud of dust with the waving of her tail in reply to her master's attentions. Flower's head was moving first in one direction and then in another, as if it were on some form of hinge.

"OK," as if a huge deliberation was now resolved, "... one cookie." Turning back to Bernhard as if needing to be thoroughly understood, "She is as fat as a hippo and she needs to go on a diet!" This was said very sternly with a good deal of finger pointing to Flower. "AND, not a cookie diet either, you BAD, BAD DOG."

Bernhard already was up and slowly moving down the steps, holding out his cookie to Flower. She was stretching an impossible length of neck and nose to reach the attractive smell. Flower seemed to have acquired an Alzheimer's remembrance for the earlier disturbance. Her entire body was shaking as if some gigantic current had connected to her toes and legs.

It was clear from Flower's eyes that her self talk went something like:

Why, this was her best friend "man" was it not?

Why, this was her bosom buddy, "the boy" was it not?

Why, this was the cookie boy; that was clear ... was it not?

The nice, nice cookie boy ... the nicest of them all ... was it not?

And with the gentlest of manners, and a nibble first, then a full-on grasp, the cookie was gone, followed by some finger licks and a new friendship bonding ceremony.

The dog approached the stiff, blond-haired, blue-eyed boy who stood at attention. First a sniff-down initiation, followed by a face licking that brought smiles followed by hand waving and laughter. Soon it was clear that some form of adoption had taken place. Clearly the boy had become the property of the dog.

Bernhard was soon petting Flower from one end to the other, and then all over again, to the great delight of animal and child. Flower ultimately rolled upside down for a belly rub while the opportunity was so generously being accepted by her new "puppy".

Alice shook her head in a knowing way, just short of full approval. She placed her milk down by the cookie plate, helping herself to a remaining warm one, before the rest could be devoured. She was certain they would be, now that the "adopted" boy took his marching orders from the dog. She plopped down on the porch stoop and watched the boy and dog in delight, displaying all the wrinkles that her face had to offer.

After a time, Bernhard returned to his stair chair, and one by one the cookies disappeared. One for him. One for Flower. One for him. One for Flower. Alice was certain a telepathic agreement had been reached.

As a milk line formed around his little boy "O" mouth he said (as if continuing a conversation that in fact had never begun), "It's getting dark! If I don't get home by dinner, I'm going to get in a lot of trouble."

As if she had always possessed such information Alice said simply, "I know boy, I know. We had better be on our way."

And then, to the boy's astonishment (as he could not recall having mentioned such a secret thing earlier), she said quite matter-of-factly, " Boy, get your magic stick and let's be off. "

He, for the first time, wondered the question of questions, "How did she KNOW?" (Over the following years he would ask this same question too many times to score.)

He picked up his magic stick, looking up at her quizzically, and followed her down a wide path away from the house, a path in shadow and forest which he had not walked or seen before, a path of pine needles and dried redwood bark, that led to tiny earth stairs that ran off into the darkest, deepest forest. Tree ferns reached out from the side walls like micro monsters wanting to test the passer's resolve. Some looked exactly like creatures, with their weird spores like hairdos.

Bernhard had never seen, over his entire four and one half years of living, anything like the rose garden. As he ascended the earth stairs from Gingerbread House to higher trails, he turned to take one last look at the colors. It was like bright candy in the best stores and he cast the vision into memory. Using his magic stick like a cane, he followed the wide square back of Alice Mahoney into the lower woods.

Tiny bridges marked the point between paths and way off below was yet another GREEN fence gate that led to even lower trails, trails that eventually led them to an old dirt road. Alice was already down to the second bridge when she said quite as if the boy were heel and toe with her, but loud enough to carry,

"I've told you I'm Mrs. Mahoney, what's your name, boy?"

"Bernhard Dohrmann," came the instant reply.

"Ah. I knew your grandfather," as if that were a normal retort, but Alice never looked back and soon was opening the gate. In a twinkle both boy and witch were out of the fenced enclosure of the Rose Garden and proceeding into the jungle of a redwood gorge. A whine from Flower left no doubt how irritated Alice's dog was at being left behind. Soon the whimpering was lost in the blend of other sounds from the cool deep forest.

By and by they came to the old dirt road. Here Alice stopped and pointed up and down.

"Mark the way boy. Mark it well. Take a look at these marker trees, and the bend in the road. Make a picture of my stairway. Grab it all into your mind. This is the short cut. And anytime you wish to return to my Rose Garden you are welcome. Day or night. Come anytime. Know the way. Make good note of it. Quick, quick, we don't have all day. You'll have to come and go on your own in the future, you're way too big to have me walk you everywhere you want to go," and with those words, she began walking down the old dirt road at a pace that stretched the little legs that followed her.

His head was turning this way and that, seeking out landmarks. Touching unique stones, trees and other plants, as many as he could with his magic stick, he tried to think what a "marker" was. He felt he could use his magic stick to make sure an invisible twinkle light (that only he could see) would guide him back. Pure Pixie Dust. He was sure of it.

He could see it being sprinkled on each item as he tapped it. Alice didn't talk much and never seemed to notice his magic ways.

Now and then when she did talk she said things which meant something (unlike many adults he had met).

Things like:

"Need a boy to weed when you come back," and,

"We can play games ... have lots of games," and,

"Like to read ... can read stories to you ... great stories, you will like them"

and

"Like to bake ... brownies ... cookies ... pies ... things like that....."

Alice was puffing a bit and it was clear to young Bernhard that walking such a distance was not something to which her roly-poly legs were accustomed.

Finally, as if a tarp had been rolled back from a twist in the road, the remaining sky was filled with sunset. The winding dirt road (the short cut) ended, and much to Bernhard's surprise, exited on Old Marin Drive right by the Piambo gate. In clear view, and just up from the first stand of redwoods, was the gate trail home. The Boulders had come into view as they walked the few more steps to the chain link gate.

"I believe that's you, I believe that's YOU," Alice said, pointing up the way trail to The Boulders.

To which Bernhard, running past the old witch, keeping firm hold on his magic stick said,

"I won' t-tell a-anyone you're a witch, Mrs. Mahoney, I promise."

To which she answered ... as if a sadness had come upon her, "Tell your father and mother ... and tell them Alice Mahoney says hello."

The next time he looked back, almost at The Boulders, he could see nothing of Alice Mahoney. She had vanished behind him ... poof! just like magic.

(Authors note: If I exercise a little license with pictorial language years removed from the telling of Master Bernhard's story, I assure you the spellbinding

saga held us all captive at dinner that night while one four-year-old upstaged his father. We had all traveled to the Rose Garden and fixed our gaze from the windows of the tree house. Every child, and every adult, was capitvated that night ... and unknown to anyone was the many times this story would be retold as the years pressed forward.

This was my first experience in the Dohrmann home, and so all the more delightful. I would much later discover the children's enchantment was the norm rather than the exception. In fact, as I would discover over time, not one child among them understood how special was their circumstance, for each of the Dohrmann children believed that these adventures were simply the "way of it" and for each, their life was that of Alice in the Looking Glass. *This was the reality that each child saw as their day-to-day living experience. In time I came to join them on the "other side" of their looking glass, and the world of the children became so completely my own that my life path was forever impacted. However, that part is yet another story.....)*

MR. DOHRMANN

As the story came to an end, Mr. Dohrmann ᵣsed up in his chair and folded his arms. He leaned ᵣrward on the large dining table staring at his son as ᵣf he just had recited the Bible out loud, cover to cover. He cleared his throat, and then in a somber voice.....

"Is there MORE.....?" A long, silent pause followed as all the children stared at Bernhard and then at their father.

"No Dad. No more."

The other children were focused on their father now. Mr. Dohrmann looked at his wife and said, "Children, your mother and I have been very careful to teach you things about nature and how we live. We live in the country. We therefore must have respect for the things of nature.

"If young children wander very far off from their home, they might get hurt." (Eight heads were nodding; baby Melissa had not quite reached the age to be able to grasp these concepts, but even she watched her father intently, and as she saw the motion of all the others, her own head began to bob up and down.)

"They might fall. They might get lost. They might even be attacked by animals in the woods. We have set the limits of where the children can and cannot travel ... and you all know the limits. We have an enormous yard for you to play in. We have the upstairs yard. We have the downstairs yard. We have The Flats at the top of the hill. We have The Boulders and the "monkey grinders" for you to play in.

"Bernhard, do you know the limits set by this family?" The stare was now so fierce, blisters were welling up in young Bernhard's eyes, as the tears started to come.....

"Yes, Father," he wavered.

"Bernhard, do you know that you went outside the limits?"

"Yes, Father."

"When did you go outside the limits?"

"When I left the Boulder area, Father?"

"And why are The Boulders the off-limit point, Bernhard?"

"Because that's where you can see from the house, Father?"

"That's right, that's where your mother and I and the family can SEE. So what do you think the punishment for a mistake THIS LARGE should be?"

"I don't know, Father."

"You want to teach the other children about what happens when you break the rules, don't you?"

"I don't know, Father."

"You know that God has rules, don't you?"

"Yes."

"You know that God has laws and what happens when you break his rules, don't you?"

(A very shaky sigh) "Yes, Dad, I know."

"Then what is the punishment that is fair for the Rule you have broken, Bernhard?"

"I don't know, Dad." The answer was very mournful now. The little head was hung way over his place at the table, and all the children were fixed on their sibling. It was odd as I think about it now, but none, not even one, seemed to enjoy the moment.

"Well Bernhard, I DO know ... so let's go through it. First, you will apologize to your mother before you

go to bed. You will find a WAY to let her know HOW
SORRY you are for how scared and worried you made
your mother feel. Do you understand?"

"Yes, Dad." Large tears were shimmering in his
eyes now .....

"Second, you will have no privileges or playmates for one week. This is because you didn't ask for
permission when you broke the rule. Do you think this
is unfair?"

Dejectedly: "No, Dad."

"Then, family, let's clear the dinner table and
adjourn to the living room, because tonight is LESSON
Night. It's time for your lesson. So let's begin."

As I didn't know what "Lesson Night" was, I had
no way to know that my first dinner with the
Dohrmanns was not yet complete. Dessert was coming!

THE FIRST LESSON

I remember there was a twinkle in Mr. Dohrmann's eye, as a flurry of commotion began. The dishes evaporated and the lights came down low, and before many moments had passed, the children had scurried. I was escorted during the moments that followed by Mrs. Dohrmann on a tour of the house, room by room. I would later learn that a regular drill was taking place. A drill to be completed within a five-minute timetable. A drill everyone but the guest knew was a very serious "rule."

Mrs. Dohrmann ushered me by the arm into the smaller of two large living rooms upon completion of my house tour. There were only three items of furniture in the large, open room. Off alone, along the long wall was Mr. Dohrmann's prized grand piano. In the center and facing the large white piano was a generously-sized, high-back easy chair with an ornate footstool. On either side of the easy chair was a handsome side chair, framing it in a cozy grouping. The pale yellow pastel flower patterns for the three matched chairs went very harmoniously with the hardwood floors and the tall recessed ceilings with their carved moldings. The simple setting and graceful proportions made the room feel complete, even without the customary sofas and tables.

Mr. Dohrmann was inquiring what period of music was my favorite. As I was explaining that I felt Bach and the pre-Romantic period was my first choice,

Mr. Dohrmann listened, nodding and commenting on various pieces with a considerable knowledge of the life of Bach. He lit his pipe while we chatted, and the scent of the tobacco wafted towards me, a fine and pungent aroma that I enjoyed while we stood looking out the windows, watching the lights come on in Marin County.

I had just finished telling him that the Toccata and Fugue in D Minor was my favorite. I was describing how the design of this piece was tempered to repeat every potential of the seven-keyboard organ, and all the notes that could be delivered from this complex instrument. Mr. Dohrmann was walking over to the piano, nodding his head in rapt attention to my discussion on music.

Twilight was fading into deep dusk and the lights were illuminating the walls now, as Mr. Dohrmann sat and simply began to play. And as his fingers came alive upon the keyboard, the children came in, one by one, or in clusters, until all nine had arrived. They formed a semicircle around the great easy chair behind us. Each had a favorite blanket or pillow, upon which they sat. I noted each child had returned in silence while the concert was underway. Some dragged their blankets along the hardwood floor, others clutched pillows nearly as large as themselves. I recall Bernhard and Sally were blanket-draggers, while Susan and Melissa opted for pillow-clutching. Each of "the nine" as the servants called them, took to their places, oblivious of the others. Each paid attention to fluffing up his or her own area, to being comfortable in what was clearly their accustomed positions. There was no talking and each child gazed at their father as he played from a place of deep ritual and understanding.

I would later learn that Mr. Dohrmann had written his first concerto when he was twelve. He had played solo piano in Carnegie Hall at age sixteen. And tonight he was playing a medley of Bach, commencing with the Toccata and Fugue in D minor. As the notes, like dandelion silk-seeds, drifted through the screens of the oversized windows, it seemed the valleys beyond were smiling. The rendition of Bach was amazing not only for its perfection of timing and tempo, but for the fact that Mr. Dohrmann played the piece from memory alone. No sheet music, just the easy virtuoso's rendering. Then he broke into a personally-assembled medley of the ancient master's works. Applause from the family marked the performance's end. Picking up his pipe, Mr. Dohrmann paused a moment and then moved off from his piano, leaving us all a bit breathless, perhaps myself most of all, since this was my first experience of his ability at the piano.

Mrs. Dohrmann had taken my arm and unfixed my gaze from the piano keys, to deliver an evening coffee. As the last notes sounded with power and magic, I found myself sipping coffee, planted on the floor amidst a half moon of small children, gazing at a Grand Piano and a virtuoso musician who had paid his guest the incomparable compliment of a private concert solely designed for my pleasure.

As the children laughed and clapped, their father moved like the elf he was, to sit in his large arm chair. He gestured for me to sit in the chair to his right, and Mrs. Dohrmann took the one to his left. It was my feeling that I was sitting in a playhouse, and that the curtain in the theater of this first evening was about to rise on the final act. I was mesmerized by my own easy integration into a family whose rituals I was only beginning to know. I had the distinct feeling they had somehow adopted me, and it lit a happy glow in my soul that remains to this day.

It became so very quiet that I could hear the whispers of the bay trees in the early evening winds. Mr. Dohrmann was tamping his pipe and relighting it, as deliberate as if he had been alone. He carefully put one cube of sugar into his coffee, and enjoyed a lingering sip.

Mrs. Dohrmann, assisted by Forest, had brought in a large Italian chess table and placed it into the area between the children and the three chairs. I noted she required more than a little help from Forest to carry the oversized weight. Next, Mrs. Dohrmann set a small battery-operated pen light on top of the chessboard, and returned to her chair to sip her own freshly-served coffee.

As Mr. Dohrmann set down his cup and the children were settling down to wait for the story to begin, I found myself studying the chessboard. As I pondered the detail, Forest returned to the room and set two candles on the side of the board that faced Mr. Dohrmann and then retired from the room by turning out all the lights.

The chessboard gleamed in the candlelight. The squares were of the finest green Italian marble separated by white clean squares of the same stone. The marble was thick, perhaps four inches from base to top. The paws and talons of large animals and birds, sculpted in ancient pewter, served as feet at each of the four corners on the board. A border of delicately complex carvings, with figures from the middle ages, traveled around the entire frame that held the game board. In the flickering light, the animals and carvings seemed to breathe and come alive.

I was still absorbing the exquisite detail on this rare art object, when Mr. Dohrmann began to speak and took the attention of the room.

"Children," he began, with an effect like a church bell.

"I want you each to know how you came to be in this world. It all began a long, long time ago. Your mother and I were very much younger then. We would sit in this room, only we would be all alone. We would sit here all by ourselves, and very much like tonight, we would have our coffee, and watch the night kiss the daytime good-bye. We would talk about what we planned to do in our life together, what would happen to us when we grew old together. Most of all, we would talk about having children.

"We longed to have our children come. We would talk about you all the time. We would name you, calling each one by his very own name. We would walk around the house, into your empty rooms, and we would imagine just what it would look like when you came along to occupy them.

"It didn't take very long before you all came. Each one just as in our secret hopes. Each of you more than any of the dreams we ever could have dreamed.

"In a short time your mother and I became very, very happy because you had each decided to join us in our life.

"Have you ever wondered how it was that you were born? Have you ever talked about it with your brothers and sisters?

"Who has?"

(Hands went up around the half circle.)

"And who has talked about it to their friends at school?"

(More hands.)

"And who thinks they really know how they were actually born?"

(No hands at all.)

Mr. Dohrmann sipped his coffee and looked at his wife as if he had just fallen in love that moment, and then continued, as her responding smile glowed brighter than the candles.

"Let me tell you ... all about the day you were born.

"On that day, you were only a breath in the lungs of God. It was a very magical day for your mother and me, because we had been on our knees praying that each one of you would be born. We prayed and prayed for over nine long years, until each one of you arrived.

"In the morning, on the day you were born, we knew the day was special. The golden way the dawn threw back the night, like old bed sheets, brought us fully awake immediately.

"At the time that we first held you, your mother and I received a new lesson ourselves. We knew that the Lord had sucked way back into those great lungs, and had spoken a huge sound, a huge out-flowing of his breath, and when he was all done blowing, and there was no more wind or breath left inside those lungs, that all that life force had been blown into you.

"You were blown up like a tiny balloon, full with the breath of God. Your mother and I knew this because in those first moments, in the hospital, you had a glow that was left over from God's work. You had a special golden pulse, that moved in and out all around your little bodies.

"Here, let me show you!"

And here, Mr. Dohrmann got out of the large easy chair and knelt, placing his hands as if they were cupped to shield back the wind, around the candle in front of the chess board. First one candle, and then the other. As he did this, the shadows from the candle fell across the chess board. Mr. Dohrmann would then gently move his hands down and away, and then back into a cup position. The candlelight would swish outward and flash out into the room, dispelling the darkness, and then once again be trapped within his cupped hands. And after Mr. Dohrmann had done this with both candles once, he continued, but this time spoke as he was doing the work on his bended knees ... keeping his curved pipe stem tightly clenched in his teeth with practiced art.

"I want you each of you to notice how the light is greatest when the light is BREATHING and traveling out in all directions. When the light is breathing, the light is replacing the shadows and darkness with illumination. Notice as the light is breathing how far it can travel ... right to the walls of our world and to the edge of where our vision can take us ... do you see it?"

I found that Mr. Dohrmann transformed as the story unfolded, presenting an enchanting blend of ancient wizard mixed with the unbridled excitement of a child. As a teacher, I would soon discover Mr. Dohrmann embodied the magic mix of scholarly seriousness and eternal childlike enthusiasm. In a wink he could be both, or switch between the two. I have never seen it again in all my years.

With his last words he rose and placed his hands on his back, stretching as if he were a thousand years old, and settled back down into his easy chair. The children giggled at their father's portrayal of creaking age, and he winked at them before continuing.

"Children, you, each one of you, had a light like the candle. For when your mother and I first held you in our arms, the breath of God was still fresh on you. Your light was still BREATHING! Your light from the breath of God was still "LEAKING" out of your body bag. Your light was glowing like the candlelight. Your light was traveling all over that hospital room. It was the same for each one of you.

"Your mother and I were always amazed and delighted to see the work of God in your faces. Each one of you had such strong, strong light. I can remember how the shadows would disappear when your light would shine and pulse over the hospital room. For awhile your mother and I could not even speak, because you were so close to God in that moment, you were like little angels that had come to earth. You each had such brightness and light.

"But that's not the lesson.

"The lesson IS, that everyone, every person, every baby, everyone you ever will meet, or see on television or in a movie or anywhere in all your life, also had a time when they were born. Each one of them had their own time and moment when they had the BIRTH GLOW in their lives. When the light that is the breath of GOD was LEAKING from their body bags. Then as we all grow up, we forget.

"We forget who and what we are. We forget how we are made in the image and likeness of God, until all the memory of the magic inside us is erased, for a great many people erased forever and ever." (Mr. Dohrmann was staring very hard at each of his children, and I noticed with a start, even at me.)

"For you see children, you see the world, even at your young ages, through the eyes of an ADULT. In many, many ways you already have grown all the way up. Let me tell you how old you are when you see things.

"You see people in the way that adults see people. Adults who have forgotten all about their BIRTH GLOW when their light had the power to take away the shadows in life. You see people as tall, and as short, don't you?"

Heads nodded.

"You see people as men and as women, don't you?"

Heads nodded.

"You see people as fat and as thin, don't you?"

Heads nodded.

"You see people as pretty and as handsome and as ugly and as not pretty sometimes, don't you?"

Heads nodded.

"You see people who talk or walk funny and those that are 'normal', don't you?"

Heads nodded.

"You see people in wheelchairs, and who are deaf or blind, and people who are walking and who see and who hear, don't you?"

Heads nodded.

"You see people as adults see people, don't you? But do you see their zippers?"

"Uh?"

And no heads nodded at all.

"DO YOU SEE THEIR ZIPPERS?

"No, of course you don't. Because then you would need to have the eyes of GOD and you only have the eyes of adults.

"For you see, my children," (and he tamped and puffed at his pipe until the embers glowed red.) "God has the eyes to see what is real, while adults have eyes to see only the reflection of what is real. The reflection is not the truth!

"In God's eyes, he makes us all equal. You have heard this from when we read the Bible and study together, haven't you?"

Heads nodded.

"I want you to do an exercise." (And here everyone paid very close attention. I would learn in a minute than even Mrs. Dohrmann participated, and so, therefore, did the guest.)

"Is everyone ready?"

Heads nodded.

"I want you to stand up. I want you to stand behind your pillows and blankets in the candlelight.

"Keep your hands at your sides and be calm while I tell you what to do.

"While you are standing, I have asked God to give you the sight that the Lord has. I have asked that just for a moment, in your young life, you have the eyes that GOD looks through.

"Does everyone want to look through the eyes of GOD?

Heads nodded. (Mine, too.)

"Then I want you, each in your own way to do the following. I want you to realize that your bodies are not the truth of who you ARE.

"I want you to look at each other. Carefully. Look up and down from feet to head and see if on anyone you can spot the ZIPPER." And here the children giggled and looked at one another, up and down, until finally it was quiet again and everyone was looking back at Mr. Dohrmann.

"Anyone see a ZIPPER?"

And everyone shook their heads ... no.

"I thought so. You still can't see with the eyes of God when you look, even upon your own brothers and your own sisters. How much harder must it be when you look upon your friends in life, or even upon strangers, to hold the GOD vision in your life path ... hmmmm?

"I want to teach you the lesson. God sees you in a special way and I want you to see as God sees. I want you all to pretend that inside you is the same BIRTH LIGHT that you held when you were born. All that you are, and all that you will ever become is contained in the musical notes and breath of God, that IS you, and IS me and IS everyone else.

"I want you to find the light that is inside your body bags. Your body bags are born and your body bags die. But the LIGHT that IS *you* is trapped inside, and will one day be released again. I want you to find your own zippers that hold the light inside, and I want you to UNZIP your body bags. I want you to wiggle out of your body bags and then just sit back down and float for a minute without them.

"So now, children, unzip your body bags and let them fall to the floor. Find your zippers and let them fall and then float to the floor in any way you want to."

Now, children are amazing little actors and actresses. With the minimum of cues they will assume the roles that are set upon them, and perform each role to virtual perfection. Somewhere along the way to total amnesia, we forget this acting skill as fully functioning adults and never again experience quite the perfection our childhood delivered each and every day. As an adult I was privileged to revisit that perfection on the evening in which the children of Alan G. Dohrmann unzipped their body bags.

Mr. Dohrmann watched in some delight as we all wiggled in our own way. Some of us took hold of our zipper and moved it down, and then wriggled out, until the body bags were deposited on the floor. Some stepped out of them. Some brushed them off. Some separated in other ways. We all watched the way the others did theirs. It was a partnership in becoming.

Quietly, with an un-childlike like calm, each of them when done, sat in their position on the floor and looked at their father.

Mr. Dohrmann leaned forward in his chair. He had placed his pipe into the great ashtray. He had his elbows on his knees and his hands were open and reaching towards the children in explanation. His eyes wandered over everyone in the room with equal measure to all.

"Children, you are now orbs of light. I want you to close your eyes. I want you to see each of your brothers and sisters with their BIRTH LIGHT. I want you to see what happens when you step outside of the body bag you have chosen to play in during this life.

"See one another as brilliant orbs of light, that are flashing, in and out, breathing, in the image and likeness of GOD. I want you to float just above your places, each a bright ball of light, each moving in and out, each expanding and contracting, each breathing in God's Breath.

"As you sit in this glow, I want you to feel perfect. I want you to hold an inner knowing that you no longer have colds, or coughs, or get sick, or have hurts or pains of any kind.

"I want you to slowly notice that you don't have any anger, you are no longer holding hurt feelings from some word or phrase, and the idea of these hurts and pain is like a WEIGHT, like putting a coat on that you don't wish to wear.

"I want you to GLOW and feel LIGHT.

"I want you now to turn to your brothers and sisters but only in your mind with your eyes closed, and I want you to see an amazing sight, as you LOOK THROUGH THE EYES OF GOD.

"I want you to see that there is no big or small, there is no tall or short. There is no fat or thin, there is no boy or girl, there is no pretty or not pretty, there is only Light. Just the same stuff. Turn and see in all directions. And then see that Al Dela Rosa and your mother, and yes, your father, are just the same. The same light in the eyes of God. All around the world there are no blacks, or whites, or Chinese, or Japanese, or Europeans, or native peoples, nor are there any other points of separation in the vision of the LORD, children. The Birth Glow is all there ever is. The rest is not Light, but reflection. Reflection is not truth, children.

"For all reflection is light that has become distorted through time and perception, the limited perception of adults.

"In these few moments, just breathe. See the BIRTH GLOW in your family. See the birth glow inside every eternal spirit that has come into this life. Have a deep knowing that it never matters if they can see their own light, or share a knowing of the light within them. That is important. Create a warm fire inside your own soul that signals that the only life event that matters, in all the many things that will happen to you in your life, is if you can hold the MEMORY of the Birth Glow in every thought, every word, every action you ever take in life. For you, if you think and speak and act in the light of the breath of God, then you will experience all things through the eyes of GOD.

"Learn the lesson that there are only two kinds of people in this world, children. The people who remember the Birth Glow, and the people who have forgotten. Try and seek out those who remember and live your life beside THEM. For if you choose to live beside those who have forgotten, you will forever be alone, even when surrounded by many friends.

"Remember not what is different about us. Remember only that in the sight of God, there are only orbs of Light, and the Light is always the same. Remember that in this Light there is only love. Love that fills you with peace and joy as you cast your thoughts to one another. Joy that is fulfilling and perfect in the LIGHT.

"It is only when you put your body bag back on that the WEIGHT of separation will come upon you again. The heavy burden of seeing with adult eyes, when your judgments hold truth as reflection rather than truth from the Source of all Light. Then and only then will you once again be boys and girls, and will you be big and be small, and will you be old and be young, and will you be thin or not so thin, only then will the heavy weights once again, like an old fisherman's overcoat covered with lead fishing weights, be taken upon your ORB Of LIGHT.....

"Do you like your BIRTH LIGHT, children? Do you like your Birth GLOW? Do you like seeing and feeling it once again?"

All heads nodded. (Including mine. I realized that somehow I had become, in this evening, one of the children. I can't explain it. But I knew it.)

"I want you to know this lesson, children. I am your father, and I will always love you best when I can see you floating, flickering, with your body bags off rather than when you zip them up and carry the weight around, forgetting the power and peace that is within your soul.

"Now! Everyone stand up.

"I want you to carefully reach down to the floor, and I want you to pick up your individual body bags, the ones you have chosen to play in while you are going through this life. Be careful of them, children. I want you to hold them and look at them as old familiar friends ... a costume. I want you to see that you are playing a role, of all the millions of possible roles, you have chosen to play Bernhard Dohrmann, or Mark, or Geof, or Melissa, or Pam, or Susan. I want you to think as you hold onto your body bag, that you will play this role the very best way you know how.

"I want you to give the LORD GOD the best performance for a Geof Dohrmann that the Lord could ever receive. I want you to GIVE the best CARL, the best SALLY that the Lord God could ever receive. And I want you to learn the lesson......

"IT IS FOR THIS PURPOSE THAT YOU NOW PUT YOUR BODY BAGS BACK ON....

"I want you to wiggle back into your body bags and zip them up."

I can remember how it took some time for several of us to start. Most of us were not eager to put our body bags back on. All of us looked at one another one last time. I know in my case it was to fix in my mind the candles, the light and the memory of the Birth Glow from each one of the spiritual beings in the room, into the fiber of my being for eternity. As I began to step into my body bag I remember how unpleasant it was. I could almost smell things I found too opaque to inhale. I noted how heavy the body bag was. I could see each of the children struggling to lift their body bag over their shoulders. For some it was a colossal effort. Swaying this way and that and using every last bit of strength. I found half of the children had tear-trails as they began to zip them up, and was surprised how wet my own face had become. As I zipped, I remember thinking how wonderful it would be if all peoples, in all countries, could have a day, once each year, to unzip their body bags and see with the eyes of God.

Mr. Dohrmann allowed a good deal of time to pass until all of us had once again returned to our places. As I returned to my seat beside him and looked at the children, there was an indefinable feeling of power emanating from that circle of innocence, a self-awareness that had not been there before.

"Children, I want you to remember this lesson as one of the most important of all the lessons I will ever teach you. I won't always be here to teach you, my babies. I want this lesson to be as a thread the angels give to you, to stitch together the quilt of all my other lessons, so that when you remember your father's stories you will always remember to see the lesson, with the eyes of the LORD.

"Now I want you to help me with one more part of the lesson.

"I want you to take your hand, and I want you to lower your zipper on your body bag just a bit. Everyone do it to just where you want it to be."

Some of the children took theirs down to their eyes, some unzipped themselves to their chest and some, including me, took their zippers down to their waist. The candlelight flickering like a blessing on the room gave a feeling of ceremony, and accented the children's faces in colors that only rainbows could have improved upon.

Mr. Dohrmann, I noticed, had his pipe lit again as he continued. "Children, you recall I taught you there were only two kinds of people in all the world?"

Mr. Dohrmann had settled quite far back in his chair now, as he looked up at the candle flickers on the ceiling, perhaps seeing things that were beyond our capacity to perceive.

"Oh, I know there are children that tease you. There are children that say that your Banana-nose Sally, or that your Markie Darky Larky if you're afraid of the dark, or that your Big Butt this or that, or a thousand things that hurt your feelings. Isn't that right?"

Heads nodded.

"And I know you sometimes tease back and hurt the feelings of other children, isn't that right?"

Shamefaced, the children nodded again.

"There are adults who are almost shaking as they cry out in secret pain, children, 'I am NOT a spiritual being, I am not an eternal creature of LIGHT, I am not the breath of the Lord God, I have no LIGHT to LEAK out of my BODY Bag. While I go through this life, no LIGHT must come from me or leak out and make me wrong. I must be RIGHT in this, I need to be RIGHT!' and the *up* pressure on the zippers grows and grows.

"They cry out as well that they must seal their body bag tight up, they must keep it so tight that NO LIGHT FROM YOU or FROM ANYONE can ever get IN, can ever reach them, can ever pierce their heart and their secret place. The upward pressure on that zipper to keep the light of others from entering is just as strong as the pressure to keep their own light from escaping. It is this balance of fears that makes movement so difficult, because fear can only be moved by the power of love and light.

"Do you know children or adults you think might be keeping their body bags very tight and zipped?"

Some of the heads nodded.

"Children, I want you to know that many adults grow up and they forget so completely about their Birth Glow and their connection to the God that has created them, that they become what the Teachers of Masters call 'Thumb-Worn'."

"We call them 'thumbworn', because they apply so much pressure upon their zipper to assure it won't slip, not even an inch, that during their lifetime they make a small mark in their thumb. You may not be able to see the mark on their thumb, but you can feel the 'thumb-worn' in your heart if you examine your feelings.

"There is nothing bad or wrong about the 'thumb-worn' in life, children. They are just sleepy. They have fallen asleep and no longer are awake to the bright Light that is inside their body bag. Because they live in a world of dreams, they believe it to be real when, in fact, they are only dreams, and someday, no matter how long it takes, they each, when they are ready, WILL WAKE UP. For in God's perfection he has made one dramatic and unbreakable rule:

'The eternal soul may never remain ignorant of its own true nature.'

"Think how awful it would be if you, who now have your body bags unzipped so far down, some to your eyes, some to your chest and some to your waist," as he carefully examined us and the zippers we were holding, "were to be compelled to live only beside the 'thumb worn' in this life. How lonely would you be? How frustrated would you be? How angry might you become? How much less laughter would you laugh? How much less happy would you be? How much less fulfilled?

"Think then, how perfect God's Plan is that you can seek out and find others, who like you have found they DO REMEMBER the Birth Glow. Others who, like you, have taken the pressure off their zippers. Others who wish to have movement in their life. Others who have chosen a new path, a fresh way of giving glory to God. For these we call THE RUNNERS, for they run their zippers always downward. They have the runners of their zippers in motion.

"In the Lord's perfect plan, as the runners have eyes to see, they, without accident, will always find one another. They will form friendships and marriages, they will create their own children, and they will have grandchildren and families. From the safety of their neighborhoods of Light, they can then wander out among those who are thumb-worn, those who are in pain and struggle. And simply by being themselves they can reduce the pain that others feel. Simply by being happy. Simply by being awake. Simply by being at all. Just being. They will make the pressure on the thumb, of the thumb-worn, so much less. The pain will be so much less.

"So in this lesson, children, when you find those who hurt you, who cannot understand you, who make you feel ashamed or less than, or in any way under the pain of forces you do not understand yourself, just examine your feelings. You will come back many times to this lesson. Discover when you come back to this room, to this chessboard, to this candlelight, and to our story, you obtain a KNOWING that those who hurt you are only causing pain because they are asleep. The pain is their own pain, children, and is not of your creation.

"Do not attach yourself to their pain or to yours.

"Simply focus your attention on the person you wish to be in the moment that comes NEXT. Dwell only on the future you choose to have. Keep your attention on the Birth Glow and the Love that God has for you as well as for those who are only temporarily asleep.

"Remember, you cannot wake those who are asleep. That is the work of God.

"Your work is to APPRECIATE the others who are AWAKE beside you as the agents of the Lord to grant peace, joy, and fulfillment to your life. Always pay attention to which way your zipper is moving.

"Up, with less light and more pain or ...

"Down with greater illumination and less pain.

"You will receive many lessons in life. You will have many hardships and trials to learn from. And in all your tests in this life there is only one real lesson you must learn. Will you move your zipper down in forgiveness and love, accepting your lesson and increasing your ILLUMINATION for the Lord, or will you move your zipper upward and add to the darkness with anger and blame, rejecting your lessons?

"You either reject or accept your lessons in life.

"If you want more Light to reach you, and you want more Light to reach from you to others, examine your reactions to any circumstance, person or thing, and ask yourself, 'Which way will I move my zipper?'

"When you know the answer ... you will have learned the lesson!"

With some signal only the children knew, everyone recognized the lesson was complete, and all the children were applauding. Forest and the family governess, Blanca, rolled in a dessert cart, which signaled it was time for a break. Everyone was eager for the dessert and to my surprise the conversation was primarily about life in the monastery, with myself becoming the center of attention. We never once discussed the lesson, which I would come to find was the manner of it in the family. When each was complete, they were like spent flowers, discarded and moved into the fertilizer that would replenish the soil of the children's growing.

It wasn't until many years later that I would come to discover that my own notes had trapped these stories in amber, as it were, in a way that the world might see value in them for the generations of children yet to arrive. Mr. Dohrmann would only wink at such a notion and remind me with his smile, that "there are, after all, absolutely NO accidents, Brother Al."

Chapter 2

The Second Lesson

THE SECOND LESSON

As dessert was winding down, the baton of story telling passed from me back to Alan Dohrmann. He gestured for the dessert cart to be removed when I had finished explaining about my life in the Abbey. The children were each wiped down with a clean warm towel and settled in for what was to come.

Mr. Dohrmann explained, because we had a special guest, there would be a second lesson for the evening. In this family, one day of the week was Lesson Day. One day was reserved for music, one for reading the Bible. And one day of the week was reserved for reading fairy tales out loud from cover to cover. The children's favorites, I would soon discover, were *The Thirteen Clocks* by James Thurber, some obscure stories by Ambrose Bierce and the *Alice* stories.

The lights were turned off, and once again the firefly lights of the candles and the chessboard stood between this patron and his children.

Mr. Dohrmann began.

"Children, do you remember the stories of *Alice* and *Wonderland*?"

Heads nodded.

"And the stories of *Alice* and *The Looking Glass*?"

Heads nodded.

"Do any of you know anything about Lewis Carroll, who wrote the stories?"

Everyone shook their heads "no."

"Well, then, let our story begin.

"A long, long time ago I met Mr. Lewis Carroll. He was very old then and I was able to spend some time with him.

"Mr. Carroll was a professor of mathematics at a university outside London, England, children. All of his publications, with the exception of the *Alice* stories and a few odd poems, dwell on mathematics. Children would find most of Mr. Carroll's writings very boring." His eyes twinkled in my direction. "So, in fact, would most grown-ups!

"When Mr. Carroll was a young man, he took a fancy to the three daughters of the Dean of his Campus on Mathematics. During the warm lazy summer days, he would row the girls around a lake in back of the grand castle-like buildings, and go for long picnics in the flower-filled meadows of the English countryside.

"It was during these journeys that Mr. Carroll created the *Alice* stories for the girls. They would giggle and clap and demand more and more. The stories became so popular that sometimes Mr. Carroll would have a good many children sitting around while he invented his charming nonsense.

"The parents kept pestering him to write down the tales and one day he did. When he had finished only part of the first part of *Wonderland*, a copy of the manuscript, written in long hand, was brought before the Queen. By Royal Invitation he was asked to bring the complete works to Buckingham Palace.

"Mr. Carroll sent the Queen a cedar chest of all his mathematical works. Later he would follow them with a set of the *Alice* stories tied with a large red ribbon. The printing press was coming into wide use, and the *Alice* stories soon became the fastest-growing publication in all the world, next to the Bible.

"Mr. Carroll, who led a very simple life, never really understood his fame, and eventually gave up any association with the stories. He spent most of the remaining part of his life in establishing new ways of thinking about mathematics.

"There were some scandals in his day, regarding his interest in children. Having known the man, I find his love and affection for the girls for whom the stories were invented to be genuine and of quiet charm. These were more than his girls, like a gift of flowers that God had provided to this rare man, to bring forth something special, that would remain in the treasury of humanity forever.

"Everything about Mr. Carroll had some hidden meaning. In his stories about *Alice*, and *Wonderland*, and *The Looking Glass*, you all remember the ingredients?"

(Heads were nodding)

"You remember the many strange animals that *Alice* met in her travels from one land to another? You remember the even stranger people that ruled the various lands *Alice* crossed on her way to meet the Queen?"

(A half-moon circle of children, framed in candlelight, nodded to their father.)

"When you become older, you will all learn, as I have already taught some of you, how to play a game called "chess." For you see, *Alice in the Looking Glass* is not just a story, but it is in fact, a game of chess. Perhaps a perfect game of chess. Each chapter and each move within the chapter, is a move of pieces on the chessboard.

"When the babies are older I will help you read *Alice In The Looking Glass* and we will actually play the game of chess as we read. Would you like to learn THAT lesson?

(Every head was nodding.)

At this time Forest brought in, on a lovely crystal tray, the chess pieces that went with the chessboard. I will never forget how they looked. The knights, hand-sculpted by Italian artists hundreds of years ago, reared high on their horses, with lances in the air. The Queen and King were more ornate than any I had ever seen. One army was covered in gold, and the other in silver.

Mr. Dohrmann took a large castle from each side, with flags waving from long-ago turrets, and placed first one, and then the other, in the hands of a child at each end of the half circle.

"See how heavy the pieces are?" he asked as the small hands grasped the weighty little sculptures.

"These chess pieces belonged to my father, and to his father, and ultimately came to America from the King's Court in Denmark. These are very special chess pieces and I want you to always remember how special they are, because they alone can move on the chessboard that stands before you."

Mr. Dohrmann lit his pipe as the children shared passing the chess pieces around. They would stop and talk in private whispers about how heavy the pieces were. I would learn that the chessboard resided in Mr. Dohrmann's private study. The children were not allowed into the study. The children were especially not permitted to touch anything IN the study. It was a rare treat that the magic of this amazing work of art would be shared this night with them. I found myself compelled to reach over without permission to pick up one of the knights and gently toss it up in my hands to judge the weight. I have never touched any chess pieces to match these for detail of carving and balance in the hand.

"Children, I want you to put the chess pieces down, and I want you to remember them. Remember that you are very much like the chess pieces. In your body bags, you are much heavier than you might otherwise seem. And I want you to remember that God, like Lewis Carroll, is a mathematician. I want you to understand that God had his own plan, for the game of life, when he set each one of you down upon the chessboard."

...And here Mr. Dohrmann reached over to the chessboard, and took the small penlight Mrs. Dohrmann had earlier deposited on it, into his hands, and replaced it with a single golden pawn. The pawn he chose was set on a white square, in the middle of the chessboard.

"I want each one of you to focus your attention now, upon the white square and not the chess pawn. I want each child in this room to BE HERE NOW. I want you to pretend that you ARE the chess piece.

"I want you to pretend that the Lord had a big plan for your life. I want you to pretend that for all your years of life, *everything* you know right now fits inside the chessboard square your feet have landed upon. Only I want your imagination to see the chessboard square as God sees it. For inside this chessboard square are *all* the things you ever learned up to right now, this night.

"As the candlelight flickers this way and that I want you to see that the square, as God has placed it before you, is HUGE. The square is bigger than all the stars and all the planets and all the universes you will every study. Everything you know from school is inside this square, even the things you can no longer remember. Every book you have ever seen. Every television lesson you have ever learned. Every radio program. Every conversation with every friend, with every adult. Everything you ever knew or will know is now inside this chess square.

"This one chess square.

"Only it is not day time, it is dark, late, *NIGHT.*"

...And here Mr. Dohrmann came off his chair, and knelt down, and holding his pipe in his right hand, he leaned over and BLEW OUT THE CANDLE to the right side of the chessboard. This left only one candle, and the chessboard was in shadow.

"Children, it's a very dark night. And you have been standing a very long time. For years you have been standing in only one place.

"God has created a chessboard that is millions of miles long in every direction. And although you do not know it, there are teachers who have learned enough, have studied and thought and prayed so intensely that they have all the information that is contained in two or even *three* chess squares.

"And although you do not know it, children, there are MASTERS who, with their Light, have many more squares lit up, for they know the information in all of these squares. They make their choices and decisions in this life with all the information in many more squares than you presently have lit up in your young lives.

"And when I see you, both as your father and your teacher, I find you nearly frozen on your square. In fact, I find many adults this way as well. I find them bent over. I find them fascinated and fixed inside their life, to the information they have at their feet. Most never even look up. For the entire journey they will make in their lives, they simply never look up.

"If only I could command them to look up, to look around, to witness all the wealth of choices and abundant information that the Lord has put in their way.

"But no, these multitudes, these students, sit on bended knees, locked down to only one square (Mr. Dohrmann was still kneeling while he spoke), and these who study this way are shallow. They monitor life in the pitch-black of night, and the night is so dark they can't even see the board itself.

Mr. Dohrmann leaned to his left and in a *poof!* blew out the second candle and the room went from reflected children, all leaning in on their elbows to see the chessboard, to complete and total darkness. The board simply disappeared. All that could be seen was the glowing embers in a pipe bowl and nothing more.

That was when Mr. Dohrmann switched on his powerful penlight and its narrow beam which, because of the way he held it, made a perfect DOT at the foot of the golden pawn, inside the one white chess square.

"When I find you, there is no moon. There is no star in the sky. There is only the small, little flashlight each child holds, shining between tiny feet, as they scan back and forth, back and forth, all the information that exists in their entire world. All the information between their feet. They kneel and spend all their time studying life, one simple line at a time. Never do they stand and see the information in the dot all around them. Never do they see the entire chess square and all its possibilities. Never do they see or even feel the existence of all the other chess squares God has laid around them, the unlimited potential, just waiting for human discovery.

"In fact, children, I often stumble over my students and fall, so dark is the night that I will miss them entirely in the shadows." (Mr. Dohrmann was a Santa-like figure, and at this point he rolled over in a large *"thunk"* on the hardwood floor, and some ashes fell from the pipe, tiny fireflies of light in the darkness.

Thunk!

"Children, when I pick myself up," (and here Mr. Dohrmann stood as high as possible, on his tiptoes as he positioned the light moving back and forth as a tiny dot in the one white square ... there was no other light in the room and our eyes were riveted to the beam.....)

"I always watch THEM.

"I watch them fascinated.

"I watch them hypnotized by the events of their own small lives.

"I watch them limited.

"I watch them beyond salvage as they are bound, as certainly as if they were chained, to the habits of their own existence.

"And I will sneak up behind them in the dark ... when they least expect it.

(At this point Mr. Dohrmann snapped out the light. We could hear a strange scraping noise, but we did not know what it could be.)

When the light came back on Mr. Dohrmann had a huge stepladder that nearly touched the ceiling, moved right up against the chessboard.

"Children, as I sneak up behind the new student I all too often find them not even aware that I have come. So as not to cause any unwanted FEAR, I will gently lift them under their arms, very softly, whispering in their ears, about their bigger future, until I guide them with me up higher than they could normally stand. Together we will journey up an enormous ladder.

"As we rise the student keeps his dot upon the square, but becomes amazed, for as the light rises it expands." (Here the dot began to expand, as Mr. Dohrmann took it higher, until it slowly began to light up the entire white square of the chessboard.)

"Children, I am always amazed." he said as he stood a little up the ladder holding his light over the chessboard, "how my students are stunned at the new information they have discovered. Information that is as old as the stars, and has been surrounding the students all the days of their lives. Yet, as if sampling air for the very first time, each student inevitably fails to learn the lesson, and begins instead to digest the information they see inside their new field of illumination, mere moments after observing it.

"They literally soak in the information they can now see. The student dwells on each new line. Each begins, in turn, to study one new line at a time, as they become numb to the new possibilities held in fresh options that lie before them.

"It takes all the strength of the teacher to raise the student from this locked-in view, and to help them even further up the ladder. Finally, after the longest time of trial and study, I arrive at the top of the ladder before the students that follow me."

At this point Mr. Dohrmann turned his penlight off, and the night fell again. The room was dark enough that we couldn't see what was under the black cover on the shelf near the top of the ladder. We were about to find out that Mr. Dohrmann had brought in an 800 candlepower battery-operated Navy Searchlight. This may not seem much of an item in today's world, but back in 1952, such portability was a highly classified research project. It made the effect even more dramatic.

Mr. Dohrmann reached over his head, and holding his search lamp, he continued his lesson.

"I try to break the students' fascination with the information they see in their past, and refocus their ATTENTION on the information that lies in their future.

"No, children, I say to them ... NOOO!

"Please look beyond where you can see.......

"Look to the edges of the chess square you are in now. See the borders. See the new ideas, the new creativity, the new possibility that touches in each direction, on all sides, and flows into directions beyond where you can see.

"What if there were a brighter light?

"What if there were a light INSIDE you that was so bright you could see beyond this point?

"What if you had enough LIGHT?"

(And here he switched on his searchlight.)

"So that you could SEE the entire chess board, children?

"You could see God's chessboard with the eyes that God has to see!

"You could see square after square, moving ahead and off in all directions.

"You could turn and spin," and the light swept the room so that the walls and the ceiling became illuminated, and the light spilled into the next room. We all turned our heads and looked three hundred and sixty degrees, while Mr. Dohrmann continued teaching us.

"Children, what if you had enough light to see all this information and you could now see so many squares.....

"Would you live richer lives?

"Would you make more and better choices?

"Would you have better tools?

"BUT THAT'S NOT THE LESSON."

Mr. Dohrmann turned off the light, and the room became even darker than before.

"THIS IS THE LESSON!

"I tell all my students, no, no, no! Do not now refocus on the information you can see. Continue.

"CONTINUE.

"Look beyond what you can see!

"Consider, what if we were in a blimp rising, and rising. Taking our light higher and higher?

"What if we were in your Uncle Walt Disney's idea for a space station that could orbit the earth and we were looking back with all that information?

"What if we were in Flash Gordon's space ship heading outside our solar system, looking back with all that new perspective?

"What if we were in Dr. Einstein's magic ship that travels at the speed of light, at speeds so fast your vision flows in all directions?"

(And here Mr. Dohrmann turned the searchlight on the ceiling ... and then moved it out the window. The research light from the U.S. Navy sent a shaft of light, as far as we could see out over the hills, and across San Francisco Bay).

"No, NO, students!

"Look UP. LOOK beyond what you can SEE.

"The lesson is ... always, ALWAYS increase your field of illumination.

"Always, always increase your field of vision.

"Do this, and your life will contain the most information.

"Do this and your life will be about the journey to come rather than the journey that is already over.

"Do this and your life will illuminate others as your vision is always reaching for tomorrow ...

"As your vision is reaching for the stars."

Mr. Dohrmann snapped off his Navy Search Light ... and the room lights were turned on by Forest.

Mr. Dohrmann gestured to the hallways from the top of the step ladder, saying, "... And now, children, say Good-night to Brother Dela Rosa and run off to bed. Your mother and I will be up to tuck you in, in just a minute."

Each of the children then got up and came over and, rather than take my hand, they openly displayed their affection with a hug. Some said the sweetest things in this first evening, and each ran off to their bedrooms, gone in a wink.

By the time it was done, Mr. Dohrmann was back in his chair, the stepladder was removed and new coffee had been served. I remember I wanted to say something, but the only thing that kept coming into my mind was "WOW!"

I had, of course as part of my training, read the works of many prominent and many obscure, philosophers and theologians, both historical and contemporary. My enjoyment of the writings of the great teachers continues to this day. It is nonetheless true that I have never since met anyone who could explain the mystery of the soul within the body, at a level easily understood by a child, as well as the man who had just done so that night.

Nor have I met one who could reveal to a child the infinite love of God, the infinite possibilities we are given, as graphically as this man. The excitement of all the many choices, the love with which the lessons are given to us, and the loving insistence that we explore and learn for all of the lifetime we have been given, all of this was contained within the lesson I had just heard.

I knew that these lessons would indeed be a part of the lives of these children forever, as they would be for me. I was beginning to understand why Father Abbot had sent me to this man, and my gratitude was immense.

Mr. Dohrmann didn't ask "What did you think?" but rather said, tamping his pipe, "So did you learn the lesson?"

I said that I had.

He said, "Well then off to bed with you, and we will continue our play in the morning!"

I thought at the time, this was a perfect ending to a perfect day. After receiving a hug from Mrs. Dohrmann, and once again being escorted down the outside stairs to The Apartments, I remember thinking about a four-year-old boy, a tree fort, and a rose garden set in a redwood forest. I remember thinking that the telling of the lessons, although not consuming much time in actuality, had seemed to possess a quality of *timelessness*. That is, the time seemed to fly by, and at the same time, it seemed as though we were together for a long period, listening and learning. I would, over my many visits with the family, learn that time stood still during these evenings, and that the magic of the storyteller's art held full sway on Lesson Night. On the first of these nights, I found myself able to sleep in the deepest way, dreaming of chess pieces, and witches with plates of cookies, and lights glowing from the unzipped body bags of all the people I had so recently met.

Chapter 3

Why

WHY

The adventures continued for me over a period of thirty years. I made more than a hundred personal visits to the Dohrmann home during this time. There are so many amazing safaris to share with my readers, that future works will be required to unleash all the lessons.

It comes to mind, at this late time in my life, how at the end, the magic never lessened. It remains fascinating to me, all these years after his passing, how this strange and wonderful man could command himself in the way that he did. Even as his children grew and had their own children, he would continue to teach them, and always in the same fashion.

I can remember Thanksgivings and Christmas holidays when almost fifty of the "marrieds" as he liked to call them, and their children, and grandchildren, would all arrive, with some of the uncles and aunts in attendance. And even in those times, as he was failing in his health, toward the late 1970's, it was the same. There was always the grand piano. There were props and lessons the world has never heard before or since, always reserved for "the children." And there was always the tradition.

The original nine children always sat first in a semicircle, on the floor before the large easy chair. The "youngers" would then sit in front of them, in their own easy circles. The "babies," whose attention was apt to wander, were retired to a family playroom. There was some competition to be with the "youngers" and no one really cared to be in the group known as the "babies." It was a sort of initiation to be allowed into the "youngers", a family rite of passage.

During all the years, and all the lessons and the growth I saw bestowed in his classes and his work, nothing so fascinated me as the essential self he would devote to his nine children. If I had to put a label to it, I would say for a great part of my life, my highest self worth, my highest honor, was my attendance to the purpose of these lessons from Mr. Dohrmann. These lessons not only did not conflict with my vocation as a monk, but as my Abbot had surely intended when he sent me to the Marin woods, they reinforced and affirmed the teachings and disciplines of my brotherhood.

I have been told by the children that I am the only remaining person that has the content of the stories in such a condition so as to render a worthy publication. They do not know whether the world will treasure the tales as they unfold, but it matters only to me, that for the legacy of Mr. Dohrmann, and five girls and four boys, the stories are recorded.

Should they entertain you, that is sufficient. Should they move you to future courses of action, we have a miracle. Should they move someone you love to find a better way through life, we have a completion ... a completion to my life, and to each reader so benefited.

Being old is one thing. Being old and retired within the stone walls of a cloistered abbey is quite another. Most of my brothers who were alive through the time of these stories, have gone before me. Each passed into their own graduations as the ceremony called to them. I can envision my own cap and gown waiting in the hall.

Each morning, at three and at five, we rise to sing our hymns, as is our way, and to pray. Each morning our simple breaking of the day's fast fortifies us for contemplation and fruitful labor. Father Abbot has recently assigned, as my sole responsibility, the completion of this manuscript. I rather think he fancies the stories as much for his own pleasure, as for my health. There is some gossip in the priory that since I have taken on the burden of these writings, I have been less ill either in body or spirit, I could not catch exactly which. I heard by the rose garden the other day, when on the back woods path, from no fewer than three brothers doing their labors, that "Brother Dela Rose will outlive us all, if Father Abbot only permits him to complete ALL the stories," and there was some friendly tittering behind each word.

I have taken you into the start of my life with the family, because the environment has some merit in bringing the reader into each story. I have been told, as I have repeated many of the more important lessons, that there is a "belonging" to them. Certain stories seem to find just the person that requires them most, just at the moment they require that particular story most, and the results have been quite dramatic, in my experience. I always find it amazing the power that seems to be stored within any given story.

Hearing such a story, one that seems tailored exactly to your needs of the moment, is like finding a treasure chest on some magic beach. The sand is white. The breeze is warm and gentle. There is no other living creature to distract you. Not even the nearby waves render enough movement to take your gaze from the jewels that await you. It is as if once you lift the lid of life, there is no disappointment. The jewels are really and truly there. Each is bright enough and perfect enough with its own divine beauty to satisfy your hunger for a thousand lifetimes.

THE THIRD STORY.....
THE STORY OF THE RUNNERS

In the summer Mr. Dohrmann would take the children in his Woody station wagon to a location approximately one-half hour away. The roads were winding and slow, and the views were extraordinary. Part of the mystery of the short journey was the increasing density of the redwood forest. Part of the serenity was the curvy, deep gorge that ran with water all summer long. As the roadway, broken by tar expansion lines, twisted and wound its way deeper and deeper into the forest, the shade blocked out virtually all sunlight. The warm 90-degree summer afternoon temperatures plunged to the mid-seventies. The Woody wagon made strange thumping noises as it went across various old bridges that linked the sides of the stream below.

Eventually, driving through what seemed more a secret opening in the forest than a real-world entrance, Mr. Dohrmann turned off the roadway into what is now known as Camp Taylor. Today, Camp Taylor is a California State Park.

Mr. Dohrmann drove into the "grove" until he brought his car to rest facing a grotto of ferns beside the stream bed. A steep incline down off the roadway, marked by a tiny little trail, led to several picnic tables, surrounding a concrete barbecue pit.

Mr. Dohrmann's chase car brought up the staff and supplies to dress the area with checkerboard tableware, wicker picnic baskets, and prepare for a feast. Soon the smell of hot-dogs and hamburgers rose in smoky fingers into the overhang of Redwood boughs. Once each child had enjoyed their afternoon dining, the fun was about to begin. The adults had been treated at the "elder's tables" to wine and story telling, both in generous measure, while the "youngers" had their own tables and play areas. Each seemed to know their place in a tradition that was a regular respite from the hot summer suns of the inland Bay Area community.

I found myself looking upward into the twisting canopy of entwined boughs, thinking that they had marked the shade and storms for more than a thousand years. So insignificant was our place in the Universe next to these lofty giants that stood guard on a millennium. I marveled at the plan of God, with a deep thankfulness to be in this place with the children's laughter as abundant as the pine needles.

The conversation had reached the stage of comfortable lapses among friends. Mr. Dohrmann shuffled himself out of the picnic table bench, and began moving with his elf-man walk, further down the tiny little trail. As if the Pied Piper were blowing the magical flute, the children, almost in the exact order of age, one by one, got up from their picnic tables and followed their father down the narrow trail, with its dark foliage branching over the walkway on either side.

Little feet made little sounds along the walkway, background to a sudden giggle or comment. It was unusually quiet during the walk.

I waited until the last child was being picked up into a stroller and escorted by adult hands down the trail to follow. The Dohrmann family ran on some interior schedule, one that everyone in the group knew. It was also obvious that this regimen was beyond explanation to guests. Somehow, as a new arrival, one just arranged to "fit."

It has been more than four decades since I walked down that hidden trail in the Camp Taylor redwoods with the children. I hunger for the words to share with you what the feeling was like. The scent that the air held: a mixture of earth and bark and greens, and the occasional salt water breeze from the nearby sea. The whisper in the branches that towered above us, the chuckling of water over polished stones in the stream bed ahead - a time and a place so fresh, so innocent, that every footfall was sacred.

As the trail twisted back and forth, it unwound like a ribbon into a circular grassy meadow, surrounded almost perfectly by tree ferns. Bernhard, who was walking ahead of me, informed me as the last bend came into view, that the "Fern Grotto" was just ahead.

I remember pausing. I was wiping my face with a linen handkerchief, when I realized all the family was sitting on stones in the now familiar semicircle around their father. Behind the children was a wall of tree ferns, with their wide limbs swaying gently, making a green curtain for the play about to begin. Mr. Dohrmann was sitting on a huge flat rock that was dead center in the tiny green meadow. The trail continued on the far side, marking this as a transitory resting place on a hike ... a place for telling stories and regathering energy.

As I took it all in, looking up to the two-hundred-foot peaks of the redwood sentries that surrounded the place, I realized that everyone was looking at me, including Mr. Dohrmann. I must have cut quite a contrast to their regular routine with my drab monk's robes, and my arms enfolded in wide sleeves, save for the wiping of my brow just completed. I returned the warm smile from Terry, who was the eldest, as she patted the larger stone next to her at the end of the half-circle of children. It was time to take my place and let the story begin.

Mr. Dohrmann carefully lit his pipe, while we settled in, and let the silence embrace us.

LET THEM BE RUNNERS.......

"Children," Mr. Dohrmann began all at once as if some cue had been given which only he understood, "look around you."

"Take some time, and look all around you."

Mr. Dohrmann turned his own head from left to right, and then spun around 180 degrees on the large flat stone, so that his back was facing us. We turned around ourselves. Slowly. Looking deeply at what we were seeing. There was really little to see. The wood was deep. The sunlight only penetrated here and there. It was very dense. Very dark. Very ancient-looking. The massive trunks of redwoods are beyond description to those who have never seen them. So enormous is the scale that everything in the line of sight is redefined against them. The forest is the game board itself. Everything else composes the squares and the pieces on the board ... all life.

In his own time, Mr. Dohrmann turned to face us again, pipe jutting from his mouth, with a sense of seriousness upon him. He leaned forward, both elbows on his knees, with his head like a lion's mane, bowing inward toward the children for emphasis.

"Children," waving his pipe toward the woods, "you have to see these forests as the place that God created to serve as the home for man. I want you to see with eyes you seldom use, so that you will see how the forest that God created really works. You may have missed this lesson. I want the lesson we learn here today to remain with you children for your lifetime. "In those years when I will not be here to sit with you and to remind you of those things you already know, I want **this** story to bind you. I want this story to take you forward and keep you open to all the other lessons we ever have shared or will share. I want this story to be part of your foundation, as the story of the Birth Light and your body bags is part of your foundation. So I ask as our afternoon begins to fade, that you listen with all intent, as the story begins.

"In this world, there are millions and millions of people. You have seen on television how the great cities are filled with people. You have seen in books the images of China and of other far-off places. When your heads rest lightly on little pillows at night, there are places in the world just waking up. There are places with millions of people doing their lives, raising and feeding their children, and taking their children to their Camp Taylor parks, all over the world. There is never an hour, nor a second in which someone is not very busy, "doing" their life, and thinking thoughts, and feeling feelings, and this is going on no matter what you are doing at the moment, or feeling at the time. They will never know how you feel, or how you will act. They will all proceed with their busy lives, each just as important as your own, without ever knowing you, ever understanding you, or ever coming to love you, or you them.

"We are born naked, like savage warriors before God, each without pretenses, simply standing alone, and unclothed before our Maker. The great teachers in life know the entire journey is taken in loneliness that at times can be as painful as a raw abrasion. For, children, we are all, each in our own way, ALONE. We never really know anyone else, never really understand anyone else, never really appreciate anyone else, unless that person takes time to slow down from their busy life and to share with us what they feel, or think, or wish to do. Even then, we may not pay attention or understand the value of the conversation.

"You will find in this life that you will give away your message, your precious secrets, with all your love and heart, to others. And you will find that they do not pay attention to you. You will find that so many you chose to share your soul with, cannot see inside and refuse to pay attention in the way that you had hoped they would.

"Some may hurt your feelings.

"Some may betray you.

"Some may show you meanness or cruelty.

"You may react and become more like them than you ever believed was possible, when you allow your feelings to rule your line of sight. When your feelings rule your line of sight, you become truly blind.

"In this life, we naked warriors are alone, by God's design, so that we can apply our FREE WILL to pick and choose our way. For in all the opportunities of life, each must be decided by the free will inside your human heart. Only you can decide.

"I cannot pick and choose for any of my children the way they will follow in their life. I cannot pick and choose to make it easier or harder. I cannot pick and choose to provide any advantage or disadvantage.

"Your brothers and sisters cannot pick and choose your way for you.

"In your choices, each will stand alone.

"If you blame others for the things that befall you in this life, you have lost your sight. You have lost your vision. For God and your soul will always know that only you have made your choices. Only you have created your possibilities, only you have selected which way to go, which way to 'be'.

"In so many ways, life is like a primordial forest. The forest is as you see here," and Mr. Dohrmann spread his hands before him. "Tall trees. Dense plants. Tiny trails leading off into the ground mist. Fallen logs. Small streams, along with a shroud of darkness.

"For the primordial forest is always in a pale of darkness. The canopy is so dense that the eternity of the LIGHT is blocked as the forest, lungs of the earth, prevents light's penetration.

"Naked Warriors, we each, off by ourselves, each alone inside our own minds, and each wandering forever lost in the vastness of the ancient wood of the Lord. We often rest and cling to tall trees. Our fingers grope into the folds and cracks of the timeless bark, to fix our place and bind us to the earth.

"All around them, those who rest "clinging" hear the sounds of life that pass them by. The conversations. The laughter. The never-ending secrets. The noises of the Forest of Life, which frighten and bind them even more tightly to their safe positions.

"Children, those who cling, these naked warriors, are known in the Forest of life as the MAYBES. For these few of all the millions will leave their safe little section of bark, the secure place of their clinging. Maybe once. Maybe twice. Usually, but not always, more than once. To maybe become more. To maybe discover. To maybe become all that they imagine.

"As they carefully search the forest, attracted by the noises of life, they find, rarely, a brilliant illumination. These Maybes find their eyes growing larger as their hearts begin to beat faster and faster. All other sounds for them temporarily fall still, as if the forest itself had grown impossibly silent, waiting to see what the Maybes will do.

"In this moment, a preordained shift in the canopy has taken place, as the living earth breathes. And in this breath the canopy parts and a single blazing shaft of LIGHT pierces to the heart of the forest floor. A clear open pool of BRILLIANCE circles in place and stains the carpet with warmth and possibility.

"After staring with single focus on this golden circle of potential, the Maybes among us will almost always relinquish their grasp of perceived safety to journey very cautiously into the tunnel of LIGHT that has entered the whispering woods. Once illuminated, the Maybe will rise and stand tall and soak in the rays from on high. Staring full into the sky, the Maybe will reside for a time in pure joy, pure bliss, pure happiness as they stand open and empowered by the SUN.

"As an adult you will learn that all such moments last only their own time, in mysteries never made known to us, to vanish as easily as they appeared. The circle of each field of illumination will dwindle. The light will fade and the canopy will again make its shift. The great Light will disappear so totally that the Maybe will once again seek out the safety of the tree trunk by their side. To cling ever tighter. To review and reflect on the past decisions they have made.

"Many millions learn only this single lesson, to rest lower on the tree of perceived safety. As adults grow older most of the olders in life reside on the floor of the forest. These naked warriors, men and women, will be found with their legs wrapped around the tree they have chosen. Dark with bark fragments, their fingernails dig into the soft wood of the redwood tree. They sit with their legs and feet grabbing the lower trunk of the tree. The heads of these fallen warriors are bent in, as close to the tree as possible, and their eyes remain closed and sightless. Their fear has become so great, children, that they fear the Forest of Life.

"Oh, they hear the sounds. They remain open to the whispered conversation and the shared secrets of humanity. They only fail to participate as they once knew how. They have forgotten the earlier way of their life. No longer can they remember the way of the Maybe. Their pain has become too great.

"These naked warriors, children, are known as the FROZENS. They are frozen, to never again stand in the warmth of the sun. Never again to see the light.

Never again to be one with the source of life itself. The Light!

"Why?

"The Frozen, children, have been forever damaged by the way in which the Canopy removed the LIGHT from their lives. The *betrayal* they remember, while forgetting their *greater glory*.

"The Frozen only dimly remember the great moments when they lived their life in peace and joy and happiness. The time of their marriage. The time when the birth of their children occurred. The time of the perfect career. The time of the new car. The time of the new home. The time when flowers bloomed. The perfect vacation. A time when the light was shining.

"Those who grip the tree of SAFETY with fingers forever frozen into the bark, dwell upon their inner betrayals, forgetting all the joys they have also been given. Only dimly do they hear the remaining sounds from the Primordial Forest of Life that surround them in their misery.

"As you come upon these Frozens in your life path, children, and there are many, you must know you cannot help them. You cannot pry their fingers away from the bark of safety, for their need to cling is too strong."

Here, as the sunlight faded, Mr. Dohrmann rose off his large, flat, stone chair, stretched slowly and fully, and then with his unique, slow gait, went behind the children. I remember he stuck his pipe in his mouth and with fierce concentration penetrated the Tree Ferns, shifting branches this way and that as he peered deeply into the depth of the redwood forest. He didn't speak any words for those moments. He didn't continue with his lesson. But I can recall the emotion of the moment, for I was, in that moment, only one of the children, who knew in their hearts that their father was indeed seeing many, many Frozens, within the ancient forest. With a long, slow sigh, he let the Fern Curtain fall closed, and he returned to his teaching position. Puffing his pipe back to life, he continued, the story drifting forth into the twilight.

"Children, these Frozens were once Maybes in their life. Once they heard the noises from the Forest of Life. Once they "let GO" as they would take first one step, then another. Once they journeyed into their life. Once they took risks. Once they made decisions. Once they left the Tree of Perceived Safety and once, maybe twice, maybe three times, they would rally enough courage and be FREE. Once, they would live, if only for some kind moments, in the pool of light from above the canopy, and children, then, and only then, during an entire lifetime, did these children of the Forest become most alive. For then, and only then, did the Frozen live in the splendor of the SUN!

"The sun, the teacher that light always is, moves forward, leaving the Frozens behind. For these find the return of the coolness of the Forest of Life far too harsh. These find the moment when the light winks out altogether, a betrayal too mighty to bear. They blame God, so great is their despair.

"They blame God for their mistake in trusting the sun in the first place. They blame God for the loss of their relationships, their divorce, their friend who betrayed them, their career when they first heard the word "fired", their children when they found drugs. They blame God for when they lost that one child, that car accident; they blame God for their lack of success and joy and peace in this life.

"Rushing, these Maybes return from the only true HAPPINESS they ever knew, the happiness of the memory when they stood, if only for a moment, in the fullness of the SUN while they were alive. These Maybes return to their chosen Tree of Safety and they rest, breathing so deeply in their anger and blame.

"Their legs grow weak as they sink lower and rest close to the ground to seek comfort in the soils of victimhood and martyrdom. Wiggling to sink as far as they can go into these deep, rich soils, they allow their fingers to cling to the deep ruts and scars in the ancient bark of BLAME which they will grasp for life. It will become as much a part of them as their inner nature, whose Light amnesia faithfully hides, allowing them to become Frozen.

"So hurt and so damaged by life have these children become, that they populate the Forest of life everywhere, my children. They cling to their trees of safety as far as the eye can see. No longer can their eyes feast in the light, for their eyes now only see shadows and darkness." Mr. Dohrmann was standing and pointing across the forest and virtually shouting, before he sat once again in sad resignation with his thoughts.

During a period of quiet, Mr. Dohrmann held his head in his hands and, staring at the ground, just shook it back and forth several times. I know a great sadness came over all of us. More than once our eyes wandered out into the Forest to see so clearly, the FROZENS and the MAYBES at almost every tree.

As Mr. Dohrmann raised his head to gaze at us again, his face took on an expression that contained the quality of hope. Moving his hand through the air he proclaimed,

"Children, this is NOT the lesson. For YOU, children, are made in the image and likeness of God. And in this you are most like the very source of creation in your perfect illumination.

"Your future life belongs to a simple knowing ... a knowing that lies deep within you. You will be largely alone in this Primordial Forest of your Life, children, make no mistake about it.

"In the journey of your life you will travel roads no one else can take for you." He looked at each individually to make sure we understood. "Your sisters cannot help you. Your brothers cannot take one step of your journey for you. Your mother cannot walk your journey for you. Your father cannot unpry even one finger from the bark of your tree of safety.

"Only YOU, by your own act of free WILL, can ever lift a finger from your own chosen trees of safety.

"Your hope lies not in what we have discussed here. Not in what we have seen or imagined here.

"For as you walk through your own Forest of Life you will be largely naked and alone. You will pass many. Most will be Maybes or Frozens, and few will know the Forest of Life surrounds them. And in moments when you are most afraid, and most fearful, when you feel most alone, and when you are sinking, your legs will feel weak. Your fingers will slide, and you will be drifting into the soft, damp soil that binds the Frozens.

"I call upon you, my children, to remember this day when you were very young, and you were very much with your family, here in Camp Taylor, in the ancient, holy precincts of this redwood forest and I ask that you listen." Mr. Dohrmann placed his hand to his ear and leaned toward the woods, actually listening harder than anything yet in his story.

"Do you hear it? Can you hear? There is the sound of movement. There is the sound of another in the forest. This sound is heard by every Maybe in the moment when they first let go. This sound is heard by every Frozen, but long ago they have forgotten what this sound means.

"For in the Forest of life, there LIVES another.
"These, children, are known as the RUNNERS.
"You can hear them.
"As they move more swiftly than the wind.
"The RUNNERS.

"These runners are leaping over the obstacles of life. These are running across the streams and around the giant tree trunks and dodging the barriers as they leap and playfully scream in their delight for life itself, searching with hungers born of inner knowing, for the impossible warmth of the sun.

"For the Runners, children, will pause only here and there, to spend the time they have in the glowing circle of light. For the Runners seek and never rest until they have found a fresh moment to bask in the light source of all life.

"The Runners, like everyone in the Forest, will experience the same sadness when the light begins to shrink. When the shaft of brilliance from far above the Forest Canopy begins to become smaller as the light moves to another part of the Forest, the Runners linger until the last of the illumination winks out completely and is gone ... then they bolt. They never pause or slink toward any tree of safety.

"Rather, they RUN.

"For in the vision of the mind they see the Forest as the eagle sees the ancient cradle of all life. They see, with the eyes of creation, their Forest of Life spread itself thousands of miles in all directions. As the Runners fly off a fallen log into the trail of life, a mighty eagle lifts off from a branch behind them, and follows sweeping with its giant wings behind the Runner, watching and searching beside this adopted traveler.

"Then, the powerful wings move and open to soar. Piercing the Forest Canopy, the Eagle rises and the mighty flyer sees the Forest Canopy is filled with illumination. Billions and billions of points of light have penetrated the Forest and shafts of brilliant light source are flowing to the floor, enough to surround every living being within.

"Of these it is only the Runner who will seek and find so many of these sacred shafts of life.

"For, children, the lesson is this: The Forest of Life is as real as any breath you will ever breathe in this life. The Forest of Life is as real as the forest you see surrounding you this evening.

"The shafts of sunlight, children, represent all that is conceivable, all the possibilities, all the rich, unlimited potential locked inside one human life.

"The Runner seeks out and finds the potentials of life. The rich marriage. The glory of children and family. Fabulous career. Adventure in vacation and exploration. Spiritual growth and purity. Truth and freedom.

"The Runner experiences tragedy. Betrayal will find the Runner. For when the joy and peace of a great moment in life winks out, there is no greater sadness than the sadness held by the Runner. For the Runner alone has worked so hard to stand with an open heart.

"The Runner's vision becomes an instant hunger in the absence of light. A hunger that must be satisfied by searching for the next potential to be explored. The higher truth to be discovered. The greatest of the joys yet to be uncovered. And the Runners RUN.

"Run with all their might.

"Run with all their strength.

"Run with all their purpose.

"Run with all their being, in every footstep.

"To rest only when they next land inside the light.

"For alone in all of life, children, the RUNNERS within the Forest of Life will live IN THE SUN, in the warmth of the source from one moment of joy to the next.

"For the Runners have chosen.

"The Runners have made a choice.

"The Runner has no time to freeze by a tree of safety.

"For the Runner, the RUN leads only to the sun.

"I have asked in my prayers, children, that each of you find your ways in life. I have asked that when we are no longer with you, each would find peace and joy every day of your lives." (And his azure blue eyes sparkled as he took his time to hold us each in his vision, if only for an instant.)

"Now learn today's lesson, children. For when I am no longer here to teach you...," leaning forward slightly, he held an imaginary strand of gems and gestured with his hands, as if he were examining each gem carefully, as he entreated his children, "make my lesson today, this ... the lesson, the MASTER LESSON to tie **all** your other lessons from your father into one necklace. A necklace of DIAMONDS that the Lord God has filled with all the colors of the rainbow for your spirit eye to reflect itself within. Master this one lesson, children, and you master all the lessons"

He paused and shook his great head, as if pondering a mystery known in secret between the man and wife, as she shared his look until he finally looked up as we all stared directly upon him.

"For your mother and I do not care nearly as much as you now believe, whether you have the best grades in school. Or the best anything as you move ahead in your lives. Did you know we cared so little?"

Heads shook, NO, Dad.

"Your mother and I do not care if you become ditch diggers or President of the United States.

"Your mother and I do not care if you become famous or if you are unknown by others.

"Your mother and I do not care if you become rich or if you are poor materially.

"Your mother and I do not care whom you may choose as your friends.

"We do not care if you are popular, or if you are unpopular.

"We do not care where you choose to live.

"We do not care what lifestyle you choose.

"We do not care if other people laugh at you or if they applaud you.

"We do not care how you make the choices that you make.

"We do not care about most of the things you may think are important to us as parents, or that YOU believe we care about." (He flashed a quick beaming smile at us as he looked up from his children...**his** necklace of nine diamonds from the hands of the Lord God.)

"Most of all, we do not care if you please us.If you act to please us. If you speak to please us. If you think that we care ... that you PLEASE us ... we do not care about THIS selfish idea, children.

"We simply don't care! It's not what you THINK.....

"But mark my MASTER lesson, my sons and my daughters,

"Because there is something that we DO care about. There is something that we care deeply about, so much in our "core" ... of self ... that your mother and I would give up everything we have in life to teach even ONE of our children this one magical LESSON in living LIFE fully.....

"We would give up our homes.

"We would give up our cars.

"We would give up our friends.

"We would give up our jobs and things that we love.

"We would give up all these things, and so much more, for only one of you, just one child among our nine, to learn this lesson of lessons.

"Children," as he stood he had a full command of authority in his voice and gestures. "I want you to know what your mother and your father DO WANT for their children in this life.

"Children, your parents MOST desire for you to simply live in this life ... as naked as life makes us all ... as alone as life keeps us all ... as afraid as life holds us all ... we ask in our most SACRED prayers children -the prayers that mothers and fathers who believe their children are expressions of God pray at night, holding hands together - in our care for this one idea.

"Yes, your mother knows full wellwhat I WISH MOST for the children of Alan G. Dohrmann ... is that I may see each one of you ... and IN all of you, that you have made in your life the choice ... the single decision, the one true choice you will make between you and God ... the core belief choice you make when you choose.....

"To LIVE your LIFE in the SUN!

"I ask that you embrace your precious life and that you each choose to FLY.

"I ask that you each hear the footfalls of your brothers and sisters.....

"That none of you cling to a tree of safety even for a moment in your life.....

"That not one of you live your life as a Maybe.....

"That not one of my children would stop and sit and become a Frozen ... not even ONE.....

"And that ... EACH ONE OF YOU," and here he stood to his full height and gestured toward the last of the orange fading fireball in the sky, "CHOSE to live your life in the LIGHT.

"That you live as you were born to live your life, my children ... for you were each born as

"RUNNERS!

"Your mother and I have only seen you as RUNNERS ... never anything but RUNNERS.....

"And we ask that when faced with all your choices in life.....

"Choices we can't make for you, or stand beside you when you choose.....

"That before all the great choices in your life, you will pause, and return in your mind to this magic grotto ... and once again you will FEEL the tall, ancient wisdom of these primordial redwood forests, and you will be still, my children, and you will listen,

"First to the sounds of the forest, before you make your decisions ... and that you will fail to CHOOSE in life from the advice of the Maybes or the advice of a spirit that lies Frozen in these woods of life....

"And that you CHOOSE to take ALL your advice, advice you apply when you CHOOSE In your life, ONLY from your FELLOW RUNNERS.

"For they WILL understand YOU.

"For they will be your company," and here with great gestures he exclaimed.....

"Now ... RUN, my Children.....

"RUN ... whenever you make your choices....

"RUN ... and help your family to RUN beside you ...

"RUN ... for the fulfillment of the Lord God.....

"RUN ... for your life of achievement and happiness.....

"RUN ... until the last of your breath is gone.....

"As you make your choice, my precious angels, to.....

"Live your life ... in the SUN.....

"Now run back to our campground with your mother, and Brother Dela Rosa will be RUNNING right behind you, but remember to listen as you run -to hear if we can - the sound of the OTHER Runners who RUN beside us, in God's Forest of Life!!!!!

"NOW RUN!!!"

........and we all did........

There are only renderings of the Dohrmann estate left on this scroll: crude and developed by my own weakening hands and memory. There is a value, I believe, in knowing a little of the terrain in which this all took place. There was a magic to it. The history of this family, so integrated into that of northern California, is also worthy of a few explanatory pages.

The estate was originally selected by Mr.
Dohrmann as a summer home•for the family. The main
home was in San Francisco, from which he continued
the multigenerational family traditions of helping to
create the city and its society. The Dohrmann family
reinvented San Francisco, and with their Emporium
stores and the Dohrmann Hotel Supply (now the Macy
Building on Union Square) and their St. Francis Hotel projects, the name was a byword in the city. Until
the mid 1970's the name Dohrmann rose on the largest sign over Union Square, up the full length of the
now prominent brick facade of the Macy Building on
Geary Street.

People at shops and stores greeted the
Dohrmanns with a different tone. It was hard to describe, but for the West Coast, the Dohrmanns were the
Mellon Family, or the Rockerfellers. The family history
held many generations of service in the city.

Mr. Dohrmann's great-great-grandfather was a
Baron in Germany, and assigned to the Royal Court as
the Surgeon General to the King of Denmark. It was
his oldest son who ventured to the "new world" during
the pre-gold rush period.

The family fortune in America was built on the
tenacity of this one young boy. It was surely one of the
original episodes of culture shock when he arrived, not
to the gentile manners of the royal courts of Europe,
but rather to the fully unkempt Barbary Coast docks
of an untamed San Francisco still in the throes of
changing from an old Spanish mission to a brash
American frontier town.

The voyage to America had been hard, nearly
impossible for the young man. There was no special
treatment for what the crew referred to as "the royal
brat." During the latter part of the voyage the seven-
teen-year-old fell and broke his arm. Treated by the
ship's carpenter to the best splints the sea would allow, and ill from a long recovery, the weakened boy was
put off on the wooden sidewalks of a San Francisco not

yet fully formed, more just a port than a city, full of bustle and commerce, unaware of the gold that lay just a few miles away.

Blonde, blue-eyed and quite striking, young Dohrmann strode the boardwalk looking for opportunity. The second day was spent in exploration, during which time he did his best to remain neat and pressed on the boardwalk, away from the horses and carriages that let the mud fly high. He found, on the wide swath of cleared dirt known as Market Street, a hardware emporium with a Help Wanted sign in the window.

He entered the establishment, and was pleased to find the shop proprietor was not only unoccupied at the moment, but upon opening conversation, he was also revealed to be German. The owner knew of the Dohrmann family. However, looking at the young man's roughly-splinted broken arm, the shopkeeper explained regretfully that he required a "whole" lad. It was also explained that he needed a lad to sweep, empty toilets, and do work unbefitting to Dohrmann's station. After a shared serving of tea, and with great courtesy, it was agreed that the position was not suitable.

As young Dohrmann left the shop, his eyes wandered to the stairway. At the top on a long landing was a large store of ship's brass. Air covers, bellstands, braces and t-bars, winches and clenches and tools. As his hand had already taken the door and sounded the exit bell with its opening, he must have seemed odd, just freezing in place and staring as if indecisive about whether to return to the harsh streets of the Barbary Coast, or to withdraw to the perception of safety inside.

Laying his bad arm by his side, the boy gently closed the door and turned to address the shop owner, calling upon the new friendship with the assurance of one who has never suffered rejection. Without rehearsal, young Dohrmann explained his proposition, as if it were the sole reason he had crossed two oceans, and journeyed eight thousand miles from home.

With a glint of conviction in his unusually deep blue eyes, he explained how the wasted brass could be restored, and marketed to German ship captains for their return voyages. He noted that he had enough influence with such seamen that a positive outcome was preordained. (Obviously, at this point, the young man took the liberty of adding to a small volume of truth with a liberal portion of optimism!)

Through another pot of tea, in this pre-gold-rush-San Francisco hardware store, the terms of a new business relationship were discussed. A fifty-fifty partnership was arranged for anything the young entrepreneur could sell.

Dohrmann moved into the loft above the store. In six weeks a number of miracles happened. First, the boy gradually regained the use of both arms. By that time all of the brass had been restored to "like new" condition. Also by that time, all of the brass had been sold. Another miracle was the way in which young Dohrmann handled the customers. He worked in the hardware store from morning to dusk without pay for six weeks. After the store was closed, he worked on his brass. At dawn, long before the store opened, he would venture to the docks to market his brass.

Dohrmann kept the loft filled with newly-acquired brass. The half of the profits he was permitted to keep was immediately invested back into new supplies. He had printed a business card that read simply, "EMPORIUM."

So taken with the boy's enthusiasm were the seamen, that they began to acquire everything they needed for their long sea voyages that was available in the Hardware Emporium. The customers that began to frequent the store increased to such a degree that the store owner was pleasantly stunned at the surge in profits.

By the end of six weeks, Dohrmann had, from his own funds, stocked shelves in the store with dry goods and food staples suitable for long voyages. Soon farmers and related customers were coming into the Emporium General Store, as it was coming to be known.

Within six months Dohrmann was made a partner in the store. In six years he owned it. By that time the Gold Rush had begun!

THE GOLD RUSH

When gold was discovered in the foothills near San Francisco, the signal went out around the entire world nearly as quickly as by today's mass communications networks. As if a whip had cracked over the flanks of the Barbary Coast, the thunderous call of "GOLD!" brought a river of treasure seekers through and by the shores of the Golden Gate. Others came the overland route, all of them eager to grub up riches from the soil of California, and most of them not particular as to their methods or manners.

The scene shimmers in my mind as I write. The noises clashing in the street: jingling harness and creaking wagons, occasional shouts and perhaps gunfire, a tinkling piano and coarse laughter from a saloon, where men pay for drinks with a pinch of gold dust, and bartenders are hired for the size of their fingers, the larger the better because their "pinch" is more profitable. The mix of languages, the smells of horse manure and leather and heated iron from the blacksmith's, the clang of his hammer traveling out along the street to mingle with the clatter of dishes and scoops scraping the woks in the Chinese chop-suey hut nearby. Braying mules and giggling women who follow the men to take their dust or nuggets and turn them over to the madam. The rough world of the men from Europe and the United States, arriving to seek their fortunes. Indians and miners bargaining over knives and pelts for a warm blanket. The Chinese who would soon complete the transcontinental rail lines. The blacks who had left the South for perceived freer lifestyles. The muddy streets created muddy faces that helped all "be created equal" in the eyes of the Coast. The Barbary Coast.

The by-now-prosperous Dohrmann had two visions of the future. First, he saw clearly that the Gold Rush was temporary, and that the foundation of wealth was not in the gold fields but rather in the streets and people of San Francisco. Second, Dohrmann saw San Francisco being built as a city of Gold, but being maintained as a city that was the railhead for the soon-to-be-completed Transcontinental Railway system to the trading partners in the East.

Having now gained affluence and traveled extensively in America, young Dohrmann made the decisions that would forever change his life and the lives of the thousands he would later employ. With good council from friends like John Muir, Mark Twain and John Sutro, he was destined to succeed.

Dohrmann believed that only the fewest of men would find their pot at the end of the Golden Rainbow. He launched into a strategy to receive gold from all of them whether or not they fully achieved their dreams. His belief was that the Gold Rush would create "no room at the inn" conditions in San Francisco first, and everywhere along the gold trail second.

Dohrmann saw that soon the stream who first flowed to the lure of gold would become a river, the people stream would become a people river, and all would be flowing toward the latest news of GOLD. Towns would spring up overnight and die overnight depending upon the discovery hundreds of feet underground. Like river beds shifting their position, the GOLD FLOW would twist and pull to places by the force of its own momentum.

Aided by his unique contacts in Holland and Germany at the Royal Courts, Dohrmann elected to develop exclusive supply lines for materials not yet manufactured in quantity in the New World. Crystal glasses, table linens, flatware, vases, furniture items, and more.

With courage and at great risk, he opened the Dohrmann Hotel Supply Company, a one-stop shopping center for the arriving river. His goal was to be the exclusive supplier to all the inns that would spring up along the road to Gold. With virtually no competition, the Dohrmann Company would expand, with offices in Seattle, Los Angeles, Las Vegas, and everywhere that hotel explosions took place.

At the same time, he expanded the Emporium Store to become a retail outlet for many of the items the Dohrmann company would sell, most of which also were suitable for home use. As immigrants moved from inn to home, Dohrmann wanted them to acquire the familiar items they would need in their households, from his now larger and much grander Emporium. Learning from Macy's, the emerging idea in the East of a one-stop department store, young Dohrmann opened what was then the first major department store in the Western States, his San Francisco Emporium stores.

By the time of his death, Dohrmann would preside over the largest resort-outfitting organization in the world, as well as the largest department store chain in the seventeen western states. The firm would eventually pass to Alan Dohrmann's Father, Alpert Bernhard Charles Dohrmann, or ABC, the eldest son. ABC Dohrmann would turn the Dohrmann success into an EMPIRE!

THE EMPIRE

Alan Dohrmann was the baby in a dynasty by the time he was born. He would spend his young adulthood during the Great Depression, virtually unaware that such a situation was taking place for other families in the nation. His father, during this time, fostered importing Jewish refugee employees from Germany, working on his own Shindler's List, which became a special treasure during Alan's adult years, a special pride he held for his father.

ABC Dohrmann was seldom home. He worked long hours in building such successes as the Ilawani Hotel in Yosemite Park, in working with John Muir and the President to secure National Park status for the wonderland created by glaciers in past millennia. He was expanding his Emporium and Dohrmann operations to become global forces.

Alan Dohrmann and his twin brother, Jerry, were among the last of the twelve Dohrmann children, and the second set of twins to arrive. As time passed most of the older children would go into the family business.

Alan Dohrmann left a world of private schooling upon completing his education, to enter the officer training program of the United States Navy at Treasure Island. Alan enjoyed the privileges of his family and was most at home in San Francisco's social life.

Attending parties with the Swig Family (owners of the Fairmont Hotels) and the Magnins, or the Gumps, Dohrmann was an obvious toast of the party in his officer's uniform, after the bombing at Pearl Harbor.

Alan Dohrmann would become involved in accelerated training programs offered by the Navy during World War II. Operation "Snap Shot" would change the future of the training industry that was to emerge after World War II. "Snap Shot" taught "spotters" to mentally record briefly viewed ordinance, planes and ships, seen from island assignments in the Pacific.

Operation "Jump Ship" taught farmers from Kansas city who had never seen the sea, to pilot liberty ships after a six-week training.

I never once heard Alan Dohrmann speak of all this. Later, I would gain a greater understanding of the importance of this work, and Mr. Dohrmann's silence on the matter was even more impressive to me. Let me digress to tell you a side story.

I was attending a lesson being taught by Alan's son, Bernhard. I attend them often if I am able to get out and support him. Bernhard's method of teaching includes having his students "share" what they learned from the day's lessons. During a share session, one student, almost my age, rose. He was old, but stronger than I by a considerable measure.

He had come in to this Anchorage, Alaska meeting, where he had had to pound the snow off his clothing. He was accompanied by an enormous Newfoundland purebred that stood next to him, shaking the white fluff off his own coat. He looked more bear than dog, and the old man looked like a postcard from the Land of the Vikings. He had sat during the class until Bernhard had inquired if anyone wanted to share. Earlier Bernhard had spoken fairly extensively with the man, as it seemed they both owned the same species of dog, and had shared stories common to such owners.

As he stood, during the share time, he said, "My name is Bill Bacon, and I want to give young Dohrmann a gift that I have carried for almost thirty years," and he handed an old, soiled, large brown envelope to Bernhard Dohrmann at the podium, limping slightly as he moved his large snowboots to the front of the room. It became quiet in the room, while Bernhard opened up the tarnished envelope.

When he saw what the envelope contained, hidden from the audience by the lectern, we were moved to see tears glistening in his eyes. Bill Bacon was a three-time Academy Award-winning photographer for the Disney organization. He had brought to Bernhard photographs that he had saved from a film shoot with Bernhard's father, Alan, and Walt Disney. Each photograph with its own story. Each signed by Bill. Bill Bacon remained in the front of this Anchorage hotel room, and turned to tell his story to the attending audience.

He said that he had never really to gotten to "know" Mr. Alan Dohrmann. He recalled how he first heard about Alan Dohrmann when he was a young man, doing field work in the Pacific for the Navy; how he and many other sailors and soldiers had heard about the Snap Shot program, and the other advanced training programs Alan Dohrmann was part of in those years. He went on to tell of how many lives were saved, how many men lived, because of the work of these programs, developed over such a short period of time. Bill had a way with words, and he emotionally indicated he felt Alan Dohrmann was a hero, and that what had come from his mind had saved thousands of men, who themselves later became fathers. He explained how through his efforts the war was shortened by many months. He said, "No brass band will play about it, Bernhard won't talk about it, but he knows what I am saying is true, and I want all of you to know it."

It marked me, that night, because I had been with Mr. Dohrmann probably as much as anyone who was not a direct member of the family, and I had never once heard him mention anything about this work, or those years. It struck me, looking through Bill Bacon's eyes, that long after his passing, I was still learning who this teacher of mine really was.

Bill went on to recall a spring day when he was filming with Mr. Walt Disney on location for a picture, away from the studio. Bill said that he was filming because it wasn't every day that Mr. Disney came on site for a shoot. "Then Mr. Disney turned to me and said, '...I want you to meet MY teacher,' and he introduced me to your father, Alan G. Dohrmann. Later I would reflect I was sorry, that I did not turn the camera around from Walt, and take Alan's picture as well. It was like that with him. He was always invisible, standing behind the great ones he would mentor. I wanted you to have the pictures, so you would always recall the day that Bill Bacon almost took your dad's picture. I have held on to these pictures for just such a time, and I have thought about what Mr. Disney said that day many times, because I thought it was so extraordinary ... 'I want you to meet my teacher' ... it was something!"

Alan Dohrmann was infected from his Navy years with the idea of how a human being could excel, if just the right training were provided, particularly accelerated training. He began to master everything in the field of accelerated learning. Pioneering in work with Super Learning and related disciplines, working with government and private industry assignments, his work would take him all over the world.

He was so influenced by the possibilities of "accelerated training" it became his passion for the remainder of his life. Alan felt that accelerated training or SUPER TEACHING as he would later call it, would be an agent for preventing war in the future. Alan believed that "only through retraining human beings could the spirit of war as a destructive force be harnessed for the spirit of cooperation and creativity."

The Dohrmann family was not overjoyed to see their young son so influenced by the war. Their plans for Alan to enter the family business did not include his appetite for experimental teaching.

ABC Dohrmann was once heard to say to friends at a San Francisco party, "School teachers, we hire them; we don't invite them into the family." ABC Dohrmann was careful of his appearance in the community. He had spent the war years entwining his considerable resources to become a key war effort supply line. He was frequently in photographs in the San Francisco Chronicle, accompanied by VIP's from President Roosevelt to the Secretary of Defense.

ABC was not amused when, following the war, his young son expressed a desire to work in the "Human Potential" business. He told the President of the Emporium in that year, "Imagine, the 'human potential industry' he calls it ... whatever *THAT* is. I can only hope he will gain a responsibility that puts out of his head this silly notion of teaching adults who have already completed their education, silly notions they don't require or desire."

Jerry Dohrmann was a family man, a business man like his brothers and sisters. Alan Dohrmann's twin tried to influence his brother back into the family business. Jerry would invest a lifetime in supplying materials to the military worldwide. Alan Dohrmann would never match his siblings in business passions. He never cared for it. Money was not his motivation ... people, however, were!

By 1948, Alan's daughters were complemented by the birth of his first son, Bernhard. ABC would never know him, however, having passed some years prior with the "family" taking control of the empire. After years of bickering on how things might be best run, the

Dohrmann and Emporium holdings were sold. The family members each went their separate ways. The only reunions the Dohrmann Family would ever host were created in the 1970's by Alan, and his oldest sister, Edith. Only brother Bruce and his sons, Bruce and Eric, would decline to attend. The rest of the family, including all the branches and offshoots, have remained in touch through the auspices of the reunions created by Alan and Edith in the 1970's. The stories of the various family factions is a huge work and is reserved for other tellings.

The history we share now is a flash bulb. A *POOF!* A flash that opens the lens of the reader to the history of Alan G. Dohrmann, to the roots of the man...a Baron from birth, and accustomed to the rich associations that had made San Francisco Society.

In 1948, Alan Dohrmann created a program known as Marriage Encounters for the Catholic Church, of which he was a lifelong member. This program took two years to perfect and was created originally by Mr. Dohrmann for the young men returning from the war, to resolve what he perceived as a growing lack of skill in relationships.

Mr. Dohrmann had no idea that this course, designed for a single parish church, would one day influence courses to be translated into more than twenty languages, offered by over 200 denominations in one form or another, and to be instructed by the year 2000 to millions upon millions of couples around the world. How many families have remained intact? How many marriages have remained whole or been revitalized?

Perhaps it is this work, rather than all the other attributes of the family, that best represents the "EMPIRE." The empire that said, "Teachers ... we hire them; we don't invite them to become one of the family....."

Chapter 4

Wonderland's Garden

WONDERLAND'S GARDEN

As I remember it these days, all the past decades seem like only yesterday to me, almost a gentle amnesia that sweeps by like a blanket gently lifted into the air and laid lovingly back upon me. The sea noise disappears, and the air and sounds of the deck by my hospice room seem to all but evaporate, replaced by redwood forests and the scent of pine and a hint of roses. Yes, in the memory of an old monk leaning now on a wooden walking stick, but gazing on that remote day at our young pioneer, the narrow trail we followed seemed to call with impossible magnetism.

Led by the tiny hand of a five-year-old child eager to share a magical treasure, I was laboring in the steep walk this hot summer day, a long, long time ago. The flowing robes provided by the Benedictine abbey do not represent in any age appropriate "hiking" apparel. In the tradition of the 1950's, it would have been unthinkable to de-robe, and nearly unpardonable to find my way along the trail in "street" clothes. One rapidly-aging Benedictine monk, and one blond-haired, blue-eyed boy sometimes running, sometimes rushing back to check on his hiking companion, but always breathless with excitement, made their way deep into the ancient redwood forests of Marin County.

We stopped to rest, I recall, far more often than my young guide would have preferred, but each new outcropping of rock required my testing its quality to perform the function of serving my derriere as a chair. Would the impossible path never cease rising? It seemed a never-ending trail, as even the air temperature began to fall. My guide's seamless chatter provided visuals of the feast that was certain to come, someday, if we only kept up our walking.

Sometimes, as we passed through minuscule clearings that seemed never to have seen the sun, with patterns of leaf-weaves to make Picasso mad with envy, I would pause to consider that God's divine plan needed no more proof than this perfection. Passing a forgotten stream driven from ancient springs, shiny stones glittering with its passage, the confirmation would come again. As we entered into grottoes of redwoods with towering boughs that whispered to tree ferns twice the size of my young companion, I entertained for a time the wish to make a new home, to replace my Abbey with God's own cathedral.

Near the apex of this hiking experience, during the period of my second doubts about the destination, the boy had turned back twice, agitated and impatient, over a knoll past which I could not see. "Come on, Brother Al," employing a movement in his great futile gestures suggesting I actually pick up the pace and RUN. "Come on, Brother Al ... it's right up HERE," and "Come ON!" ... and ... "You can see it now.....," and then he scampered ahead, out of my sight once again. Although I considered a wonderful rock chair for a just a second, I passed it by to favor my young enthusiast with my total attention, admittedly lacking up to this point in our safari.

A prayer for strength was sent heavenward, and legs in denial picked up the pace for the final distance up to the crest in the narrow path, at last reaching the tiny knoll, the place where one could finally see "IT".

I had, in my mind, discounted the many tall tales this imaginative youngster had been spinning about his adventures during the long winter and spring months. In my life I had inevitably been disappointed in so many missions of childhood fantasy, where the reality is so much the lesser in comparison to the imagined vision that shot from the mind of innocence in its telling to adults. Such was the norm, such was the anticipation.

It was, therefore, with great surprise, perhaps TOTAL SURPRISE, that my hiking was stopped short. I found myself actually holding a hand over my heart for several moments with heaving breath that was more gasp, as the full impact of the experience held me fixed. All my previous doubts were put into suspension. All my distractions were placed on hold. All my outside predeterminations had been shattered like an old mirror carelessly dropped.

It was a minute, perhaps longer, before I realized my other hand, the draping hand, was being tugged repeatedly by tiny fingers once again.

"See? I told you, Brother Al, I TOLD you....."

And indeed he had. However, he had not prepared the mind of the doubting adult for the smells, the sights, the vista of what lay before me now.

I can remember these many years later, how, like warm milk, I felt my smile leak across my face. I stood with the goofy grin adults own in surprised discovery, basking with my own inner child coming up to gasp for air in the pond of unlimited imagination gone wild. In that single moment the boy knew he had made his first CONVERT, at age five, the first of many stages that would mark his later life with drama, as he could feel that I honored him with my surprise.

I had to stop a little longer just to record the experience for a lifetime of memory. Something (was it angels brushing me with insistent wings?) suggested this was one of a handful of "meanings" for the life journey, not to be minimized in passing.

Never in all my earlier travels to Europe had such a magnificent or magical garden ever been discovered. If I had to describe it to the reader, I would simply say, "It was perfect".

It was as if I were lying down, looking through the keyhole of Alice in Wonderland's tiny hallway, under the rabbit hole. Lying in that long hallway, and seeing WONDERLAND for the very first time as the tiny door was first opened to her magic garden. This garden was created by another Alice from another time altogether. It was a sight for Gulliver rather than for a real-life boy and a monk standing high on a knoll in a redwood forest upon a real-life trail.

As I began to adjust to the effect, I was able to let in the other sensations. It was only at this point that I realized one could almost taste them. The scent of ROSES. It was so powerful that no flower shop could ever match it. Every time I would again be around live flowers, I would always return to this moment, on the knoll, standing beside HIM.

The awesome fact of actually seeing over 2,000 of the rarest roses in the world, virtually every living species of rose, in a collector's garden, held its own magic far beyond these words to convey. Like a stamp collector inspired, the roses were placed in their catalog positions, perfectly mated to companion flowers. Daffodils on one side for the yellow roses, Sweet Williams on the other side to accompany the red roses.

There were pink-and-white striped roses, and green roses, and blue, there were jet black roses and vast vines of climbers on trellises that framed the fence for hundreds of yards, completing the canvas. No painting could capture the mystical reality. Carved like a work of art in an amphitheater featuring showers of color, the entire setting framed a gingerbread house that even I was tempted to believe was from Hansel and Gretel, just as he had proclaimed in his story on that very first night at the Dohrmann home.

I found myself walking by compulsion (not just led, but *dragged,* although not at all unwillingly) as I noted the tree house, off to the left on the other side of the large fence, just as he had said. He scampered and half slid under the fence like a trained athlete and stood waiting and smiling on the other side.

I chose to lift the latch handle on the giant gate and open it, to step inside a strange new world, held out of time from the rest of space.

COMMON SCENTS IN WONDERLAND

I have tried to recapture the scents present upon entering the place the children referred to as simply "the rose garden." Prior to this time, I had prided myself on being a practiced observer. My trained eye has many times since taken in the impression of these first experiences in Alice's rose garden. The impact of that first moment is forever caught in the word "proportion".

The mere act of fastening the gate altered realities too numerous to describe. Rather than a list of incidents, the surrealistic proportion began as a FEELING.

The trail was transformed by passing through the gate into a place of magical *proportion*. Part of the feeling was the sensation of TIME held at bay, as if the soul knew it was coming home to God.

Like a giant step into the kingdom of Lilliput, standing on the downhill side of the trail, the average person was forced to reach up, to fasten the gate. Whether by plan or accident, I found myself caught in the feeling of being a very young child. The large, green gate (perhaps eight feet high) was made far taller on the downhill side of the trail, as one reached upward to pull it closed and re-latch the fastener home.

As I quickly turned to glimpse my young blond guide, already skipping far ahead down the winding path of redwood chips and needles, I could only see the roses.

Before entering, I had thought the scent to be overpowering as the breeze carried the fragrance to the tiny knoll overlooking the snapshot of her garden. Once within, the sheer vastness of what greeted the senses became overwhelming. To my right as I walked down stood a citadel of giant redwood trees like four stationary guards, creating the impression of a gate within a gate. Running off into a dense forest of tree ferns were finger paths, some going down and some seeming to run level to the place where I stood rooted in astonishment. The finger pathways were lined with sculpted rock walls, that made an ordered perfection out of the chaos of color.

"It's awesome, isn't it, Brother Al?" The young hiker was now far below me with tiny hands cupped around his mouth to magnify his cry.

The grotto to my right was framed in magnificence by aging railroad ties, that formed a gentle recreation area providing privacy and shade. I saw that one could enter this pool of shadow from other trails far below, climbing carefully constructed rail tie stairways to the semicircular alcove, a reprieve from the eons of work that must have been required to construct the garden itself. A life of labor fixed in stone, pathways and roses.

My guide, having hopped onto a stone footstool, launched himself into one of the two large, green hammocks hung by chains around the mighty girth of the redwoods. He proceeded to make the chains creak, rocking back and forth in his hammock bed. As his little hands went behind his head, his blue-eyed stare was so intense and silent that I turned to consider, why was he resting all his attention on me?

I returned the smile in recognition of his delight at my overloaded senses. This was HIS moment of confirmation that the "disappearing place," as Mr. Dohrmann would refer to it (upon relenting to allow Bernhard's visits), was no longer to be considered an exaggeration.

No one could deny the "why" of it.

The child within me was newly reborn in the feasts to follow. I paused, continuing to rest on the wooden staff I had picked up along the forest walk. Turning left from the grotto off to my right, I was met from my trail line, with what seemed like hundreds of perfectly designed circular trails, each off its own main trunk path, and reconnecting eventually, each larger than its sister, upward, and higher until far off into the forest I could see no end to it, always with roses, more and unending roses ... thousands and thousands of roses. Each pathway off to infinity lined on either side of the first and then the other of these circular trails with roses.

At the very top, after so many tiers and rows of rock walls and sculptured trails, one could see blossoming orchards bordering the trunk path. Fully in bloom like some grand frosting for young master Bernhard's magical Cake of Roses. How long was I drinking in the smells and sights in this fashion I cannot recall. I know the youngster never said a word. I was lost in thought a long while as I perfected a memory I was certain few would ever or could ever hope to witness.

I was pulled out of my quiet meditations by the voice of the plump "witch," who materialized from nowhere with her bellowing dog Flower, calling for me (by name as Brother Al, I might add) to come down to the house. I was provided with detailed instructions of how to get to "Gingerbread House," the centerpiece of the mystical creation of Alice Mahoney. Smiling as my guide left his hammock to show me the paths with personal attention, for quicker ways down than my bemused state might have allowed me, I was nearly instantly down to the lower lawns and cottage. Indeed, the walk was too brief; I would have, if left on my own, paused many times to admire the stunning beauty on all sides.

Tea and cookies were ready, as though prearranged, with milk for young Master Dohrmann, served on the outdoor picnic tables as if I were a returning guest. My arrival obviously had been both planned and expected.

Not knowing how to address this strange reclusive woman that young Mr. Dohrmann referred to only as his "mentor", surely a word learned from his father, I continued to gaze at her work, each tier of rose after rose framing the eating area. I was silent, as if I had known her a lifetime, with no need to feel awkward when words were not immediately available.

Her dentures were the worse for wear, leaving cookie crumbles falling in place, and she began talking while we ate, as though she had left off from some earlier conversation. It reminded me of the manner of the boy's father when he was teaching a lesson. Alice Mahoney spoke her first words to us and the lessons began.

TALKING WITH ALICE

"We are both alike, you know?" She was staring to see if I was paying attention. Her white hair and pale soft eyes, made one think of being adopted into a family by the most perfect of all grandmothers. Not knowing how to respond with a mouth full of freshly baked cookies, I nodded.

"You see, Brother Dela Rosa, we both have chosen our own monasteries in which to serve.

"Each of us has left the world of people and busy thoughts, and chosen to serve in a quiet form of isolation.

"Oh yes," she went on, picking up tone and enthusiasm with a wave of her hand, scattering cookie crumbs and a chocolate chip in a dramatic arc, "You have chosen a monastery of stone and cement. I have chosen a monastery of redwoods and roses.

"You have chosen a monastery of discipline and liturgy. I have chosen a monastery of divine breezes and the scent of angels.

"You have chosen to pray in your way for the salvation of every soul on the planet. I have planted a rose for each soul and cast their petals to the wind."

And here, having her fill of cookies, and with young Bernhard lying himself full out on the green bench soaking up the sun, this strange woman sat back in her large wicker chair. She was so large one would have thought her a direct descendant of a Lewis Carroll character from Wonderland ... perhaps the Duchess. Her chair quivered and the opulent rounded back looked like a crown of glory, creating the sensation that she was resting in her Throne of the Roses. Patting her mouth and moving forward just as Mr. Dohrmann so often would, without preamble or small talk, she began again.

"Brother Dela Rosa, let me tell you a story about my garden."

With only the occasional animated gesture to break the rhythm, or the peep of a blond head now and again over the rim of the table top, the story flowed uninterrupted. Alice Mahoney's story, which has been retold many times in the family, went like this:

ALICE'S STORY

"As I built my garden I came to union with the first of all creation. I can't recall how long exactly, but it was many years ago. I was young then. Some say I was pretty.

"I remember the moon was full. Very full. The garden had already become quite large by then. As was my custom, especially on the warm nights from late spring 'til fall, I would work quite late into the darkness in God's garden, as I liked to call my work. Extending a rock wall in perfect symmetry or matching other flowers to the petals of each and every rose.

"After some time at work, that first time, I remember simply turning and looking down the many lower tiers of the garden. Only for this moment, Brother Dela Rosa, the garden had disappeared altogether. I was so utterly amazed I could not think of where I was or what had happened.

"I do recall that the peace and joy in my turning at this moment of discovery was so complete, such a moment of purity that there was no fear. No fear or apprehension at all. In fact, I was somewhat concerned, if my memory serves (and it often doesn't these days) that the Garden might return in its illusion and destroy my new found reality.

"For long had I studied the early writings of this one phrase 'and the word was made flesh' to contemplate the meaning of life. The true meaning of life once the onion peel is stripped bare. Always seeking the underlying meaning, Brother Dela Rosa, to those words, 'and the word was made flesh'.

"And after years of poring over the well-known and the obscure commentaries, my husband Bill and I (no minor scholar in his own right was Bill Mahoney), we landed on the conviction that the soul itself cannot be defined in words. The soul can be defined, we came to believe, in sounds, by vibrations.

"The spirit that is our reality plane, the plane in which we call things 'this' or 'that', is nothing more than the conscious notion of GOD expressed in the form of a beam of light, a beam of light that is so unique and pure it has a vibration that defines it from every other possible beam of conscious light that ever was or could ever be. And within the magnificence of the perfection of this beam of light, God has chosen for his own delight, to sprinkle in his music, a simple tone or vibration that is the expression for this perfection. Sound, like a DNA code, wrapped vibrationally to a beam of pure conscious light.

'And the word was made flesh'

"Peace had been ours, Bill's and mine, a long while when we drifted into the knowing of our nature, Brother Dela Rosa. Our one TRUE nature. For the beam of light of which we speak, may in one form be nothing more than a weed here in my garden. We were now certain another beam would become a rose. While another becomes the redwood. And of course another becomes Alice Mahoney, or Bernhard Dohrmann or Al Dela Rosa. For each of us flowing from the single source of impossible perfection in light and sound, are in our own world, never-ending and connected.

"Which brings me to the story of our garden on that evening when "it" happened for the very first time.

"I remember I could still see myself, although my garden had actually disappeared. I appreciated however, that even I was altered from this very first experience. For long trails of silky-weave light were flowing, and fell off all my fingers and flew from my toes sticking through my sandals. It was as if I was made up of silver threads connecting at every point of motion with 'the others'."

"And what 'OTHERS' they were, Brother Dela Rosa." Alice paused a long while and we just waited as she glowed in her memory, weaving her hands and seeing sights only she could see as the thin threads wound off her hand movements and the wiggle of her toes on the porch.

Opening her eyes as though she had forgotten her company, and shaking her head a moment, she first reached to sip her cooling tea. Then the story continued....

"So you would like to know what I saw, wouldn't you?" I could see she was looking at the blond mischief whose head just rested on the picnic table and had begun to nod. I smiled.

"I had always wondered how the eternal soul would see a rose. I suppose in my prayers I had requested to have the truth of this vision more than once.

"As I turned I first thought, perhaps a trick of moonlight? Or even an indigestion? Some trick of mind or lack of sleep?

"But no.

"I knew when I turned what a gift this was.

"For I could also hear the sound.

"In my garden's disappearance I could see the field of creation with the vision of the angels.

"And in the world of angels there are no roses.

"There is something even more profound.

"For in the midst of my labors, my garden was transformed into a river of light and a symphony of sound. Replacing all the flower beds was a river of pure white light containing bursts of color and solar flares more magic than the sun.

"Each ripple was a cascade of bursting, never-ending showers of movement, expressing the true vitality of life itself. Colors changing and reshaping themselves in endless variety to the winds of time. Each was unique unto itself, no two were alike in any way.

"The ancient depth of the redwoods in the river of life were so profound and moving, no words can be said here,to paint a mental picture for what I bore witness to that night, save to say that each redwood was like a universe of stars with a wisdom pleasing to creation and roots that, like a supernova, touched upon the river of life in God's garden of creation, connecting one to all. Each redwood was like a spider web of new universes touching an impossible dimension of creative stars within the flower beds, each alive and each in a motion of living light!

"Some of the little flowers, now pulsing ripples of energy, had sounds like tiny bells almost unheard. Large orchard trees made oboe-like response to the blend of all the sounds around me. The sound was unlike any symphony or blend of information you have ever known or ever will know, Brother Dela Rosa.

"The sound was itself a miracle. The sound heals. The sound blends into the heart. The sound connects the soul to God. The sound completes the unseen. The sound conveys the garden to the vision when the organs of vision are closed to sight. Only with such sight can one truly see.

"Many times I would close my eyes, and the sight was always the same. Unchanged. It mattered not if my eyes were closed or open.

"There was no way to turn off the hearing either, and the sound was with me during the whole experience. Perhaps the magic is the sound itself, and once heard, it never leaves. The soft power of the moment transformed a life of work to the inevitable peace of full oneness with all things.

"Make no mistake, Brother Dela Rosa, I knew then as I know now that each and every creation in the river of life could hear the sound that I made, even as I could hear them. Each could be enjoyed as one ... or as many ... or as ALL ... with only a thought ... a reflection ... within the feast of it.

"I remained in this state, learning so many of the connections between each life source, and with the sound of myself, until the dawn. The time seemed only moments. There was no need for rest, for this was perfect repose, perfect balance.

"I remember the sad sense of lonely separation that came when the fingers of dawn quieted the oneness, closed the sounds and lights to dense and solid forms, and left a quiet breeze as memory for the fading vision of my gift that night.

"After some time I rose and went into the house to make breakfast for my husband.

"Braced for the inevitable incredulity that must come from him as I shared my story, I discovered that Bill Mahoney only smiled as my excitement increased.

"After I finally finished, my husband Bill told me how his night had gone. He had made a note to come and get me from the garden around 9:00 PM. Somehow he dozed off in his reading chair and didn't wake again to come for me.

"However, he explained that he felt his arm being pulled. He thought it was me and in his sleep brushed the hand away, only to have his arm pulled again. This time more firmly. When he opened his eyes, he found his small gingerbread home had been turned into a castle of light. A flowing creature, an angel of light was floating just off to the left of my Bill's easy chair.

"Bill said his first observation was that he could see through the walls of his home, suddenly transformed into a castle of light, and into the garden of oneness. He saw me as a sphere of brilliant rainbow light, and heard the sound of me, and was at peace, knowing that I was safe.

"Bill was beginning to bask in the colors and sounds of the garden when the floating light creature filled his mind with words. The words did not come in sequence like our talk, nor did the words sound like words. The communication was through pictures, sound and knowing. Bill told me that morning, he reviewed each message as it had been given in its entirety, with the first thought that woke him. Bill described the sensation as 'pleasant'.

"As Bill conveyed the angel's communication to me, it went something like this:

THE ANGEL'S STORY

" 'Bill Mahoney, hear me!' The light creature began. As attention was centered, the conversation flowed.....

" 'Great Spirit has shown you this garden so that you would know how Great Spirit exists. Bill Mahoney, see all creation through the eyes of illumination. Great Spirit has sent a message for you. The garden you are now seeing is no more nor less than all the gardens of all the creations in all the possibilities. This garden of life you now witness is ONE. There is only one garden and there is no separation between the flowers. There are two parts, two messages.

" 'In the great garden of light, for the time and space in which you reside, Great Spirit has chosen one, and only one, who is to become the gardener at any point in time. This one, this chosen gardener, will tend the garden until the work of illumination is complete for their journey in life. When this work is complete, God's gardener of light must choose another.

" 'The two messages are:

" 'First, it is the time of the choosing.

" 'Second, there is no separation between the flowers in Great Spirit's Garden.'

"Bill reported that as these final thoughts came upon him it was dawn. He indicated he had felt as if he'd enjoyed the best night's sleep he had ever known, even though he remained in his easy chair throughout the night. Bill said that he remained still until I came into the house; his revelation of the river of life remained intact until the surrounding noise distracted him and the vision faded.

"We didn't talk that much about the subject after that day, Brother Dela Rosa, although on more than a dozen occasions we both were blessed with the GIFT of true sight again.

"I have often questioned the children who have come into my garden, Brother Dela Rosa, for I know after all these years, that my rose garden is not a garden at all. Rather, what you see as a rose garden is, in fact, God's lighthouse."

I felt that Alice was about to impart something of great importance to me when I heard a lower gate bang, and the cry of a loud "HELLO!" from a lower trail off in the redwoods below the cottage. Mr. Dohrmann was coming to take us home.

THE ROAD HOME

The spell of Alice's story kept me quiet, able to offer only small talk. After several minutes, Alan Dohrmann arrived on the board walk from the lower trail. He was wearing khaki shorts, a bright green shirt, and a broad-brimmed straw hat. One hand carried a walking stick upon which he rested as he looked at us, and the other held a bright green pipe that matched his shirt. His broad smile was infectious.

With only the shortest of chats, we turned to depart. A bit of dialogue ensued that has remained with me for a lifetime.

Alice said as we were turning to leave, only to Mr. Dohrmann who was in the rear, "I just finished introducing them to your work here."

I remember he beamed upon her and turned to give her wrinkled face the most tender of kisses.

"Did you tell them about the garden?" he asked as he started walking.

"Just the first part."

"Did you tell them I have chosen?"

She shook her head "no," as a little blond head ran off into the garden.

I can remember it was strange to me at the time that as she was watching the youngster she had tears in her eyes.

Mr. Dohrmann waved to her as he began to step onto the stair path and raised his walking stick and said, "There is no separation between the flowers," and he was gone, winding his way up the knoll onto the forest trail.

During the long walk home we talked of sealing wax and sailing ships, of rings and kings and lots of things ... and we talked of roses.....

My feelings, as I put these memories to paper? Knowing that half the parties to this story have moved forward from this plane, and I am sure to soon join them, the colors of past memories hold special impact to an old man. I suppose I look forward to seeing my mentors again, my many teachers, my sacred time with Mr. Dohrmann, and Alice Mahoney, with an ancient abbot in from a timeless monastery, and the One who taught them all they knew. I know I will find them waiting for me, playing and laughing inside Alice Mahoney's garden of roses. For I know she tends it still, and I see her often in my mind, looking up as her garden disappears, to be replaced with the True Garden she was tending.

I suppose I wish I had her GIFT, and just a few more years, (the only reason now to really hang on to life a little longer) ... just enough more years ... to see who HE will chose to tend the garden.....

.....as ... the story of the roses ... never ends.....

But wait ... there IS more!

THE THREE BRICKS

It was late August, nearly September, in Marin County, warm and full of a feeling of mellowed richness.

The scent of the bay drifted into the large open area around the window seat where I was reading. I liked to have the large windows heaved all the way into the "open" position, leaving breeze and sounds to keep my meditations company. Screens kept the summer pests away. The breeze sounds from the garden forests made my readings that much more serene. I was thinking how much this place had become like "home" to me.

My cloistered life of service, bound by vows of silence, was held in momentary reprieve as the balance of the secular home delivered experiences I knew to be yet another blessing to my life.

One of my favorite privileges when residing in The Apartments was the many "browsing" opportunities. There was always something different to discover with each new visit. I can remember the "thank you" mementos that Mrs. Dohrmann left in place around the Apartments.

It was like a museum of sorts. Hanging on the walls were featured notes from Israeli General Moishe Dyan and his wife, Rachel. I remember the note from Buckminster Fuller and the model Geodesic Dome. There was a hand-signed copy of the EPCOT treatment in full color from Walt Disney, made more impressive because at the time EPCOT was not yet under construction, but only a dream on paper. There was a series of letters from Napoleon Hill. On the wall was a note from Harry Oppenheimer, Chairman of Anglo-American, the largest mineral extractor in the world. Later would come notes from Warner Erhardt, and the writings of Tom Wilhite and William Penn Patrick; the dream work of Bill Dempsey and Marshall Thurber; the teachings of Alexander Everett and of John Hanley.

Some were obscure intellectuals or mystics from India or Tibet while others, like Dr. Edward Deming, were icons in Japan, made even more immortal in the setting of the Apartments each had visited. The common thread though, was a union at a cushioned window seat, the smell of bay, and a soft autumn breeze. For these, I knew in my browsing mode, were shared by all, even as I shared them at the moment.

I would imagine the face of Werner Von Braun sitting in a chair in the Apartments, or of Walt Disney having his own "stories" told and retold. I would often think which of the beds they might have reposed within, as I myself selected them each over time. I would see their news clippings and read *their* stories. I would see portraits of their faces hanging on the Apartment walls. I would often be moved to pause, and dwell on the values that we shared, as each had shared this space. I know the others felt it as well. Perhaps it was a feature of the period, there was a kind of reverence for the deliberations, the leisurely thinking and talking that had gone on there.

In these latter days of the Internet, and the fiber optic virtual world exploding upon us, I think of these things now ancient and buried, with a kind of wonder. Perhaps "his" stories are after all out of place, lost in time, and without significance to a present human race gone wild. And then again, in writing them, I think, perhaps, from this tranquil period of the 1950's, just perhaps a ray of illumination might inspire the mind of one more child yet, in the coming millennium. I know I won't be here to witness how his stories might be finally received, and it seems not to matter as I write today.

As I review my notes on the story of the *Three Bricks*, I know that one child, if only one, MAY be chosen to carry their own bricks forward in time ... and I know Mr. Dohrmann would smile then and wink, and say in his manner, "See, Brother Al ... it's all worth it ... more than enough ... all the while."

THE TIMELESS WEIGHT
OF THE BRICKS

I am amazed at the fragmented detail I will remember about a given story. I often sit for hours before I prepare to pick up my monastic quill to write on a new scroll about one or another of the main stories. Most of my time is spent in the outline work on the many tributary stories that were also told over the years, the minor lessons as we call them in the family, or as his wife refers to them, "the corrections". Phylis Dohrmann has been such a blessing in the work, with memories even more venerable than my own, she tirelessly makes herself available. I find in discourse with her on a given story, the laughter of her husband returns to us both.

As we both remember it, I had elected to dine in The Apartments alone on that August night. It was quite late when Forest returned to inquire "Would you like to participate in the "lessons" tonight, sir?"

"Yes, yes, of course, Forest, thank you," I said as I placed my Bible on the nightstand and stood to follow.

I noticed it had become quite dark outside ... I often failed to notice the passage of time while visiting The Apartments.

"Your meal was satisfactory, sir?" Forest, always the caretaker, inquired as we walked the outside stairway to the great double glass doors on the upstairs landing.

"Yes, as always, it was wonderful. Please thank Mrs. Dohrmann and the staff for me, Forest." ... as I followed the good fellow inside the main house.

"I shall indeed, sir," was his reply, holding the doors open for me. I passed him and went alone into the area reserved for the family storytelling.

When I arrived, the evening's events had already been set in motion. Mr. Dohrmann was finishing his evening pipe. His grin was every bit the Cheshire cat's, as I approached. The children were dressed in their customary night clothes, and sitting in their traditional semicircle around their father's easy chair.

Mr. Dohrmann's house staff had placed a circle of candles around himself and the children, as was the rule on "lesson night". The candles formed their own half moon, just behind the children, having the effect of making it appear that the area in between was a formal stage, upon which the children and Mr. Dohrmann were the touring company. Tonight the circle was broken near Mr. Dohrmann's footstool, where three neat knapsacks rested. One was red, one was silver and one was bright gold.

THE GOLDEN KNAPSACK

"Children," he said as he removedhis pipe and leaned forward with his elbows on his knees to stare at them, "do you know what is in these knapsacks?"

Heads shaking "no" with few words to add.

"But would you like to know?"

More heads nodding.......

"Well, you can't know. At least not yet. First I want you to wear each one of these knapsacks tonight.

"I want you FEEL as you wear the first knapsack, one at a time, then you will take your places as you are now.

"So come up and try the first knapsack on, starting with you, baby Missy!" He held the knapsack to help her put it over her tiny baby shoulders.

And they came, first one and then the next. Each tried on the first, red knapsack. Each carried the first knapsack one full circle around the outside of the flickering candle markers. Some went directly. Most modeled and feigned mock expressions to their brothers or sisters as if it were some form of exotic fashion show.

When they were done, Mr. Dohrmann asked the children to come and perform the same task, but this time with the second, silver knapsack. The others watched their sister to understand there was a big difference, with the silver knapsack.

Missy had great trouble putting on the silver knapsack. She didn't offer any fashion show this time. She seemed to be struggling and wanted only to remove the knapsack when she got to the other side. Mr. Dohrmann just smiled and nodded to her brother, sitting next to her, to rise off the floor and repeat the performance. No one was laughing halfway through, as everyone could see it was a struggle to wear the second, silver knapsack.

When they were done, Mr. Dohrmann said that it was now time to put on the third knapsack, which was the color of pure gold.

No matter how hard little Missy tried, she could not lift the third knapsack and wear it. Mr. Dohrmann suggested that she wear it right where it lay. Although Missy could struggle into the knapsack, she virtually lay upon it. She was not able to lift the third one onto her back. She toddled back to her place inside the circle of candles.

Her stronger brother had no better luck. In fact, none of the children could lift the Golden Knapsack from the floor at all.

When the last child was done and rested back in place, Mr. Dohrmann just leaned back in his giant easy chair, with his hands folded in his lap, and looked at each of his nine children.

"What have we learned so far, children?"

"We learned one knapsack is heavier, Dad....."

"We learned that you can't move the gold knapsack, Dad....."

"We learned the silver knapsack is too heavy, Dad....."

And so it went.

Finally, after a long pause and a nod of his head noting he was not pleased with the answers ... he leaned all the way forward and began to open the first knapsack, which was colored red.

In a ritual that took more time than would have seemed strictly necessary, Mr. Dohrmann carefully unzipped the red knapsack that had been so easy to wear while going around the circle of candles. Each child had had no problem carrying it. Each had clowned around almost dancing while they wore the red knapsack, like a game they knew well.

Reaching deep inside, Mr. Dohrmann lifted out and placed into the circle of candles a large red brick, and then sat back and looked at the brick, which he had set on end.

The children were staring at the brick to see whether, with eighteen eyeballs, they might find out the secret. A father's secret of just what was so special about this ordinary-looking red brick. For awhile some leaned on their elbows looking at the brick with chins on tight little fists. After a time, each of the children rested back on their pillows and blankets. I found I myself trying to figure out the puzzle's secret like another child, when Mr. Dohrmann began to speak again.

The candlelight dancing on the children's faces made our despair all the more poignant. You could easily sense the frustration.

"Children," Mr. Dohrmann began as he saw he held their attention once again. "I saw you put on quite a fashion show when you wore the red knapsack that held this single Red Brick. You danced around our circle of lights having quite a time of it. You performed for your brothers and sisters. You were "light" and you were happy when you wore the red knapsack which held the bright red brick you now see before you." He gestured to the brick standing on end, inside the circle of flickering lights.

"Do you know the reason that you found it so pleasant to wear the red knapsack, children?"

Heads shaking "no" from all the children.....

"You found it so pleasing, children, because you will wear this knapsack all your adult lives. You will never take it off. You will never set it down. Every waking moment you will take this knapsack and you will tie it on your back. For, of all the knapsacks you will carry in your life, my children, this one is most FAMILIAR to you, even though your souls are very, very young.

"For the Red Knapsack, children, contains one of the bricks of pure human nature.

"The red brick of human nature is the brick of *POPULARITY AND ACCEPTANCE.*

"Human beings love to be popular. Human beings love to be accepted. And when God made human beings, he made the red brick perfect. The red brick is light. It is easy to carry.

"When you wear the Red Brick Knapsack, children, you can dance and play and spin all around your friends. You can show off to your brothers and sisters. There is no weight to the effort. For the effort of seeking our Popularity and Acceptance comes naturally to each of us as human beings. Everyone snickers and thinks you're funny and important when you are playing with the Red Brick of human nature. You were winning acceptance and popularity as you each walked around our circle of light.

"And I want you to remember how it FEELS to be popular and accepted.

"It FEELS good doesn't it, my children?

Heads nodded.....

"Next, can any of you tell me the lesson of the silver knapsack?" And once again he sat back in his large arm chair in silence, with his arms folded and waited.

More quickly the children conveyed they didn't know the lesson of the silver knapsack.

Once again, Mr. Dohrmann leaned forward, this time as if the effort was far more important. I remember the anticipation as his hands disappeared like spiders into the Silver knapsack. He was waiting for a moment, and then he lifted.

He brought out a small bar of pure silver. I can remember the mint stamp impressed upon its surface. As he set it down into the circle of lights, the candlelight jumped and licked the bar of silver, causing flickers to dance on it like fairies. The light spilled off the bar of silver and fell onto the waxed hardwood floors.

"Children, take a close look at God's bar of silver. I noticed you didn't want to wear God's silver knapsack. It was harder and more difficult for you to carry this bar of human nature. You each had trouble getting the silver knapsack onto your backs. I also noticed you did not want to keep this knapsack on. You couldn't wait to get this knapsack off. I could tell that you wished you had the red brick knapsack back on, as the red brick knapsack was far easier to lift, and to carry in your life than was the heavy weight of the silver knapsack.

"For, children, the lesson of the silver bar is that the silver bar is the weight of *YOUR HONOR and of TRUTH, yet another quality of the potential within your human nature!* The silver bar is much heavier because it carries all the weight of the first bar, the red brick of popularity and acceptance, but it also carries the full measure of its own value, the weight of Honor and of Truth.

"Honor and Truth are qualities in human nature that are far more demanding than the easy burden of Popularity and Acceptance." All eyes were fixed on the two bars and the flickering light that flowed across them both.

"For, children," Mr. Dohrmann was very stern and sincere. "it costs something to HONOR another human being. It costs something to carry TRUTH in your words and your deeds as you move forward in the path of your life. And the weight of silver is far heavier if you choose to HONOR every other human being that you come across in your life. In the end, children, you will always be far more popular and far more accepted in life if you choose to meet every other human being with your Honor and your Truth fixed firmly on your shoulders. Notice that it is the silver brick which SHINES.

"Do you see it? The silver brick, children, is SHINING for the Lord God!

"You can FEEL the SHINE of TRUTH and HONOR!"

.....*And we all felt it!*

"Now remember how the silver Bar of HONOR and of TRUTH felt this night.

"And when you grow up, never forget how the badges of HONOR and TRUTH will FEEL in your life, when you carry them. If you ever feel a little weight when you are faced with the honorable action, or the truthful words, remember this night, remember your home, remember the silver BAR inside a circle of light and your father's words!"

And as Mr. Dohrmann sat back in his chair one more time, he asked, "And so what did we learn from this point in the lesson?"

.....And after some discussion it was considered and agreed by virtually all the children that they had learned the secret that the BEST way is not always the lightest and easiest way.....

"Very good, although ... that is not the lesson....." His huge smile made it clear we would soon learn the lesson of the Golden Knapsack.

THE HERO'S GOLDEN BURDEN

It took much longer to unzip and grab what was in the golden knapsack. With a nod, Mr. Dohrmann indicated that he would need assistance. Forest came from the side wall, and together both men were able to grasp and lift what was hidden inside Mr. Dohrmann's knapsack of gold.

When it was done they stepped away, and we could see that he had set down a very large bar of pure gold into the circle of light. The light that danced off this item was spectacular and filled the entire circle with golden sparkles flowing over the other two bricks. The circle of sparkles was far larger than from the circle of the flat silver bar. The bar of gold seem to glow with its own light. It was spectacular to see.

As Mr. Dohrmann settled into his chair, he leaned forward to explain the lesson of the golden bar.

"Children, you may recall that none of you could lift the knapsack of gold. Not even when two or three of you tried together to do it. Why is that, do you suppose?"

"It's too heavy, Dad."

"The answer, children, is that the bar of gold was made by GOD to hold a weight so vast it is beyond the strength of children to lift. Yet the bar of gold is also a quality of the human spirit.

"But what is this weight you may ask?" And he stared for a moment at all nine children.

"The weight of the Golden Bar, children, is the weight that God has reserved for the HERO.

"Oh, not the hero you see on television.

"The person who draws the fastest gun. Or the one who wins all the medals in sports competitions.

"We are talking about the Hero inside each one of us, the Hero who CHOOSES, the Hero who wears all the bars at once. For this hero carries the full weight of popularity and acceptance, as well as the full weight of truth and of honor, while also carrying the huge added weight of the HERO's bar of gold in their life.

"And you may ask what is this weight of the Hero that contains each of the other qualities in full and complete measure?

"The answer, children, is that the HERO is a person who has learned the lesson of Sacrifice.

"First, the Hero will sacrifice in little ways. The hero may give up the need to be RIGHT in front of another. The hero may gift the "right" that the other needs, putting their own "need to be right" away, in a small self-sacrifice of their own inner feelings. And never will they tell a soul that they have done this deed, such is the way of heroes.

"A hero will stand up for those who stand beside them, not when it is simply RIGHT to do so, but also when it is inconvenient and costly to stand by a friendship or a mate or a child. A hero will sacrifice whatever it may cost to do the RIGHT thing, even if it is unpopular or costs acceptance from another, or a group of other human beings. The hero will sacrifice popularity and acceptance in favor of the TRUTH, children, such is the way of the hero in life.

"Heroes, in the end children, will sacrifice their own precious life, to protect the life of another human being. A hero will carry the full weight of GOD'S true power in the choice they make to lay down the things of this life so that another may keep those very same things.

"This is the way of the HERO, my children, and I want you to learn the way of the Bar of Gold.

"Come, each of you and see how it FEELS to be a Hero. And we did. I can remember as I touched this bar, that because of the words of this magical man, what was after all a simple bar of metal, felt especially wonderful. Our fingers turned golden with reflected glory in the candlelight, and he let us linger to have as much of the FEELING of the Golden Bar as we required. Some took more than one turn. It was smooth and his words had warmed a part of the soul, holding a magic power to bind us together. We shared something that night that words cannot impart. The IMPACT was at a level too profound to be expressed.

Finally, as he began again.....

"And the lesson, children, is THIS.....

"I want my children to learn that when you grow up and you choose which knapsack you will wear in your life, by far the most difficult and challenging will be the knapsack containing the bar of God's gold. But this my babies, is what I wish for you to choose when you grow up.

"In fact, I dream of all of you choosing God's Bar of Gold, as soon as you are old enough to lift the gold knapsack onto your backs.

"And yes, you will be less mobile. You will not be as free as you may have been with the red brick of simple popularity and acceptance.

"For when you wear God's Bar of Gold, the knapsack of the HERO's qualities, YOU, my children, will become much more rooted in your life. No longer will you need to run here and there in FEAR of your own popularity. No longer will you have to banter around with your lighter knapsack, hoping for acceptance and always in FEAR of losing either one of those two elusive qualities.

"The hero is afraid too, but the heroes choose COURAGE that overcomes their fear, as they make their stand in life, a stand that always FEELS like Truth and Honor to everyone who is a witness.

"The HERO, children, is HONORED for the truth that they alone display, for the TRUTH of the HERO is forever fixed, immobile, eternal. The truth of the HERO is made in the image and likeness of God.

"And so are you.

"And when you were born, your mother and I only saw in you the golden shining of the HERO. In each of you," and he pointed, "you and you and you. You were all born HEROES, my children. We brought home babies with the flickering golden light of HEROES in their tiny eyes. A shining that remains in their eyes to this day.

"For in this lesson you are learning that as you grow up, you will always hold the magic of the golden knapsack inside you. Adults can only free themselves, one life at a time, to behave in a heroic manner, my children, if they CARRY the bricks from within their own knapsacks.

"And adults can miss being the hero by stopping in life to remove one or more of God's great bricks from within the knapsacks they were born with. It has always been a matter of free will and choice, what each one of us will decide to carry, my children ... the choice is always ours. For we were BORN TO CHOOSE!

"Have you DONE THIS? Have any of you removed even one brick from your knapsack already?

"Have you done this terrible thing?

"Have you removed the brick of truth and honor from your knapsack?

"Have you taken away the weight that GOD has placed upon you, the HERO's weight from your birth-ride into this life?

"For you see, children, when you choose to wear the knapsack of GOLD, the HERO's Knapsack, then, and only then can I do, what I am made to do as your father.

"I can," and here he looked very hard at each child "... LOVE YOU with all my heart and all my might and I can provide to you the LOVE that only HEROES know ... one from the other ... for in giving you all the love that I have to offer to you ...

"MY HEART WILL KNOW.....

"That YOU, my children, are indeed my HEROES ... and you will then and only then, DESERVE it all!

"For now though, the night is tired and so are we, so run to bed ... but run as HEROES ... and then your mother and I will come and tuck you in with all our love ... the love we reserve for God's HEROES ... scamper off to bed!"

I found I wanted to "SCAMPER" too, as the children ran full speed, off to bed, HEROES one and all.....

Chapter 5

When It Rains........

WHEN IT RAINS IT POURS..........

It was almost two years between my visits in the late summer of 1955 and the winter of 1957. I remember seeing the shiny red and white, now-classic 1957 Chevy in Mr. Dohrmann's driveway. I had heard he acquired the new item from the dealer showroom release in the fall for Mrs. Dohrmann as an anniversary present. Forest had driven me to the back entrance, with its flat, enormous parking lot above the main house.

As we had come across the Golden Gate Bridge, I had noticed the effects of winter on the hillside meadows of Marin. The usual golden color of the dry grasses had been transformed, and now a lovely green startled the eye of one who had not seen the gradual change. When it was pouring rain, as it was this chilly winter's day, the back entrance was the shorter way to the main house. Standing there with Forest holding the umbrella, I paused at the landing, looking down at the green roof of the estate. It always felt like a homecoming.

I gazed at the terraced lawns sloping down toward the main house, with the little outcroppings of level ground in pools of contrast stretching like arms to either side. It was as if the tiny paths and trails that wound their way through the property had some plan to circle back on one another to provide a secure embrace to the home site itself. Other buildings showed corners or rooftops, like the Lath House, amid various gardening sheds which marked the way from the orchards or were sprinkled amidst the flower beds.

At one level on a separate landing stood a large new playground for the children. I noted some sawdust had replaced a piece of garden in the exchange. Swing sets and merry-go-rounds offset the colored animals that were mounted to fixed springs. It was a magical place for the children and it was all new since my last visit. The frosting was a full-size doll house built to scale as a three-room "fortress" for the children's imagination. Forest and I had to stop, even in the rain, to explore the new surroundings. He took great delight in pointing out every detail.

It was winter, the roses and related flower gardens were bare, and the cascade pummeling the large umbrella provided all the incentive necessary to convince me that I should be moving indoors.

I laid my dark Benedictine greatcoat aside on the coat tree in the breakfast nook, Forest beamed with pride as his legion knocked and delivered my traveling bags. Not only delivered but completely unpacked each bag, as was their custom, while Forest made fresh tea, my favorite blend. It was a marvel how detailed the welcome always was whenever a "homecoming" was to take place, as the Dohrmanns called it. We sat awhile on this first arrival afternoon in the breakfast nook in The Apartments and caught up on the family news from my two years "away" as Forest like to refer to it, the same way he referred to Mr. Dohrmann's many travels as his "away" time.

I learned that Mr. Dohrmann had been in Japan, and had only just returned. In fact, the family was preparing for the first "story" in almost three months. I was told the children were delighted, and Mrs. Dohrmann was visibly happy I would be participating.

Forest explained the plan tonight was to repair to the Great Room following the evening meal, due to the chill and rain, so that a large fire might be enjoyed. I was anticipating the evening with pleasure. Our tea time complete, Forest left, allowing me to rest and refresh.

In my browse I noted that Dr. Edward Deming had been to the Apartments while I had been away, as had the Dalai Lama. I also noted that Richard Nixon had visited The Apartments during my absence. A gift from each guest spoke oceans about their stay. I often wondered about the stories I had missed while "away".

THE FIRE

Before long, I had had a festive and loving reconnection with the family at dinner. Sitting later with a rainstorm pounding at the giant windows looking out to a fierce night sky, we snuggled in the circle of light the fire offered. The huge, walk-in, stone-crafted fireplace, with its bonfire roaring, spread mixed light across the walls and windows. Coffee had been served to Mr. and Mrs. Dohrmann, who sat in large easy chairs. Tea was replenished for my comfort without the asking.

I had already enjoyed a warm reception from each of the children, who (older now) had come to regard me as a member of the family. My funny robes and clerical mystique were by now casually accepted, and Mr. Dohrmann's permission for the children to call me "Brother Al" gave our relationship a cozy familiarity. Brother Al was asked to read bedtime stories. Brother Al was asked to play games until the rain stopped. Children fought over who would be permitted to sleep over in The Apartments during Brother Al's visit.

I came to understand that the "off limits" Apartments sat like a magical playground for the children, just beneath their feet. I also learned from the servants that few of Mr. Dohrmann's callers were visited by the children in The Apartments. The meetings held in The

Apartments equated to a global "think tank" in which the topics dealt with "visioneering" as Mr. Dohrmann commonly referred to the work. We believe the common phrase "imagineering" that Mr. Walt Disney so liberally applied in his later work came from a visit to The Apartments in 1951. The Apartments were a holy ground to the children who delighted in being included when permitted. Brother Al shared The Apartments, so that they soon were filled with laughter and falsetto voices. For the children, being able to visit there was a rare delight, and one they knew would be a daily occurrence when I was the only occupant.

As my eyes fell to the playful eyes of the children, reveling in Mr. Dohrmann's homecoming, I thought what a magical setting it was. The fire was to the back of the children and the enormous blaze in the walk-in-size portal was well stoked by Forest and his watchful professionals. Light flew out in crackling orange hues, which, when the embers exploded, sent virtual meteors of color across the hardwood floors. It was as if some super nova had suddenly created a universe of crackling and hissing sparklers like wee dragons, each fixing their vermilion eyes on the upper chimney as they flew in a mad dash for freedom. The aftermath of such a half-life left impressions of radiation bathing the Great Room with a magnificence only the descent of Santa Claus could have challenged.

A long while we sat in silence, listening and watching the fire tell us its own private stories, as the scent of wood smoke evoked ancient memories of tales told long in the past by other master storytellers sitting around their fires in caves, fires in teepees, fires in small houses or great castles on the moors, fires in the desert.....

As splendid and evocative as these sights, these sounds, these smells were, we could not help but wonder what was symbolized by the props Mr. Dohrmann had set in front of the children. We were beginning to try and decipher the unique code of the master teacher, eyes wandering more and more often from the fire to the collection of objects sitting inscrutably before us, within the half-circle of candles that always accompanied the Lessons.

THE CODE

Mr. Dohrmann had assembled a pile of what appeared to be tiny leg irons, made of a silver metal, in front of the children to the left of our position. In the center was what seemed to be a large printed document, very thick, with a shiny blue cover that simply read CONTRACT. And to the right, a large set of what I thought looked to be green gardening shears.

I was noticing that the older children had abandoned thumb-sucking or Binki-holding, and other quaint habits that I rather missed. Their attention was now riveted...their replies compelling. They were after all, growing up. I felt a shadow of what it must be to be a parent ... the longing to keep them small and innocent, the determination to prepare them for life.

As they stretched to still their little arms and legs, and studied each of the props carefully, Mr. Dohrmann, seemingly failing to notice it all, tapped one of his famous pipes upside down until the red glowing embers died in the large crystal ashtray. Turning his full attention to his nine children, he began to speak. There was no warning. There was no formal starting. There was just a tone, that indicated that the informal conversation had "slid" somehow into the lesson about to unfold.

OF OWNERSHIP & LOVE

"Children, tonight's lesson is about OWNER-SHIP and LOVE. My first question to you tonight is a simple one.

"Who owns YOU?"

In his usual manner, he sat back and with hands folded patiently in his lap, he stoically waited for answers to come.

Little mouths twisted. Bodies pulled to sitting positions. Some whispered discussion between the elders, indecipherable from their father's throne position. More than one got up to join the activity center in the middle, cupping hands to ears and checking to see that Dad was not listening too closely to the suggestions. When all had settled back to their semicircular configuration, much like some queer television game show, a look of victory came over the contestant winners.

The answer was given by Terry, the oldest.

"Why, you own us Dad," ... and there was some confidence in it ... tiny heads were nodding in agreement, and some were smiling confidently.

"So you believe that your mother and I OWN you?" Mr. Dohrmann had leaned forward to check the belief system of his nine children individually.

"Is that your answer then?" His eyes burned into the children waiting for confirmation as if testing common resolve.

There was some positive head nodding at this point ...

Terry repeated ... "Yes, you own us, Dad, we all belong to you and to Mom....."

"Well, what I want you to DO, children, is, I request, starting with the oldest, that you place the leg irons I brought here, onto your legs. I ask that the oldest help the youngest until it is done. Let's start one at a time."

Now, this took some time to accomplish. The oldest in the family had no easy time of it. Mr. Dohrmann sat back watching, offering zero support. The task was made more challenging because the younger children could easily step out of their leg irons, and so the elders had to instruct them how to shuffle their feet to keep the bracelets on their tiny ankles. Finally it was all done, if somewhat awkwardly, and every face, smiling, turned in victory to their father ... I can see them standing in their semicircle, with the fireplace illuminating them from behind, as if standing at attention. I thought they might soon salute their father in military style. However, they kept their hands at their sides, each chained to the others now, and waited for further instructions.

Without speaking, Mr. Dohrmann rose from the chair and approached his oldest daughter, Terry. He stooped over her, his frame hulking over the child, and picked up the end of the chain from her leg irons. We saw that it had a kind of handle fastened to it, with a length of chain leading to the first leg iron.

Again without so much as a word, Mr. Dohrmann began to walk. At first, as he pulled the chain, the children didn't understand. With his back to them and his pressure on the chain very slight, it became quickly clear that he wanted his children to follow his lead.

And so it began. The little shuffle of feet. The clankity-clink of the chains dragging across the hardwood floor, and the procession taking form. I recall Mr.

Dohrmann was careful not to pull on the "runner" in front. Mrs. Dohrmann, first smiling, left the room in part to shelter her giggling, and in part to retrieve her Brownie camera to frame tonight's lesson in time.

Back in the room it was inevitable that a leader or follower would jerk and pull the person they were chained to, which created some friction. A little back pull made one or another child almost fall.

Mr. Dohrmann circled the giant sofa, and the Great Room's half-moon of candles on the outside, to pass three times by the fire before he was done. Watching as he went behind our chairs, Mrs. Dohrmann and I noticed that the smiles from the experimental chain gang procession quickly turned to effort in the second pass around the track. The children were learning to cooperate so as not to pull and jerk one another.

In the first pass there was a lot of pulling and jerking. "That's not funny," and, "You're yanking," and so forth were common remarks. In the second and third pass everyone was focusing on cooperation and a rhythm in their steps to make a smooth passage. The third loop was by far the most difficult.

Mr. Dohrmann was picking up the pace by the third go-around, clearly wanting to remain out front. As his lead chain pulled, the children would shuffle and try to keep up. The occasional jerk on the chain of another became more frequent as did the exclamations.

Finally, Mr. Dohrmann stopped the chain gang in more or less its original position. Once this equilibrium was reestablished, Mr. Dohrmann simply dropped his lead chain and returned to his chair.

He watched the children in silence for a time. Facing him like a platoon ready for inspection, the children waited with hands at their sides for further instruction. There was a fantastic discipline about the family, that one must have witnessed in order to fully appreciate.

"Children, take off your leg irons and put them where you found them, and return to your lesson positions." He then waited with folded hands in his lap. He didn't even reach for his oversized pipe resting silently in the crystal ashtray.

After the children had unfastened themselves and whispered about their own conclusions for this "game", they finally sat in silence waiting for further direction.

"So children, tell me. How did that FEEL when we shared our procession of LIFE?"

.....And here there was some discussion that went on for awhile, most of it whispered. I could catch a word here or there but in the end the conclusion stated by almost all was, *"It didn't feel GOOD, Dad."*

"So you're telling me that the procession of life exercise DID NOT FEEL GOOD?"

All heads nodded ....

"But let's stop to think about what we have learned so far in our studies tonight.

"First, we learned that you THINK that your mom and your dad OWN you. You feel owned. Owned by your parents? Isn't that right?"

More nods without words.

"So then we chained you up like we do Alexander, the dog, so that he will be safe and secure. We made you safe and secure. Like we chain our bikes. Like we chain up all things we OWN. Like we protect all the possessions we have. We treated YOU just like our other possessions, because you feel OWNED. We made everything safe and secure. You were safe with one another. You were chained to one another. You could SEE one another. You could FEEL one another. You could HEAR one another.

"When I jerked your chain, you jerked someone else's chain until everyone's chain was jerked.

"And we found we didn't like the way being JERKED was FEELING, did we? We learned a little how it FEELS to be owned, if only for a minute. And we didn't like it, did we? We began to FEEL a little of what it was like to be forced to do things, all nine of you together, no one an individual, all of you tied with a common chain, the chain of OWNERSHIP. For just a moment we suspended what we THINK and we were able to focus on how we FEEL about ownership. And we discovered what it is like to consider the FEELING of what happens when one HUMAN BEING tries to OWN another Human Being.

"This bad FEELING of OWNERSHIP might be the OWNERSHIP of a husband for a wife, or a parent for a child, or a boyfriend for a girlfriend, or a friend for a friend, or a brother for a sister, one human being owning another human being.

"And we learned that OWNERSHIP chains us to FEELINGS we do NOT like.

".....But, of course ... that's not the lesson!

"Now, sitting next to the pile of chains is a legal agreement. I want you to learn that God's universal law is stronger than all the chains in the world.

"Yet how does our human law FEEL? Can you FEEL the human law of ownership? Do you think you can?"

"We don't know, Dad.....," came the uncertain answer.

"But do you think you can FEEL human laws of ownership?" Without waiting for a reply this time, with a lean forward, Mr. Dohrmann continued with the lesson.

"See the legal agreement in the middle of our circle here?" His gestures made us look.

"That document is a bunch of agreements. What it says is that you children are all adopted. All nine of you. You're old enough to KNOW what adopted IS.

"What this document says to you is that your mom and I adopted all of you when you were very, very little, and then we brought you home. This paper says we OWN you. The paper says we OWN you right now and forever. This paper says we own you in the future for as long as you will live. We don't know who your real mommy and daddy are or where they are. We just know that WE OWN YOU because of this paper."

Here Mr. Dohrmann paused and leaned back in his chair to let the children think about what he had said. He asked again, "SO HOW DOES IT FEEL, CHILDREN, TO BE OWNED?"

"......It feels terrible, Dad......"

"Now the part about being adopted IS NOT true, my babies. You ARE our real children," which was a good thing, as some of the youngest were starting to become upset at this point, "but I want you to tell me HOW IT FEELS to be OWNED in this way."

Now, it got somewhat emotional here. Although Mr. Dohrmann permitted some time for the elders to make the youngers understand that they were NOT adopted, it was a little while before the answer came ...

"It doesn't FEEL GOOD, Dad......"

"So again you tell me that OWNERSHIP doesn't FEEL good, no matter how we do what you said, as we TRY TO OWN YOU.

"You said, after some while in thought and discussion with each other, that you believed, and we have many times learned how powerful a belief IS, that your mom and your dad OWNED you. Yet each time we show up to OWN you, we find it DOESN'T FEEL good to you.

"HMMM.

"Let's see.

"What have we here?"

And at this point Mr. Dohrmann reached all the way over and picked up the scissors and examined them as if he had never seen such a item before. After a time, with the reflecting firelight reddening his face, he said, "Why, these are not really scissors. These are wire cutting tools." And with this he bent down and carefully asked each child to help him cut the chains that held the shackles. One by one he cut them all.

So now the shackles lay in front of each child, but freed, and no longer connected to the other shackles.

Next Mr. Dohrmann asked the youngest children to help him to carry the shiny blue legal document that said CONTRACT to the fire and burn it up. First he showed us, however, that all the pages inside were BLANK. Then we watched the contract burn.

I know in my case, I felt relief, in knowing the very idea of an adoption for even one of these nine precious children had become vapor. In the process of examining how I was FEELING about it, I reflected on Mr. Dohrmann's earlier words. Indeed, how powerful a belief can be upon our core being. How powerful can a suggestion become in our core being. I was thinking how important it was to GUARD our FEELINGS and BELIEFS from "unwanted intruders" when Mr. Dohrmann and the story continued.

THE MEASURE OF LOVE

While we were watching the fire consume the last of the contract, Forest had placed a folded wash rag with a little colored pail in front of each child. As he finished he placed in front of Mr. Dohrmann, a thimble, on a little wash cloth, a bucket and finally, a large, waist-high barrel.

This took time and required two servants in the doing.

The barrel had a lid which was removed after being, with some struggle, placed into position by the household staff. This had become a major event by the time the legal agreement had burned.

And we knew the lesson was about to continue.

Leaning forward with his arms on his legs, and his hands holding his chin, Mr. Dohrmann began.

"Children, we have learned that ownership is a funny concept. It's not exactly what we thought it was, this thing called OWNERSHIP.

"We have learned that anything you really, really CARE about is best left free of chains and shackles, and should have no binding agreements of any kind to control or limit the LOVE you possess. We have learned that only GOD owns that which is created and GOD made sure that we were all set FREE from birth. We were set FREE when we were created, with FREE will. We have always been FREE and we must always BE FREE.

"Free of any chains.

"Free of any agreements.

"Free to return or withhold love. The one true freedom.

"However, we put chains upon ourselves, and we limit ourselves when we make binding agreements, that seek to grant ownership to another to control our lives. We have learned that only when the SHEARS of PURE LOVE go to work to set free our beliefs and our prison chains, do we begin to FEEL really FREE again. Only when we burn our limiting beliefs and self-imposed agreements, so that the transformation of such illusional beliefs of ownership is complete, do we become truly FREE to choose.

"For you see children, it will never FEEL good to you if I own you, because you believe you have the obligation of BEING owned. It will only FEEL good to you when you surrender ownership VOLUNTARILY because you FEEL the desire for such ownership as a condition of LOVE. You give your love. You surrender your SELF as you surrender your love, as a partnership to spiritual union. Union to God first. Union to family second. Union to mates and friendships next. Spiritual union is the expression of selfless love made free of any and all conditions of ownership.

"However, this is not the lesson." The smile that came when Mr. Dohrmann leaned back tickled him and the children, for they knew then that the magic would continue.

THE LESSON OF LOVE

"I have had Forest place a different-colored small pail in front of each of you. Nine children, nine colors, one for each.

"I would like to have you come, one at a time, each with your pail, forming a line over here at the barrel that Forest and Kris Major (Forest's second in command) have brought into the Great Room. Be careful you don't spill even one drop as you learn this lesson. So fill your pail carefully.

"Set each pail, without spilling even one drop, on the washcloth that is laid in front of you."

So, starting with the eldest, the children began to line up by the waist-high barrel. Each with the help of their dad filled the bucket assigned to them and, with slow deliberate steps, walked back to their places. The youngers where helped by their mother, Forest or Kris, so that not even a drop fell to the hardwood floors....

As the rain continued to pound, and the storm pummeled the night, the warmth of the fire formed a comforting contrast and illuminated the next part of the lesson.

"Now that you have settled back into your places, children, I want you to know what you OWN inside your pail. Each pail is a different color because each of you experience your WAY in life individually, one from the other. Each of your pails is the same SIZE, however.

"Exactly the same size.

"For your pail is, in truth, the vessel that God has given to each human soul to hold ALL their love, the special LOVE that innocent children reserve for their mother and father. The water inside your pail is ALL your love, my children, all the love you possess for your mother and for your father. The water is all the love that can fit into your vessel. All the love that your vessel in this life will hold for your mother and your father. Remember always that the vessel God gave you to hold all the LOVE you possess is of a different color than anyone else's.

"For even though you all have buckets that are FULL right to the top, you also have buckets that are different from one another. This is because the hue, or the color, of your love is experienced differently, one child to the next, even though your bucket is completely and absolutely full.

"Now that you know about your bucket of love, I want you, one at a time, to carefully pick up your *love bucket* with both hands, and ever so gently, one step at a time, cross over the area to my big bucket, and dump all the water back into that great bigger bucket," which was sitting next to the waist-high barrel, "right in front of your dad and mom." And he patted his leg.

"Don't spill even one drop. Now, oldest to the youngest, let's bring your buckets of love up here.....

"And when you DO this and you HEAR the water flow into this bigger bucket, I want you to THINK in your mind that you are pouring all the love you have back to your mom and dad. You are GIVING all the love you have in your hearts to your mom and dad and putting this love into their big bucket over here." He tapped the big carwash-sized bucket next to the waist-high barrel.

.....And so, one by one, very slowly, almost reverently, each child set a pattern for how they would carry and give back their love. Based on how the olders did it the youngers followed. It seemed that they poured their water so slowly, and so deliberately, as if trying to stall the inevitability of the last drop that would drip. To the last child they would tap, in their own way, as if to shake another miraculous final drop into the larger bucket ... and then ... it was done!

Mr. Dohrmann peered over his bucket for some time. He nodded in satisfaction. His smile was always infectious and made everyone feel lighter.

"So what do you FEEL now about ownership? You have given away all the love you owned from the vessel that GOD gave to you. So what have you learned?"

Considerable whispering at this point ... a debate and shifting of positions. Then the contestants of the world's greatest game show returned to their home base positions with a smugness. The answer: *"We learned that we all want bigger buckets....."*

At this, Mr. Dohrmann beamed as he looked knowingly at his wife. Without saying anything more, he stood and stretched his back. Then he bent over and with his wife's help, he began, without saying a word, to take the larger bucket, (and here I must say I will never forget the feeling or energy in that moment, as if an angel had brought its presence into the Great Room, and a warmth settled over every heart that was monitoring Mr. and Mrs. Dohrmann) and each lifting one side, they duplicated the slow way the children had poured. I recall that they even tapped the great bucket when they were done, to secure the very last drops into the waist-high barrel.

As they both emptied their bucket, Mr. Dohrmann spoke of what was taking place.

"Children, the bucket we are lifting represents all the love that your mother and I have in this world." (The emotion was thick, because Mr. Dohrmann's voice was cracking, as he said his words from a deep heart place we all were connecting to). "And while we give the ownership of this love away, we like you, are wishing, with all our hearts, with all our souls, that the Lord God had given to us a much BIGGER BUCKET. A much, much bigger VESSEL for all of our love. However, this IS the only vessel we have been given.

"And as we pour this love away, children, we pour this love into the waist-high barrel of all the LOVE we hold in our hearts for our FAMILY. For the giant barrel that is waist high is the largest of our vessels, one that has been given to your mother and I, by the Lord God, to hold all the love we are able to give. This waist-high barrel contains the love from all of YOUR buckets, blended with the love from our own giant bucket, into one enormous barrel of love. And, children......

..... I clearly remember this part ... as he was crying ... his voice was cracking and Mrs. Dohrmann was crying as she faced the children, then the children started crying ... and then I was crying ... as he said to us, "Your mother and I pray each night that GOD will give us a bigger BARREL to hold the love we have for you ... for it is far too great for the vessel we have now ... FAR TOO GREAT....."

Here he did a funny thing. He patted the top of the water.....

After a pause made more dramatic because, with his back to all, he just stood awhile and gazed at his wife.

When he turned back to us he asked that the children come up one at a time to see something magical.

He held each child's hand and gently, one at a time, patted the love that had filled the barrel. I know I watched it nine times and I still wanted to see it one more time. Knowingly, he called to me to come and I did. For when you patted the water you sent a tiny connection motion across the barrel. It was a wave. The miracle was that the love in the barrel rested on the top of the rounded lip. We knew that with just a bit more force the love would pour over the top. The pat just completed the wave which touched all points across the barrel ... a barrel that was FULL to a point that one more drop could not be contained. It was a feeling of GREAT LOVE that we each felt that night, a feeling that came from TOUCHING the LOVE ... a feeling of connection ... of being full ... of longing for a LARGER vessel.....

As I took my seat, so did both Mr. and Mrs. Dohrmann. Sitting on the edge of his chair, he said again,

".....And, children, ... that is NOT the lesson."

THE THIMBLE

Mr. Dohrmann picked up the tiny thimble that was set over to his right on a small white washcloth. He held it up in the firelight and examined it from all sides.

"The lesson, children ... is that many do not have the family you have. Some come into the world without moms or dads to love them. Some come in and have very hard times when they grow up.

"Some are adopted and find loving families, others are not so lucky.

"Some are abused.

"Others are abandoned.

"And it affects them, children. It affects how they carry and protect their vessels.

"Many, many never discover that the vessel they own is FULL!

"And for all too many, the vessel they OWN to hold the love they have to give away in this life, is just this tiny thimble.

"For children, the one truth you can rely upon is the truth that every human spirit will indeed OWN their OWN VESSEL for LOVE.

"You will find, children, that when we give our love away, when we give the love that is in the barrel of our family away," and he stood up and walked over and patted the top of the barrel, "that there is NO ves-

sel LARGE enough to contain all the love we pour when
our heart IS on fire. For this love will fill a lake like
Lake Mead." (The children had been inside the great
Hoover Dam, and they had felt the mighty turbines
come on to feed Los Angeles with power, and they appreciated the awesome depth of Lake Mead.)

"For even Lake Mead is not large enough to contain the love of our sacred FAMILY, my children, for
this love is REFILLED every time we let it flow out.
Refilled from the endless source like the Colorado River
which is God's Divine Grace.

"And the more you give away, the more the lake
REMAINS full. In fact, like your lessons at Lake Mead,
the more Love you give away, even when all your power
turbines are at full heart power in LOVE, and the Love
is flowing through your dam at its greatest power, so
is the Lord God providing storms such as we have this
very night, to the Colorado River, with so much Divine
Grace that the FLOOD GATES must be OPENED to
let the LOVE FLOW through, because the LAKE becomes SOOOO FULL at such moments, the dam or
vessel could break ... as so much love is passing
through.

"For we can fill all the thimbles and all the
buckets and all the barrels in the world, and we will
still remain exactly as you see this barrel," and he patted the top of the water again, "FULL. For when you
give away the love of this family children, you must
know.....

"THAT GOD WILL RAIN ON YOU.....

"And this rain will fill your barrel and your lake,
for God's Love is the ocean, and like the ocean, children,
is always, in every way, FULL. And from the ocean
comes all the rain that flows into the rivers, that flows
into the lakes, that fills all the barrels, that fills all the

buckets, that fills the thimbles, and all the LOVE VES-
SELS remain always and precisely FULL.

"As you grow up you will choose friendships.

"You will choose to be married and you will, God
willing, have your own children, with their own pails
and your own family barrels.

"And as you choose your companions, your partners, your mates in this life, children, ask yourself.....

"Is this person
"a Thimble,
"a Pail,
"a Bucket,
"a Barrel,
"a Lake,
"or an Ocean...........?

"Ask yourself and be very careful that you
KNOW the answer before you match up your own family love, for when you begin to make your choice,

"You will learn the lesson of ownership.

"For you are owned in life only by the love you
give away ... and never by the love you seek to receive.....

"And when you learn this ... lesson....."

And he turned his bucket up and tapped it, and
when he did he filled the thimble ... right to the top ...
with what all thought was an empty bucket.....

"When you learn this ... lesson.....

"Your vessel will be FULL.....

"For you will GIVE your LOVE away to EVERY-
ONE and you will FILL every bucket and vessel you
can find, without FEAR, knowing that GOD will rain
on you, filling your bucket which will forever remain
FULL.....

"Full for YOU.....

"Full for LIFE.....

"Full for everyone IN your life.....

"And you will learn that the one truth you OWN in this life is the ownership you have for the LOVE you GIVE AWAY ... for the lesson IS, children.....

"..........you ARE God's RAIN.........

"Now run to the bed you OWN, and fill your dreams with LOVE ... as you sleep listening to the rain....."

.....and the children were told to take their pails with them.....

Chapter 6

The Tall Ship

THE LESSON OF THE TALL SHIP

It was many years after my first visit that I came to meet Lt. Bill Roberts of the San Francisco Police Department. Bill was Mrs. Dohrmann's oldest brother and something of a hero to the children in the family.

I first met him during one of my many week-long stays. As I walked toward the giant, green wrought iron gates, the breeze on my face gave a refreshment to my soul. The children were spread out to my left on a makeshift baseball diamond, with chatter rivaling that of the sea lions basking at Seal Rock across the bay in San Francisco.

I knew it was past the time that Mrs. Dohrmann's brother, Bill, was expected to arrive. The sun was blasting at high noon and I was ready to seek the beckoning shade of the large oak which was serving as the batter's box for the third baseman, Geoffrey.

It was with no small gratitude that I saw Mrs. Dohrmann and a servant approach, toting a sturdy table with folding legs and a large pitcher of fresh lemonade. We were all drinking Mrs. Dohrmann's famous lemonade, with terrific appreciation and playful banter, when a dust cloud appeared in the lower driveway. A full-blast siren announced the approaching police car, and up thundered (almost airborne with the power of a specially-adapted Dodge engine) a San Francisco police vehicle with all the markings, a single spinning light on top flaring its nostrils like an angry bull.

The children and I were entertained, but it was quickly apparent that Mother Dohrmann was more than put out at the reckless nature of her brother's grand entrance to the children's playground. The moments went by while Mrs. Dohrmann explained to her older brother, the new rules for entrance and egress.

"Ah, Sis, you worry too much!" I remember he said, as he unfolded himself from the car to reach for the lemonade Mrs. Dohrmann was extending his way. He had already grabbed his shiny hat, fixed neatly at its regulation angle of officialdom, either for shade or for the children's apparent joy, I couldn't determine which. I was now even more out of place in my loose-fitting robes, as I leaned against the giant shade oak to see what would come next into the theater of a day with the Dohrmanns.

"That's what sirens are *for*, Sis," Officer Bill exclaimed after a long slug of his lemonade, followed by another. By this time "Uncle Bill" was lovingly surrounded by children who were clambering up his legs and causing his drink to shift on unsteady ground.

"One, two, four, seven, NINE ... yep, they're all here ... not one under the car," as he looked just for good measure, to the children's delight. "Nope, all nine alive and well," as he picked Melissa and Geoffrey up, to thrill them with proximity to the badge shining on his uniform. Mrs. Dohrmann gave Forest and me the look that says, "It's hopeless ... as you can see ... it's hopeless with this man-child," and converted her dignity to lemonade sipping while she watched her brother shed his adulthood like an uncomfortable pair of new shoes.

I would learn later that Officer Bill always wore his street blues when he came to visit the children. He was basking in the reflected glory of the new television hit, *Streets of San Francisco*. The way Bill saw *Streets*, as the "boys" already were calling it, was that *Streets* would forever link his chosen vocation to stardom. A stardom he was now playing for all it was worth. For the next hour or so I found myself reliving my own childhood as "Uncle Bill," took the nine along walks of fantasy.

I think my abbot had held quite a different vision of my Dohrmann "training" than traveling with The Nine as we went for a ride in a fancy new San Francisco police car, quite against, I believe, local police regulations. I was never clear whether the vehicle was really supposed to be in Marin County at that day and hour, or indeed ever. I can only say that the San Francisco police car weaving its way, at great speed, around the winding passages of the streets of Fairfax, California, stopped many a local out for an afternoon stroll.

They took turns with the siren and lights for short bursts of fun. A few pets in their yards and a few drivers in their cars were suitably impressed.

We heard stories of Uncle Bill's most recent arrests, and we were invited to "see, feel and touch" his two scars from "heroic" (as Bill told the stories) bullet wounds, one still very much in the healing stage. The children had had lessons of respect for weapons and the law, which Uncle Bill had concluded by wrapping his own holster and weapon in a locked car trunk at the beginning of the excursion.

The protruding Irish chin and the humor to go with it, made Uncle Bill one of the most charming individuals I had met. He was a man's man who spent equal time with the girls, making time to include everyone. I found I was very sorry to see him depart in the late evening and hoped I would see him again soon.

I would, to my delight, see the children's Uncle Bill on more than three occasions over the next five years. And it was no small surprise on one of my subsequent visits to find a fog bank of sadness over the entire family as I unpacked upon arrival. I spent substantially more time writing and reading in The Apartments and the gardens than was my custom during my Dohrmann retreats. It was clear some space for the family was the order of the day. I knew them all well enough to understand when they wished for my company I would be fully included.

I had learned from Forest upon arrival that Uncle Bill, due to complications from a badly-healed gunshot wound, had prematurely passed away that night. Mrs. Dohrmann was inconsolable at the loss of her older brother and dear friend. Uncle Bill was so young, so strong, so vibrant in his use of life, that his absence left a huge vacuum for everyone who knew him.

I can remember falling to sleep more than once to the sound of weeping that swept through the valley of the Dohrmann estate and affected us all deeply. I can also remember counseling more than one of the nine, who, each in their own time, would come to visit with their questions about their uncle. Death was a new story.

Mrs. Dohrmann had left little notes in the fruit baskets of The Apartments to inform me how she had been relieved at my timing for this visit, alerting me to the comfort my presence had meant to her. She was most thankful for my walks with her, in complete silence, which she said had provided her more solace than all the words she had been receiving from a wealth of friendships. I am unashamed to admit that the memory of those days still causes my eyes to water.

Mr. Dohrmann had been away when it happened, having been delayed in Japan with his colleague, Dr. Edward Deming. I had been wondering what it would be like when Alan Gerrard Dohrmann returned home to his family this time. I remember vividly the golden afternoon that brought the sea wind and the Master home.

Everyone was tense with anticipation. Even the animals seemed to adopt peculiar behaviors. The cats played with the dogs in a more friendly way. The birds were unusually quiet and polite.
And then, he was there. The long trip from Japan was more demanding than it is in today's time. I noticed with some amazement, respectful of his schedule, how fresh, clean-shaven and ALIVE he looked. He had a clean new suit on, and seemed more appointed for Church than for retiring after a long, grueling trip. I found that he had had Forest deliver clean outfitting to him at the airport, where he had taken the time to freshen up prior to his return home.
He blazed up the steep drive to the "flats" in a large new Cadillac, which we knew Mrs. Dohrmann had adopted as her favorite car, the one she would have someday. It seemed today was THE DAY. He had a large bouquet of splendid white roses, to accompany his huge smile as, holding one child in either arm, each helping hold the flowers for mommy, he descended the stairs.
We had hoped all the tears would have passed by the time of his return, but upon seeing her husband, Mrs. Dohrmann almost fell into his arms. As servants took the children and flowers on the kitchen landing, Mr. Dohrmann held and with gentle pats, comforted his wife.
He delicately guided her, as if she were made of feathers, back up the steps, and with hand motions invisible to anyone not looking with utmost care, encouraged us to join him. In moments we were inside the new Cadillac, and motoring our way into the countryside of Marin County.
There was little talk during that drive. The children sensed the mood was sacred and somber. The normal banter and laughing of childhood was simply suspended. I remember the tenderness with which first this daughter and then her brother would reach over the seats, to stroke their mother's hair, or to pet her

arm softly, or to hold her hand. I can remember Mrs. Dohrmann's manner as she leaned her head on her husband's shoulder, and the comfort that seemed to pass upon her as the forest shadows swept across the interior of the vehicle.

I cannot remember her face looking more lovely than on the day of this drive. It has stuck in my mind as one of the clearest memories of all my times with the family.

Mr. Dohrmann had taken the slow winding road up Bay, and across the Meadow Club Stable and its sweeping fields of grass, framed by rolling hills that seemed never to end. Far above the rural community of Fairfax as it existed in the early 1960's, the twists and rolls of the roadway rose higher and higher. Up higher still came the ancient Redwoods, always home to Mr. Dohrmann's soul, and host for many of his famous stories. The old, twisted, concrete road, with its thumpity-thump expansion grooves held by tar in the old way, wound its way ever upward across the steep wonder of Alpine Dam, and the lake that sneaked into the mountain valleys like a thief. Modern and timeless became one here. The car would make double switchbacks until we emerged upon the upper ridge road, above the steepest grassy slopes, that tumbled downward to the mountain foot and Stinson Beach. Our gaze flew from the ridge tops to the sea. One minute an impassable canopy of forest towered hundreds of feet overhead, the next, wide open expanses of slopes and the Pacific Ocean, a sea that had no border, merging perfectly with the sky.

The air held a chill that was immediately apparent. With the windows down, the sea breeze filtered peace into the car. The Pacific Ocean was kissing the toes of the sun, which was lazily settling toward the waters on the horizon, creating a soft cloud bed for itself. The children seemed fixed on the huge orange ball that was floating without apparent movement above the thread line of the ocean's extreme edge.

It was magic.

All by itself it was there!

I think I wanted this ride to never end. With children on either side snuggled into the folds of my robes, I felt as at home and beloved as I believe a man had the right to feel and still be alive.

My prayers were for Uncle Bill and for Mrs. Dohrmann's grief as we wound our way ever downward toward the sea.

AT THE BEACH

Mr. Dohrmann parked in the sand, near a tree bent from a hundred years of determined resistance to the prevailing winds. Like an elf's mushroom shelter grown immense, the circle of boughs made a cover for the car as all four doors spread open and eager feet emerged.

Mr. and Mrs. Dohrmann led the way, holding hands like teenagers. Sometimes Mrs. Dohrmann would lean over on her husband, and squeeze an arm or hand. The tiny sand trail did not permit everyone to remain together. It was not long before we were in single file, making our way between giant dunes. The ocean could be heard but still lay beyond our view. Shrubs and scrub oak dotted the sandy valleys of our walk.

I was struck with surprise at the expanse and nearness of the ocean as we walked through a break in the dunes and found ourselves at the sea's edge. The sheer immensity and staggering beauty of the sea always presents me with a slight shock, no matter how often I visit it.

No one had spoken a word. To say the lack of noise was unusual was to minimize the sobriety of this journey. Nine wildly active, alert, curious and playful children made the journey in total silence.

The ribbon of our trail disappeared into the wide expanse of sand and open beach, which we crossed, fanning out to either side of Mr. and Mrs. Dohrmann. I could see the tender sparkle as Mr. Dohrmann looked into his wife's eyes, and her almost-smile that promised healings to come.

There is a spot where the sand grabs the ocean and the temperature, texture and color of sand is altered, shifting its reality until the sea leaves, allowing it to return to its dry self. It gradually becomes parched and easily moved by the slightest wind, awaiting the kiss of the living waters with the next tide. As we crossed this wet area, our feet made impressions and our tracks became more pronounced.

For a few moments we quietly stood gazing at the sunset, in a long straight line on either side of the mother and father of this special family, although it seemed then to have taken an hour or more. No signal or command was ever given when,as if rehearsed, we all stopped in perfect procession and stared at the sea, absorbing its healing powers. Not even one of the children ran up to the water breaking only feet away, as was their usual custom. No one spoke. Everyone had joined hands.

There was no one else on the beach and, as we could see for miles, it made the moment precious.

In silent prayer, united, everyone held the moment. The sun was only seconds from nibbling at the sea. Larger than imagination, the giant redness was now a perfect painting. The breeze made the fading heat a memory, and a promise for tomorrow.

Forest had placed a folding director's chair on the sand, near the damp verge, but a bit on the high ground behind us. It was customary that when the entire family traveled together, a staff car would follow, carrying all the items that could not fit into the family car when it was full of children. Mr. Dohrmann turned to us and walked us back to the folding director's chair, now the focal point.

Mrs. Dohrmann sat as though she sunk into place carrying a thousand weights. Pain was a visible presence on the beach, hanging in the twilight.

The children spread out, on either side of their mother's chair, with only a single hand gesture as instruction from Mr. Dohrmann, who even at this moment was working his pipe, with much frustration in the afternoon wind, as if some universal problem were deep in the meerschaum bowl.

The children, once seated, focused their attention on the sun. I must say, having traveled from Rio to Jerusalem, I am unsure if ever in the world a sunset was more perfect than the one seen on that day.

There was a gift within it.

After some moments, as if there had been much preamble and discussion on the topic, Mr. Dohrmann continued. I say continued, because there was really no beginning or ending in his story telling. Each lesson was on its own a partner with every lesson he ever told to us. He seemed to hold some magical abacus that contained the sum and totals of all the ingredients a spirit in this life would require, and at just the right time, with a formula he alone commanded, he would release one more bead.

If I wrote it any other way it would mislead the reader. Mr. Dohrmann looked up and simply continued as though we had been interrupted only for a second or so, and it was time to go on with the story. I know we felt at home with this notion, and accepted his assumption of continuance; years later I talked to the brothers and sisters at some length about this curious phenomenon which felt so natural in the presence of the master story teller.

I noticed as he began to speak, that the beach was entirely empty. There was not one third party to witness the moment. Oh, there were seagulls landing around the place where we sat, and a stray sand crab would rush off into the foam now and again, but all in all, the solitude wrapped around us like a pleasant blanket.

Looking up, his words louder than the sea and pounding surf, his wavy hair blowing and ashes falling away from his stormy pipe, he began:

"Children, this is my first day home now, and I want all of you to share with me the love I hold for the sea. In just a moment, children, the sun....." and here Mr. Dohrmann turned his back to us, with a grand gesture as if he had purchased the setting sun for his personal theater, "this SUN, this incredible perfect red ball, is about to kiss the sea. And when her lips touch the magic sea, the day is kissed good-bye. This kiss of good-bye sends many subtle changes flowing everywhere upon the earth."

Mr. Dohrmann turned to tamp his pipe and ponder his next words with brow furrowed, but we already held the sense a great story was unfolding.

"Subtle changes, children.

"The mountains that tower behind us, will now become less tall. In only moments, the outlines of these mighty peaks will soften in God's twilight. The trees upon the slopes will lose their definition and contrast. As long as the sun remains hanging, the trees hold dominion, each with sharp spires and individual authority. Soon, however, after even a single kiss to the sea, each tree will begin to blend with his neighbor. Each will become first a small group and then a vast single shape of gray. The very colors of the day will begin to fade. The greens and the goldens of our state and all the rainbows in our flowers and even the contrast between mountain summit and sky, between cloud and ocean, will disappear into the new night.

"The day can be very hot and harsh, children. Things happen in the day. Most of your life is spent in the day. Think about it. At night we eat. We talk a little. Then we sleep. The vast amount of time we spend awake with one another is invested in the day. Most of the decisions we will ever make will take place during the day, children, not during the time we spend asleep in life.

"Eventually the day will become so soft and so faded we will sleep. Can you imagine how it would be if we never slept, children? Can you imagine if we could never stop, and reflect, and remember and look back on even one day, because the day itself never, ever ended? Isn't it perfect....." as he waved to the red orb hang-gliding in the sky, "how God has engineered it so that the Sun would kiss each day good-bye, just for us, children? Always just for us."

He held some tears in his eyes as he talked on, compelling us all to follow suit.

"It is this kiss that lets us know that this day is coming to an end. Each day when you see a sunset, children I want you to stop, and pause a moment. I want to you to embrace how IMPORTANT one day of time, each day of time is in the flow of your human life. Your day. This one day. Every day.

"There never comes another like it, you know."

"This day is the only day, THE ONLY DAY, on this exact date at this precious time, that you will ever have to share your hopes and dreams. For in an instant it winks out and is gone!

"And some day in the future, some day in the year 2005 on May 2nd, in the sunset, when I am no longer here to teach you such things, I want you to re-alize that never again will Terry, or Pam, or Bernhard ever know, or see again, a May 2nd in 2005, such a sun-set again. For the ONLY individual day you were given with that particular number, is the day that will then be passing. So pause in your life and remember to watch God's special marker for creation, that which God calls "a day" as each sunset kisses the day good-bye.

"Mark each day. Pause and remember the worth and value. Replay each memory. Hold them as fragile truths in your life and then forever let them go.

"Twilight time is a time of wonder, children. I want you to witness the WONDER of Twilight. I want you to embrace, if only for a moment, the importance of marking each and every day with a spot of WON-DER.

"Wonder for God who made your day.

"Wonder for all the choices and decisions you made this day.

"Wonder for the other spiritual beings who came into your life on this wonderful day.

"And in some way, become like the SUN as you find your own way, your own WONDERFUL way to kiss each day good bye.

"It takes so little time.

"It means so much if you learn to hold a spot of wonder for God's special day...

"......But, children ... this is not the lesson......

TALL SHIPS

"For today's lesson is one of tall ships.

"Now, children, can you see how the sun is resting? The sun is tired after a full day of labor. God has granted permission for the sun, His brilliant motor of fire and life, to rest. To lie down and sleep. For the sun, my children, lies in a very special bed made up of the horizon," and here Mr. Dohrmann made a grand sweeping gesture as if he could contain the entire vista of the horizon before us, with the cauldron just tipping a path of gold into the water, leading to the spot before us on the shore.

"God made the sun so that it is tucked in each and every night, like your mother and I tuck you into your safe warm beds, only God personally tucks in the sun, each and every night like the good parent, using the covers of the eternal sea. See! The sun *is* sinking...it's diving into the sea on the far horizon ... isn't it? It seems about to be tucked in for one more night of well-deserved rest."

We felt like we wanted the sun to be rewarded for the warmth and life shared with the planet Earth and with all of us. Mr. Dohrmann had a way of making you FEEL something while he told his stories. These feelings grew deep and rose high, originating from something entirely nonverbal that is, in these later years, simply impossible to bring forth for the soul of the reader. The FEELING was like an electric whip that ran through all of us in each and every lesson and the FEELING was building to critical mass as we monitored the progress of the sun, folding into sleep as twilight spilled over into the night.

I remember with a smile ... eighteen little eyes, all shaded with lifted hands, scanning the blazing glory of this huge red sphere as it began to impair its own shape, as moment-by-moment the orb sank lower, until only half of "the magic" was visible above the far distant waves.....

I remember how Mr. Dohrmann shaded his eyes with his hand upside down on that day. He stood on his tiptoes as he looked far off onto the sea. As he turned back to us with some excitement he exclaimed, catching us up in the FEELING, even more than was his custom. His shaded eyes kept roving the horizon as if for some magic vision he alone could see. All began to look with more diligence.

"......THERE! Do you see it?" Pointing. "No, there!" slightly adjusting his pointing finger, "NO! Over there just a bit more. Do you see it children?"

Some had risen to stare as everyone sat higher in the sand, still looking. Nine, all facing the sea, trying to discover the mystery. There was plenty of light. The horizon had become a burnt offering to the day, with spires of color sweeping into the towering clouds dotting the blue remains of this early twilight.

"THERE! Do you SEE it?" Mr. Dohrmann was animated. He would skip up toward the water, and then virtually run back to us, pointing.

"The tall mast of a ship? A really big ship. Did you see the tall mast?"

He seemed to ask each of us individually. We shook our heads "no" together, as we strained to see the tall-masted ship that he was obviously spotting directly in front of where we sat in the sand, at the edge of a rapidly-drying, high-tide line accented with seaweed and little shells.

"There it is again!" he cried, "just coming up here!" (pointing) "and there!" (turning and pointing).

"Dipping around the horizon, children.

"Do you SEE IT?

"For you MUST SEE, my children, that just a moment ago,

"Just an instant ago,

"Just the snap of two fingers ago, to the old sailor's eye, that TALL SHIP was resting right here," and he swept the ocean in front of our position.

"Right here ... directly in front of my family.

"Right HERE where all of US could see this tall ship, with its many sails and personalities, catching the full breath of the winds of the day.

"And how you longed to visit that tall ship, my children." He came up close now, and sat with his legs crossed Indian-style in the sand, and revisited lighting his pipe as he shook his head with affection for his private memories.

"Oh, I CAN remember, children," he said, looking more at Mrs. Dohrmann than the children, "just the way you would tease your mother and I. Using almost any excuse over the years to get permission to visit that great tall, tall ship.

"For this tall ship, my babies, has a name.

"And the name of this ship, has always been how you said it ... when you said the words 'Uncle Bill'!"

"The tall, tall ship that I have seen this night, the ship I have just shown you IS, to God, the ship known as your Uncle Bill ... for the ship and Uncle Bill are one, my children.

"And oh, how the ship of Uncle Bill would love to carry you over all the waves of life. To make you safe. To keep you dry. To carry you through any storm. To provide shelter and a nest for you to wage war against all the storms that life could bring. Safe and secure in the arms of the great tall ship, UNCLE BILL.

"This is a very tall ship, this ship that God made. For like the big man, our ship is filled with impossible surprises.

"Did you know that each of you had your own special places on board the ship? Oh yes. You each have had your own nooks and crannies in the mind and heart of your Uncle Bill. Didn't you?" (and the heads nodded).

"Private places?"

Heads nodded.

"Secret places?"

Heads nodded.

"Places only you and the ship himself ever knew as you both shared such wonderful treasures on board?"

Heads nodded.

"You would always feel safe on board Uncle Bill, wouldn't you?"

Heads nodded.

"You would almost always giggle and laugh to run and play when you were on board "your Uncle Bill" wouldn't you?"

Heads nodded.

"You would find those quiet places in the riggings or down below the decks. Those secret hiding places and those fun, adventure-filled journeys in this place or that. Down this corridor or up another passageway. Always safe in the LOVE of your UNCLE BILL.

"For all these winding passageways on board led to some other new place of discovery inside the imagination of your tall ship UNCLE BILL.

"Eventually you would giggle and play held up high in the upper wind, caught up in the RIGGING of your Uncle Bill. Caught in the full sails and lines that supported how this tall ship would catch the breath of God and float FREE on the sea of forever.

"Taking you along for the ride of all the possibilities that your Uncle Bill could give to you."

Mrs. Dohrmann was crying softly now ... her tears making tiny indentations in the fresh warm sand.

"Safe! On board your Uncle Bill.

"Laughing! On board your Uncle Bill.

"Playing! With your loving, magical, wonderful Uncle Bill.

"Held high and firm in the bold, strong RIGGING of your Uncle Bill!

"For this rigging, this place you spent so much time represents the ARMS of your Uncle Bill, as well as ALL the love that Uncle Bill could provide to you children. From the space below decks to the cross bars of the highest rigging, contained all the full measure of LOVE this man could muster.

"Love that ran from his base foundations and keel boards to the very top of his main mast, your UNCLE BILL loved his children. You were his babies. You were why he sailed here in the first place.

"For children, your Uncle Bill sailed here in this life, just to be with you."

Some of the children watching Mrs. Dohrmann took her hand, or leaned over on her, and most of the children had tears themselves as their father shared his feelings.

"And as you search for him......," here Mr. Dohrmann turned around and looked at the horizon again. I noticed no rim of the orb remained above the sea, just the fading shadow fire. Mr. Dohrmann's face was brilliant in this reflection, as if painted in red by some hidden lens. "You look everywhere." He turned his head this way and that. "Don't you?"

Heads nodded.

"Looking.

"Hoping.

"Wishing.

"To BE with.

"To see again.

"To climb into the arms of that great giant strong rigging again, as you are held once more by all the LOVE that IS your Uncle Bill!"

Tiny tears, nodding.

"For your hearts have become so very heavy ... while I have been gone.

"Your hearts are like the lead weights seamen use ... so heavy is your heart tonight isn't it?"

Heads nodded.

"And some of you have become so sad, you don't know if you can ever be happy again, isn't it true?"

Heads nodded ... and Mrs. Dohrmann nodded more than once.

"SO sad.

"Your mother here is like a child herself today."

The great master had turned to hold his gaze on his one most priceless treasure and smiled upon her comfortingly.

"For your mother is looking for this ship, just like you are searching for this great tall mast.

"For your mother's gaze is even more compelling than that of your young eyes.

"For children, always know your MOTHER has had more TIME with this tall ship, we call UNCLE BILL.

"Time when she was little as some of you.

"Time when she was older, just like some of you today....times together in school....

"Time as adults, like your mom and dad, just as we are today.

"TIME. So much time.

"So many memories.

"So many trips into the RIGGING that IS your Uncle Bill.

"Your mother has tied her childhood and her adulthood and her many journeys to and from so many ports with this great tall ship into a place she knows as HER LIFE.

"She has sailed through too many storms with Uncle Bill to stop looking now.

"She has been through so many adventures with Uncle Bill she must find him.

"And through all this TIME and LIVING your mother has known the tight, tight LOVE rigging of the tall ship we call UNCLE BILL.

"And now, she feels maybe she will fall.

"Maybe the rigging is not so safe.

"For she can no longer, even when she strains her vision, SEE her tall ship floating upon the sea of all possibilities ... this sea of forever," and he gestured to include all of the sea from side to side.

"For you see, your mother feels because she can no longer SEE the tall mast of the ship we call UNCLE BILL, she might be stranded here upon the ocean, and actually be all ALONE when the next storm arises."

Some of the children had been crying and some hugged and held on to Mrs. Dohrmann for she was crying very hard now ... and Mr. Dohrmann paused again and was silent, smoking his pipe ... and then at just the right moment he continued.....

"Let's wait awhile to see if we can help your mother, perhaps we CAN see a bit of that great tall mast.....," and he shaded his eyes and turned to look again upon the fading blaze on the horizon.

We sat quite a long while snuggling one another, each holding our gaze far upon the sea.

Finally he said, " No.

"No. Children.

"I think it is beyond us to see it now. And soon it will be dark." He tamped his pipe upon his shoe and the ash flew like the Yosemite Fire Fall to the wet sand at the edge of the sea.

"The sun has finished with our day...," he was studying the fading light, "it will become very dark soon.

"The ocean will turn to black ink, an INK that reaches far beyond these waves to nowhere.

"Soon even your shadow will disappear into an ancient blackness. We must then rise and we must go home. For all creation will be blended into oneness and the time to rest will be upon us.

"We will use the light of the car to find our way home.

"The day that held the tall ship Uncle Bill will be gone.

"Vanished forever.

"Complete.

".....But tomorrow my family will learn another lesson....."

Here a very strange thing happened. I had never seen anything like it before in the many years of Mr. Dohrmann's lesson telling, nor anything to match it since.

Mr. Dohrmann gently raised his hand to the horizon, and as if a signal had been given, a great star appeared. The star seemed brighter than any in the moonless sky that night. The way the star rose, as if on command from Mr. Dohrmann's softly gestured hand signal, it appeared, to some, to be the running light, twinkling like a lantern, from a very tall ship ... floating just off the horizon.

Mr. Dohrmann quietly rose.

He again struck his pipe on his shoe several times, until the red burning ashes had fallen completely to the sand.

He next took his wife's hand ... as all continued to look at the sea. It had become very dark.

It was more than a little challenging to find the ribbon path, through the great dunes that led to the car. I don't recall much of the ride to the house that night.

We literally returned home late enough to find our way to bed, following snacks the servants had prepared for us in neat little baskets, to draw from as we drove.

I was therefore more than surprised to find that it was still dark when the servants came to wake me.

I was asked to dress without even bathing. When I arrived at the car, the children were all waiting as if we just returned home. Everyone was in need of more rest. Everyone looked somewhat rumpled.

Mr. Dohrmann did not speak to us on the drive back to the beach. He played classical music softly on the car radio.

Some of the children slept.

As we returned to the spot of our vigil the night before, the indentations of our bodies were still apparent. Nothing had been disturbed in the hours of our departure. We nestled into the same positions.....

It was growing lighter ... as Mr. Dohrmann simply looked out to the horizon.

He sat in the same exact spot.

The servants brought fresh, cold orange juice.

We watched without talking, and with blankets wrapped around us to keep out the morning chill. I remember thinking what a special woman Mrs. Dohrmann was for the trust she placed in her husband's intuitions at these times.

She always acted as if the process we were living through was as normal as brushing teeth, or reading stories, or making a barbecue. Just a normal conclave on its way to bring a family of nine forward into the future. Normal as any habit of busing the children to school, or making lunch or any custom of parenting. And yet we sat, alone as for a thousand years this morning, on an ancient beach watching a newborn sun rise over the mountain.

Of all the thoughts that went on this morning, the thing I remember most was the silence. The total silence in this family while we waited.

I remember there was a golden hue that came across Mr. Dohrmann's face first, for he alone sat further out from the mountain's shadow, as the first sliver of the new sun rose over the majestic Marin County hills behind him. It was then that he began to speak, as though he had never stopped ... from the evening before.....

He jumped to his knees as if a signal switch had been thrown. He turned and again with his hand, upside down, shading his eyes, he searched.

"SEE IT?" (He exclaimed).

"I can see it!

"Do you see it?

"The tall ship, mast first! Only that!

"Confirmation!

"Did you see it over there?" Pointing.

Some stood up on tiptoes to look.

"Do you see it?

"Can't you see it?!

"There!" Pointing dramatically.

"And again ... there!" Pointing, finger shaking for emphasis.

"Plain as the nose on your face! THERE IT IS!!!!!

"I see the rigging! Now more. There! The rigging!"

.....for this rare man had hired a tall ship to sail just outside the horizon for this morning ... only later would I know ... nine children rushed the shore. Mrs. Dohrmann hurried a bit herself. For the FEELING of actually SEEING the RIGGING break the horizon and a REAL SHIP show up just out of VIEW ... to only now and again see the REAL SAILS ... full of power and wind ... FULL of LIFE ... to see the MAST ... to actually SEE IT!

Whispers.....

"I see it!

"I see it!

"I see it too!

"Look. Over there.

"There it is again!

And always Mr. Dohrmann with:

"Do you see it?" Pointing.

As it fell back beyond our point of view, Mr. Dohrmann sat again and simply shook his head looking down at the sand; as he looked up he said,

".....But, children ... that IS NOT ... the lesson....."

THE LESSON OF THE SUN

We sat looking to see whether those masts would appear again.

Turning ... he gestured and said,

"Children ... look behind you!" It was such an emphatic command, all stared. Mrs. Dohrmann and I had sat arm-in-arm and we both turned together.

"Look behind you!

"Do you see the sun is waking from sleep? To rise and play in God's playground of the SKY? See how the sun leaps to play in this first new day created just for YOU?

"This rare and precious new day. Like no other before or ever after.

"THIS NOW DAY.

"THIS NOW MORNING.

"OUR NOW MORNING.

"Do you see how sharp the hills and the trees have become again as each new finger of light tickles them to see this day as well?

"Do you see how you can now, with fresh vision, gaze out upon the sea of all God's possibilities? Gaze far upon this ocean of forever?

"Look now and SEE!

"Now stand with me, children."

And soon all of us were holding hands equally spaced on either side of this man, with the wide brimmed Panama hat moving gently in the morning breeze from the Pacific ... facing the mountains and our future.....

"See the sun rise. UP. UP! LOOK!

"Again in silence we shared a FEELING as the miracle of the dawn washed fully over us, vibrant and alive.

"Let TODAY'S sun fill you with how different it FEELS when the new dawn sun KISSES each new day HELLO.

"Witness as the sun rises and lets go of the mountain to tease the valleys with her charms.

"Witness the power of the LORD who lifts the SUN as a miracle higher into the sky.

"Witness the majesty, children, of the ONE POWER who raises up the SUN.

"And consider.....

"As the sun rises and the distance between the mountain grows and grows and grows ... how high ... how terrifically high is the throne we call the SUN.....

"How many miles.....?

"How many units of measurement.....?

"HOW HIGH is the PLACE where now the sun RESIDES ... think about it, children ... HOW HIGH IS THE SUN?

".....But children, even that is not the LES-SON.......

"Not for you," and here he turned us toward the sea.

"No, not for you who have played on God's special tall ship,

".....The tall ship we call UNCLE BILL.

"No, not for you who have been held and loved BY this tall ship UNCLE BILL.

"No, not for you who will know and receive love from tall ships you will choose during the sails of your life or other tall ships who WILL CHOOSE you......

"No, for you, the lesson is greater than all these words of truth up to this moment.....

"For the lesson is this, children.....

"I ask that you close your eyes," watching them ... "Close your eyes.....

"And feeling the warmth of this great sun on you ... with your eyes closed.....

"I want you to imagine that there is One who is so great, so powerful that for this ONE LORD, the sun floats low in the sky rather than high in our mind's eye.....

"For this ONE LORD turns the sun on and turns the sun off like we turn on and turn off a switch in our kitchen or bathroom or bedroom....

"For this ONE LORD simply commands, and the SUN switches on this day, my children.....

".....And you know that for this One, this GOD, there is no TIME in which the sun is hidden ... no night ... for the LORD GOD is illuminated with perfect vision.....

"Now open your eyes, children, and look again upon the sea..........

"The sea that this same God has created to catch and hold the reflections of his SUN....

"Do you see how the sun rises and the rays catch along the water as far as your vision can take you?

"Miracles ... little mirrors that return the light in showers of spectacular colors from wave top to wave top ... do you see it?"

Heads nodded ... some of us were still holding our orange juice.

"You believe these truths I tell you, and yet somehow you fail to believe the greatest of ALL these truths.

FOR THE LESSON IS THIS.....

"The tall ship, my children, that you search for, has never gone. Your Uncle Bill is not ... GONE!

"Your Uncle Bill, just as we have seen this morning," mighty gesture toward the sea, "floats just over that Horizon. Just beyond your field of VIEW. Just beyond the point at which YOUR tiny vision can hold the top of the mast for your great ship, UNCLE BILL.

"Uncle Bill has not changed or been taken away from you.

"Uncle Bill has simply moved forward ... while you, my family, stayed here on the beach.

"I saw Uncle Bill last night just as clear and true as you saw your tall ship Uncle Bill this morning!

"Uncle Bill floats just as high and with all the power and strength you ever knew.

"Unchanged. Unchanged at all.

"Uncle Bill, children, is waiting.

"Uncle Bill is waiting ... for YOU. Waiting for this family.

"Uncle Bill has you still wrapped up like tiny little Christmas presents, in the unchangeable rigging of his giant love for you.

"You, Bernhard, are held just above the mizzenmast sail. And you, Mark, are held behind the main sail. You, Geof, are being held by the main mast and you, my pretty wife, are being held higher than the crow's nest ... caught up and entwined in the LOVE RIGGING that is this tall ship's HIGHEST POINT this .... Uncle Bill.

"Held tight against all the storms, you rest, the mother of this family, entwined in the strong forever shrouds and lines at this HIGHEST OF ALL POINTS, you remain ONE with a tall ship ... known as UNCLE BILL."

Mrs. Dohrmann was standing looking at the sun, and she wasn't crying.

"And I say to you," and he roared the words, "how dare you, that's right, HOW DARE you sit here

STUCK upon this beautiful beach and fail to believe my words?

"How dare you consider that one single word of what I am telling you this fine lovely morning is anything but the truth?

"For there," and here Mr. Dohrmann pointed up to the sun which was quite elevated now, "HERE," as he pointed upward to the light, "rests a pair of eyes that carry a vision that is higher than any vision we hold down here upon this beach.

"There ... rests a vision that can see beyond the remote horizon, and all horizons off this shore. Horizons that your frozen and stuck eyes can never see beyond.

"There, way up there, children, stands a vision that can SEE ... see clearly ... SEE NOW ... IS SEEING THIS MOMENT all of what is the real UNCLE BILL.

"All of your Uncle BILL.

"Just as you have always seen him.

"Nothing changed.

"Not one thing.

"Not one part of the decking.

"Not one part of the cabin.

"Not one part of the sails.

"Not one part of the love rigging.

"Not one part of ANYTHING.

"Nothing changed at all.

"Uncle BILL *IS* alive and complete and whole.

"WAY UP THERE," pointing high.

"As Uncle Bill was yesterday, was the day before, or will be a million years from now.

"It is only YOUR VISION.....

"Your limited, frozen vision, my children, that has been changed.

"It is only YOUR VISION, my children, that has compelled you to remain here, with your sightless eyes, so low to the ground, frozen here, on this special beach.

"IT is only YOUR VISION that is limited now, so limited to its line of sight, my babies ... that separates your seeing and feeling your Uncle Bill." He ruffled Bernhard's blonde hair more than once.

"IT IS ONLY YOUR VISION that can't see the tall mast.

"Only your vision that fails to see the truth.....

"Just your limited view, nothing more.....

"For your Uncle Bill floats with all his majesty, with all his heart... his love... his spirit... his soul, just beyond this horizon of your sight, my children....." He waved toward the sea.

"Just over there....." and waved again, pointing this time.

"No, just there ... for Uncle Bill is MOVING.....

"Right over THERE!" and he pinpointed the spot. At that moment I swear we saw a billowing sail and a wisp of a mast spike roll beyond a wave of the great ocean once again.

"And one day, all too soon children, you will move FORWARD, as Uncle Bill has done, within your cruise of life, and when you do, once again you will sail right by the side of YOUR UNCLE BILL.

"For your Uncle Bill is not alone.

"He sails with a FLEET of TALL SHIPS that sail beside him ... each a beacon for those who will soon move FORWARD to FOLLOW in the journey of life.....

"For now ... this early morning ... just remember, when you THINK of your Uncle Bill.....

"To always in ALL WAYS, adjust your FIELD OF VISION ... and as you do ... you will SEE with the eyes of a higher point of view.

"From this vision point you will actually SEE the tall ship we call Uncle Bill, even as we saw the tall strong mast this early dawn. So it will be every time you remember.

"And as you remember, KNOW that you, my babies, are forever entwined in the rigging of all the LOVE that IS what your Uncle Bill uses to sail with.....

".....And that, my family, IS the lesson ... Now, let's go eat!"

..... And for the first time in a long while.....

.....The family was hungry once again.....

Chapter 7

The Balloons

A BALLOON FOR ALL SEASONS

I often preferred to return to Marin County in the long, hot summers. The time away from my mountain Abbey was welcome, as the chores and routine confined the mind. The fresh smells opened the heart. Forest would pick me up at the San Francisco Airport, the airport everyone remembers from the television series *Streets of San Francisco*. Burned forever in my mind, I remember the San Francisco of those days as if it were only yesterday afternoon.

By the time we reached the Golden Gate Bridge, the Pacific was washing away the memories of cloistered living in the Benedictine way. The gentle hills of Marin rushed up to greet us. There was less traffic then with the new freeways. The off-ramp at Greenbrae led you to Sir Francis Drake, then narrowed. This reminder of the rail days deposited you through the old town of San Anselmo, exactly where the raised rail bed used to be. I missed the old trestle sounds of the train which had originally brought me as Forest ushered the Cadillac easily along Center road toward Fairfax.

As we turned off Sir Francis Drake on Old Olema Road, I knew that we were in the land of bay trees, oaks and tall pines. In only moments I would be returning home to The Apartments.

There was no "story" on my first night back in the Apartments. Mr. Dohrmann had just returned from working, yet again, with Dr. Edward Demming in Japan. As was his custom, he preferred to follow his body clock and rest, letting nature provide relaxation and readjustment to California time. Saturday was a calm day of sitting out in the gardens. The sounds of children laughing, teasing and calling to one another in countless games gave charming background to the passing of the hours.

Mr. Dohrmann created a feast for the evening meal, with his famous barbecue in the giant outdoor Lath House. Facing the boulders and wilderness beyond, the Lath House was the last outpost in the Dohrmann gardens. Surrounded by giant shade trees that towered over all sides, the Lath House was always an oasis of cool breezes, hidden from hot midday sun.

By late afternoon, Mr. Dohrmann had the coals glowing. The smells of barbecue began to waft through the yards and called every neighbor to join the opportunities for discussion as the juicy steaks and ribs sizzled on the grill. I remember these lingering feasts as times of debate and conversation unlike any I have ever known.

Attorneys and philosophers, physicians and architects, artists and mathematicians, all the folks in the neighborhood would drop by for long periods of fraternity when the barbeque was in operation. Mr. Dohrmann was known for his wit and humor, which increased with the length of time the bar was "open."

The Lath House could easily hold fifty guests, with outdoor picnic tables in the gardens and lawns for children to overflow. The bright checkered table covers on the Lath House refectory tables gave the visits a more familial, intimate feeling. Little outdoor easy chairs made of redwood with Mrs. Dohrmann's floral cushions lined the walls of the Lath House, providing comfortable seating for this enormous outdoor conference center. The slat walls, or laths, allowed for filtered viewing of the terraced gardens, lawns and walkways, and the breezes passed through easily, refreshing those within.

The broken light from the long straight slats made shadows as the twilight advanced, illuminating the guests. The scent of flowers surrounded Lath House like a giant flower lei from the Dohrmann's home in Hawaii.

As the Saturday evening turned to glowing banners in the sky and the children, one by one, kissed their father good night, I was missing the story I had felt "for sure" was coming from the good feelings of this special evening. Mr. Dohrmann retired without saying good night to his guests. After some while, one of the servants returned from the main house to indicate that "jet lag" had overtaken Mr. Dohrmann, and the guests should continue to enjoy the hospitality without interruption. I became resigned to the fact that a second night would pass without satisfying my hunger for one of Mr. Dohrmann's private "family" lessons.

THE RIDE

Early the next morning I was delighted to discover that the entire family was being divided between the old Woody Wagon and the servant chase car. The old Woody, which was Mr. Dohrmann's favorite picnic "cruiser" as he liked to refer to it, was still a frequent weekend road warrior, polished to the new car luster in which all family vehicles were maintained. After attending Mass at the new St. Rita's Church where Father Gleason, an old friend of Mr. Dohrmann's, celebrated mass and gave the sermon, we drove up the long way toward Stinson Beach, along the back side of Mount Tamalpais, Marin County's three-thousand foot spire of legend, myth and lore.

I remember how cramped the windy ride was. For some reason, large balloons were crammed into the back space. This space normally held some children and the picnic lunch. Today was more than odd, although we didn't speak about it, since Mr. Dohrmann's "story props" were always explained eventually. Six of the children were in the chase car behind the Woody Wagon, while the others crammed themselves in the best they could, with most of the wagon space reserved for the enormous balloons.

The children were in limited view amidst the balloons, and the chase car remained at all times in plain view behind us. Only the youngest children were in the car with Mr. and Mrs. Dohrmann and myself: Melissa, Geoffrey, and Carl. The rest of the children were in the Cadillac which followed us, bend for bend along the road. The division seemed to follow a plan for which I had yet to discover the meaning. As with all Mr. Dohrmann's lessons, the anticipation charged the experience with colors enriching every detail.

The lazy day ride continued, up, and higher up the twisty way of the mountain road. As always, the scent of sun-warmed sage along the way mixed with the pungent aroma of eucalyptus and the haunting fragrance of redwoods, to give a feeling of having taken some wonderfully refreshing and energizing medicine that was administered by inhalation.

THE BALLOON CHILDREN - OVERLOOK POINT

It was an absolutely gorgeous day for the San Francisco Bay area. I can remember Mr. Dohrmann announcing his plans for all of his nine children plus the servants, plans committing us to be sitting on top of one another other along the way, as we proceeded to a place called Bolinas Beach. Being fifth generation San Franciscans, this beach was a familiar place to even the youngest of the children, and all held an anticipation to get to the quaint seaside fishing village of Bolinas.

Unpolluted seaside ride,
The only sounds - a sea gull cry ...
Or ocean breeze ...
And the ever-crashing surf appearing far below the slopes we now drove upon...

My mind strolled to the sweetness of Alpine Lake and the Meadow Club stables we had recently passed. The redwoods along the upward slopes were like blankets to the morning's fading dew, holding the damp scents within their shadows, as the rest of the land quickly grew dry with sun and wind. The ancient trees were like a prelude to the symphony of the open meadows at the crest of Mount Tamalpais, with their majestic views of the rolling Pacific. The contrast as we burst from redwood canopies into open air theaters, returned my thoughts to the here and now, perched like eagles above the sea.

In less time than my mediations allowed for, I was brought back from the classical music on the car radio by Mr. Dohrmann's announcement that we were overlooking Stinson Beach State Park, just beyond which was the village of Bolinas. I was impressed by how the green cliffs plunged dramatically, like diving gulls rushing toward the sea. To the right, long, clear beaches swept up to the short drop from the cliffs. The sand stopped directly in front of our meadows, as the sea attacked with a vengeance the rocky crags which rose to our level. Splashes arched above the overhanging banks, and patted the grass with salt water kisses.

A dust cloud plumed as Mr. Dohrmann brought the car to a halt, so sharply as to skid the tires on the gravel, ending with a perfect landing inches from the line of grass. Mr. Dohrmann had already bolted from the car with the door left open, to stand regally as was his way, shaded by his wide brimmed hat and gazing far out to sea.

His commanding presence was such that everyone would feel compelled to take note when he was so engaged; surely some matter of great importance must be mere inches outside our limited view, and with his guidance, we were sure to find it. We too would soon be hungry in the search for opportunities only temporarily misplaced.

Shortly, the Cadillac had joined the party as a line of nine reunited children stretched to either side of their parents, all looking toward the far horizon of the Pacific Ocean.

SO CAN YOU SEE.........................

Mr. Dohrmann left the scene amid whispers of,
"What did he see......?"
"I don't know, what do you see....?"
"I don't know, look again...."
"I don't see anything, do you....?
"No, did you.....?" and so forth.
Mr. Dohrmann took a little paper bag from under his front car seat and proceeded to place the
lunchbag-sized sack upon the waxed hood of the old
Woody Wagon. At this point, Mr. Dohrmann (with exaggerated care) unrolled the folds of the brown lunch
bag, as he removed a beaker of pale greenish-looking
water and placed it also on the shiny hood. The science
beaker had measuring marks upon its side, and looked
like a laboratory container of some sort.

I remember how Mr. Dohrmann looked at the
beaker, crouching down and staring close and making
the beaker appear to us as if all the magical secrets of
the entire universe were held inside this one glass vial.
The children had assembled themselves in a semicircle
in the grass right around their father, and had sat
down. I found myself sitting in my usual position beside Terry. It was always amazing to me that the "knowing" from all nine children of what to do was carried
on in silence, with a ritualistic behavior rare among
those so young.

A sense of awe and wonder descended at such moments. It is a great frustration to me as a writer that my skill is inadequate to convey the feeling to those who read these words without having experienced it.... the feeling of impending Mystery and joyful knowledge which would give the reader a clearer understanding of the man and his effect upon me and upon any who ever met him. I was then, and shall forever remain absolutely convinced that he was divinely guided in his "stories," parables for the times that illustrated so clearly and easily the moral and ethical precepts he wished to impart to his children.

The next "story" had begun.

Finally, Mr. Dohrmann held the beaker flat on the palm of a fully-extended hand, gazing at it with reverence. All the while facing the children, he continued to look into this beaker as if all knowledge sought by him lay contained within it. He spun around, intently absorbed with some mysterious information inside his strange beaker. The sun was fully reflecting off the large open glass as Mr. Dohrmann began to speak his thoughts out loud.

"Children," he began, with his back to the sea,

"Do you know what is IN this beaker I am holding this morning?"

....Some shrugs and a few "No, Dads"......

"No? Well let me tell you, then! What is INSIDE this beaker is all of the power and all the WILL and all the CREATIVITY of our Lord God!" (And here he stared most solemnly.)

I stared myself, waiting for the wisdom to come.

"For IN this beaker my children, is enough power to create all the electricity and heat and energy that the entire planet earth requires. That all mankind require. Forever and ever.

"The resources required to replicate all life on the planet are frozen INSIDE this beaker children.

"The secret DNA codes that can create and evolve all life are fixed within the Magic Beaker I have brought to share with YOU this morning!

"The seeds of the planet earth are held inside this beaker." (Still the liquid inside the beaker rotated, glistening in the bright morning sunlight, held as high as it would go above Mr. Dohrmann's head, on the flat open palm of his large, raised hand.)

"The source of operating a Breeder Reactor that promises to create more fuel each hour than it uses, hides inside this single small beaker of eternity, that I am holding this morning at Overlook Point on Mount Tamalpais."

(Mrs. Dohrmann, in a happy summer dress, had come to sit beside me in the tall summer grass that had become my chair.)

"All the ingredients, children. The total formula for life. The recipe for creation itself. All the power to turn on the sun, and all the SUNS in the universe are contained in the blueprint I hold in my hand, if we only knew what the Lord God knows in this instant.

"For it is only the KNOWING that makes these ingredients one form, or another form. Only the knowing.

"But what is this magic green fluid I hold within this beaker of life?

"Why is the code of life so complete in the secret blend of what is inside the beaker?

"What blueprint does the Lord God require to replace the earth itself, children?

"The plans held inside this beaker are the blueprints of all that is required, children, to sustain life forever on this planet or to rebirth the earth over and over again.

"And all that men must do is be close enough with their God, and mankind can discover the secret code, the secret information, of how this blueprint works. For when mankind is one with creation, the

Lord God will surely reveal all the hidden secrets once again.

"For only that BEING with the Lord God, as ONE, is missing.

"We have yet to learn the language of life because of our separation from our Lord. The secret hidden language that God uses to communicate every signal in the universe is waiting for our discovery.

"For all things are connected to the word and sound of God.

"All things hear the whispers of HIS word.

"...........*and the word was made flesh*.......

"As ... All things reply.

"Only we can't YET read God's newspaper.

"We can't hear God's phone calls.

"We can't see God's movie.

"We can't understand God's language.

"And yet, children," (still holding his beaker up to the sun at varying elevations and pointing) "this single container has all the language required to turn on the sun.

"Just as we turn on a light switch.

"Just as we believe when we turn that switch the light will illuminate, so is the energy inside this beaker transformable to a sun that will operate for a millennium, at the whisper, only the whisper of even one sacred sound from the memory of the Lord God.

"And you, my babies, are made IN the IMAGE and the Likeness of the Lord God as surely as the word has been written and this beaker contains the code of life.....

"For what I hold in my hands children ... is a simple glass of sea water.

"A container of ocean water, which later, I will have you return to the Pacific.

"And when you do, you will know, that every single drop of information you place into the sea, is connected to every other drop of information that is already IN the sea.

"You won't ALWAYS be children, you know," he said, making a sweeping gesture with his arms toward the ocean.....

"There will come a time, in only a very short while, when you will sail out upon on this beautiful ocean of fantastic possibilities ... an ocean of unlimited fruits and choices that the Lord has put in front of you." It was as if he saw things, far away, at the horizon and if we only looked a little harder, we would see these sights of wonder as well. He stood there with his elbow leaning on the hood of the Woody, near a brown paper bag and a beaker of plain green sea water, gazing under his wide brimmed hat, off to the horizon, and I longed to see what he was able to see, to have his sweep of vision for even a moment.

"For you SEE, children, this is not really an ocean as you see it with your eyes," and here Mr. Dohrmann reached up and shaded his own eyes as he stared with ever-greater concentration off to the edge of forever, "No! God's ocean is more than what you see reflected in the bright summer sun this morning.

"Children, see how the sun is turning the water into a dance of light that flows far off into the horizon ..." and every child could see the shimmering light as it ran off to meet the sky. It was as if the morning sun had painted a causeway that rushed to greet the sky on the other side of the world, a salutation from the rising orb, now floating in the pearly daybreak, risen over the mountain and smiling down at the sea.

Mr. Dohrmann crouched down upon his knees like an Indian elder, as if by doing so, he could gain more distance with his eyes, and see farther from this new position. His body language told us at a level of inner knowing, how far away into the future he was attempting to place his vision.

"A highway of LIGHT, (gesturing at the sun) children, that will turn PURE GOLD by the late afternoon. A river of GOLDEN LIGHT that runs off our

planet to meet the sky with an embrace. But wait, our
river of light will then turn RUBY red, by the late afternoon as the sun hides away for yet another new
dawn, waiting like a Christmas surprise ... on some
new morning ... but that's yet another story."

Mr. Dohrmann's eyes twinkled and his upturned
lips almost went into a smile, as his gaze fell upon a
line of quail far off on the high meadow trail. (I think
I alone of his listeners noticed that the quail family
included mother, father and nine chicks precisely; I
shared a knowing exchange with Mr. Dohrmann at that
instant.) Stretching and waving over the ocean one last
time, Mr. Dohrmann continued.....

"God's ocean of UNLIMITED possibilities actually safely HIDES the secret location for all the invisible choices and potential actions you ...

"And you and you ...

"And you and you" (pointing to each of us in our
turn) ...

"Will ever TAKE or MAKE in your lifetime.

"For hidden within this ocean is all the life and
substance of the Universe waiting for those who are
AWAKE to discover!"

Mr. Dohrmann then broke his story, purpose-
fully turned and walked off to the car, crunching gravel
sounds filling our ears as the big man moved out of
sight, only to quickly return. He brought out one thermos and one clear plastic cup from the Woody Wagon.
He placed both the thermos and the clear plastic cup
on the large shiny hood near the paper bag and beaker of green sea water.

He then poured from the thermos into the plastic cup.

He said, "MORE SEA WATER, for as I pour,"
(and he took the beaker and the plastic cup and mixed
the water back and forth) "All the information of the
entire ocean, the vast ocean, the ocean beyond your
vision children, the ocean you cannot even imagine
from this tiny point of your observation, the huge vast

ocean, every drop of the ocean, every atom is here IN-
SIDE the drops of sea water flowing between these
cups.

"For not only is every part of the blueprint of life
in every drop I pour right here on the hood of my car,
to the mind of God...

"And not only is every part of every drop one
with the entire sea, the entire ocean, the entire web of
life...

"But in every drop is contained every atom of
the ocean, and every part of the ocean is here, just as
it is behind me, for what you see is not the sea, for the
sea is right before you in the cup of life I pour on the
hood of your Woody Wagon. The closer you are to your
GOD, the greater will be your gift of vision. Then, and
only then, will you see the flow of energy that binds us
all and wraps itself around and within us to show you
that the drops here, the drops I am pouring, are in fact
ONE with the sea and the sea is one with the drops ...
the farther away from GOD you rest, the more limited
your vision will be. Until, almost blind, you may swear
that there is just one cup here on the hood of the car,
pouring a small limited supply of sea water from one
vessel into the other.

"Your Father above, however, is witnessing that
I am pouring an entire ocean from one vessel into the
other, and each time I pour I give glory to the Lord God,
for the blueprint of life is a treasure that I adore my
Lord for creating. With each pouring I make a prayer
of gratitude so profound, to pour not sea water but my
heart into the heart of my Lord God, so that like the
drops of sea water I pour here, your life and my life can
be poured out to become merged into ONE with the
ocean that is the heart of the Lord God. The miracle of
our VISION is to know, even to be aware of this small
miracle of the story of life ... standing here ... with one
lunch bag, one thermos, two cups and the entire ocean
on the hood of one Woody Wagon...."

Then Mr. Dohrmann turned, and made the sign of the cross, marking the end of this prayer ... and said:

"But this ... is not the lesson......"

_____

FREEDOM & A WOODY WAGON

The next episode of this morning's story took a matter of time in the telling. I remember the entire procession of events from the view spot that morning. Leaning on Mr. Dohrmann's classic Woody Wagon, I must have presented quite a sight to the cars that passed: A lone Benedictine monk, in rapt meditation of sights below they could not see or know. If one of the many famous authors who made their homes in Marin County had happened to pass at that moment, who knows what creative spark might have ignited a mystery novel or existential short story?

Mr. Dohrmann was busy leading his nine children down a narrow pathway in the tall meadow grass, looking more like a park Ranger on a field trip than a father taking his family on a summer safari for the soul. The deer path traced its way through green seaside meadows of tall waving mountain grass quilted with native California wildflowers. Children who might be caught whispering as they marched (in single file) made a rustle in the reeds as the path wound this way and that, ever downward. There would come a giggle here and again, as one grabbed the garments of another, or a comment came unbidden from an elder to a younger. Nevertheless, it was an orderly progression as we made our way into the slopes of the meadow that summer day.

With a hand motion, Mrs. and Mr. Dohrmann had stopped the procession short of the Pacific cliffs, overlooking the froth of the ever pounding surf below. With words lost to those that were not in his presence, each child, one at a time, came forward to their father, held the beaker of liquid high over their head,and then took only a small pour, as they added their innocent spirits into the mix of life from which the water was taken ... the sea!

By the time it was over there was still enough remaining in the beaker for Mrs. Dohrmann to join her spirit into the ocean beside her children, after which the beaker was completely emptied as Mr. Dohrmann shed the remaining green ingredients into the mighty Pacific.

I would learn later that the only words he told his children at the cliff site were these....

"Children, when I am no longer here to coach you in the journey of your life, and your troubles seem impossibly LARGE, and you lose sight of God's unlimited possibilities; when your life problems cloud your beaker of unbridled potential, I ask that you come HERE, back to this spot in your MIND. Come to the SEA of LIFE on such a day. As you stand back here, beside your family, I request that you pour your beaker of cloudy trouble into the sea of all possibilities, KNOWING that the Lord God has unlimited choices for your future. As you pour out your cloudy beakers on such a day, back into the sea, remember the moment we share now. Remember THIS moment. Remember the breezes... the smells, remember the way the grass feels against your legs, and the mist from the surf below, remember the love of your family, and the unconditional love from your mother and your father, remember all these FEELINGS and remember it well. Feel the release that is provided by God's ocean to your inner self for all your problems and troubles ... and as you do this.... you will be made FREE. "

Then Mr. Dohrmann asked each child to hold the beaker high over their heads, and focus on their biggest problem in life. Each child was asked to look at the beaker until they could see God's light from the sun shining through their problem, and then, only then, were they permitted to release the idea such a problem represented, back into the sea. As they poured, Mr. Dohrmann's guiding hand drew attention to how small the splash of each problem was in the vastness below. He explained that the small beaker was large enough to hold all the problems the family would ever know or experience.

Over many years to come, I would discover that the Nine would often come back here to this spot they later named the CLIFFS OF HOPE.

And as they walked back up the trail, I know they were thinking of his last words by the cliffs of the Pacific Ocean, as was I.

I did not hear him, but I knew what they were:

"......But, children ... that's NOT the lesson ..."

DAD IS MAGIC, BROTHER AL........

He rested a bit when he returned, and then continued the story.

Looking at each of the Nine intently, he took a tobacco pouch, and a large orange pipe to match his Sunday blazer, and began to tamp and light his peace smoker. The gentle late-morning Pacific breezes were calm enough that with only his second attempt at flame, long columns of smoke arose, accompanied by sucking noises, completing the familiar pipe-lighting ritual. As he performed this task, he cast his gaze over the brim of his pipe bowl, like an impish dragon, to catch the eyes of each and every child. It seemed to be a moment for him to assure that the attention of each ear and every eye was upon the lesson to follow.

I can remember that his "setting" of each scene for each and every story commanded such total attention that all of us felt pulled out of our body bags, if only for an instant, to attend to the detail of it all. There was a quickening, as the moment of great truth came upon us, that welled up from an impossible place deep within the knowing of the soul. Now that so many years have passed, it may be a trick of failing faculty or memory, but the sensation I recall most is one of time. Although the stories each took only a few moments to complete, I can remember every one as a monumental work, one that seemed to stretch far beyond the time of the actual telling. It was as though some spiritual truth were imparted at such a vital level of being, that one held this truth like a "heart diamond" as Mr. Dohrmann often called them, woven now into the fabric of the vital beingness of the individual. Time seemed suspended as the story continued. The sensation of the "heart diamond" had the effect of creating the notion that Mr. Dohrmann was moving and talking in slow motion, and that every word was a note of music which, once-played, would continue forever.

When later I would ask a few of the older children about this observation, (with some delicacy) the reply was simply:

".....*Dad is Magic, Brother Al, and when he uses his magic, time stands still........*"

It was some time after this, that I began to believe in magic all over again. I was wearing a necklace of heart diamonds.

LESSON OF THE BALLOON CHILDREN

"Come follow me," ... and he went toward the back of the Woody, which Forest had turned around, so that it was now facing away from the sea.

As all nine came 'round the car, I can remember seeing the Giant White Balloons straining against the impassable barrier of the Woody Wagon's doors. They seemed like living animals, each struggling to be set FREE, squashed one against the other, all bursting for release.

As Mr. Dohrmann turned to face us, he continued his story.....

"Children, I know that all of you have seen the balloons that have been inside our wagon in the place you normally sit." (Mr. Dohrmann tapped the back windows of his station wagon for effect.)

"I know I asked you not to question me about these balloons, and I am happy not one of you did. You're "good dogs" (a common expression in the family ... Mr. Dohrmann often referred to his children as "good" or "bad" dogs, which was always said with his infectious smile and a tone of endearment.)

"For you see, children, these balloons represent each of YOU, my babies. There are exactly nine balloons inside our Woody Wagon, and all NINE balloons are straining to get out ... straining to be FREE, straining with ultimate strength to ... go BEYOND. To travel fur-

ther than the Woody Wagon can carry them. You can see yourself if you stand on your tiptoes and only look."
(Which, of course, we did.)
Nine faces pressed against the windows.
He paused awhile until the children settled in again to listen.

"I want you to understand, children, that the safety and familiarity of our Woody Wagon is much like our family itself ... The borders of our family ... The rules of our family ... The love of our family.

"For even the love of our family cannot contain the bigness of you forever. The bigness of the lives that each of you will soon choose to live. For each of you must soon, REPRODUCE the love of this family, my children in the only form love can BE replicated ... you must GIVE AWAY all our love, the love we know IN our family so that others may RECEIVE this form of perfect love.

"We call this kind of giving, in the adult world, by a word. The word is known to you... It is FREEDOM.

"Freedom means only that you are GIVING all of your love away.

"All the love you have learned. All the love your mother and I have taught you about. All the love you know today or will ever know in the future.

"You must, however, discover, how to CREATE your own love. ...Your own loving mission in this life ... Your own WAY to discover this simple truth that is the only MEANING for all my lessons.

"The truth. The ONE TRUTH that you ARE made in the image and likeness of GOD ... that you are truly only magical beings of LOVE and, in the end of your life, there is nothing left inside your body bags, children, but the LOVE you have chosen to GIVE away within your lifetime. Everything else returns to earth and only the LOVE you have GIVEN AWAY is lifted beyond the possibilities of the eternal sea directly to God.

"Everything else which you do or say that is NOT Love Given Away, everything else you think or feel, everything ELSE is trapped here within the Earth, children. Only the LOVE that you GIVE away ... is carried beyond the sea of all possibilities (and he gestured outward toward the expanse of the rolling waves of the Pacific Ocean) to reach the heart of the Lord God. "........But, not even THAT is the lesson........"

THE CONTRACT
OF THE HEART DIAMOND

"Always remember what I have taught you about the truth today. The truth about a cup of sea water and your future of DISCOVERY in the way you will each CHOOSE to GIVE your love away." Mr. Dohrmann stared at each of the nine children.

"For someday, children, and this day will be so soon and so sudden for your mother and me, you will LEAVE the SAFETY of this Woody Wagon ... this Wagon we call OUR FAMILY. You will, first one, and then another, begin to bounce down, off the bumper here," (and his foot tapped the bumper) "to bounce further down the road of your life, just like a balloon filled to bursting with the Breath of God, to flow towards your destiny in life.

"Like each of these balloons," (and he gestured at the huge, beachball-sized orbs pressed together inside the Woody Wagon) "your body bag balloon has indeed been filled by God with all HIS LOVE.

"Not even one small breath was withheld from even one of you special children, when God blew your body bag up, just like the balloons inside our family wagon.

"For you see, when you were born, I made a contract with the Lord God. Your mother and I each made our own special prayer for the start of your new life. In my birth prayer, I asked that God see into my heart. I have always believed that God, during this prayer time, held a knowing that I had agreed to GIVE all my love away, and the Lord, in return, would give all of HIS LOVE away, to each of my children. I prayed that God would show his LOVE by blowing his breath into your body bags ... your baby-size balloons.

"I can see on this Sunday, in the sun, that He has kept His part of the bargain. "

Mr. Dohrmann looked, with some water in his eyes, at each of his nine children for what seemed like a very long time.

"For I can see now that each of you, my children, is FULL.

"Filled with the LOVE of GOD. And I can see that each of you has all the love that God, in all his wisdom, has the power to blow into each one of you.

"*And I can see ENOUGH ... more than enough!*

"But now, my children, comes the lesson. The lesson has to do with how your mother and I keep our part of the prayer.

"For your mother and I know all too well that the road of Balloon travel in life is not always easy. Sometimes balloon children WILL fly HIGH, and it will seem as if your tiny fingers can reach the sky. At other times you WILL impact and bounce down on the sharp stones on the roadway of your life, or land in a stream or river, fearing that you have lost your way within a dark forest, always moving... always flowing through the challenges and natural way of life and growth itself.

"And as you travel, I am convinced that each of you will make more than ONE new discovery. In fact, I know that God will help each of you to make many, many fresh DISCOVERIES along the journey of your lives.

"Each of my children will uncover one more new truth about our simple cup of sea water, more than all the world has ever known ... such is our time of illumination. A new dawn is arriving that we are destined to contribute to......"

(And then he thumped the back-door to the wagon and the balloons seem to quiver inside with each thump of his fist, moving with an eagerness to escape).....

THUMP!

"One new truth."

THUMP!

"One new discovery."

THUMP!

"But each Child MUST always take their OWN steps forward in life, each one with the strength gained from WHAT you RETAINED while you grew INSIDE the safety and the love, while you lived inside OUR FAMILY wagon."

...and here Mr. Dohrmann made a latch sound like he was opening the double handles on the back doors of the Woody Wagon, the doors that held the giant balloons inside ... but it was only the sound and the doors did not open.....

"For, children, when you set yourselves free, truly and all the way FREE, you will also discover that you can never again come back together in the same way. For the original way of FAMILY that you know NOW is only a fleeting thing.

A thing we call ....your childhood.

"I NEED for you to see ... it is not your mother and it is not your father who open the door and set you children FREE to explore your lives as adults. Yes, we can OPEN the door to adult experience. Yes, we can point the way to the sea of adult possibilities." (Here, he pointed down the wildflower meadow path to the ocean.)

"But it is only YOU who can LEAD.

"It is only you who can choose to take that FIRST GIANT step toward your individual adult freedoms in life. It is in the end ... only you who WILL decide when the time is right ... and HOW you WILL go about taking your first steps into your own adulthood!

"In this you act ... in this first true adult choice ... you must each ACT *alone!*

"And once you have taken this first giant step ... your first truly ADULT step...

"You can never again be family in the same pattern as you know the word family on this day. Here on this Sunday. Here with your mom, with Brother Al and with your father ... here with all your brothers and sisters beside you as they are beside you today...."

Little faces looked one to the other and back to their father ... in rapt attention.

....again Mr. Dohrmann made the double-latched sound with the Woody Wagon doors. Once again the doors did not open.....

"For, once you take this first great ADULT leap in your life ... you must then go forward. You must always then proceed to move ahead in your life ... always ahead in all of your choices.

"Children can replay and step backwards ... but adults, my babies, must always and FOREVER ...move forward in their life. No longer can they backtrack like children........ for new rules will forever apply in the adult world.

"You can never return here once you choose to begin to live your adult life, my babies, as choices will always be different for you. Never can you play here at the beach in this same way. Although nothing has changed on the outside ... everything will change on the INSIDE of God's magical balloon, which is all that you really are ... the YOU Balloon is a body bag filled with the divine expression of the Lord.

"Oh, we will share our Christmas together,

"And our Thanksgiving ...

"And our LOVE forever...... as family."

....Some of the young children were sad at this point in the story and began to look at their older brothers and sisters in a new way. Two were holding on to one another and rocking......

"But at this precious TIME, this impeccable moment, here beside our Woody Wagon at Stinson Beach ... in this way today ... on this special Sunday in this magical summer, the way we live right now ... children ... this is TIME more priceless than all the diamonds ever mined, all the gold ever discovered, and all the buried treasure that was ever hidden away. This, my children, is the most fragile gift in the world. This Time MUST be treasured by you inside your hearts over an entire lifetime.

"For once undone, it can never be reclaimed in exactly the same way.

"For in this INSTANT, this speck of time and only at this place and moment ... you are all TOGETHER with ONE ANOTHER ... AS ... CHILDREN.

"You are all together as family, but you are fixed for the only the shortest of TIMES here in your balloon bags, inside your CHILDHOOD.

"Your love and playful ways are gifts for you and you alone to harbor for all your adult lives, to cherish for all your adult days, and to never, EVER be forgotten.

"All your memories. All your teasings. All your laughter. All your games. Even your disagreements, which you settle together, knowing that the love you have for each other underlies any argument, and remains there long after the dispute has ended. All your comings and goings are the comings and going of CHILDREN.

"These are the only MOMENTS of your CHILDHOOD that you will ever know or ever remember. I call upon you children to hold them dear now. Grab them, as memories, deep inside your heart...."

(And in a whisper he went on)

".... for they last not long at all ... they move away so fast, my children ... so fast...." (the last sounded like air hissing from a tire ... or a balloon).

"For it is this single KNOWING about the IN-NOCENCE and LOVE you hold as MY children, that supports you and lifts you in all your adult journeys over an entire adult lifetime."

(And then came one of Mr. Dohrmann's favorite sayings, in a way only an elf could render the words.....)

"Youuuu'llllll SEEEE!"

(And there was a special twinkle in his eye.)

"Now I know you children wish to know and understand what happens TO you in your ADULT life ... when you throw the doors of our safe and protecting Family OPEN and the Balloon Children inside are released. What happens when YOU make your decision to GO FORWARD in life and move BEYOND your CHILDHOOD. Always too soon. Always too much in a rush. Always without understanding how much you GIVE AWAY the first time you take on those truly adult choices.

"We know you wish to SEE, to FEEL what it is like when you give away your CHILDHOOD and begin to travel the adult road as our balloon children."

FREEDOM COMES

"And this begins the lesson.

"For, children, in all the lessons you will ever see from your father, I cannot TEACH you the lessons of your adulthood. You must learn these lessons, one at a time, each on your own. I cannot teach you HOW to live nor may your mother or I live your life FOR you.

"We cannot protect you from pain.

"We cannot solve your every problem.

"We can not undo the things that you will choose to do for yourself.

"My only gift, when it is all said and done ... at the end of the long, long road of life ... will be the GIFT of the rosary of YOUR CHILDHOOD memories.

"Your memory of a summer day...

"An ocean breeze...

"Your mom, here beside...

"Your father...

"And one comfortable old Woody Wagon we call our FAMILY ... a time when your father and mother stood beside the DOORS of your TOMORROW opened wide, and with fear and pride waited for YOU to step away from the safe and warm INSIDE of the family we have made for you.

"Today there are still nine big balloons inside our family ... Balloon Children that represent YOUR Childhood, all straining to become grown up and to go their SEPARATE ways on their individual journeys in life.....

"But that is NOT the lesson....."

...and here he made the double latch sound one more time.....

"I ask you to visualize with me that the Balloons inside will find a moment in life when they SUC-CEED... an instant when YOU succeed, when you take that first adult step outside your family ... and although you won't see it ... or feel it, this whole story of life, at this place, today, in this time ... I can see the ENTIRETY OF IT ALL, I can see everything I wish for you as my children, to own as your DESTINY.

"But I ask that you imagine with me...

"Really imagine... moving forward from the first moment the doors of our safe and loving Family are THROWN OPEN... THROWN OPEN BY YOU ... so that each of you can spread your WINGS and FLY....."

(And I can recall eight of the nine children had shut their eyes, and then I shut mine.)

"Imagine with me, children ...

"That the first bounce from the safety of our Family and this Woody Wagon, for each and every Balloon Child, will become a long, LONG fall... a long and scary FIRST step DOWN into a place we call THE REAL WORLD... and yet it is this single fall that provides the momentum for each BALLOON CHILD to take their NEXT step, and then their NEXT step... and each of you... on your own... will be compelled to take this FIRST GRAND STEP... to BEGIN IT ... and then move forward ... always ahead in adult life ... always forward ... and away from HERE ... this place we have known together as YOUR CHILDHOOD ... with ONE ANOTHER........

.........*OUR FAMILY IN CHILDHOOD*........

"And on your way down the path of adult life much of what Mom and Dad have provided to you will

be forgotten... forgotten in this first GRAND and GI-
ANT STEP of your willful adulthood.

"That BIG, GIANT TEDDY BEAR that symbolizes the 'things' that mean the most to you about being a Child INSIDE this FAMILY, may vanish or be entirely GONE ... and you will SUDDENLY hear a BELL,
a Tone, each of you WILL know when that FIRST GI-
ANT STEP in your ADULTHOOD has taken place.....

"Oh, you may often wander back to this place in
your mind, children, and you MAY remember your Dad
and the Woody Wagon and this summer day ... you may
even drive back here once in awhile and remember the
place of this story, and your old Dad holding these
handles on a Sunday morning by the beach......

"And you will recall, with the perfect memory
that only childhood can record, the day you VEN-
TURED through your safe secure hallways at home,
and held that GIANT TEDDY BEAR that symbolizes
your CHILDHOOD memories, held your FAMILY
BEAR so high that you recall with a small tear in your
eye the moment...... the very second...... that you cast
aside that wonderful Childhood much like a teddy bear
tossed out a high window from our hillside home ... cast
it aside.... to explore YOUR ADULTHOOD... you WILL
remember the sight of how your TEDDY BEAR fell ...
fell, as if in slow motion, and finally disappeared from
view altogether ... into our family garden of flowers and
memories.......

"But wait ... there is more.....

"For a long while you may forget much of your
family life, here in the family we have made for you ...
and some of you may find the way BACK home will become fuzzy ... and lost ... for awhile......

"Some of you may forget how to FORGIVE your
mom,

"Some of you may forget how to forgive your
father,

"Some of you may forget how to forgive your brothers or your sisters,

"And some of you may forget how to forgive even the little child inside you, that IS you ... nothing more than a BALLOON CHILD of the LORD..... the ultimate amnesia, when you forget the lesson of how to forgive yourself.

"You may fail to forgive yourself for the failures you think you have made in your life, as you forget the Lord God has never made a mistake, especially with YOU.

"You MAY focus on the bounces and travels your balloon path will represent. You may focus on the rocks and pricks and roughness along the roadways of your life journey. You may focus on the bridges and stone walls and tiny narrow passageways you will pass through on the adventures of YOUR adult discoveries.

"For much of your adult journey you will be at the mercy of the winds of TIME ... winds that will carry you down roads you cannot imagine as we gather here today ... as you try and remember your father's cry...

.... *THERE ARE NO ACCIDENTS!*........

"There will come a time for your schooling in your adult life ...

"A time for your adult possessions in life ...

"A time to travel down the narrow hallways of religion and truth...

"A time to travel the broad earthly hallways of family and futures and discoveries too numerous to name.....

"And through all these journeys of MY Balloon Children, there will BE snatches ...

"Fleeting snatches ... of THIS knoll ... right here above God's ocean of unlimited possibilities," as Mr. Dohrmann swept our attention again out across the horizon to the unlimited sea.

"This view ... will return time and time again, as a MEMORY for MY CHILDREN,

"A vision, of your dad and mom, and an old Woody Wagon.....

"And in these fleeting moments, you will RE-MEMBER

"your childhood ...

"You will smile ...

"And you will, for an instant here and there...

"As my BALLOON CHILDREN, take on new dimensions.....

"For you MUST, as this memory does its work, have a glow that floats inside your heart, my little ones.

"For You, and you alone, must hold the candle of your Childhood in your adult life....

"You must hold the tiny little light of the child that lies within each one of us, whenever your thoughts will take you back to this day, back to this place.....

"You must warm your outer self with the memory of your inner self.....

"And you, my children, MUST SMILE ... with JOY!

"For only you have the power ... TO KEEP YOUR CHILDHOOD ALIVE!"

And here Mr. Dohrmann put his hands upon the two large chrome latches to the back-door of the Woody Wagon.....

And said.....

"CHILDREN ... I am going to SHOW YOU my lesson as a physical truth ... but before I do ... I want you to IMAGINE what it is like at the very end of your life ...

"At the time when you will be very old.

"Imagine the oldest person you know.

"Imagine the most old, wrinkled person you have ever seen ...

"And pretend in your mind that this is YOU ...

"YOU and your brothers and sisters,

"YOU, old on the outside, but still a BALLOON CHILD on the inside ...

"Unchanged ... Always the same ......on the IN-SIDE.....

"Containing all the memories from an IN-STANT on this grassy place, to the end of your journeys in your life.

"Always the same ... A BALLOON CHILD... now and forever more.

"Know, my children, that your mother and I see you ... see each of our children as mighty FLAGS ... FLAGS that reach far up to the sky billowing a hundred stories into the winds of TIME... and only for the shortest of moments has God entrusted us to briefly anchor the edges of these GIANT FLAGS beside our hearts, hearts in our family that beat as one today ... for it is impossible to hold the MAGIC and the GLORY of what GOD has made inside you CHILDREN, to bind you or contain your spirit ... and you MUST KNOW that a time will come when your mother and father... MUST LET YOU GO.....

"And the flags will fly free, up to the sky, as the anchor is released, and you make your own way back towards GOD in the life journey.

"When parents do that which is most difficult ... that which is not natural to us, freely performed, this letting GO ..."

....Here Mr. Dohrmann made a gesture like releasing the base of a kite or flag so that the entire huge object just flew off into the sky on its own ... I was sure some of the small eyes could see it all before them.......

"...First one flag ... then the other ... WILL ... FLY FREE ... truly FREE to see with your own eyes, in your own ways, the FUTURE that God has planned for you ... for each flag is the symbol of the Lord for your FUTURE.......

"And remember, my children, that in the end I want you to imagine that in the twilight of your life, at the very end of this life ...

"You may all return here to this early place where we all began.....

"You may always return to this place and re-member these Symbols of your Childhood, in your mind ... in your heart....

"You may always return here to once again see your mother's FACE, her face in youth and as she is now, as she has always loved you," (and here he ca-ressed her face).

"Like a GIANT and HUGE STATUE carried by the brothers and sisters together, you will see HER FACE being carried off into the twilight of your own life. And as the shadows race across this fading statue you will know the love your parents held for you ... see your mother as this great soft statue being carried off into the shadows by her nine children who have agreed to never ever leave her ... in this life we travel........

"The symbol of your father ... standing by his Woody Wagon ... will come upon you ... now and again in life.....

"And you will see, in long lines, the children of other families, NINE families, all joining you ...

"As everyone ...

"At one time ... or another TIME.......

"Returns back here, to THEIR childhood.....

"And in the final moment of life ...

"My children, there is only a sound ...

"A soft note ...

"For the ringing of the Bell of Truth ...

"Is KNOWN by all.

"There is not one of us who does not know this sound.....

"And in hearing it we are granted Peace,

"Peace in our memories,

"Peace for all our travails,

"Peace on earth as it is known even in heaven,

"I want you to know the lesson ...

"And the lesson is this ...

"The journey you take does NOT matter,

"The places you travel to will not really count,

"The end will always be the same,

"The same for you,

"The same for me,

"The same for mom,

"The same for all of us.

"The only thing that matters is here ALREADY

...

"INSIDE this FAMILY, children.....

"For it is the very BREATH of GOD that has granted LIFE to each of you.

"It is this same breath of God that transforms a simple cup of sea water to a breeder reactor, or unlimited loaves to eat, or turns on a star called the SUN, much as you may switch on a light bulb, to light a solar system.....

"It is this same breath of God that takes a simple BALLOON and puffs the balloon into the shape and mystery of a Child.....

"It is this same ...

"Exactly this same breath of God ...

"That fills the Balloons that are the LIGHT in EACH of you ... each one of my children ... filled with love, with playful giggles, and yet" (as he turned once again to the back doors of his Woody Wagon) "you strain so to move into larger possibilities along in your journey ... back HOME.....

"And the lesson, children, is to always, always look INSIDE your balloons for the answer of how to enjoy your life in just the way you DESIRE your life to be.

.................Always look inside..................

"Always, always return to your CHILDHOOD ... to the safety and strength of a FAMILY that loves one another, and that cherishes the very idea of FAMILY, and never allow the path of life to rob you of your VICTORY for being here in this Woody Wagon, and having

been so close together if only for a precious short second of time in your life ... never forget the memory,
children, of your summer day ... THIS summer day ...
looking BACK upon the sea of possibility...for in only
moments from now ...

"THIS ... BEGINS!"

And without warning Mr. Dohrmann threw
open the doors to the back of the Woody Wagon ... with
a crack ... a sound I remember as rolling off the green
and golden hills in Marin county.....

And the Balloons expanded and came out ...
driven by the wind.....

First one fell and then bounced...for each was
so large when expanded to its full size ... each seemed
as large as the child who watched it.....

Then came another,

In a perfect Parade.....

(It was only then we noticed that on each balloon, appeared the NAME of one child ... Terry, Pam,
Sally, Susan, Melissa, Carl, Geof, Mark and Bernhard
... in crisp green printed letters) ....

And as the wind caught them, the balloon children began to flow down to the meadows and toward
the sea,

Through the wild flowers and beyond.....

And as they each

Formed their way,

I was impressed how they traveled in a line, one
behind the other,

Along the pathway in the grass,

Until they met the sea itself

And then scattered upon the waves .....

Turning to the children, I could see the effect it
was having as the balloons separated, and scattered,
each alone, upon the sea, moved by the vagrant winds.
I was asking myself....was this indeed the wind of
TIME that caught the children and took them.....

All away........

Drifting right and left around the bay perimeters ...

Seeking and finding a way out to the open sea...

Until soon there was not a balloon left to be seen at all.....

We sat awhile in silence, hoping one, even one, would return into view. But none did.

Mr. Dohrmann had returned to the front of the car during this time.......

...And taken from the front seat an ancient Bell, a gift from Tibet, from a monastery, I would later be told. An old treasure unseen by we who stared out to sea, remembering when the last one of the Balloon children had faded from our sight.

Then Mr. Dohrmann simply ... Rang his Bell of Truth.....

And a long, solitary tone rolled across the mountain in contrast to the Sea.....

Mr. Dohrmann looked up at us and said ...

"Children ... Today's Lesson seeks to have you understand that each of you offers to the other the invaluable memory of your Childhood ... and I ask only that you ...

"KEEP ... YOUR ... CHILDHOOD!

"ALWAYS AND FOREVER REMEMBER, KEEP YOUR CHILDHOOD ALIVE!

"That you return to this instant, if only in your memories, when called upon to do so.....

"As you return, hold the power to recall the Love that your mother and I have held for you in our hearts...

"In our thoughts ...

"In our very being ...

"And the love that you have held for one another.....

"And I ask that you always remember ...

"That this is the essence that fills the BALLOON CHILDREN ...

"And the remainder of your lives You are free
"To return to a grassy knoll,
"A Woody Wagon,
"An ocean of unlimited possibilities ...
"With a Mom and Dad who will always love you,
"Under the sun of an eternal God who loves you bigger than the sky.

"And it is THIS more than any sound from any man or woman in your life ...

"That will always be the BELL of Truth for MY CHILDREN"

"Always remember the tone of it, in all your adult wanderings......"

(And he once again rang the bell.)

"Now, let's jump inside and go to the beach.....
.........like children."

(And we did just that!)

Chapter 8

Perfection

PERFECTION CAN BE HAD

Some of my best lifetime memories are of the travel adventures that I was able to enjoy with the entire Dohrmann family. My favorite of these has always been our visits to Hawaii. In the 1950's Mr. Dohrmann would take many trips to the Pacific for the Dohrmann Hotel Supply Business. This was in the days before things changed to the present emphasis on tourist-oriented industry there, before something very special was lost in the feeling toward visitors, before the Aloha Spirit became something to exploit more than exhibit.

During his long stays in Hawaii, at the Bishop Street home (long since torn down), Mr. Dohrmann would enroll the children into local Hawaiian schools. I would often accompany Mr. Dohrmann on what he called "all-nighters" to remote villages. Mr. Dohrmann spent much of his free time studying the ancient rites and teachings of elder native Hawaiians, the *kupuna* and *kahuna*. I would come to discover that a story of his, here or there, would belong to the ancient peoples of Hawaii, and that their timeless Aloha had spread its way into a Dohrmann lesson.

I recall one occasion in the mid-1950's. Mr. Dohrmann bundled all of the children into an odd transport, even for his style. A huge green military vehicle had arrived at the Bishop Street home. A United States Marine, in uniform, approached the front door in a quick march, to stand quietly at attention while the bell was still ringing.

The servants announcing the visitors caused Mr. Dohrmann to drop his pen in the study, and to call for all children to assemble at the front door. As in a navy submarine drill for battle stations, this "alert" always caused a terrific commotion. Tiny feet would scramble in anticipation from the upstairs and downstairs rooms to the formal section of the open-air home and down the main hallway to the carved stained-glass door.

Standing by the flower trellis, Mr. Dohrmann assembled the children on the wide front lawn, until he had completed a counting ritual, assuring himself that all nine of his nestlings were front and center. At this point Mr. Dohrmann invited the children to march up the gangplank that led to double rows of facing benches inside the canvas-covered military transport truck.

The children were a little cautious, and the eldest tended to encourage the youngers to move ahead first. As soon as all had taken their place, with Mr. Dohrmann and myself up the plank at the last, a well-decorated uniformed officer joined the party, which caused considerable saluting from the honor guard, prior to closing the tailgate.

Mr. Dohrmann stood and shook hands warmly with the military man, saying, "George, thank you so much, I know this will mean a great deal to the children...I really appreciate you taking your afternoon."

George provided a beaming smile in reply, (I noticed they both smoked pipes) and saluted the children as the truck began to roll. "Future officers, I take it, and fine examples, too...not a bit too soon to begin their training today." There may have been a brief wink, but I lost it in the ongoing discussion.

Using Hawaiian words I never could decipher I was told that we would be going onto a restricted Military base, on a mountain cliff near Diamond Head. The cliff was an ancient site used by Kings and their family to control the "gathering place," or Oahu.

I remember how we could see out through the back canvas flaps, as the truck went up a rough, winding small road, high into the mountains. It was cooler as we rose higher. We stopped once, and I could hear the cranking of a gate and the clatter of the chains as locks were undone and refastened.

After we went through the no-man's-land of a large military compound, we drove for another good distance before coming to a final halt. I remember the truck backed into a turnabout, which looked to the children and me like nothing more than a large circle with huge tree ferns lining the amphitheater.

A tiny trail led up even higher, the only break in the fern-lined ring that framed us like a picture in this magical place. The gangplank was lowered to almost touch the base of the ancient Hawaiian trail, and following "George" (we didn't learn until much later that Mr. Dohrmann's friend was *Admiral* George), each child proceeded up the trail. We didn't have long to travel before we came to an abrupt halt on a spit of lava that created a rim trail which went left and right in both directions.

As I rose to my full height ("Never a very long trip," I can hear Mr. Dohrmann say with a chuckle), with my hand on my back to stretch, I can remember feeling as if we stood on the edge of a knife blade. One side of the blade fell without deflection, in the most direct drop I have ever seen, to the sea. Some three thousand perfect feet of free fall, with only the seagulls using the cliff effects to their full value.

Much later, in the 1970's, Hawaii's infamous stunt man, John Thorpe, would secure access for this very same property, to make the land headquarters to the world's most foolhardy hang-gliders club. However, even as it stands today, home of the Hanglider Daredevils, attracting stunt folks from across the globe, the way up still includes the same creaking of the iron gate, and the clanking of chains, and a long drive through the compound, the only access to the spot where I stood all those long years ago.

On the other side of this volcanic knife edge lies in more gentle repose all of Honolulu and the bays from Waikiki to Pearl Harbor and beyond, up the leeward coast. What is desired here is a way to recreate the picture my mind still holds of this view in the 1950's. Pearl Harbor was still so fresh in everyone's mind.

Few of the "newer" jets transversed the way from the West Coast to Honolulu's old airport. Most of the traffic was still Pan Am prop Clipper Ships, with their eight-hour flight to Hawaii. Waikiki was not a "place" so much as a "swamp" in those days, particularly in the area of the Ala Wai.

Kalakaua Boulevard, in the 1950's, was a small single-lane road that brushed an enormous wide beach, primarily populated by native-born surfers, swamps and palm trees.

The majestic Royal Hawaiian was still only the second hotel property on the beach. Arthur Godfrey had elected to broadcast his world-wide radio show from the Royal Hawaiian Hotel. The unspoiled view of Honolulu, as yet undiscovered, made the word "paradise" seem somehow inadequate.

Mr. Dohrmann, having let the children dance up the trail ahead of the adults, preceded only by the military honor guard, finally, puffing from his years of smoker abuse, drew himself up beside us. The honor guard were busy watching the children on their "cliffside maneuvers" to assure none ventured too close to the sharp edges with their sheer drops to the sea. There were no rails, and it was more than conceivable that a wrong shove could end in dire consequence for the playful brigade.

More than once I felt myself looking over the south side and down the cliffs to the ocean in awe and wonder. How the Hawaiians must have worshipped God who had carved such a splendor. Even standing here to appreciate the carving was itself like a healing prayer.

My view to the west, however, was by far the best. As we reached a grassy knoll everyone was sitting out in front of Mr. Dohrmann looking off to the west. I noted that "Admiral George" and Mr. Dohrmann were enjoying cigars, both men gently puffing white circles of smoke into the trade winds whispering over the bluffs.

George would spend most of the next half hour telling the sad history of the Hawaiian people. Speaking as a military man, George noted, he believed it was the only time the United States deposed a Head of State (the Hawaiian Queen Liliuokalani) at gun point, and appointed their own government in the place of a free people. In fact, George pointed out, contrary to the history in the children's history books, the Hawaiian Government had been hugely popular. The Hawaiian people had emissaries and ambassadors established in over twenty countries. The royalty and aristocracy were well-educated in Europe's finest schools, as the trade and wealth of the Hawaiian Islands grew rapidly. Never had America so violated a free and sovereign people against their will as on that January 17, in 1893.

The illegal take-over came about almost solely due to a handful of local plantation families, still large powers in Hawaii today. The Hawaiians had the law on their side in all their protests, but the United States had gun ships. I thought it odd that George would bring the long version of this history up before the children, when I noticed that some of the Marine Honor Guard were Native Hawaiians.

Only recently, I read that the Congressional Representatives for Hawaii have introduced a bill, in which the United States government will formally issue an apology to the people of Hawaii for the illegal overthrow of their legally-constituted government. It is my fervent prayer that this will eventually be made into a law, not merely for the belated recognition it will give the Hawaiian people, but also for the cleansing of a national shame it will afford the country as a whole. As I read the news article with the eyes of an old man, how the memory of a much younger man returned with longing to the KNIFE EDGE, the grassy knoll, Admiral George and Mr. Dohrmann, surrounded by nine children in the island sun, and the first time I heard the story, the true story, of the Hawaiian nation as it once was.

On November 23, 1993, President Bill Clinton signed a proclamation extending the apologies of the United States to the People of Hawaii for the illegal overthrow of their rightful Queen Liliuokalani, on January 17, 1893. Brother Al had already left us, but we know that he heard the answer to his prayers ... BD

SUNNY DAYS AND RAINBOWS

"Look," said young Bernhard, "a rainbow." As we turned to the sea side, we saw it. From horizon to horizon a huge rainbow, correctly framed by clouds, bent itself to the ocean floor on one end and into the Ko'olau Mountains on the other. All paused to enjoy the spectacle.

One could not focus on any other sight for long, as the afternoon sunset commanded everyone's attention. The sun was hanging like an ornament on a Christmas tree. So enormous and red with the spent splendor of the day it seemed, demanding to enter its sleeping place underneath the sea. In only moments the first contact of its great lip would come to kiss the ocean horizon point.

Mr. Dohrmann, taking his cigar into his hand and gesturing to the sun, as if we had been discussing it all along said...to George rather than to all of us...almost as if we had become staging for the play......

"George, you have all your military might and know-how. You've just harnessed the atom and ended a world war. Perhaps no other endeavor in the known history of mankind has inspired such cooperation in a single endeavor. And yet look out there George." (as Mr. Dohrmann directed his cigar towards the sun blazing just above the sea line).

"Look at it, George!

"In all your imagination...consider the idea I am going to propose to you this afternoon.... Let's say that something goes wrong somewhere. Something huge.

"Something with the war machine.

"Something with the Presidency.

"Something with the democracy.

"Something with other world leaders somewhere.

"Another Hitler.

"Another something.

"You'd fix it wouldn't you, George? You'd just mobilize those vast resources you command and you'd fix it.

"Say something was wrong with the Planet?

"You'd fix that too, wouldn't you George?

"In these times the idea is that we can 'fix' anything, isn't it? We can resolve anything if we really put ourselves into it, isn't that the feeling?" (Mr. Dohrmann's cigar was continually waving now, almost always into the sun).

"But look out there, George.

"Will you just look at it?

"Someone has set up a machinery so perfect, so vast, that when all the Hitlers have come and gone, and all the heroes with them, that machinery will still do its service as though not even one of us had ever been born.

"Machinery that knows not whether we live or we die. Machinery that comes each morning and performs its labors, and travels its way, and does its tasks so brilliantly not even the most renowned among us has a limited clue as to how it all works.

Machinery that in its timeless way, gives us all life. Our lives George, our entire framework would be meaningless, save for this item of machinery we see disappearing now into the sea once again.

"Machinery that provides the reference of night and day, of time that is forever passing, of warmth and cold, and of too many contrasts to enumerate here.

"Now, George, in all our greatness and in all our self-importance, think how each human problem, as it is thought and rethought, has impact on the SUN. Think how each morning as the hurt or pain regains its power over a human mind, how the machinery of GOD simply performs its task, unknowing, unfeeling of the misery down here among us.

"How, in perfect operation, the Machine just delivers its mission and continues.

"When you experience your worst day George, when things don't work the way you designed them to, or someone near you is suffering, remember this knoll George, and say to yourself, fully facing this machinery of God, say quietly in such moments...simply 'THE SUN DOESN'T CARE..,' for all of God's Machinery is working just as it should, and even if you fail to know it, so are you, George, so are you. BE HERE NOW on this grassy knoll and everything that needs fixing will simply vanish before the phrase, THE SUN DOESN'T CARE....

"Now 'SWITCH' your thoughts, George, to consider that something is wrong with God's sacred machine. Consider that we wake up one day to discover our scientists reporting that something is terribly amiss with the mechanics of the SUN.

"The machine is now malfunctioning.

"First, think, what could you, or what could all your teams with all their egos and all their fine theories do, to fix this thing we call the SUN? How would they begin? What could they possibly DO to fix the machine we call the SUN George? What?

"Second, think, how impossibly remote and insignificant every human problem would FEEL, in the instant mankind was awake to the notion that something was not quite right with God's machine. The machine we know as the SUN. Think of how all the problems that create all our human feelings, would simply vanish. All focus would be on the PROBLEM with the sun. All else would fade to insignificance.

"Think how silly the divisions among men would feel then, George" (and all our eyes were fixed upon the huge glowing sunset in Hawaii), "and how uncomfortable, how petty, how terribly INSIGNIFI-CANT our bickering would be then...should something be truly wrong with the SUN."

By this time half the sun was behind the distant waves with only moments left for the image of the giant Red Ball cut clean in two by the horizon line.

"Think how many men and women have pain in today's life, pain created by a memory. A random firing of a brain cell, that develops a chemical pattern, that is no more an *experience* than the idea of Pearl Harbor, now years past, is to our memory. How many men and women focus all their attention upon the brain cell firings we call 'memory' in order to bring their memory into their precious NOW MOMENT in life? The moment when we are alive, the NOW moment from whence all decision and choice is made.

"No choice was ever made in memory.

"No memory was every created from its brother or sister memory.

"All memory is created by being...by BEING ALIVE....fully ALIVE in the NOW moment.

"For the only moment you and I George, are truly alive is right here. Right here with this cigar, the view of the sun now fading into the sea, and the now moment with these nine children, a handful of Marines, and a monk. This is our memory generator. This is the point from which all possibilities flow FORWARD.

"Let us wash away our memories, as the sun cleans itself within the sea." (And here only the top of the sun remained above the horizon, a tiny ember of molten ruby).

"If the SUN is broken, George, there is only one source you can go to and find a reliable mechanic. All your money, all your power, all your scientists, and all your resources will not lay one ratchet upon the sun. You can't rewire the sun, George. Not now. Not ever.

"You can only come here.

"When the problems get too great for us to solve.

"When the cold war seems too cold.

"When the choices seem too multiple.

"When the decision stream seems too wide to cross.

"You can always come here with your problems. Come to this place, George.

"You too, children. You can always return here, to this spot of the ancient Hawaiians.

"Come here to this sacred vista of the Kings.

"Take a handful of this grass," (and here he grabbed a giant handful of hillside grass and held it over his head) "and pretend each blade is a problem so large, so huge in your life you can't begin to solve it.

"And as you see the rest of the SUN washing itself in God's ocean, the ocean of unlimited possibilities....

"Throw your grass into the SEA."

He got up and walked to the back side of the cliff, and standing with the full red glow of the sun upon his back he cast his grass into the ocean, what seemed to be at least three thousand feet, straight down below.

And then each did. One by one.

Each focusing on a personal problem, problems that were just too big to solve at age five, at age twelve, at Admiral George's age, at any age. At the age of a Benedictine monk who lived virtually problem-free in a stone monastery; I noted my hands held more grass than anyone's.

When we were done, I remember watching the last of my own grass fall into the sea. Everyone sat again in the now-indented grass, in the traditional half-moon circle around our teacher.

Mr. Dohrmann went on waving his cigar as if we had never stopped.

"Once we have thrown our memories, our pain, our problems, into a bigger ocean of thought, and have let the blades of our individual problems be washed with God's love and possibilities, we become once again FREE.

"Truly FREE.

"Free to enjoy the perfection of the sun. Of God's machinery. Here. Now. IN the now moment. Watching this last bit of sunshine disappear, we see that as the twilight comes, we can no longer see our blades of grass. We can no longer see them nor can we feel them.

"Our problems have vanished from our now moment. Our memories have no power in the now moment. We are FREE to own our destiny with full gratitude for the inner workings of God's SUN.

"For we know that inside ourselves there is a peace. An inner peace for today, as if it were the first of all days, we have awakened with the KNOWING that there IS indeed nothing WRONG with the machinery of the SUN. Nothing that requires mankind's DOING to repair or make right.

"Just the knowing the SUN is working as it should is enough.

"That tomorrow the sun will rise again.

"And so shall we.

"Each new rising is a time to give GLORY, our entire being of glory, to God for making this simplicity, that we will not have to worry or be in pain that something is WRONG or BROKEN with the sun. And in this glory, this gratitude, the rest of our worries disappear and as they become so tiny in the new day's sun.

"Each new rising is a time to remember it was only LAST night, not today, that we threw our pain, our sorrows, our problems, like so many blades of grass, into the sea of God's unlimited possibilities. We pulled our very being into the sunset of the NOW MOMENT and we gave GLORY to GOD for his twilight to our problems, which seemed so large in one moment, and so small, like tiny blades of grass disappearing in the great ocean, the next.

"And in this knowing, we recognized the LIGHT that is the way of the sun in our lives.....the inner light as well as the outer light....

"If we can only master the lesson of a handful of grass, a huge ocean of choices, and the splendor of living in the NOW moment of every sunset, then PER-FECTION *can* BE HAD....my children, ...insist on it!

"Teach your men to live only in the NOW MO-MENT, George.....and your leadership will be as great as your vision.........

"Now children......let's get back home, for its time to solve the problem of making a fabulous dinner for nine starving hill critters......"

... **and we did.**

Chapter 9

Dad.....

DAD ... AND TO ALL A GOOD NIGHT!

Once upon a time, a four-year old, blue-eyed, blond-haired boy child woke up and walked out into a hallway that led to a family Christmas tree. It was midnight exactly. With his tiny right arm dragging his favorite binki, his squinting, half-opened eyes spied an elf man with a pipe (his father, coming into focus) balancing on a ladder. The elf man seemed to be struggling to re-suspend one Christmas ornament that Circe, one of the five Persian cats, had playfully adopted earlier as a personal toy from the family Christmas tree ... such "adoptions" were not uncommon at Christmas time.

Mr. Dohrmann was carefully repositioning the cat's chosen plaything, far from harm's way on the upside of one of the twenty-foot high boughs. Unseen in the picture was the Benedictine monk having his hot cocoa on the far side of the room. Father Abbot had acceded to the family's request that I spend the holidays with them, and as the small boy entered the room, wiping sleep from his half-opened eyes, I felt a tingling *knowing* that this moment, this little drama about to unfold, was the reason that I was here at this time. At times, God sends an angel to tap us on the shoulder ... sort of a heavenly heads-up when something special is coming.....

He entered and glared at his father (a drowsy glare, but a glare nonetheless). Father was wasting precious time. Santa might come at any moment, and find the room occupied. Who knew what catastrophe might ensue? He might not even descend the chimney! Look at that blazing hearth! Visions of singed Santa danced in his sleepy head.

His father switched on his largest smile, as his head turned from the ornament, to face the boy. The boy shuffled his feet as he trailed his binki, occasionally jerking a foot across the path of the ill-fated comforter. A bit tattered for indoor-outdoor wear, the binki literally went everywhere the boy went, which was now a place near the foot of the ladder to one side of the roaring fire.

The huge grandfather clock was still striking midnight when the boy circled the magic blanket around him in a pile, as was the custom when a Lesson was about to begin. I wondered what was coming next as I observed, still invisible to the boy. I sipped the steamy hot cocoa Forest had offered me and waited. From far below on the hardwood floors reflecting the fire in mirrors of wax, the boy stared balefully up the tall ladder toward his father.

The Dohrmann Christmas trees were a special tradition in the family. Mr. Dohrmann's many brothers and sisters, especially Bruce, Bill, Bob, Edith, and Barbara would invest a long evening of labor to assist the family in the annual decorating ceremony for the towering green pyramid. What made the Dohrmann trees famous in the neighborhood was their sheer size, reaching nearly to the arched ceilings above them. The Dohrmann Christmas tree for the year 1952 was almost twenty feet high, with room for the large angel on the top near the ceiling cross beam.

The children would point out in years to come that "their" tree was taller than the tree selected by the City of Fairfax, and the municipal tree was outside, while "their" tree was inside the house. This seemed to have relevance in the Olema Drive neighborhood of the time, but tonight a sleepy set of very blue eyes matched the fire with their heat, not caring a whit for the height of the tree, and a twin pair stared back from a very high ladder.

Mr. Dohrmann's twinkle that night was more complete than Santa's. It glowed out from the piercing lapis eyes that always held a magical love, tempered with a "wisdom river" as broad as the Mississippi.

As if the two had already been engaged in an extended conversation, Mr. Dohrmann "continued" speaking. I remember that he kept holding and staring at the large frosted ornament which reflected his image, multi-colored from the lights of the tree. From my hiding place in the shadows of the room I could see Mr. Dohrmann's expressions in the reflecting orb as he went on talking.....

"You know, Bee," (the boy could not pronounce his own name in those early years so the child had been labeled by the family for what he COULD pronounce. From age two, the first-born son had been known simply as BEE.) Writing these words now, I know the family, when they gather at Christmas time, continue this affectionate appellation, so that even the youngest of grandchildren call him, "Grandpa Bee."

Mr. Dohrmann held the bulb in one hand, and carried his pipe in tightened teeth as he twirled the sparkling bulb, using only his fingers. His other hand now and again steadied him on the ladder as he spoke...

"..... some folks think all these bulbs are real and hang on this tree to decorate the branches ... is that what YOU think Bee?"

"Dunno, Dad." (Always a safe answer.) If I leaned over and around, I could see that Bee's answer was muted by the insertion of his thumb, for a bit of security sucking, much like a nervous student wondering if the test was coming. The sleepy four-year-old mind was not certain what importance questions at midnight could possibly have, on a night when everyone knew SANTA CLAUS was coming. Bee wanted his Dad to damp the fire and go to sleep so that Santa would not be frightened off. He wished his brothers and sisters were here to help.

But his father went on talking......

"As I'm looking with my magic eyes....... what I see from up here, Bee, is not just ONE ornament.

"Nope, what I can see, if I look really, really hard into this one ornament, the only one that Circe chose to play with on the floor," (here he stared putting his face up close into the ornament itself) "....I see the dark hallway reflected in back of you, and the movement that took place when you stepped into our Christmas room."

The boy looked back over his shoulder......

Mr. Dohrmann then twisted the bulb as if that were going to give him a far better view.

I felt myself wishing I could see the magic inside the ornament a bit more closely than from my hiding place, although I could catch many reflections from my spot of vantage. I had placed my cocoa down so as to gain better concentration and a clearer view of the unexpected lesson.

"Yep," Mr. Dohrmann continued, "I see magic here, Bee. Because I have always known something special about our family Christmas tree. Know what that something special is, Bee?

"What do you think is special about our family Christmas tree?" (The giant elf leaned back on his ladder to look down upon the boy...still holding the magic orb high overhead in one hand.)

Now remember, the boy had just awakened from a sound sleep into a time of night that was never mated to his metabolism. This boy was and remains a Morning Person. He replied in a sleepy, rather sing-song voice, not quite giving vent to his impatience with a parent who just *wouldn't* go to bed....

"The tree is filled with our memories, Dad?"

"That's right, Bee. That's the answer. Only there is more to it. This tree is filled with our memories and because it was filled past the *critical point,*" (which was said with emphasis) "...the critical point, Bee...this Christmas tree IS ALIVE. I select each tree for our family, every Christmas, using all the power I have, so that I can seek and find the most ALIVE of all Christmas trees to place inside our home. Did you know this is how it is done?

Someone very little was shaking his head, NO, he did not know.

"Know why?" his father asked him, still fixed on his giant frosted orb of magic.

The boy, sitting partly on his binki, and partly on the hard wood floor, with reflections like tiny fireflies skittering all around him, again sent the "NO" signal from his bobbing head motion.

Bee was staring up at the GIANT on the ladder looking into this mystical ornamental world ... but all the boy said was:

"Dunno Dad," in an impossibly sleepy voice, that made him seem as he if were in a dream world, in a room with the blazing fireplace; the sparkling Christmas tree; and his father; only dreamy illusions, coming from a pre-Santa reverie "almost" remembered.

"I'll tell you why," his father continued, commanding firm attention with another twist on the bulb as if the rear side held an entirely new view of EVERYTHING.....

"Magic is waiting for ALL OF US, Bee, waiting for us in lots of ways." (and he was so animated and excited as he told his story that surely even Santa would wait.)

"You can only see my LIVING ornament ONE WAY from so far down where you sit. But from up here, Bee, it's not a big frosted crystal ornament at all. Why, it's actually a WINDOW ... a magic WINDOW into a world that IS more real than anything we think we know ....as REAL... why it's more like the world I know you children live in each and every day!

"In my CRYSTAL world," (he held the ornament in both hands, with his elbows on the top of the ladder, and stared as if in some trance induced by fairies) "I can see our fireplace and all the Christmas lights that are now spilling and twinkling all over our floor, Bee," Mr. Dohrmann never stopped spinning the Ornament over and over again, to stare at first one quarter, then another, in the large Christmas room, attempting to see all the Magical Views being displayed at once.....

"Why, I can see the aliveness of the tree in the back light of the fire. I can see the true TREE Bee, the Tree that is really ALIVE from up here.

(And the boy was standing now to get a better look, with his own hand on the ladder as he stretched his gaze).

"I can see, Bee, that every branch has a magic white light filled with all the memories of our family. Each and every branch, Bee." (and Mr. Dohrmann's voice caught in his throat, as if life were happening to him for the very first time this Christmas Eve. I noticed that Forest, by the side wall with a linen towel over his arm, was watching the drama in rapt attention).

Mr. Dohrmann continued with his Christmas story. "In fact, wait a minute ... yes, YES ... every NEEDLE has the light of LIFE ... and the needles are LAUGHING ... yes, they are LAUGHING ... because they are so happy you and your brothers and sisters took the time to honor their life, and to decorate them so that GOD would see how happy they were when serving our family and adding their light to our Christmas.....

"...Their life light, Bee, is so bright...so very bright and it jumps off every needle and kisses every

other object in the room. I wish you could see.....how
the needle light flows off every end point like tiny fingers to blend into the light sources all over the
room....for in the crystal ball Bee... everything I see is
at Christmas just another light source. A source light
for God like some magic playground.....all lit up."

.....More spinning of the ornament, and intense
staring....

"I can see reflections of Mom and all the kids
still lingering here inside, as they giggle and make the
popcorn strings, and place the tinsel up high and down
low...I can even FEEL it, Bee...I can FEEL the spirit
of CHRISTMAS here...it's leaping and spinning out of
this magic place..."

He shook his head but we both could tell it WAS
real, from the way he went back in and looked even
harder.....his body language simply confirmed that
what he was seeing and saying to us was REAL and
everything else was UNREAL.....

"Bee...wait...I can see you coming out of the dark
place in the hall ...and, yes, you are SHOWERED in
Magical Red, Green, Blue, White and all the colored
lights from the Christmas Tree, but you are so
bright...you seem to have a light from the fire behind
you that is flowing off you in all directions.....

"Wait....."(here Mr. Dohrmann pressed his face
to what seemed like the inside of the frosted ornament,
as he held his gaze only an eye lash away from the bulb
surrounded by fiery reflective light).......

"WAIT A MINUTE!!!"

The boy was frozen in total attention now, his
head arched back and his eyes wide as saucers, so involved had he become in his father's Christmas story.

Mr. Dohrmann moved the Ornament lower (because he knew the boy was not completely certain
whether his father was telling the truth)...one step at
a time as if he were carrying the most precious treasure in the Universe, always staring mystified into the

depth of the giant Frosted, Twirling Orb protected by a father's big, strong hands...one proud step on the ladder at a time....

Step. Down.

Step. Down.

Step carefully with one hand holding, step finally off the ladder ...one last foot (big as Santa and just as round) ....Bang! To the hardwood floor.

Slippers reaching to an inch of where the boy now stood staring up... squatting again, with his secure binki circled around him. He pulled the binki in for further protection as his eyes penetrated to the depths of the magic sphere his father was holding between them. Four eyes staring into a wonderland of magic.

Mr. Dohrmann squatted down...even lower...and lotus positioned into comfort next to the four-year-old, as though he were another child and this was the most natural thing in the world to do at midnight on Christmas Eve...

....and placing his arm as far as it would extend....Mr. Dohrmann held the ORB in front of the boy's eyes, sideways to the heat of the fireplace rippling over the scene...so that the Christmas Tree was on one side and the fireplace was behind the duo, while Forest and I remained unseen inside this Orb of Christmas magic.....

Mr. Dohrmann's words took on the emphasis of an important lesson as he continued ... "For the Christmas Ornament distorts light and image and creates its own world, Bee." ... something the young boy would soon discover.

"See YOUR OWN LIGHT IN THE CHRISTMAS WORLD .....?" as he spun the globe without moving his hand, or sparing even a glance toward the boy beside him.

"I see it, Dad." The sleepy voice was waking up now and the child's blue eyes held a fascination only the best teachers in the world will ever really experience.....

"It's MAGIC, Bee ... this light that God has put around you."

Forest and I both were transfixed, without noticing the cookies and milk on the hearth behind us for Santa, or any other thing in the room...for we were focused upon this father and son, who were seeing and feeling THE LIGHT... together at midnight.....

...The next day the boy would tell me that he saw inside this bright frosted ornament the most amazing sights ....

He told me, as naturally as if it were the story of putting on his shoes, that the fire had cast a light that ran off every part of his tiny young body. A light that flowed like foxfire in back-lit illumination, and spilled forward to mix with the twinkle and sparkle of the distorted and far-elongated lights of the Christmas tree needles, as they became one. He explained he could see that everything in the room was really alive with light, and that everything in the Christmas room had its own color, its own light, that pulsed and glowed. Every chair. The mantelpiece. Every item of furniture. Every piece of carpet. But the most intense lights were flowing from the Christmas Tree and from his father and himself, he explained. These lights would reach out to touch one another.

He felt it was like hugging. He said there was no fear anywhere in the lights. He said he would always see these lights at Christmas time, he was sure of it. But this came later.

At the time Mr. Dohrmann was telling his story softly to one boy, and in an empty room there were four eyes, a little space, and a frosted ornament in an oversized protective palm.

".....Real Magic, Bee, is YOU at Christmas time. Oh, I told you all about the Magic of Christmas many

times, but down deep in your heart you don't have room
to FEEL the REAL magic sometimes.

"I KNOW this is true.

"So, as your father, I want you to FEEL that the
lessons your Dad has given to you, each time you hear
one of your father's stories, are more important than
all the Christmas presents under the tree.

"Many children, Bee, don't have a father to tell
them stories at Christmas time, or at any time. And for
the millions of children who do have a father, somehow,
somewhere, along the way of a father's life their
MAGIC burned itself out, Bee, for these children never
receive a father's story, never at all. Not even once!"

At this point Mr. Dohrmann, even more fixed on
his Globe of Magic...simply and gently, without the
boy's knowing or thinking about it...for buried in the
magic looking glass world was a boy's soul...the father
lifted a tiny arm and stretched little fingers...and he
placed the ornament into those two little hands for the
very first time....and as he did so, he began to feel all
around the boy, patting the air as if something around
the boy could be moved into proper position...

Mr. Dohrmann's hands flew to their mission as
he continued to stare into the magic ornament...feeling
all around without so much as touching the boy, but
rather tracing his entire three dimensional being in the
firelight, the reflected light in the WONDERLAND
Orb, that was flowing from behind like fingers of the
aurora stream off the Northern Lights, jagged and
pulsing, rippling and surrounding the boy's entire body
with colors, mixed with the lights and colors of Christmas   as   they   shed   themselves   forward,
tremoring.....ALIVE!

The boy began to notice that when his father
moved his small hands for him that the light moved
as well...the light raced and shot from each tiny finger and reached out and touched the tree light and

connected to the light of all the needles, each on fire...and then the next hand...and in this orb...

(I shifted in my corner in the shadows to get closer as my eyes danced inside the vision that seemed to be unfolding.....)

I could SEE for the first time ... the TREE did have LIFE Lights, as Mr. Dohrmann would call them later, and the LIFE LIGHT was surrounding every NEEDLE just like he had told us....you could see it so clearly in the reflection in the ornament....first as if each needle had a jacket of ice, one might mistake for only ice, until it MOVED and spread to become unmistakable LIGHT.....

And then the father's free hand grasped the tip of one of the boughs that was closest, to move it up and down, whimsically ... and the light from the needles SHOT forward and grabbed hold of the reflected light that was shooting off the boy's fingers and for a MOMENT the communication in that room HELD, became an actual FEELING....a tingling.

A feeling of ONENESS with all creation....a feeling of being connected....a feeling of what is the SAME about all life, all creation...*only* of what is the same...the light, the source...the illumination....and we watched the boy turn his hands in amazement as he saw the light shimmering over his arms and out from his fingers to touch and become ONE with the light from the LIVING Christmas Tree.....for me I know it was as close to magic as I have ever felt in all my life......

I came off my chair and spent some time looking at my own hands, with their impossible light source zooming into and around the room, objects and tree needles all made ONE at the center, with a single magic Christmas orb, held in the hands of a tiny boy at midnight.

Smiling his grand beaming smile warmer than any fire.....

Still moving a new branch or two.....his father spoke:

"This is the LIGHT of CHRISTMAS, my son ... and it is always the LIGHT OF GOD.

"For all living things to be SEEN they also must REFLECT the LIGHT of the LORD ... however only a special FEW can ever see the true wonderful light of Christmas. So few have the sight. Very few.

"For most the SIGHT of Christmas light is hidden from them.

"Most will never find the truth we feel and see this Christmas, Bee. These will never see...they will never know.

"But the Christmas Light is always here, all the same, always touching them, for it matters not whether they see the LIGHT of CHRISTMAS. For the needles of life are always ALIVE as are all sights in our Christmas world, and each will always be laughing in their own true service to God, and to each other.

"One of the Ornaments each year, usually only ONE, Bee, will become your magic WINDOW to the true inner light of Christmas.

"But the real MAGIC, my son, is YOU ... for what you can't know is a father's feeling on this night. For your father, the only gift that you could possibly bring to me that would fill my heart so completely full, is the vision of MY SON and HIS LIFE FORCE touching the MAGIC LIGHT of CHRISTMAS as together we are sitting here on the floor, a son and his Dad at midnight, and KNOWING

"that MY son can SEE the one true LIGHT of Christmas with me...

"You, my son, represent a great LIGHT in my life and the light you see this Christmas Eve, is only ONE of the many lights of Christmas..."

".....there are eight more lights in your brothers and sisters....and your mother is a huge light that fills the room like the sun...as all these lights come into our

Christmas room, whether they know it or not the Light of Christmas,

"this Christmas,

"our Christmas,

"flows off THEIR hands and fingers and faces and feet as it spreads around the room to touch and mingle and to become ONE LIGHT...

"We are so lucky, Bee, because we have a real magic here that we call our Family.....the lesson being that FAMILY is a blending of our lights, yours and mine....your mom's and your brothers' and your sisters'...Forest's and Brother Al's and all our Family Lights......just as you discovered this Christmas...in a magic orb that hangs high on a special family Christmas tree.

"This is the one present you can unwrap all your life, Bee. The gift of your family and the light that is contained inside...a light...to shelter, protect, guide and nurture in all the Christmases to come.....enriched by your family MEMORIES."

Then Mr. Dohrmann wiggled all the way in back of the boy. The youngster was going to turn when his father said, "Don't turn..." and he reached both his great hands over the boy's head and held the MAGIC ORB out in front of the four year old's eyes.....and began a final time to turn the Christmas Orb once again......

.....As Bee told it later, he remembered the image exploded into his vision of two silvery silhouettes, two auras, two blended beings of light and color expanding, moving...and with his arms extended the LIGHT along his arms and from the ORB shot in pulsing tones over and surrounding the father and the boy's own arms. The light of his Father's own body was pulsing and encompassed the boy's. I could see tiny hands resting on a father's secure redwood arms. Bee said that each light would be broadly defined in the teacher's movement so that one could see the boy's light reflected, dancing within his father's own brilliance...shimmering together as ONE and as TWO... as he had said.....becoming one light....

From my corner it seemed that all four of us were bathed in a search light of the white illumination which filled the room, to slowly fade to a warmer hue that lingered....when Mr. Dohrmann spoke....

"The real Magic is that YOU, my SON, are the LIGHT within ME for all my Christmases...all the Christmases I have known or ever will know...for all our light together is the LIGHT OF THE LORD....... and it is THIS truth that IS the Spirit of my Christmas." (And still he twirled the orb in front of his son.)

For moments that seemed much longer they just sat holding their arms and fingers entwined, in silence. Bee remembers he touched the ball once or twice. He remembered that as he turned to look up, his teacher was crying.

I recall how Bee reached up to hug the big man and how small the little boy looked in those great arms as the Master held his oldest boy tightly....was it the boy or the monk that was now four years old....?

At last, I turned to see the boy moving back down the hall with its dark forbidding fringes ...

I could see Mr. Dohrmann once again on the ladder as if the entire evening had never taken place.....

....but he took one last look at his firstborn son before putting his frosty Christmas ball carefully back upon the tree ... when he said ... never turning to look ... as if to no one in particular......

"....KNOW how Christmas FEELS my son ... go to sleep now and dream about the living lights of memory...but, Bee, NEVER forget our Christmas story.....

"For what is important is not how Christmas looks to others ... the lesson is how you and you alone will KEEP the FEELING of Christmas.....

"...for as you grow into adults you must choose how you will keep FEELING for the Christmas Lights as precious GIFTS for your own families.

"Tonight is only one memory, wrapped as a gift from a tired old father for his eldest son. A gift that you may one day, many years later, open each and every Christmas, to knowingly look inside, and to SEE, once again the true LIGHTS OF CHRISTMAS........

"Simply come back in your mind, to this ladder, this night, this tree, this hearth and fireplace, with Brother Al sipping hot chocolate in the corner of the room and Forest close beside him, (I thought he had forgotten our presence) and you will always remember the LIGHTS.....of THIS CHRISTMAS NIGHT......

"...and then you will keep your knowing for how CHRISTMAS is supposed to FEEL!

"....now everyone ... take the FEELING of CHRISTMAS ... and go to sleep......

Santa Claus is coming......."

The cat Circe, sitting on the large overstuffed sofa, yawned, stretched and went immediately back to sleep.

With all of us following only moments behind......

Chapter 10

Miracles
& Magnets

OF MIRACLES AND MAGNETS

After a warm summer dinner in 1959, we had retired to the family room of the Fairfax estate. I loved these evenings especially for their perfect temperature as the earth released the fragrances the sun had warmed, and the cooler breezes from the bay gave just the right hint of tangy sea-scent. I held special appreciation for the fact that the enormous windows were always open on all sides of the Dohrmann home. The ceiling height was impressive, even in the Apartments, framed by the exposed hand-hewn redwood beams which gave a feeling of great age and solidity. In later years when the Fairfax home had burned to the ground, I would be saddened with the knowledge that replacement was impossible. By then the family had moved away, and we never returned, outside our memories, to the home on Bay and Olema Drives.

A breeze was coming through the large family room as iced tea was served. There was a scampering in the lesson room as little feet trotted back, ready for their father, recently returned from travels, to complete the evening.

As each of the children completed their essential portion of the half-moon circle around Mr. Dohrmann, whose pipe, after repeated tampings and great clouds of smoke, had finally expired. He turned his attention to the evening's work.

As if a minor earthquake antedated the movement, Mr. Dohrmann struggled with an "oooof" groan into a stretch, with his hands on his lower back. The spectacle of this large, plump man rising from the seat of his overstuffed easy chair would have made a superb subject for a small, drama-laden movie by one of those artists of the film who delight in vignettes of the minuscule details of life. Slowly, as though the effort were far too great for him, he went behind his chair where he kept "story props" for each lesson. Usually such "story props" were in a large sack or grocery bag.

Pulling and sliding a bag around my feet, and past Mrs. Dohrmann's chair, never looking up, Mr. Dohrmann laboriously moved the bag to dead center in front of his own position, as if lead bars were contained within. The labor was greatly exaggerated, but was perfect in holding the attention of nine young children. Once the "story prop" bag was properly centered, with a release of air like ballast from a blimp, "Oiehhh," Mr. Dohrmann settled into his soft chair once again. The entire "set up" took only moments, but in his way, Mr. Dohrmann had stretched the impression of time spent.

Still not really taking notice of anyone else in the room, and with all of us fixed in silent stares, he placed his hands deep into the large "story" sack. For an instant it seemed that nothing happened. It took several moments for the completion of whatever task he had set for himself to reach its apex (all the while the bag bulged this way and that in reply to his fingers within), at which point he looked up and smiled at the family.

And then with one motion he raised his hands directly out in front of him. As he did so, we noted that he had tied a cord to each of his index fingers on either hand ... one on the left and one on the right.

At the end of each cord, dangling and swinging freely, were two large silver spheres. Each sphere was about the size of a lemon, perhaps a bit smaller. Each was polished so that the reflection of the entire family danced in each smooth sphere. They dangled like mirrors showing off the cloudy sky and mountain backdrop through the open, ceiling-high windows that lined the entire far wall of the lesson room.

Very directly he began to speak....

"Children ... do you know what I am holding in my hands?"

(Following some of the customary body scrunching, and whispering, and giggling and so forth, Terry answered)...

"Two silver balls on two cords, Dad ....?"

Mr. Dohrmann frowned, and we knew the answer was wholly inadequate.

"But what about the silver balls, Terry? What makes them unique?"

(Again some further whispering and coaching. Pam, the next oldest, raised her hand.....)

"Father, the two balls are identical.....?"

A beaming smile from Mr. Dohrmann......

"Yes, children, each of my silver spheres IS precisely identical.

"Even more than you may ever suspect.

"But that's not the lesson."

(Here he jerked first one ball and then the other so that it would swing like a pendulum back and forth and connect to the other with a WHACK, and the WHACKs continually emphasized what Mr. Dohrmann had to tell us that night.)

WHACK.

"You see, children, while teaching over at the University, I had the Bureau of Standards and Measures work on each of these two spheres. In fact, I chose them especially for our lesson tonight. Do you know why?"

WHACK!

(Tiny heads shaking no).

"Because Children, each sphere, the one on my left and the one on my right, is the same. Exactly the same!"

WHACK!

"In every way, the same!"

WHACK!

"The weight of both spheres is the same."

WHACK.

"The circumference of both spheres is the same."

WHACK.

"The number of molecules in each sphere is the same."

WHACK.

"The number of atoms in each sphere is the same."

WHACK!!!!

"So children ... what is DIFFERENT about ONE of my special spheres?"

It was at times like this, when the children were whispering, that I became somewhat uncomfortable with the notion of how grateful I was not to be included in the teacher's question and answer sessions. I found I was staring at each of the Silver Spheres, with no idea in the world what could be unique about one or the other.

"But WHAT makes one sphere unique and the other just a regular sphere?" Mr. Dohrmann was beaming at the consternation his question was bringing forth from the huddle of children engaging in debate before him.

After much nodding, Susan spoke.

"We don't know, Dad....." Mr. Dohrmann's favorite answer.

"Are you sure?" Mr. Dohrmann asked one last time. He still held the spheres directly out in front of him, WHACKING every second or two.....

After some minor additional discussion among the nine,

"We are sure, Dad, we just don't KNOW what makes ONE of the spheres different if they're both the same, in every way you can measure....."

Mr. Dohrmann slowly looked from one to the other and then moved his right hand higher for the first time ... making the sphere on the right rise higher in space.....

"Children ... the sphere in my right hand is MAGNETIZED....."

(Which caused a buzz through the clustered children.)

As Mr. Dohrmann held the spheres closer without the energy to create a WHACK of separation, the spheres came together as magnets do ... each yearning to touch the other.

Mr. Dohrmann pulled on his right hand until they came apart ... and then placed the sphere suspended from his left hand back into the sack and untied his finger, while he extended once again his right hand, from which the MAGNETIC sphere still dangled.....

"So children ... what is different about the sphere on the right?"

The children knew a little about magnetism, so they did their best to answer ... all in vain.

"Children, would you like for me to tell YOU the answer?"

(All heads nodding.)

"Children, the magnet in my right hand contains properties that physicists describe with great care. These scientists chose their words carefully. They use just the right words when they describe universal principles.

"The magnet is a universal principle, children.

"Although the sphere you are seeing now is exactly the same as the other sphere which is in the sack, it is also unique. Why?

"Remember: Physicists choose their words VERY precisely, children, and physicists don't say that the magnetized sphere CREATES or that the sphere GENERATES, rather they say that the sphere on the right

"DISPLAYS

a

Power.

"And the power being displayed is the POWER of ATTRACTION.

"This power RADIATES in all directions ... always with the same force, and attracts all objects, in equal manner, that fall into its POWER.

".....But that IS NOT the lesson.....

"So tell me, children, why are YOU like the sphere on my right?"

Susan again, with, "We don't know, Dad."

"You are sure?"

(Little heads nod in unison.)

"Let us look into WHY the sphere in my right hand DISPLAYS a *POWER.*

"Even though the sphere in my right hand is exactly the same as the sphere my left hand held, the only difference is the FACT that the sphere in my right hand was MAGNETIZED.

"But what does this mean?

"The answer IS that the sphere in my right hand has all its MOLECULES in alignment."

Here Mr. Dohrmann nodded to Mrs. Dohrmann, and she displayed a large photo book, with an illustration of the molecules in perfect ALIGNMENT as opposed to randomly displayed molecules.

Mr. Dohrmann continued.....

"And I believe my children are like MAGNETS of GOD using universal principles.....

"I believe that my children, each one of you....."

And he walked around the half moon, holding the sphere in front of each child's face, while he stood behind them, so each could see themselves in the perfect reflection of the magnetized sphere.

"…..Are individual little MAGNETS for GOD…..

"You, my children, are magnets….."

"And I believe," (as Mr. Dohrmann settled back in his chair, though holding his sphere well out in front)…..

"That YOU display a *POWER*.

"When you become adults, things may not always go just the way you want them to inside your life." Here Mr. Dohrmann swung a circle in the air with his sphere, as a symbol of the circle of the life each child would pass through. I noticed that the candlelights were coming on brighter as the room darkened, and began to add their own dance to the reflection on the surface of the sphere.

"You may have all sorts of unforeseen challenges along the adult journey of your lives. Challenges your mother and I could never imagine as we look upon you this night.

"And through these times, your mother and I, although you can't imagine it today, may no longer be here to make it safe for you, or to make the bad things go away.

"You will have to deal with challenges in your life, one-by-one, all by yourself.

"Even your brothers and sisters may not be around to help you on the day that you need your help the most," which caused some head turning back and forth among the children.

"For you see, children, when things are not going just the way you desire, I ask that you remember this lesson, on this evening, with your father and mother and Brother Al and our family intact together.

"Remember the lesson of the spheres.

"And when you have challenges in the way of your life, I want you to look INSIDE rather than OUTSIDE as to what might be the cause of each challenge.

"I want you to look INSIDE to see if the molecules inside YOU are in ALIGNMENT to the will of GOD.

"I want you to test the power of your own surrender to God.

"I want my children to hear the WHACK that flows from having all their molecules IN perfect alignment to the will of God.

"Are your molecules in ALIGNMENT with the values we have shared here, inside this family?

"Are your molecules in ALIGNMENT with GOD and the values you have been taught?

"Are your FEELING molecules in ALIGNMENT right now?

"Are your WORD molecules in ALIGNMENT?

"Are your ACTION molecules in ALIGNMENT?

"For I believe, children, you will always find that if you fail to receive what you most desire in life, you will also discover somewhere on the inside, your molecules are OUT OF ALIGNMENT.

"And if you will put your molecules back into alignment, I also believe.....

"You WILL display a POWER.....

And the power will be the power of divine attraction.....

"As you manifest all that is good and wholesome and perfect about your lives and your future.

"So, as you share your problems in life as brothers and sisters all growing up together, I want each of you to always look first to the INSIDE and ask one another.....

"Are your molecules in DIVINE ALIGNMENT?

"For if they are,
"For if YOU ARE,

YOU *WILL* DISPLAY A *POWER!*

"Now run off to bed ... like powerful little magnets!"

.....And once again ... they did!

Chapter 11

Oneness

THE CONCEPT OF ONENESS

That last Thanksgiving was like a summons. Mrs. Dohrmann had alerted my Abbot that most certainly, due to Mr. Dohrmann's illness, this was likely to be the LAST Thanksgiving for him. I had been cordially invited to join the entire family for the Thanksgiving feast. It was 1982.

The family arrived from the many states in which they lived. The nine had their own children, "ankle-biters," as Mr. Dohrmann referred to them. Always his favorites. Always tireless energy for them.

Throughout the dinner, we kept down the talk of how he looked. The chemotherapy had taken a huge toll. The four surgeries had not stopped the ravages of cancer. Still, he was beaming; "No pain, no gain," he joked, lightening the pain for all of us, at God alone knows what cost to himself.

He wore a Parisian artist's beret on top of his injured, hairless head. He faked the energy for every grandchild; the elders knew it was sorely taxing for the man.

The Greenbrae house was a two-story wonderful place of light. Wide vistas of San Francisco Bay with sweeping views of Mount Tamalpais made each window a master's landscape. After the feast, everyone retired into the large living room as extra chairs were brought in. The children all sat on the floor, while the Mr. Dohrmann gave a thrilling performance on his grand piano.

Finally, as the last notes died ... he rose up with his cane and hobbled over to the same giant chair that the Fairfax home had made so memorable to all of us. Sitting alone facing us, with his back to the fireplace ... ignoring the advice of legions of doctors one more time, he tamped down and lit his inseparable companion.

And smiled.

"Are you children ready for a lesson?" he said beaming ... looking down solely at the ankle-biters in the half-moon circle before him, and ignoring his own nine, sitting in sofas and chairs behind them.

Tiny heads nodded, "Yes, Grandpa....."

"Good.

"That's good ... because the lesson is ready for YOU!"

Here he rose and brought several large brown "story bags" from behind his chair, much to the delight of the little ones on the floor.

I noticed a circle of candles had been lit around the circumference of the room, now playing on the white furniture and walls. I recall thinking how I liked this new Lesson Room as much as I had enjoyed the one in the Fairfax home.

Reaching into the large brown "story bags," he began to take out ... shoes.

Shoes of all different types.

Which he proceeded to fan out in front of us.

Finally when he was done, and a great assortment of various pairs of shoes, in all sizes and shapes, were formally presented before us, he asked:

"Can any of you tell me what is the SAME about all these shoes?" ... holding his cagey smile in check as he once again seemed absorbed solely in the tamping of his pipe.

A good deal of discussion next ensued, including substantial study of the shoes before the group, without much in the way of outcome....

"...We don't know what's the same about the shoes," said more than one grandchild. "They all look different to us, Grandfather....."

"Yes, well, that is not the lesson, is it?

"Let me tell you what makes these shoes the same ... which is the featured content of tonight's lessons.

"I am sure you all know, simply to make the doctors right, as they hate so to be wrong, this is probably my last Thanksgiving. I want to thank all of you for making it also, MY BEST.

"I love you all so.

"And knowing the end is coming, I thought I'd better tidy up some things ... important things.

"Things I don't want forgotten when I am gone ... things like my prayer center for ONENESS we started a few years ago. Remember when our family and a few friends were the only members?" He looked at his children, receiving confirming nods from them.

"Well the prayer centers for ONENESS now operate in thirty-two countries, children ... did you KNOW that?"

Little heads shook, "No, Granddad....."

"Well, they DO.

"And it all started right here in San Francisco.

"For our guests, let me explain. The Prayer Centers for ONENESS meet in a chosen house of worship for a different religion once a month, every month. Leaders from every congregation and denomination are invited to attend. The meetings take two hours.

"Meetings include a group prayer at the beginning and end. Everyone sits in circles, and in larger meetings there are many circles. One person starts and everyone shares around the circle. But what do they share?"

".....They share one idea that is THE SAME about the faiths of the world, Grandpa?"

"That's right, perfect! The Prayer centers on ONENESS, focuses on what is the SAME about each faith ... and no one thinks about anything that is different, for at least two short hours.

"As it is likely to be my very last Thanksgiving, it is also likely to be my very last PRAYER meeting on Oneness, so I asked my twin brother Jerry to take me to the San Francisco Center last Sunday.

"Which brings me to the story of these shoes in front of you tonight."

The candlelight made the vast array of shoes shine with colors and contrasts I had not noticed before.

"As your Uncle Jerry fussed over me like some damaged bird-ling, we arrived at the Muslim mosque, the site of this Sunday's ONENESS service. As your Uncle Jerry and I were preparing to enter I noticed an elderly woman, who was grumbling and obviously changing her mind about attending this month's Oneness Service.

"I went over and introduced myself, to inquire whether I might help." Mr. Dohrmann was drawing mightily on his pipe, alive like a dragon with his tale.

"I came to find the woman was a delightful Jewish mother, who was attending her FIRST Oneness Session at the insistence of her son. She complained that all this ONENESS mumbo-jumbo was lost on her. She was eighty-two, 'for crying out loud' ... as she phrased it.

"She had a religion that for five thousand years already had it right, starting virtually every prayer with PRAISED BE THE LORD GOD IS ONE ... why did she need THIS to tell her about Oneness? Why did her SON think she needed this?

"Then she had to come halfway 'cross town, to this Holy MUSK' (I corrected her to know it as mosque) ... and she didn't see anything really all that much Holy about it, either.

"And now her son, already inside, was waiting to meet her. When she arrived, she gathered from all the shoes on the mats by the door, that she was SUP-POSED to ENTER with her shoes off. So she had decided ... NOT TODAY, BUDDY BOY ... and proceeded to enter the MOSK with her shoes on.....

"However, the sharp clicking noises of her heels brought on sharp criticisms ... from the security persons INSIDE the MOSK who forced her back outside, until such time as she took her shoes off. Oh, she had taken her shoes off. But she was now putting them back on.

"This was ridiculous.

"This was not for her.

All the while Mr. Dohrmann had simply sat down beside her, listening intently. And as she was putting HER SHOES on, Mr. Dohrmann was taking HIS SHOES off.

Curious and noting he never tried to debate with her ... she asked him, "So are you going to this ONENESS THING?"

Mr. Dohrmann had stopped taking off his left shoe, to look directly at her, as he began his reply:

"I thought I'd give it a try, Mrs. Silverstein.

"You may have noticed I'm not doing too well in the health department these days.

"That's my twin brother, Jerry Dohrmann, over there; now, he is the healthy one ... I want you to meet him!"

And Mrs. Silverstein shook hands with Alan Dohrmann's twin brother Jerry ... who already had his shoes off ... as Jerry went inside.

"Mrs. Silverstein," Mr. Dohrmann had continued, "... there is a lesson here somewhere. See all these shoes. They are all different. Different sizes. Different colors. Different ways of going on and off.

"When a man is dying, Mrs. Silverstein, he begins to feel the whole world is a Holy place. This mosque, the street over there, a park ... taking off my shoes is the easy part. FINDING OUT why so many different pair of shoes might be alike in some way is God's mystery.

"Perhaps you came here today to TEACH rather than to learn? Did you ever think of that?"

Mrs. Silverstein looked at the man sitting on the mat for a few moments before she, without announcement, sat down and took off her shoes. Together they walked into the mosque, arm in arm.

"Looking back on it, children, it must have been very new for Mrs. Silverstein. She was bent over, in her black mourning gown, hardly looking at the huge columns rising to the sky. It was so quiet. The rumblings of small discussions roared like distant thunder from somewhere in the belly of the vast interior of the ageless mosque. It was a long walk for Mrs. Silverstein. Her only words to me were said when she took her place in the great circle of ONENESS service that day, as she looked up, lifted the veil from her hat, and said with penetrating eyes, 'Thank you, Mr. Dohrmann.' She faced the group and her son with resolve.

"Staring back at her she would find a Catholic priest, a friendly Jewish rabbi, a Baptist minister, various Protestant ministers, Evangelical preachers, deacons, Buddhist monks, a Hindu Brahmin priest, Muslim mullahs, and Native American shamans. One Hawaiian kahuna sat next to Mrs. Silverstein, contrasting his almost three hundred pounds with her ninety.

"And it began.

"Everyone sharing a ritual of ONENESS from their faith, that united us all. Talk and prayer about what was the SAME in our humanness, our beliefs.

"Just before Mrs. Silverstein was to finish the circle, a young woman who had passed us to sit on my right, rose to share. She had tears in her eyes, obviously moved by the prayer work of the others.

"She explained that in her liturgy, the chant was the message. She felt compelled to share her gift of CHANTING with our Oneness family. After this short explanation, she broke into rocking back and forth, and chanting in a magical musical manner. Her song filled the mosque for almost ten minutes.

"There was no applause when she was finished.

"There were no words for her song.

"Many in the circles had been moved to tears, so lifting and light were her words, so powerful and entrancing the voice with which she had blessed us.

"But then it was time to complete the circle, and Mrs. Silverstein was helped to stand, after which she faced the group. There was a power in the way she slowly undid her veil and removed her small black hat. She placed the little hat in my lap, as she undid a hair pin that let bands of long, gray hair fall to her shoulders, transforming her appearance. One could see how lovely and special the younger Mrs. Silverstein had been, to, even now, command such fineness in her sharp features.

"She ended looking directly at her son, halfway across the circle. She lifted her bony hand and pointed like some witch from Oz, at her forty-year-old as she began:

" 'HIM....

" 'If not for HIM ... I would not have attended your service for ONENESS.

" 'After all, I am eighty-two.

" 'You are just children.

" 'I feel like the only adult in the room.'

"Then moving her withered arthritic hand in my direction, she pointed down to me.

" 'AND HIM ... if he had not been kind enough to share a few corrective words with an old woman at the door, my shoes would still be on my feet, and I would be walking far away from here.

" 'However, as it is,

" 'I arrived, no accidents, and I'm here, because of HIM and HIM,' and she pointed again.

" 'Then as you shared, I thought how irrelevant all the information is.

" 'That the information you share here won't change anything.

" 'Not even one point of view.

" 'A human condition forged through generations of focusing attention, RELIGIOUS attention, only on WHAT IS DIFFERENT about each of us.

" 'Like some Lilliputian story, where one society slaughters another because their hatwear is different. One wears pots and pans. One wears vegetables on their heads. Or where one society performs the racial cleansing because one group opens its eggs from the small end at the top rather than the large end at the bottom. Or a society where six million Jews are slaughtered because they read a book from back to front and wear a little hat when they pray.

" 'I thought as you went around the circle with your words, "Look for what is the essence here. After all, they have been meeting for years. They know some things. Find their essence and see if you can understand the truth within it."

" 'I had about given up searching for such truth from all the various words and sincere sharings. I could only see you picking up, going back, each into your DIFFERENT worlds, having very little new to take with you that was truly the SAME.

" 'In fact, when this young lady here began to chant, I thought, "Here it comes. The reason to rise up and leave altogether" because all the feeling of what was different came crashing over me.

" 'And I was not alone in my feelings, you see.

" 'Oh, I saw it on your face, Rabbi, and you too, Mr. Baptist Minister.

" 'The patience of the monks was also tried, as you blocked out your feelings to retain a focus for what was real and true about our circle.

" 'But then, during her long chant, something quite profound came over me.

" 'While you were watching her, I looked up. And as I did, I noticed the most pure white dove was hovering, without its wings flapping at all, just there,' and she pointed to the great dome of the mosque, open to a morsel of sky.

" 'I watched the Dove as if the bird were suspended by the psalm notes of the young lady's chant ... floating for an eternity above our heads.

" 'It created a profound feeling for me.

" 'When I looked down again, I almost gasped.

" 'Somehow my eyes had in their new focus of light, failed to reel you all back in.

" 'For when I looked back down all I could see were feet.

" 'I thought, "Well, it's dark here, and there is a dust stirring in the shallow sunlight." I looked around the circle and the focus of my attention was on your feet.

" 'Of course, you must remember how tiny this old Jewish widow woman is. My eyes were almost at the level of your feet already.

" 'However, I came to understand, as the chant was rushing over me, that my soul was doing the looking for me.

" 'For the question that was being asked of me was profound.

" 'I was being asked, as if from the DOVE, as though a voice commanded me to reply.....

" 'Where is the Jewish foot?"

" 'Where are the Baptist feet in this circle?"

" 'Where is a Buddhist foot?"

" 'Where is a Protestant foot?"

" 'Where is a Catholic foot?"

" 'Where is Muslim foot?"

" 'I looked around the feet that seemed to be staring me straight in the face.

" 'As I looked, I went around the circle more than once.....

" 'Looking only at the feet.....

" 'A circle of feet ... all pointing towards me.

" 'I heard the voice again, "Where is the foot you seek?"

" 'As the chant continued, I began to notice tears had come into my eyes.

" 'For I found, that in this room, it was impossible to find the difference that was before me.

" 'What I found was, what was THE SAME about the circle.

" 'It may have been my imagination ... but when I chose to next look up, the white Dove was still hovering. My eyes found the bird hovering directly in the sun spot above us. I had to squint and shade my eyes to see. Still the chant rose.

" 'The instant my eyes fixed upon the bird, its wings began to move and it lifted over the mosque ... hovered only a second more and was gone. However, as it drifted over the lip of the mosque a voice seemed to call within me; it said:

"THE LORD GOD SEES ONLY FEET"

" 'Again I looked at the feet in the room, as our young lady completed her chant. And as I looked I began chanting, "The Lord God sees feet, the Lord God sees only feet."

" 'I next considered how we in our human view put so much more into our vision. We begin as we place our shoes upon our feet, to make each FOOT that God is seeing in his ONENESS as different as we can make it.

" 'Then we place our different clothings and trappings upon ourselves. So that even our appearance is as different as we can make it.

" 'We invest so little of life THINKING of what is the magnificent SAME about each and everyone of us. That which binds us.

" 'Yet wherever we go, wherever we journey in life, we move toward our destinations as ONE using our FEET to transport us to the place we seek. If our feet are damaged we use our hands, then the Lord God sees only HANDS.

' 'So I suppose if a newcomer has anything to share with you, it is this:

" 'As you leave this mosque, and place your shoes upon your feet.....

" 'Whenever you are in your churches.....

" 'Your offices.....

" 'Your cars......

" 'Your streets, your stadiums, your shopping malls,

" 'Whenever you are alone or in groups,

" 'And your spirit tells you to be calm to visit with God,

" 'Perhaps you might begin your prayer

" 'Your thoughts that the LORD GOD IS ONE,

" 'With the memory of our circle on this Sunday,

" 'Beside some very magic men and women,

" 'And an old, broken 82-year-old lady

" 'Who has, with hardly any eyesight at all,

" 'Imagined she heard some angels call her,

" 'And created the illusion of a very particular white dove.....

" 'That delivered an intuition, an inspiration, an inner truth for knowing.....

" 'That indeed.....

" 'THE LORD GOD SEES ONLY FEET.

" 'And if we can hold our vision on our FEET perhaps, yes...

"'We will come to worship together as we learn to know.....

" 'THE LORD GOD *IS* ONE!

" 'and the circle is complete.....' "

_____

After pausing ... smoking ... staring ... Mr. Dohrmann kneeled down, and began to take each of the pairs of shoes and to return them to the brown paper bag. And then a special thing happened. One of Mr. Dohrmann's youngest grandchildren (aged three) began to take off her shoes. She didn't say anything. She just took them off, walked over, put them into the bag and walked back to her place on the carpet.

Then another.

And another.

Until the nine and their children had all taken their shoes off ... and the bag was so full another was brought and it was filled and removed ... and the children and grandchildren sat with their feet toward their father and grandfather ... and without words he looked at them.

As he was looking, a very old lady dressed in black came out of Mr. Dohrmann's study, and very slowly, with her hands bent and damaged with age, she unstrapped her shoes and took them off, one by one, and sat down beside Mr. Dohrmann's easy chair. She slowly stretched her feet out ... and then she reached over to take off Mr. Dohrmann's slippers, which she placed beside her shoes.

Then Mrs. Silverstein looked up and said to the children and grandchildren.....

"Happy Thanksgiving, Children.....
"...and THAT is The Lesson....."

And she held Mr. Dohrmann's hand, as they brought out the pumpkin pie ... to a perfect circle of FEET!

Chapter 11

Thirty-One
Flavors

THIRTY-ONE FLAVORS FOR THE SOUL

In 1983, I was at the Dohrmann home in Greenbrae, long after the Fairfax estate had been sold, long after the flames had eventually taken it, and many memories for the Nine and one old, tired monk had drifted into the Marin County sky.

On this wonderfully fresh and warm winter afternoon in February, Mr. Dohrmann was dying.

It had been an amazing time. The children were all present. We had been retelling the "stories" for some time. Over a period of weeks, the old sage had fooled us, and almost passed on many occasions.

The last time, he had been in a coma for some weeks. The only nourishment had been the intravenous feed that held his lifeline to the temporal world. The last rites had been administered by Father Frank Lacy, the family's favorite priest. Frank had been crying when he came out.

However, Mr. Dohrmann didn't die. In fact, although we had to use a small crane to move him from his hospital bed in the large bedroom sitting area, he rested comfortably in his wheel chair. His eyes were sparkling as he came coma-free for the first time in many weeks.

He could see his beloved Mount Tamalpais through his bedroom window, this mountain that he had loved to hike upon. He could see his Marin County and his San Francisco Bay where he loved to sail. And he could survey all nine children, and many more the number of grandchildren, sitting in front of him, as if a lesson were about to begin.

Sally completed feeding him an enormous dish of his favorite dessert. Some remained on the corner of his mouth which could still blister the air with the warmth of his smile ... even now.

I noted more than any other feeling that day, how his first words held such humor. The man, for all of us, was simply amazing. He, who had taught us so well how to live in life, was now showing the entire family how to be magnificent in the passing from life. Some stories are impossible to translate, but, dear reader, know that the feeling held in his words that day conveyed entire seas of information to the children.

"Children," his very first word in six weeks, said with a full smile and an impossible elf-twinkle in the eye, leaning forward in the restraining straps of the wheel chair, "you probably know that I have been ready to leave for a long, long time."

(Some words of comfort, some nodding and much more silence than was typical as he looked into the soul that was his family.)

"If it were up to me, I would be serving on the other side this day.

"I have said good-bye, in my private way, to each and every one of you. And there really is nothing more I need to tell you.

"And some of you, I know, realize I have been gone far, far away these past many weeks, leaving you only with the idea you must get used to, that soon even this physical form will fade away, as the work continues on a higher plane.

"In fact, I want you to embrace this idea with joy. After all I have taught you for long enough, that it is now your time to teach, rather than study, the lessons."

Huge smile as he looked upon each one of his precious children. They had come from five states, to be together with their father, in this ritual. And even as the time dragged on, they stayed for a period of weeks. And waited. I found it impossible to leave, myself.

"Children," he said, absolutely beaming, "you probably wonder, why it is that I have come back at all?"

All heads nodding.....

"There is a simple lesson in this 'coming back' that I wish for you to learn for everyday living.

"While I was offering my service on the other side, a thought came upon me that was so powerful, it restrained my ability to let go and pass forward into my next work. And the thought was this:

".....*Children ... they simply do NOT have ICE CREAM over there.....*"

And I remember he almost choked as he began laughing so hard, and recalling so completely his decision.

"Children, I have come back to have one MORE bowl of ICE CREAM!

"Today I have ordered that the doctors take off the life support, and as I place myself upon this swishing air bed you have created for me, I will sleep and remain this time in higher service. I only ask that you are complete in all your dreams and memories for your father, knowing that in his life, the magic is, that when it came to ice cream, he, at the very end, had finally had just the right amount.....

"It was enough.

"And like each flavor and every single scoop, you children with your gazes upon me now, are just like flavors of ice cream to my soul. For in my soul, so close now to the other side, I hold the taste of you, the color of your aura, the full measure of you all, and it is this, this INSIDE ICE CREAM that I will take with me when I do my higher work in just a little while from now.

"Now run off to be with your mother while they put me back to rest, and leave Bernhard with me, as I have one final lesson I wish for him to receive before I sleep; and Brother Al, you remain beside me too, as there are some words I wish to give to you as the family begins its new journey, in new ways, with my guidance expressed in new forms."

As they each came to kiss their father, there was such emotion, and crying and expression of grief, as I have never known or seen, before or since. I finally sat off in the large loveseat by the window, facing the mountain, as a tiny river of tears flowed down my cheeks onto the timeless robes of the Benedictine.

I could hear them put the ice cream away.

I heard them lift Mr. Dohrmann into the bed that was never quiet, with its ceaseless air pump and swishing noises. The sounds of the crane's winch, showing how dignity is a thing we adopt and abandon between our infancy and our leaving.

After a long while of waiting, I heard the live-in nurse finally leave. Mr. Dohrmann's breathing was loud and labored. He had had such a long, long struggle. So many surgeries. So much pain. So many punishments to his body bag.

I turned as he called his son to come be by him. He had no words for me but I had come to understand he desired my witness for what was to come.

He had been turned upon his side. His face was crushed into the down-soft pillows and his hands were spread through the rails of the hospital bed, as if pleading for human contact.

His son Bernhard, now thirty-four, came and sat beside his father and clasped both his hands. The two, with identical blue eyes made from the same divine material, shared their moment of power as they gazed for a time so perfect, so infinite, I felt as if I aged in the process.

Eventually, with a little more effort Mr. Dohrmann began ... the last lesson:

FOR THESE
ARE THE TEACHERS.....

With labor in his breathing, Mr. Dohrmann continued, staring directly into the eyes of his first-born son, "You know we have already said everything that needs to be said, Bee, don't you?"

"Yes, Dad," the younger man responded.

"And you know that I have never shared my love with my children, one to the other, differently in any way...."

"I know, Dad....."

"And you know that I have always and forever loved my children equally and the same in every way?"

"Yes, Dad....."

"And you know that your mother and I had yearned for many years to have a son, as the first four girls were born, isn't that correct?"

"Yes, Dad ... I know....."

"So I wanted to tell you in only this one small thing, it might be important for you to know later in your life ... a little secret I felt you should share with Dad....."

(More breathing.)

".....What, Dad?"

"In this one small thing, Bee, and I know your mom joins me in this, which takes nothing from the other children.....

".....We have always loved you FIRST.....

"For you were our first son....."

There was a long pause here and I saw the warrior Bee, who had led this family through the entire illness, and without any tears, now had those big, blue eyes filled and with no words, the tears just flowing, the water just falling onto the bed sheet ... as a smile came to Mr. Dohrmann.....

I was crying again myself ... as Mr. Dohrmann took his index finger and rubbed it softly on the cheek of his boy, sometimes deflecting the flow of the tears from their natural course as he said ... in his way.....

"But, Bee ... this is not the lesson....." and if a voice could smile, the voice held the smile now.

I found through the emotions I was feeling, it was very difficult for me to sit in a meditative manner. I felt nervously, emotionally, so deeply moved, that my outer body had become unstill as if a great movement was upon my world.

Mr. Dohrmann continued ... as he always had, from that very first Lesson Night ... as though the story had no start or end to it ... he spoke in labored breath and halting words:

"I have made a magic life for us, with all the children, but do you know why the magic is what it is, Bee?"

It was as if each breath were a victory and each word a conquest.

Bernhard only gestured in the negative ... I suppose my mind played the trick of inserting the "No, Dad..." which my ears never heard.....

"The magic has been the impossible circle of beings that have entwined our family AS the magic. Beings like Brother Al here," and he raised a weakened hand to almost point in my direction before collapsing back upon his son's strong hands again ... which was a signal of his knowing that his control over all things in his surroundings even now was ebbing. I found my eyes began to hurt, and tears came unbidden for us both.

"For you see, my *precious baby,*" (this name was used endearingly by the father for this son from time to time, a subject of great teasing from the others), "the greatest of THESE, that have lived among us, have been my many magic friends.

"My closest and bonded friendships.

"And of these, you have been surrounded all your life with their words, their presence, the power of their being ... and without knowing it you have been made more for it.

"For these of my friends that you have always known ... have been the TEACHERS, Bee.....

"And the teachers have come to us to SPREAD the TRUTH. To seize upon the truth as they know it to be, and to SPREAD the TRUTH to the students of the world, who need the truth like air. The students themselves will always appoint their own teachers, for the teachers rise from among the students in a timeless pageant for God's glory. Once called, the teacher being true to his or her nature, moves within and creates their own destiny of service to the students of the world.

"And we, this family, have lived our lives within the presence of the greatest of these beings on the planet at this time, and we have known them as our Friends and Companions!

".....But ... that is not the lesson....."

FOR THESE ARE THE MASTERS.....

At this point Bernhard brought the cup to his father's lips. Without turning, Mr. Dohrmann took the straw in a mouth painted with white paste from medication and drawn with dying. I could see the oxygen was making his mouth parched, leaving flakes around the corners. He sipped a moment and shook his head indicating "enough" and they resumed their odd dance of eyes, this father and son ... as I observed in silence.

Like chains dragging up anchors off the sea bed, his words continued.....

"And OF these Friends of our Family, my baby," as the breathing settled down again, his voice raspy from the effort, "there has been magic within magic. For from among these great beings, I have been blessed with my closest of all friends, those with whom I shared my confidences in this life.

"You have known them, one and all ... but of these nearest to me, there were fewer.

"You have lived your life in privilege for the knowing of them.

"However, I realized in leaving you, that you did not have the words to speak of what it is you knew and felt. My returning here is about leaving you, at this time, the words for what it is you already know within yourself as a feeling, one for which you have no words.

"For the magic continues to be the honor the Lord God has bestowed upon us, to create our closest friendships among those with whom I have spent most of my time in this, my life's journey.

"Our closest friends.

"For my son ... it is these friends that are known in this LIFE as the MASTERS!

"Masters who are chosen by their own students, the greatest of the teachers. For in their graduation they, and only they, have come to this time to PROTECT the TRUTH from Error.

"Their students, the greatest of living teachers, will always recognize within their ranks, when the chosen are ready, the qualities of MASTERHOOD that shine in their midst. The teachers proclaim their MASTERS and the MASTERS recognize their own true nature from such a place of rejoicing, that they are readied in the awakening.

"Masters are the rare ones. Masters are they who are on this planet serve, to vigilantly protect the TRUTH from Error. The Teachers rely upon their Masters to receive the truth in the form of eternity, and so recognizing the *error-free truth,* they rush to teach and instruct the perfect truth to their universe of students.

"Such is the Way of the pathway to the divine.

"And you, my son, have lived your life among the MASTERS....."

(This was spoken with some power, in contrast to the hoarse, weakened voice to this point ... and then a pause.)

The young man, still with tears flowing with his memories, squeezed his father's hand gently and nodded yes more than once, shaking a few tears off his face with each downward motion........

"But that is not the lesson ... THIS IS THE LESSON....."

THE TEACHER OF MASTERS

A pause to regain breath, as obviously this effort had consumed a great deal from Mr. Dohrmann. I found as he continued, like air rushing from a great balloon, his voice became nearly a whisper and it was with effort that I could record this last lesson at all.....

"For there are among these beings, the most rare of the rare .... the highest of the high ... and by these you have been transformed, merely by being in their presence.

"For these my son, have been during my life, my special reward for the walk I have chosen. These alone have been my ETERNAL FRIENDSHIPS, my FOREVER FRIENDS ... my colleagues.

"So few, however ...

"So precious FEW!

"And none of these in the last have been my students, for I have been a student OF ... THEM ... "

(Which seemed strange to me at the time, but soon the strangeness would pass away, like curtains being pulled to permit the sun to fill an empty room.....)

"You have lived your life among these as well.

"These beings of the Light ... and you have not known who it was that mentored, tutored and loved you so.

"Oh, you have known the names. Tom Wilhite or Warner, John Hanley or Alexander Everrett. You have known Penn Patrick and you have known Walt Disney; you have known Napolean Hill and your uncle Bucky Fuller; you have known Dr. Edward Deming and Leland Val Van de Wall. Oh yes, you have known them well these many years.

"Our family has been guided in all things by these magical beings, and we have never discussed who it was that crossed your way.

"For of these great ones,

".....these greatest of all teachers.....

".....and the chosen MASTERS who mentor each along the "way".....

"There is another,

"And this, my son,

"Is the TEACHER of THE MASTERS.....

"For the Teacher of the Masters walks this way in life, to pull from the other side of eternity, NEW TRUTH.

"New Truth in each time and space that is required in the moment, to progress life, and to manufacture the way of perfection in God's plan.

"In any time and place there are so few, so few of these great BEINGS that are alive and which a student's life path may be blessed to cross....

"...and we have known, you and I, many......

"This blessing to us is beyond prayer, and is the finger of God upon our lives. It is a continuous marker from God in the teaching work that I have attempted to deliver to the world ... He has confirmed the work through sending me another TEACHER OF MASTERS.

"It is enough.

"More than enough.

"For you see, Bee ... the Teacher of the Masters is not appointed by his peers.

"The Masters do not denote the Teacher of Masters when they appear, for they are eternally KNOWN for who they are by the Masters, the protectors of the truth.

"The Teachers and their Masters have always recognized the Teacher of Masters, as they rarely appear, and provide reverence to them, for the way of their life is a mysterious path.

"And only when a Teacher of Masters comes across their brother Masters on "the path", do they pause to teach, so that their teaching may be made known.

"For if unbidden, unsought, their hidden wisdom remains silent.

"And when these few congregate with the others, so that they may hear and know, then from their words, from this, comes the future.

"For the word was made flesh...........

"And in the beginning, it is a Teacher of Masters, in his or her special KNOWING, who will recognize another Teacher of Masters in the world.

"In their knowing, it may be years, truly years before that other, so witnessed, is awake enough to know, to gather the force to look within their own surrender, to accept who it is that they truly ARE.

"For their road is separate from the road of other men. To accept the burden is to move the transformation forward, once again. Only with enormous courage can such work continue upon the shoulders of mortal men.

"For when the Teacher of Masters speaks his truth, it may be hidden for a long while from the eyes and ears of man.

"When another such Teacher is recognized by a peer, their nature may rebel and for some time confusion may reign in the life of the newly Witnessed Teacher of Masters.

"However, the soul of the great being may not remain ignorant FOREVER to God's plan, and eventually, in just the right time, the soul will know its true nature.

"For this is the way of it.

"And now my first-born son, ...it is for you to know...that I am dying......."(said with a whispered outflowing of breath that was quite moving, as the words were spaced painfully between the difficult inhalations).....

"......*I know, Dad"* (with some tears and choking to the words).....

"I won't be coming back now, when I sleep again, Bee......"

"....*I know, Dad..........*"

Squeezing his son's hand, he spoke .....

"So I say these words as a man who is dying.......

"To a son who is living and who needs to FEEL these words....."

Here he raised his head so his eyes were level with his son's, which took an effort so Herculean that I winced in sympathetic agony.

"Then know that you, my son, ARE a Teacher of Masters,

"and you have been SO for a very long time...

"and it pains me so to see you confused by who and what you are, and as I leave you this last time, know that I will NEVER leave you and that you are among all things to me

"MY FOREVER FRIEND

"and that I will take you with me in all ways,

"and that I will remain beside you in all your days,

"Now as the father you have well loved, I command you, to go into the world and discover the true nature of your divine soul, and complete your destiny.......

TO TEACH AS A TEACHER OF MASTERS!"

(And here Mr. Dohrmann's eyes closed for the first time, and tears were flowing from them as his hands released his son. Bernhard was crying very hard now as his hands settled back into his lap and I took my gaze from him, to allow his composure time to return.)

"........You're my eternal friend too, Dad........"

and I could tell that, despite his deep emotion, these were just words to the son, and that it would be some long while before I would see this one learn the last lesson. I took him by the shoulders and walked him down to the family room....and after a time....slowly returned to sit beside Mr. Dohrmann one last time.

MY LESSON.......

After almost a half-hour of labored-breathing nap time, Mr. Dohrmann's hand rose into the air with a finger signaling for me to approach closer.

I came around the bed, still lingering on his words, and the life I had shared with them.

As we sat, and stared at one another, I found myself sharing the drinking cup and holding the old master's hands in mine.

"DO you THINK he has any idea of this last lesson, my friend?"

".....No, Alan, it will take some time......"

He nodded with a knowing I will always remember. In some moments he spoke....

"You have seen all the happy accidents that show themselves to us Brother Al?"

"....Yes ....so many........*SO MANY*......"

"It is important that the children remember that when these happy coincidences show up, they are tiny MARKERS FROM GOD.....

"When they are many it means the way is right and strong.

"When they are absent for long periods of time it is meant to mark a hunger the spirit has to take risk, and to reward the soul with tests that must come one WAY or the other........easily and flowing or challenging and unbidden.....but always the LESSONS will come.....

(We held hands and communicated our understanding by squeezing).....

"Now there are Markers I want you to keep in the children's way when I am gone and the greatest of these is a trust you know as SUPER TEACHING......

And here he provided me with the last of his visions for the future.......

But that's another story.

_____

Chapter 12

The Candlelight

THE CANDLELIGHT

On the last day, Melissa came downstairs that late winter's afternoon, and asked for Bernhard. He was being interviewed by the Wall Street Journal. I can remember him saying, "I'm sorry, I really must interrupt this now, as my Father is dying."

All the other eight children were in the room when Bernhard arrived.

They parted to let him be near their father. The breathing came in great gasps, the bellows of his lungs straining on through the pure instinct for life that was so strong in him.

He had been asleep now for many days.

The room's shades were drawn and it was dark outside. Twelve candles had been lit, one for each of the nine children, one for Mrs. and Mr. Dohrmann, and one for myself. The candles were placed around Mr. Dohrmann's room much like the circle made for the children's lessons, as indeed he had instructed us to arrange it.

Bernhard cradled his father in his arms, the teacher's head held to his son's breast as if he were a favorite rag doll. Everyone held tears and strength at the same time.

There was a power which filled the room that evening which we easily recall, even all these years

since. Everyone felt it. We would discuss this feeling
for days following these moments.

The nurse who had cared for him for these four
years, and loved him so, led us in the words. We asked
that he move toward Christ, toward his light, and release all earthly possessions, and that, filled only with
our love, he cross into the great light of a higher reality.

Eventually, in three impossibly deep but telling
breaths that filled his body with racking gasps, and the
room with knowing, he expired. And in the stillness we
all could feel POWER rise above the body bag. I remember seeing the children following with their eyes something that could not be seen. I noticed and reported to
my Abbot that the children's faces held an illumination
that was far too white and bright for the light of twelve
small candles.

When, as if to say,
"But, children....that's NOT the lesson...."

A wind came from *within* the room....and each
reported it the same way....all the candles went out as
one........and the children and their father were in total darkness.........a final moment...together.....

and their faces held only the illumination from
another Source, which was enough to allow us to see
one another......filling the room with a soft white
glow......

Then, the nurse spoke; she said simply,
"WOW!"

When, as if a switch were thrown by her saying
this word,

all twelve candles were back, ignited at the
same time,

which made us look back at him one more time,
as the nurse, who was the first to have the power of
movement, unclenched the cradle of Bernhard's arms
from his father's head, and pulled the sheets over the
body bag of an elf who had disappeared.....

The saddest of the moments was watching the workers carry Mr. Dohrmann in a different, artificial, plastic body bag, out to the ambulance. And to see Carl, Mark and Geof, standing by their brother, as if they MUST, against their will, as they remained until the red lights of the ambulance were no longer visible. I remember Bernhard spoke as he walked back in.....

"That's not him ... he has gone.....

with the candlelight!"

EPILOGUE

By: Bernhard Dohrmann

It was ten years, almost to the day, when we received word Brother Al had graduated and was now with Dad again. It was weeks after that the San Moritz Abbey forwarded a strange trunk to me. Inside was a letter from Brother Al that explained the contents.

It read:
...Dear Bee:
When Mr. Dohrmann was moving forward during that last lesson, with you, he asked that I consider taking time to record what I felt were the most important of his lessons to the family. You will find over 1,000 scrolls which seek to address the promise I made to him in that final hour. The work of two lifetimes. His and mine, now well spent, in faith.

But among these, for the scrolls have been copied for the world as preserved work to be released over time as HIS LESSONS...there is a set of scrolls that are for you alone.

Although he didn't mention it specifically, I think it was meant for me to record "your fathers stories".....I know there are so many that I was not present for all of them, and the rest must reside within your memories and the memories of your brothers and sisters. Perhaps you'll complete the scrolls one day.

Of those I was witness to, I have created THE SCROLLS entitled DIAMOND HEART - MY FATHER'S STORIES ... and as you can see they fill an entire chest. It is too much for one publication, but perhaps readers would enjoy them in some sequence.

I am reasonably certain that as the world comes to know your father, they will also remember much about their own greater family, as they may return to the truth of being children in our world family once again.

However, that is not the lesson. (Can you feel me smiling with your father as you read these words?)

The lesson is, that these scrolls my son, are for you and for YOUR CHILDREN......for these are "your" STORIES..........

I'll tell him you approved of my work.....and now if you don't mind......why don't you enjoy them like eating cherries...one scroll at a time.....which is how they were created.

And that my boy........IS the LESSON.

I love you FOREVER.

Brother Al.........

The original of the letter is framed and remains in my home. The marks on it are from the tears that the impact of receiving this gift had upon us. Brother Al's letter and a photograph of the great chest, was sent to each of my brothers and sisters. The work has never been released until Christmas, 1996.....when the first DIAMOND HEART "translation" of the scrolls was completed...(the code was quaint, Brother Al.)

DIAMOND HEART - MY FATHER'S STORIES is an adult fairy tale, as the first of the scrolls' great gifts, it appears now in published form. We are planning to release more of the STORIES if it seems the world is a better place for the receiving of them.

Each story is written upon a scroll, the monk's original. Some are longer and two-sided, some are multiple scrolls rolled together. Also arriving later, were the manuscripts of My Father's LESSONS.

The Lessons are being prepared for release in seven volumes, one each year, starting with the first in the year 2000.

All proceeds from the publications of my father's work are being donated to the not-for-profit International Learning Trust, to install SUPER TEACHING technology in classrooms around the world.

Thank You, Brother Al.

THE CHILDREN

Terry lives in Southern California.
Pam lives in Sacramento.
Sally lives in Texas.
Susan lives in Texas.
Bernhard lives in Alabama.
Mark lives in Portland, Oregon.
Geof lives in Walnut Creek, California
Carl lives in Novato, California
Melissa lives in Washington State.
...........Phylis Dohrmann lives in Palm Springs,
California ... dearly beloved of Alan Gerrard
Dohrmann..................................

"TRANSLATION" COMPLETED - DECEMBER,
1996

A BIOGRAPHICAL NOTE

Alan Gerrard Dohrmann was born into the famous San Francisco family, known for some five generations for its contribution to community. It is a family known for many things, but perhaps most for creating the Emporium Department Store chain across the western United States in the mid-1800's. After more than one hundred years of service, these once-great stores were disbanded in the mid-1990's through their sale to third party companies .

The family also spawned the equally famous Dohrmann Hotel Supply Company, a global resort outfitting business, powerful even to this day. The Dohrmanns, still well-known in San Francisco, played a key role in the progress of the city by the Bay. ABC Dohrmann, grandfather to "the nine" was pivotal, for example, in the reconstruction of the Saint Francis Hotel in Union Square. The Macy Building of today on Union Square's famous south side, was for three generations a San Francisco landmark, known as the Dohrmann Building. When I came to know them, the family had been busy for a century, creating landmarks in the downtown San Francisco skyline. Many more testimonials could appear in such a history, continuing on with various Dohrmann companies, from newspaper publishing to cold storage, details too numerous for this journal to record ... to be remembered only by the family journals and memories of the time. For this is not our story.

The Dohrmanns as I knew them then, represented a solid thread in the history and development of California. The family photo albums featured portraits with Presidents and Kings. Historic images with President Roosevelt, or tintypes with John Muir and Mark Twain decorated the family walls. I was always a bit in awe during a tour from Mr. Alan Dohrmann, of an estate that included so many precious records.

One of twelve children, Mr. Alan Dohrmann, one-half of one of the two sets of twins in the family, was virtually the only child to remain "free" of the wealth and power of the family empire. Upon exiting school, Mr. Dohrmann, somewhat by accident, found himself on a project in accelerated learning for the United States Navy war effort. Such projects had grown popular during the World War II years, when speed was essential in transforming human potential.

In Mr. Dohrmann's case, his training related to teaching others to handle warships such as mine sweepers and liberty vessels, even when the students arriving for instruction hailed from such exotic locations as Kansas, and had never before even seen the ocean.

A rather singular project he designed, code-named SNAP SHOTS, helped spotters in remote islands in the Pacific grasp vital statistics for ordinance on planes and ships and thereby saved a substantial number of American lives. There were other war projects in human training, but my memory is weak and my date line seems to waver prior to 1950.

I do remember hearing about young master Bernhard's birth in 1948, for example, but then that was notable due to the baby's being premature by several months. He almost died on the way into our world. My abbot recalled to me that after five weeks of failing strength for the infant, arrangements had been made for young Bernhard's last rites in an incubator. However, that was before he decided to fool us all, and take his throne as the firstborn son. It was the first of many "jokes" we would come to see as lessons, as we came to know the rascal.

After the war effort, Alan Dohrmann continued to design creative programs for human potential that over time, would affect millions. A pioneer, he called himself, in a strange new land.

During the period of the 1950's and 1960's Mr. Dohrmann would design or influence human potential training that included much of the work now known as Marriage Encounters, Mind Dynamics, Lifespring, PSI World, Total Quality Management, Sage Trainings, EST, Total Value Quality, Leadership Dynamics, Visioneering, Money & You, and many others. This body of his work was principally developed for major corporations or leading human potential training companies, a task that continued throughout Mr. Dohrmann's lifetime.

However, my writings have virtually nothing to do with this vast body of Mr. Dohrmann's more "classic" work. The proof of Mr. Dohrmann's life work lives on today in the lives of the graduates of scores of training programs, still taught throughout the world, and the teachers who have knowingly or unknowingly been influenced by a charming, plump, elf-like man, that only a very few ever had the privilege to know about or to meet personally.

There were those I have chosen to call the "Great Ones" who did have the blessing of gaining their instruction directly from this Master Teacher. Over the years these few came to be a unique tribe of some of the most important "light workers" visiting the planet in this time: Leaders who pursued expanded human potential in the work place...in the family...and in our society. Many of the Great Ones commonly made it their practice to visit Mr. Dohrmann, with the delight of treasure seekers finding a lost chest within the hull of a Spanish galleon.

Alan Dohrmann was known as the "Teachers' Teacher." He was always introduced by word of mouth; he never sought his students, nor did he ever promote his work. Each new leader was always welcomed the same way, with invitations to stay in Mr. Dohrmann's home in a part of the estate simply known as "The Apartments".

The Apartments were located directly underneath the main Dohrmann country home, in a village known as Fairfax. The Apartments existed as a stand-alone living complex, filled with every creature comfort for extended visits. Private great rooms, baths, kitchens, sitting rooms, and trappings more common to the finest hotels, created the special ambiance of the facility. In those days, an invitation The Apartments was a very exciting proposition.

Those influenced by Mr. Dohrmann's work included, from my own introductions, Dr. Edward Deming, Walt Disney, Alexander Everett, Tom Wilhite, Warner Erhardt, John Hanley, Bill Dempsey, William Penn Patrick, Michael Murphy, Richard Nixon, John F. Kennedy, Clement Stone, Jane Wilhite, Val Van De Wall and many other leaders in the field of human progress. The pioneering breakthroughs created by the late Alan Dohrmann and those he chose to work beside, continue to reach millions of individuals even now.

Mr. Dohrmann passed forward ("graduated," as he liked to call it) from his service to us in 1983.

These scrolls complete a promise I made to Mr. Dohrmann in 1983, as he "graduated" from his own courses. I have written the adventure of it all, first for "the nine" - his nine children: Terry, Pam, Bernhard, Mark, Geof, Melissa, Carl, Susan and Sally.

Mr. Dohrmann presided with the authority of a Pope and the magic of a leprechaun over this family of nine children, and my own life was enriched for knowing all of them. And so, as I myself will soon graduate to join my teacher, I smile as the work is now completed, for now I know his story continues. As...

Now it is your turn!
Al Dela Rosa
Benedictine Friar
Montclair Abbey

Other Books by Bernhard Dohrmann:

LIVING LIFE AS A SUPER ACHIEVER

by Bernhard Dohrmann

**Available through
ST Productions**

for $**20**⁰⁰

Call **205 830 4760**

*　*　*

Money Magic

by Bernhard Dohrmann

**Available through
ST Productions**

for $**20**⁰⁰

Call **205 830 4760**

Recommended Reading
Available in Bookstores Everywhere

Chicken Soup for the Soul .... M.V. Hansen & J. Canfield

A 2nd Helping of Chicken Soup for the Soul .... M.V. Hansen & J. Canfield

A 3rd Helping of Chicken Soup for the Soul .... M.V. Hansen & J. Canfield

A Cup of Soup for the Soul .... M.V. Hansen, J. Canfield & B. Spilchuk

Condensed Chicken Soup for the Soul .... M.V. Hansen, J. Canfield & P. Hansen

Chicken Soup for the Surviving Soul
.... M.V. Hansen, J. Canfield, P. Aubery & N. Mitchell, R.N.

Chicken Soup for the Woman's Soul
.... M.V. Hansen, J. Canfield, J.R. Hawthorne & M. Shimoff

Chicken Soup for Soul at Work
.... M.V. Hansen, J. Canfield, M. Rutte, M. Rogerson & T. Clauss

Most Chicken Soup products are available
in print and audio format.

For a complete list call
Self-Esteem Seminars at 1-800-237-8336.